£2.00

CW00470913

Lifespin.

Lifespinners

LYNN WATSON

Troubador Publishing Ltd
Unit E2 Airfield Business Park,
Harrison Road, Market Harborough,
Leicestershire LE16 7UL
Tel: 0116 279 2299
Email: books@troubador.co.uk
Web: www.troubador.co.uk/matador

ISBN 978 1 80514 106 8

British Library Cataloguing in Publication Data.
A catalogue record for this book is available from the British Library.

Printed and bound in Great Britain by 4edge Limited
Typeset in 11pt Minion Pro by Troubador Publishing Ltd, Leicester, UK

Matador is an imprint of Troubador Publishing Ltd

For Rob, Jay, Lani, Hazel and Lynn
and with sincere thanks to all my early readers

A baby is born and a trio of ghostly goddesses, the three Fates, gather round the crib. The first Fate, Clotho, spins the thread of life on her ancient spindle. The second Fate, Lachesis, solemnly measures out the length of individual thread. The third Fate, Atropos, frowns as she decides how the person will die, knowing that when the time comes she will cut the thread.

That was in ancient Greece. This is Wellowfern, 2048.

One

The pigeon cybird waited on the balcony landing pad, his neck glistening emerald green and the soft feathers showing pink as they lifted in the scented breeze. Isabel paused, leaning on the doorframe with one slender bare foot stroking the other. Caramel, that was it – usually a favourite but too rich for now; the woody aromas were more soothing. She stepped out of the apartment, pinning her hair into a neat roll and picking off a handful of grapes from the generous bunch in the fruit bowl. Her head was still pounding from last night's party. DJ Johnny wasn't the oldest resident of Wellowfern, but he could well be the first DJ in the world to run a full-on 1960s disco at his own 118th birthday gig.

The cybird tapped his claws on the pad but Isabel wasn't ready to engage with anyone, least of all Cyril. His message could wait. She looked across the tiled piazza to the arcade, with its boutique outlets and graceful stone arches. All quiet, just a few indistinct figures weaving between the columns. Bending over the balcony railings, she checked out the tree-lined paths of the park and the row of glinting, peach-tinted domes leading to the river. The runners and cyclists were out in force on their parallel racetracks, and there was Trish, of course, doing her post-run stretching exercises under their big chestnut tree. Any minute now, she would probably glance up to see if Isabel was watching.

She turned her gaze back to the piazza, letting her mind roam. DJ Johnny grew up in this city. He was still a child in 1941, when the Blitz strikes reduced this whole area to jagged remnants of walls and heaps of rubble. After that came the bog-standard high street, eventually killed off by soulless indoor shopping malls inhabited by cool, lippy kids like Isabel and her friends, the '80s in-crowd. Then a period of creeping dereliction, she imagined, before the Healthy Ageing Foundation razed it again to make way for its world-class research centre and Wellowfern, now one of the most sought-after select clusters this side of the Atlantic. Isabel was lucky, she knew that. She had managed to get away, using an astute mix of charm, insistence and well-targeted generosity to acquire this stylish penthouse apartment, with its commanding view and easy access to the roof garden. They had all escaped, in one way or another. DJ Johnny too, no doubt. It's what you did when you'd had an eventful past.

More claw-tapping, sharper this time. Cyril flew down from his pad onto the balcony rail and edged sideways towards her, too sly by half. He was clearly determined to pass on some advice or information, whether she wanted it or not. Isabel sucked in her cheeks and fired a semi-deflated, soggy grape at his cocked head, missing by a mile.

'All right, I give in. What is it?'

It was a memo from Nathan, the chief exec, inviting her to a welcome reception for the new scientific director. She had heard the rumours, some clearly off beam but others in line with what she had picked up as resident rep on the Participation Committee. Not that there was any participation; only fatuous references to "future direction of travel" and "exceptional opportunities". It involved an expansion of the Institute, its research trials and novel anti-ageing treatments, that much she had gleaned. This affected everyone: residents, university students and staff, all were involved. Isabel had tried cornering individual directors, but she couldn't get past the cloak of confidentiality justifying why no one could be brought into the loop until the key decisions were finalised. As a successful businesswoman herself, she understood the need to negotiate behind closed doors, especially in a field as sensitive and competitive as healthy ageing and rejuvenation. She just wasn't used to being kept in the dark, and she didn't much like it.

'I'll talk to Finn, see if he's got any clue what they're cooking up. Get him over here this morning, Cyril, soon as possible. Say it's urgent. If he can't or won't tell me, you'll have to make me an appointment with Nathan right away.'

She had nurtured a positive relationship with Finn, her personal lifestyle manager. He was motivated and usually tuned in when it came to analysing her biometrics, adjusting her genotype diet and deciding which research trials she should go for. He had worked as a fitness trainer and was impressed by her previous life as Olympic Team-GB gymnast and co-founder of a leading space insurance company, although she had given him no details. She had put in a good word with Nathan, so Finn could expect rapid promotion if he played his cards right and showed more confidence, made himself noticed. Even if he was too junior to have inside knowledge on the new scientific director, he might offer some insight from a staff perspective, instead of the wild speculation circulating among her fellow residents.

She turned towards the balcony door to go in, then wheeled round and raised her leg, swinging it forward to see how high the flat sole of her foot would reach up the leaf-patterned railings. Ooh, maybe not. She let it drop, gently, and looked over towards the chestnut tree, knowing Trish would be finished her stretching by now. Yes, she had gone but there was a new type of runner: men and women in uniform, sprinting along the paths and filing into lines as they approached the piazza below. What the...? They were streaming in from the other side too and massing in front of the apartment building, their boots obscuring the colourful floor mosaic. It looked like a raid, like that time with Jerome... She stepped back, out of sight. No, that was too crazy. The site security guards, it had to be, renowned for their near-invisible presence and tactfulness; she had never seen more than two at once. It was all laid out in the promotional material: *discreet 24-hour security and protection, with full respect for resident sensibilities.* And it was highly appreciated after all that had happened, or might happen, outside their safe enclave of Wellowfern.

This was anything but tactful and discreet: military-style dress, officers barking their orders, shouting over each other and piercing the air with high-pitched whistles. Now they were off, heading in ragged formation towards the university campus at the far end of the piazza, where

4

a crowd was gathering. Isabel breathed in deeply and rubbed the back of her aching thigh, feeling shaky as the sickly-sweet caramel breeze whipped up into an erratic tropical wind.

'What's going on, Cyril, by the student halls? Do they have to yell like that? So much for our so-called "*serene and tranquil setting*". It's one hell of a din when you're this fragile.'

She didn't expect him to fly over to investigate. The Wellowfern cybirds retained the legendary eyesight and hearing of their natural bird ancestors, those grey-winged heroes that saved countless lives by guiding rescue craft towards drowning sailors and passengers when stricken boats and ships went down. The combination of their innate pigeon talents and newly enhanced perception and communication skills had made them the envy of global leaders in the diverse select movements that had sprung up across the inhabitable regions of the world. The unique cybird formula was a closely guarded secret, known only to the anonymous group of scientists involved in the project.

'A young man is kneeling on the ground, surrounded by security. He is not resisting.'

'A young man, seriously? Is that it? All that fuss?'

The cybird's head bobbed forward. 'Update by real-time notification. This is a minor disciplinary incident involving a student. It's not relevant. Your daily nutritional guidance is ready, with offsetting adjustments to rebalance your constitution.'

'Later, thank you. I over-indulged last night, no need to be pompous about it.'

A minor disciplinary incident. Five years Isabel had lived at Wellowfern with no such incidents and now they'd had three within two months, with no explanation or follow-up. And this time they had deployed security like a heavy brigade, in full view. What was Nathan thinking of? She broke off another sprig of grapes and stepped into the apartment, aware of the room adjusting to warm vibrant mode in response to her pulsing headache and prickly reaction, the tingling of unease. It was her sanctuary, this place. She belonged here and she didn't want any complications or nasty reminders; none of the residents did. They had been pushed into this cluster, into Wellowfern, by the increasingly stark options on offer, their fast-polarising prospects. Mostly they felt they had done their bit, made something of it, and they wanted to enjoy themselves, stay healthy and live longer than DJ Johnny; hopefully much longer, with a fair wind and no looming icebergs.

She sat on the arm of the sofa and turned her attention to the sleek aquarium, which followed the continuous curve of the wall. Gazing intently at one fish, her current favourite, she watched it change its colour, shape, size and intricate pattern with each quick flick of a feathery tail, gloriously unaware of how fabulous it was, or how soon it would be overtaken. They lived so peaceably together, the extravagant hybrids and the natural fish, but she had often thought that one day this could be disturbed; a more aggressive variety would find its way in, whether by accident or design. And what was that, half floating on the surface? She went over to investigate. The body was pale and bloated, the orange fantail viciously picked at by its vengeful or thoughtless companions. She swept the limp creature up in her hand, cradling it for a brief moment before it was sent hurtling down the rubbish chute.

'You're not supposed to do that, die on me. This is Wellowfern, you know.'

***

Finn took the stairs, two at a time for the first three floors and the last flight at a run. It all chalked up points towards his daily target, although he was also keen to respond promptly to Isabel's summons. She could be arrogant and dismissive, but nothing unusual about that here – and anyway, she had something to brag about, if it was all true. He had grown wise to her over the last two years, figured out how to capitalise on her audacious streak and nudge her to take the next risk, make choices that other residents would shy away from. This might be even more important now, if he was to find enough willing participants for his assigned new research trials.

He arrived at Isabel's door and held back for a moment, taking off the wide-brimmed Stetson and rearranging his floppy hair at the front, where it was always mussed up by the hat. Keep to generalities, that was it; don't allow her to interrogate. As he opened his hand to activate his skin-embedded palmleaf device, the door opened and Isabel ushered him in.

'Ah, here you are, excuse the mess. I've got a zinging hangover from Johnny's party. Someone must have altered the mix to get us all properly drunk, like in the good old days of disco. Remind me to stick to our fortified brain cocktails from now on.'

Finn smiled and looked around the room, which was tidy apart from the sparkly gold outfit flung carelessly over Lottie, Isabel's homebot. She generally left Lottie standing idle in the corner, where she could be used as a late-night clothes horse. What was the point of a domestic bot, she'd said, once they were eclipsed by the more versatile cybirds and stopped developing any new skills? The household appliances and surfaces were all proactive and self-cleaning in any case, and as for food preparation, Isabel loved to cook for herself and her friends, using her spattered, full-colour recipe books – French, Greek, Indian, Caribbean, Thai. It reminded them of their travelling days, the foreign trips and holidays before all that went pear-shaped. And when you added in the fitness points gained by doing the enjoyable bits of housework herself, it left tidying away as Lottie's main task.

'Take the party things to the bedroom, Lottie, and hang them up – go on, jump to it! Sit down, Finn, and please stop fiddling with that hat. It's unprofessional.'

'Okay, strictly protein and vitamin mixes, including special birthday parties. I'll make a note,' teased Finn. He usually judged it right, what he could get away with, although her mood could shift dramatically without warning. 'You and Trish were still going strong at the disco when I dragged myself off to bed at one-thirty.'

'And Trish had to be on the running track this morning, just to show me up – so boring. Anyway, why I called you over... Nathan's invited me to a reception and it's to do with the management shake-up that's been brewing lately. Apparently, we're getting a new scientific director, no name or details and no one thought to inform me personally. It's what happens when you're "honorary", you have to fight not to end up as an afterthought. What can you tell me, who is it and why now?'

Finn balanced his hat on the arm of the chair, wondering what Isabel already knew. Perhaps a good deal more than him, despite her gripe about not being kept up with it, so he had to avoid coming across as ignorant or ill-informed. And at the same time, he didn't want to get into trouble with his managers by giving away too much, or worse, getting it wrong.

'And not only that,' said Isabel. 'There was a big disturbance on the piazza this morning. That's the third so-called 'incident' and the security guards were out in droves, it's unheard of. Something is going on over there and it's being hushed up, or was up to now.'

'So, let me deal with that one first. A few students were caught doing a private lab experiment. It wasn't important, trivial stuff, but they broke their contract with the university by not focusing on their own study programmes. One of them refused to leave Wellowfern, so he had to be expelled and evicted. That was the fracas just now. It's a shame because they are, or they were, some of our brightest talents.'

Isabel sat back. 'Come on, I wasn't born yesterday. Tell me what these students were up to, what they did to provoke that display of force. They went rogue, that's what you're saying. Don't come over all official or try being cagey with me. We know each other better than that and I can spot an evasive answer a million miles off.' She jabbed her finger at him and shifted to a playful tone. 'Go on, give me a hint, at least.'

'Honestly, I wasn't involved and I don't have any details of the incident.'

Isabel leant in to invade his personal space, her blue-crystal eyes wide and expectant. He wavered, looking for a way to deflect her.

'Look, Shani's the one who has direct contact with students, she's the scientist, not me. I only heard from someone else that… I think it's to do with the cybirds, testing their abilities, but I can't say for sure, it's second or third-hand information.'

Idiot. He had dragged Shani into it, without any prompt or suggestion from Isabel. Shani, the one person here that he really cared about, wanted to shield from any hassle.

'What are you saying? That's way out of order.'

Isabel dropped her gaze and glanced out the window, as if to make sure Cyril was on his balcony landing pad and not within listening distance – although that exact distance was a matter of debate after the cybirds' latest enhancement. She lowered her voice anyway.

'If it's the cybirds, it's not just a university issue. No one is allowed to interfere with them or delve into their workings, their mashed-up brains or whatever. We're all forced to have one and it's a mixed blessing as far as I'm concerned. I'd love to criticise Cyril as much as he does me, take him apart myself or send him off to birdy Shangri-la, but it's part of the contractual obligation, we're stuck with them. And I will admit, they're great for Wellowfern's reputation.'

Finn had gone too far, even mentioning the cybirds, let alone Shani. Damn Isabel and the way she pinned him down, her incessant questioning. But then again, she was important and he needed her to see him as a close confidant, even if there was risk attached to leaking information. And she was right: the incident was potentially serious. At least she seemed to have strayed away from the students' antics, and he could say more on the other topic she was about to grill him on – the upcoming reception.

'You asked about Nathan's invitation. I wanted to discuss that anyway, after our staff briefing yesterday. I can fill you in on some of the thinking, Isabel, but I don't know what's exactly planned or how the changes will affect us.'

'Go on then, I'm listening. And please no waffle or corporate hype. We'll have more than enough of that at the reception, I'm sure.'

'So… it's a mega success, what the Foundation's achieved in ten years. We can cure, treat or prevent all the degenerative illnesses and chronic conditions of older age, hold back ageing with rejuvenation therapies and protect our residents from heart disease, strokes and the big, long-running health threats, including cancer, new viruses and severe mental illness.'

'Can't argue with that, prizes all round. It's more about life enrichment now. You're in the right job, Finn, lifestyle manager.' Was it genuine, or was there a touch of sarcasm to bring him down a notch? Always hard to tell. Isabel stood up and wandered over to the aquarium.

'I just lost a fish. They'd nibbled its tail off.'

'I'm sorry, Isabel.'

'No point being sorry, it had its day. What next then, the future?'

'We've aced it with stem cells, gene therapies, senolytics, magic enzymes, ultrasound and tissue bioprinting; they're all expanding, reaching into new areas. Now it's age reversal, plasma infusions, soft implants, mini-organoids, courier nanobots, intelligent vaccines. And then the brain—'

She raised her hand. 'Stop, enough. Never slow to blow our own trumpet, are we? All good though, I'm not knocking it. It's an impressive list and Shani keeps me up to date on the latest advance, so I can pass it on to residents. You missed out pulse lasers, by the way. They saved my life a few years ago, before Wellowfern. And don't forget our old friend cell repair. I was in the last study, not the sexiest but still fundamental.'

'Yep, rolling cell reprogramming, sexy as ever. Now the Foundation has evaluated all our work on healthspan. No hype, Isabel, just solid scientific evidence of an incredible win, keeping people healthy and energised to the end of their lives.'

'And we're madly competitive, some of us anyway, which adds to motivation. It's good they're now publishing our collective biological age, not just individual results. Makes us feel more of a team.'

This was safe territory and Isabel had lightened up, showing her usual enthusiasm for the research programme. Probably the dead fish had got to her, that was strictly a no-no. Finn leant back, crossing his laced boots at the ankles and linking his fingers behind his head, making the hair flop forward again.

'So, what do *you* reckon, Isabel? Nathan was secretive at the staff briefing, so it's not just you feeling left out, but there's a big announcement coming. And he did let on that the new scientific director is called Georgina… something, I've forgotten.'

'Okay. No doubt she'll have her own pet projects and she'll put a lot of noses out of joint. That's inevitable when you create a top post. Perhaps we'll extend our healthy ageing approach to the local population in the Fringes. It's always been one of the goals, officially at least.' She paused. 'Pros and cons to that, of course.'

Finn nodded. He was the first in his family to make it into a select cluster and he hoped to bring his younger sisters to Wellowfern as university students, if they passed their exams. It was vital for them to escape the Fringes, which spread out from the edge of the cities and the remaining scattered towns into former farmland and open countryside. Their town was one of the better ones and he had found the necessary connections to get himself out, but his sisters were ten and twelve years younger and opportunities for escape were shrinking all the time. Even the smart city encircling Wellowfern, which offered great positions and high rewards if you had the right qualifications and tech skills, was a distant second best to a select cluster. But this wasn't the time to open up to Isabel about his family – and in any case, she had never shown the slightest interest, even when he had once tried to talk about his plans for Iris and Maya. Perhaps it touched a raw nerve if she had her own relatives to worry about. Best to keep quiet and stay in tune with her thoughts.

'Yep, pros and cons. It should be a long-term goal to extend to the Fringes but not now, it's volatile out there.

And when you consider logistics and expense, the cost of developing and rolling out new medicines and techniques, as well as lifestyle, the enrichment facilities that go with it… No, we have to concentrate on increasing our lead in global research, be the best in our field. That's where the action is.'

Really? Is that what he actually believed, or was he pandering to Isabel, trying to show his ambition – ruthlessness, even?

'Right on, Finn. You'll make an excellent CEO one day. We can't lose our edge, although in the end we'll have to do something big to benefit the Fringe public; it would be unwise not to. Anyway, I'm sure you'll find enough keen residents to join the new clinical trials, assuming it's on the same basis as now. I mean the incentive package – personal health gain, enrichment experiences and opportunities for financial investment.'

'Yeah, should all work out. Anyway, I said I'd drop in on Trish and Paul, so I need to make tracks. They had a reception invite too – or Trish did, as an active committee member.'

'Active hardly covers it. Hyperactive, more like – or dynamic, she'd prefer that. Paul, though… he's different, cautious, an outsider. She needs to make sure he's not a drag on her. You can tell Trish, next time we play table tennis I'm challenging her to the best of three. Not today though, not with this fuzzy head.'

Finn ran down the stairs to the first floor and managed to catch Paul and Trish for a brief chat. As he left the apartment building, he was still fretting about the Shani angle, but at least he had managed to move Isabel on to the positive news about research wins. He had tried quizzing Shani about rumours among the lab scientists and academics, what was planned, but she wasn't willing to discuss it; not with him, anyway. Other questions had been asked at the briefing too, about protection of jobs and guarantees on residents' accommodation and participation contracts. Nathan's responses were brief and far from reassuring, but Finn was hopeful that he wasn't first in line for redundancy, if it came to it.

No, it was his family he had to worry about. If only his parents… but it was too late for the older generations, unless they already had wealth and high status, or the special talents and expertise prized by the global movements and local select clusters. And none of his relatives had a valuable gene variant, now the prime alternative currency with which you could enter a health or family-related cluster like the Healthy Ageing Foundation. He could fantasise about grand gestures and ideal futures all he liked, but in truth there was little he could do for them; not until he rose to an important position or found some means, devious or otherwise, to raise the funds and rescue them from their life-sapping predicament.

He walked diagonally across the piazza, making his way back to the Institute. Perhaps Shani would be in the office today, or he could at least save a hot pod in case she turned up. The security guards had left and the entrance to the university, where students were usually milling about, was deserted. He stopped halfway over, sensing something out of the ordinary; probably a lingering tension from the earlier arrest, which he hadn't witnessed. Or the effects of the hot wind, the sudden flurries playing on his cheeks.

Then he heard it: a whirring in the distance, coming closer. A new type of helicopter or drone, perhaps. He was attuned to vehicles and could easily identify them; it came from his dad, who had loved doing up old bangers and once held a pilot's licence. He looked into the bleached lemon sky above the arcade, but just to confirm what he'd already concluded: this wasn't a drone, it was a car. He raced back to the corner of the apartment building and hid behind it, tilting sideways to keep his eyes on the archway leading to the main gate. Within a minute or two, the vehicle emerged from the arch, its whirring now a light purr. It glided to a stop fifty metres from where he stood, at the front door to the apartments. It was a blue and silver Rolls-Royce, a stunning classic from a different age. Finn stared, spellbound. No one had any kind of private car now, at least not at Wellowfern. The air taxis, looptrains, copters and beetledrones – these were the safe and authorised means of travel.

He ducked his head back when both driver and passenger door opened, then peeped again, unclear why he should act so furtively but following his gut instinct. The driver was a real chauffeur, peaked hat and all, like in the old films. The passenger was tall, athletic and fair-haired, wearing tight jeans and shiny white shoes. He looked around the piazza, clearly a newcomer, before the two of them carried his large holdalls into the building. Finn's eyes returned to the Rolls, longing to touch it, to feel its sleek contours and, above all, to slide himself into it and drive off. He tipped his hat forward and stepped out from his hiding place to lean casually against the front wall by the door, reclaim his territory. The driver glanced at him as he strolled back to the car, giving a slight nod before he got in and started her up. And then it was away, skimming near-silently across the paving of the piazza and slipping through the archway, his dream motor just a distant vibration, dissolving to nothing.

Two

The Institute occupied two sides of a leafy square at the other end of Wellowfern, across the river. The health centre was on the near side and the opposite side was taken up by the food labs, the vertical farm for fresh produce and the unit where clothes and other home products were custom designed and printed on demand. Entering the Institute, Shani wanted to claim a workpod before her meeting with Nathan and Isabel. There hadn't been enough time to prepare after getting back from her course, but it should be simple enough, as long as Isabel was in a good mood and Nathan eased things along.

She had learned not to expect any pleasantries or signs of curiosity from Glen, who was known for ignoring his academic colleagues and everyone else in the office. He looked up as she passed his corner space, but it wasn't to ask about the course, although he had insisted she attend it.

'A minute, Shani. I notice you're booked to meet Nathan. What's that about? Didn't you think to check it out with me first?'

'I'm sorry but I don't see why—'

'I'm your line manager, that's why. Unless you presume you're reporting to the new scientific director from now on? I can tell you it's not going to happen.'

'Fine, but you know I'm on the New Advances group and I'm briefing Nathan on research strategy. Today's meeting is part of that, talking to Isabel as resident rep and preparing for Nathan's presentation at the reception for Georgina.'

'You make it sound like you're in charge of the strategy, which is hardly the case. And by the way, we're unlikely to approve your own research proposal.'

He was needling her again and she had to stay calm, not rise to it. 'My project's still to be agreed, I'm aware of that. It's up to the Scientific Committee. For the reception, it's about goals and research methods and that's what I'm there for, to explain it to Isabel.'

Glen bristled. 'Isabel? It's ridiculous. And I might recommend closing down some of the ongoing research trials if there's all this extra work coming down the line. Nobody's talking about that, how realistic it is and if we're going to get any additional resources.'

'I'm sorry but I have to go. Can we talk about this later, Glen? I'll report back to you.'

'Very generous of you. I'm sure it will be scintillating.'

He turned away, conversation over. The odd razor haircut did nothing for him, either in its shorn or high-spiky versions. Shani saw a vacant pod next to Finn, who waved her over.

'Morning, Finn. Don't go anywhere near Glen. He's in a foul mood, worse than usual. I expect I'll get a detention or something, for answering back. You doing okay?'

'Yep, fine. I'll keep well away – not that he talks to any of us; non-scientists are pond life. I saved this space for you. Do you fancy lunch at the café?'

'Don't think I can, too much going on. Got a meeting now; Nathan and Isabel.'

'Ah, in that case I need to say something.' He beckoned her in closer. 'There was a public incident on the piazza. You might not have heard about it yet.'

'No, I did – a minor incident, so they said. I meant to check it out later today.'

'Well, it's not that minor. One of the students was arrested, then expelled from the uni and evicted. The word is that it's linked to unofficial cybird experiments and Isabel's sniffing around, she asked me straight out. She might bring it up in front of Nathan. You'll have to head her off, say you'll talk to her separately or something.'

Shani hadn't had an easy time with the students, trying to reason with them on this. They were like kids, she told them, unable to resist taking forbidden things apart to see how they worked. It wasn't a smart move, doing it with the newly enhanced cybirds. Now she felt nervous about her meeting, especially as Finn seemed to know she was involved.

'That's bad. Who was it? Hope it's not one of my tutor group.'

'A third year, guy called Josh. He was expected to do well in the summer exams, so I've heard. Which makes sense, I suppose – too clever by half. Is he one of yours?'

Shani shook her head. Josh wasn't in her tutor group, so she wasn't responsible for him. That was the good part. The bad part was that she'd done something incredibly stupid, months ago but still, she was compromised by it and now this: Josh was evicted. They must have questioned him before he was thrown out…

'You're looking worried, Shani. Do you know him well?'

It was a straightforward question but there might be more behind it. Was there any gossip, or was he picking up on her discomfort, fishing for clues?

'No, not one of mine. It's brutal but the authorities wouldn't have acted arbitrarily, so he probably got what he deserved. It's the public disorder element that bothers me, and the message it sends to residents and students. We do all we can to promote a calm, congenial environment and I can understand why Isabel might be upset. But anyway, I have to run.'

She cupped her hand to open her palmleaf and check in with her cybird, Sage, who thankfully had no new notifications. As she walked across the internal garden bridge and past the rotating art display, she tried to focus her mind on the key points of the research plan. Glen wanted to throw her off balance before this meeting, that was obvious. He was turning vicious and she'd have to defend her position if he seriously meant to sabotage her research bid. And as for Josh and the cybird episode, she just hoped that Isabel wouldn't bring up the subject. Worst case, if one of the students had referred to her interrupting them that night, she'd have to brazen it out and claim she had misunderstood the situation.

Nathan was waiting in the small, wood-panelled conference room when she arrived. In contrast to Glen, he welcomed her with his usual bland, amiable politeness.

'Good to see you, Shani. I'd rather not be having this meeting before the reception, but you know Isabel, best to tackle any issues directly and important to have her onside. I did consider asking Georgina to join us, the new scientific director, but thought better of it. Isabel was put out when she received the invitation by cybird note, rather than a personal message from me, although I suspect her real motive for today is to steal a march on everyone else. Anyway, you'll find Georgina interesting, she's forward-thinking and not afraid to push the boat out. She's been taken on by Lextar for this specific role, and she's highly regarded.'

Shani nodded. 'Okay, sounds great. But… what's Lextar?'

'Sorry, leaping ahead, forgetting you're not up to speed on all the background. We're keeping names secret to stop anyone doing private investigations and coming to premature judgements. Not that they'll find much, as we've blocked key words on our internal network and the global internet is useless for that kind of thing; far too splintered and out of date. Anyway, the Foundation is now merging with Lextar, which stands for Life Extension and Regeneration. We're adopting its name to show we're moving on from healthspan and curing ageing conditions to an explicit focus on longevity, increasing lifespan with a multifaceted approach to rejuvenation, enhancement and enrichment. It's a big shift and has to be handled right, but it's the logical next step and we need to be agile… ah, here she is.'

Isabel was wearing one of her brightly patterned headscarves, gathered and tied low at the back of the neck so that it fully covered her hair. Shani imagined she would have gone to the races in the old days, perhaps owned one of the winning horses. She waved regally at them through the glass and strode into the room, accompanied by a powerful floral scent and closely followed by her cybird, who strutted along the counter to perch beside the drink dispenser.

'Good morning to you both. I brought Cyril along. He's moody and bored these days, since his latest enhancement. He needs to get out more, find some stimulation.'

Nathan nodded. 'No problem. I hope we can talk freely and agree not to release any new information ahead of the reception. Shani has been developing ideas around our future research themes. It's contingent on the merger with our new partner, Lextar, how our joint priorities shape up. But before we get on to that, I want to stress how much we value and respect our older residents, their life experience and ambitions. It's only through their loyalty that we've achieved what we have, their self-belief and trust in the Foundation. And you've played a large part in it, Isabel, so special thanks to you.'

'Well, I do take my role seriously and the older residents are your key partners, as you're saying. However, you haven't made it easy for me, Nathan, by failing to inform us, let alone consult us, on this significant change, which is clearly going to affect the trials and treatments. We accept we're the guinea pigs but we want to be well-informed guinea pigs. We have to be confident we can weigh up risks and benefits.'

'Point taken but, in my defence, we're negotiating a company merger and I'm sure you'll have experienced this situation in your business career. You can't announce anything until it's secured and you've agreed the high-level goals, which is now done, I'm pleased to say. We can move on to the research strategy and I hope you'll take the lead in canvassing the views of the residents as that develops.'

'Certainly, and I should have been canvassing their views from the start. These high-level goals, what are they? And why this partner – Lextar, is it?'

Nathan repeated what he had explained to Shani about the shift from healthspan to extended lifespan, adding detail in reply to Isabel's probing questions. Normally, this kind of conversation set Shani's brain buzzing but she was struggling to focus, still digesting the news about Josh's disappearance and its possible ramifications, if Finn or anyone else knew about her impulsive, fleeting thing with him. And where was Josh now? That was the other worry…

'Shani?'

Nathan's voice was too loud, almost a bark; he had noticed her wandering off.

'Yes, no, sorry, I was thinking about it, new ideas. Shall I do the plan for the trials?'

'Well, as I say, just the key points for Isabel, how it affects the participants.'

This wasn't difficult, Shani reminded herself, and it mattered how well she did it. She took a quiet deep breath and launched straight in, as if giving a lecture.

'Okay, so the new research trials will be organised into three tiers.

'Tier one continues the current programme; prevention and treatment of illness and age-related conditions. This will include stem-cell and gene-therapy interventions, our latest anti-ageing medicines and cocktails, nanosurgery, bionics and organ regeneration.

'Tier two involves similar methods but with accelerators and combined approaches, as well as testing of novel medicines and biosynthetic innovations. The aim is to speed up age reversal and rejuvenation and work towards radical life extension.

'Tier three focuses on the brain and mind, as this is where regeneration is most complex and there are still many challenges, following our success in the detection and prevention of dementia and other neurodegenerative conditions.

'Residents will be required to participate at a minimum level but they are free to choose which tier to join and whether they take part in any particular trial. We'll carry out rigorous risk analysis and there are no plans to alter our generous incentive arrangements.'

The delivery was rapid but she had managed to propel herself to the end without tripping up. Her stomach was contracting with nerves, like it was a tricky job interview or she was defending her academic work to a fierce external examiner. She generally got on fine with Isabel and she probably liked the brisk approach, but you could never tell what was going to bug her, apart from any threat to her own superior position. And Shani wasn't sure that Nathan would come to her aid if things got difficult. Line of least resistance, that was him every time. They both waited for Isabel's response, while Isabel herself sat back, pursing her lips and fiddling with one of her dangly gold earrings.

'Thank you… Radical life extension – it sounds momentous, I like it. Keeping tier one makes a lot of sense, as some residents will be anxious otherwise. I need to get on top of the detail but I'm confident I can bring people round if they're wavering, and mostly they're adventurous or curious types who'll jump at it anyway. But we're an awkward bunch too, very contrary. Do you really want to keep us going indefinitely, Nathan, make us immortal?'

He smiled. 'No, your age group will avoid that, we can safely predict. But the idea of longevity escape velocity, a dramatic lift-off towards life extension and immortality, is on the horizon. With our considered approach, the research will take time and some trials will go on longer, which is why we're widening the age range for participants, starting younger. It also means extending our collaboration with other select clusters.' Shani was giving him a subtle hand sign. 'But I expect Shani has to get back to her work. If you like, Isabel, do stay and I'll tell you more about Lextar, our new partner.'

'I will, but while Shani's here, there's something else.' Shani knew what was coming, although Isabel's searching blue eyes were fixed on Nathan, not on her. 'Why did you bring out all the security guards to arrest and evict a single student, like it was a riot? Is this a change of policy and are we going to see more of it in future? Because I'll tell you now, it breaches the Foundation's contract with residents and won't be tolerated. We want a quiet life and discreet security, not a show of force. And if it was just a one-off, what did this young man do to provoke such an extreme reaction?' She flicked her head, turning to Shani. 'You know the students; can you enlighten me?'

Shani froze, her mind going blank. *Answer, say something.*

'I can't discuss that now,' said Nathan. 'Another time. Thanks, Shani, you can go.'

Wow, that was decisive; he should try it more often. Shani walked back over the garden bridge with a great sense of relief. She had carried it off okay, Isabel had given her backing in principle and Nathan had saved her, unwittingly she assumed, from having to be evasive or tell outright lies. Even disregarding her brief personal entanglement with Josh, she knew too much about what the students had been doing with the cybirds. She should have reported their activity when she first got wind of it but she had held back, for all the wrong reasons, and now it was too late.

**

Paul and Trish had visited all the natural environments the Foundation had acquired along with Wellowfern, but the coastal path was their clear favourite. The looptrain took just six minutes to reach the coast, and it was a half-hour walk from the station to the cliff top and the rocky track down to the beach. You could only ramble so far as the area was bounded by security gates and fences on three sides and they preferred to turn around before they were close to the perimeter. Their route involved an easy stroll along the top path, then a scramble down to the beach and a splashy walk back along the sea's edge until they reached the next headland, meeting the track again where it wound up from the rocks and caves.

There were several boats out in the bay, including a luxury yacht, a fishing vessel and two sailing dinghies, but none was near the shoreline. The security guards weren't in sight, of course, but they had hidden viewpoints and would be ready to deal with any threatened landing on the sand. Knowing this fact disturbed Paul's sense of freedom and his enjoyment of the peaceful scene, but he was used to it now; it was still a delightful, unspoilt place.

'Is here okay for our picnic?' asked Trish as they completed the circuit, pulling the strap of her timeworn canvas shoulder-bag over her head. Paul squatted and sat back on the soft grass, legs apart as he took out the two water bottles and popped open their shared lunch box. He unlaced his tough walking boots and started to eat a sandwich wrap with both hands, gazing out towards the horizon. Trish sat beside him and laid her hand on his knee.

'I'm so glad we did this, Paul. I know it was rushed, they wanted a quick decision and you had other ideas, other places—'

'It's fine, really, Trish, don't keep worrying about it. I want to be with you, that's why I'm at Wellowfern.' He put his hand over hers and nudged against her shoulder, unbalancing her. 'Hey, see the seagulls following that yellow boat. They must have a net or a line out, however they do wild fishing these days. Looks quite traditional.'

'Yeah, I don't know...' She turned towards him. 'And think of our parents, what they went through. Your dad struggling with dementia, it must have been awful for both of them, and my mum, the pain... We're spared all that and we've got so much to live for, so many more years of these lovely walks.'

'No, yes, it's good. I do feel very... privileged.'

He knew this was inadequate, too half-hearted. There were some great aspects to living at Wellowfern, he appreciated that, but something still jarred with him. The Healthy Ageing Foundation presented itself as progressive and enlightened, while it exuded privilege in every way. It wasn't what he had expected to do and it continued to surprise him, landing up here. He had returned to England from heat-stroked Australia before the legal channels were blocked off, finding a remote cottage high on the edge of the moor where he had kept hens, bees and two friendly nanny goats. It had been another huge wrench, leaving there, but in the end it wasn't tenable, being so isolated and with dwindling resources locally, and the stifling summer heat taking over, invading spring and autumn. The cherry tree would be flowering about now, two months early, the bluebells carpeting the dell in his little spinney at the bottom of the garden.

'Are you worried about the new scientific director, Paul, how things might change?'

The yellow fishing boat was circling, tracing a ring of small white crests on the sea. It went around once more and the sight stirred something in Paul, a faint memory. It was too indistinct; he couldn't recall what it was, except it had to do with Trish, their first summer.

He stood up to brush the crumbs off his trousers.

'Not worried, that's too strong. You know Wellowfern wouldn't be my first choice if I was still on my own. I'd have gone for a different cluster, Education and Human Skills or one of the environmental movements. It's working out here, though, because you've got enough idealism for both of us, and being half of a couple I'm not compelled to buy the whole deal. I might even sign up to a research trial, not impossible, but generally I'm happy to keep my head down and get on with work. That's going well, it suits me. It's just all this secrecy and anticipation, the silly rumours; I could do without it.'

He was aware that Trish had begun to cover for his scepticism in front of others, but why should she have to? Their friends held a wide range of views and weren't all crazily enthusiastic about the trials, or the lifestyle regime for that matter. Isabel was committed to it all, but she seemed more intent on her personal mission to rule the roost, while Suzanne preferred mysticism to cutting-edge science and DJ Johnny just wanted to have a good time and play his music. All good reasons to stay young and keep going longer, but it wasn't some kind of religion. And although Trish *was* idealistic, it wasn't the only reason she'd wanted to move to Wellowfern. She had reached the point where running the wildlife park with her ex, Matthew, was no longer viable. They were outpaced by the surging rates of extinction, the problems of transporting wild creatures across hot, desolate and lawless territories and the steep drop-off in interest and support as people turned to more urgent and immediate priorities. She could have stayed to develop the fruit-farm idea with Matthew, but without the animals her passion for the joint project, and her love for him, had wilted and died.

And then Paul's stark message had dropped on her out of the blue, a blast from the past throwing everything up in the air. He was just as responsible for upending Trish's life as she was for dramatically changing his direction.

'Look, Trish, that yellow boat's going round in circles. Does it remind you of anything from when we first met, that summer?'

Trish watched for a few moments, then picked up a mottled pebble and stroked its surface with her thumb. 'Was it that time we borrowed a boat for the evening and then lost our way back in the dark? Or when we got picked up by the police on the beach and had to sit in their car for hours, blue light flashing, while they checked to see we hadn't run away from home... we were that young, just imagine it. Or after that, when we rented the old van and drove south – what was the name of the island? God, Paul, this was so long ago.'

Paul struggled to think of it. 'I forget the name, it was off the coast of Yugoslavia. Camping on the beach, skinny-dipping, collecting wood for the fire. Amazing.'

'And it was completely isolated, do you remember, all ours? We had to park the van on the road and slide down a sheer rock face to the beach, more or less. Scarily steep.'

'Yes, only it was more like scree, loose gravel where you couldn't find a footing.' He closed his eyes to concentrate, conjure it up. 'Hang on... yeah, got it. There's the yellow speedboat swerving round into the bay, the woman water skiing behind and the next thing, it's way out of control. The man's standing at the wheel, all frantic shouting and waving, and then he tips overboard, just like that. The boat's going round in smaller and smaller circles, trapping her inside the ring, and he's thrashing about trying to grab her.'

'Zeus, it's coming back to me,' said Trish. 'She was all cut up by the propeller, deep slicing gashes down one side of her body and criss-crossing down her legs. How did they get to shore? What the fuck did we do?'

'We waded out as far as we could. He was carrying her in when we reached them. He stank of booze. We turned our tent into a stretcher and somehow we managed to drag and bump her up that cliff. I've never seen injuries like that, exposing everything and spilling out of her like clear jelly – like… human frogspawn.'

'Yuk, don't.' Sitting close, Paul felt her shudder of repulsion running through him too. 'And the guy had the nerve to come back the next day, didn't he? We'd driven them to the hospital, skidding round those hairpin bends on two wheels, and in the morning he turned up in another flashy speedboat and paid us off, cool as anything.'

Paul frowned. 'Hold on. What do you mean, paid us off?'

'He suggested we pack up and move on, so we wouldn't get drawn into an inquiry, that was the gist. Except we took it more as a naked threat than a suggestion, but then he was understandably distressed. His girlfriend had died overnight.'

'She'd died? No, that's not right. I'm sure we heard from them soon after, a postcard or something when we got home, and she was okay.'

'No, honestly she did, Paul – she died of her injuries, or perhaps it was a heart attack, I don't know. The guy gave us a shedload of money, in dollars it was, to make ourselves scarce. He'd been drinking, you said it, he was well up shit creek. And we took the dosh, no scruples.'

Paul shook his head, puzzled. 'That last part, that's not how I remember it at all.'

'Well, as I say, this was sixty-odd years ago. Maybe it's surprising that so much of the story actually matches up. They often don't, when you get to compare notes.'

The yellow fishing boat had found its straight course again and was moving away. A seagull landed near to Paul and waited expectantly for them to leave their lunch spot.

'Strange… we packed such a lot into that one giddy summer.' She paused. 'Wish we could hire a boat here, take our best friends out, drop anchor and picnic in a pretty cove. A small sailing boat, that's what I'm imagining, so no risk of water skiing, although I'd like to see Isabel give it a try.'

'We'll probably find she's three times world champion, from way back.'

He picked up a random pebble, heavier than the one Trish had chosen, and aimed it at the cheeky seagull, almost hitting it as it flew off to a safer distance.

'Hey, don't, what the hell's that for? It was only hanging around for the crumbs.' She jumped up and began to run on the spot. 'Time to go home anyway – race you back!'

Paul got up and stretched out his arms, as if making peace with the gull, showing his underlying friendliness. The bird ignored both him and the sparsely scattered picnic crumbs, looking directly out to sea before flying straight upwards, wings flapping as it hovered oddly in mid-air, like a giant hummingbird. This acted as a signal to other birds, which flew up simultaneously out of the rough patches of vegetation around them. It wasn't just seagulls but smaller species too, the sand dwellers and cliff nesters that still clung on precariously to their traditional habitats.

Trish had set off at a fast jog. 'Wait!' shouted Paul. 'Something's happening – look over there!'

It wasn't the noise, because there wasn't any; no sound at all. The dark shapes of the copters appeared silently above the two headlands, to left and right of the bay, perfectly choreographed so the two groups sliced gracefully between each other before they dropped to land on the opposite cliff tops. There must have been around forty in total; it was too quick to count.

And then came the boats, again skimming silently but high-powered and very fast, their bows lifted up in the air as they navigated the rocks around the headlands. The yellow fishing boat was almost out of the bay, keeping a middle course, and the other vessels had already gone, perhaps given a warning or instruction.

'What is it?' whispered Trish.

'Don't know yet. We should leave, go home.'

'Ah no, let's watch, it's exciting. We're protected here. The guards—'

'You are so bloody trusting, Trish.' He felt torn but the need to understand this situation was going to win out, so in a way he was grateful for her confidence and curiosity.

'Let's get closer to the edge and lie down. We can't be seen to be spying on them.'

They had wriggled forward into position when the copters all lifted at once and formed a circle in the sky. The boats were spreading across the bay in different directions, still moving fast and swerving at the last moment, almost playfully it seemed, to avoid direct contact. Then the attack began: a hail of soundless missiles striking the boats, sending them sideways, the targets split in half or upturned, their hulls gleaming white. But no one in the water; no splashing, no climbing the hulls or attempting to hold on to floating debris. The copters had regrouped, reverting to left and right flanks and advancing on the cliff edge, where Trish and Paul were now lying prone, their arms covering their heads and faces burrowing into the ground. It was more than a whisker but very close, maybe five metres above them, the sensation barely registering as the fleet of aircraft passed over.

'Whew! Have they gone?'

'Can't hear anything.'

Paul raised his head, spitting out the pieces of grass in his mouth. Trish had a mask of dirt covering her nose and cheeks. They started to giggle as the tension eased, then heard a polite cough behind them.

'Excuse me.' The man was on the path, a coastal security guard with a weapon slung over his shoulder. They sat up instantly, recovering themselves, although Paul still felt dazed and disoriented. Luckily, Trish was more on the ball and quick to respond.

'Hi. We're residents of Wellowfern, just out for a walk.'

'I know who you are, I checked and it's okay. Hope you enjoyed your walk.'

'Thank you,' said Paul, 'we did. What was this going on? Should we be alarmed?'

'No, not at all, sir. It's an exercise, testing out our tactical force, air-sea combo.'

'Looks pretty effective to me,' said Trish. 'Was anyone in the boats?'

'I can't say, madam. Just that it's new and unique – we're the first to have it.'

'Was anyone in the copters?' asked Paul, pushing it.

The guy was clearly proud of the display and he might even be tempted to share his knowledge or conjecture. He perhaps hadn't twigged that it could spell the end of his role, the old-fashioned cliff-top watch.

'I can't say, sir. Now you must go straight back to the station and catch the looptrain home. You shouldn't have been here; it was an oversight not closing it for the day.'

'We're going… very happy for you to escort us.'

'I'll stay at my post, there's a high risk of incursions. We're here to defend Wellowfern, twenty-four seven.'

Three

Isabel sent Trish up to the roof garden to see who had turned up, while she filled bowls with nuts, berries and mushroom bites, selected the wine and opened a box of her home-printed dark chocolates. She was impressed by Georgina, the incoming scientific director, who had given an engaging talk at the reception and fielded the stream of questions and comments smoothly and with a nice touch of humour. She wondered what her friends would pick up on this evening; there were many angles and intriguing possibilities. Hopefully the vitality snacks and nootropic chocolates would liven things up as the conversation progressed.

'Four in the roof garden now, so that's six with us,' called Trish, as she came down the external steps. 'Paul, DJ Johnny, Suzanne and a new resident called Harvey. He's moved into Esther's apartment. I missed that somehow, Esther leaving us. Didn't she celebrate the one-two-five a couple of years ago? What happened, do you know? Did she die, go to live with family or transfer to another cluster? Surely we should have been told?'

Isabel reached up for an additional wine glass and clunked it heavily against another as she thumped it down on the tray. The glasses were tough and durable, although designed to look expensive and delicate like the high-end crystal glassware she used to own.

'No idea. It's news to me and you're right, Trish, it's unacceptable to hear it from this Harvey, whoever he is. I'll take it up with Nathan, let him know it mustn't happen again. And who invited Harvey tonight? How did he get in on our little gathering?'

'Don't know, Isabel. He probably met DJ Johnny in the bar this afternoon.'

'Ah Johnny, yes, that makes sense.'

It was after nine-thirty but still warm outside, the temperature nicely moderated by the solar shield. Apart from this invisible effect, the roof garden scene could have been one from thirty or forty years ago: wooden flower tubs and herb beds, simple solar lighting on the pebbled path, a wrought-iron trellis, a grassed area and beautiful red sandstone paving. The first residents had co-created it to remind them of their previous gardens, and Isabel thought of it as her special retro-retreat, although it was open to everyone in the building.

The small group had collected at the far end of the terrace, no doubt because Johnny liked to stretch out in the hammock. Yes, there he was with Suzanne, who was using her feet to push herself back and forth gently in the hanging swing-chair. Paul and the new guy sat opposite each other at the nearby table, Harvey facing towards Isabel as she picked her way over the pebbles with the loaded tray. He jumped up and came towards her with a wide smile, his hands outstretched. She stopped, instinctively wary, trying to gauge him.

'Please, let me.'

She held on to the tray, hugging it closer to her chest. He moved back with a slight bow, giving her space but still standing ahead of her on the path.

'I'm Harvey, it's great to meet you. I'm the new kid on the block, number eighteen.'

He was tall and nicely tanned, with a distinct American accent. He also looked youthful. Nathan had said they planned to widen the age group but she didn't expect it to be this quick. And Harvey was probably much older than he seemed. She found herself gripping the tray more tightly, creating a solid barrier to his amused, open gaze. He nodded appreciatively, as if confirming something about her. DJ Johnny could have made an outlandish comment over drinks at the bar; that would be par for the course.

'Yes, eighteen, that's Esther's apartment. No one said she was leaving. Did you move in suddenly, I mean at short notice?'

He straightened up, perhaps taken aback by her semi-belligerent tone. Isabel was tall as well and it was unusual to find someone towering over her. She wished she'd chosen a pair of heels for this event, ideally her vintage leopard stilettos.

'No, I guess I went through all the usual preliminaries, no stone left unturned.'

Isabel softened her expression; after all, it wasn't his fault about Esther. But still, there was something unsettling, as if they were playing out an already rehearsed encounter.

'Well, it's good to meet you, Harvey, and welcome to Wellowfern. Thank you for coming along tonight, it's a kind of informal briefing about the changes at the top, what's going on. Can I get past, please? This is getting heavy.'

He stepped onto the grass. 'I'm deeply honoured to be invited. Johnny assured me you'd be cool with it.' His smile was sudden and lopsided, making his hazel eyes crinkle up nicely, like an older man or perhaps revealing his true age.

Trish poured the wine while Isabel told them about the reception, the merger with Lextar and what Nathan and Georgina had said about how it would affect them. She was careful to stress that much would stay the same and they could choose their level of involvement, plus they would have expert advice on risk-benefit trade-offs, particularly around new types of research trials.

'So – questions, comments? What do you think?'

Paul leapt in first. 'But it's a *huge* change, surely? I understand why they'd move on from healthspan, given the drive to keep ahead of the game in biotech advances. There's a whole argument about who gets the benefits and who loses, but aside from that, it's a big difference between extending lifespan by degrees and what they're calling radical life extension, making longevity the goal and accelerating it by whatever means. It raises lots of issues for us as individuals, for Wellowfern and also for the Fringe public out there.'

'They didn't say by whatever means, Paul,' countered Trish. 'You're reading that into it. It's still going to be based on scientific and medical trials, properly designed studies.'

'That doesn't mean it won't have unpredictable effects, things we haven't even—'

'For God's sake, that's the whole point, isn't it, discovery? It sounds exciting to me.'

Isabel had anticipated disagreement between Trish

and Paul, knowing their different stances, but she was determined not to let it overshadow the discussion.

'DJ Johnny wants to say something. Go on, Johnny.'

'How ancient will we get? That's what I wonder,' mused DJ Johnny, twisting into a sitting position in the hammock. 'They've always been coy about it. They should come clean and give us a firm EED, Expected Expiry Date. And a free one-way ticket to heaven.'

'Only if we can override it,' said Isabel, 'if we can choose our end date. I'd insist on that, Johnny. We've come a long way since the Fates chose our destiny, and we have most of the tools now, medically and scientifically. It's a little scary, I admit.'

Suzanne leant forward, twiddling with the red ribbon at the end of her long plait.

'You can't override luck or destiny, Isabel.'

'Or someone else's malign intervention,' added Paul.

Trish threw up her hands. 'Hey, come on you two, lighten up! We'll have to get a few more gigs out of you first, Johnny, and definitely a fantastic event for your final fling. It'll be a complete sell-out!'

'Okay,' said Isabel, 'here's one of Georgina's nuggets. Some scientist has calculated that the lifespan of a medical immortal, someone who's immune to diseases and ailments, would average 5,775 years before they have a fatal incident. And for most of history, death wasn't particularly associated with old age, as there was so much danger at every stage of life. It was child mortality that was the most… but I'm digressing, let's go on. Suzanne, you always have an interesting take. Anything more at this point?'

Johnny put his hand up. 'It'll be a race to bump your partner off, that's what.'

Suzanne fixed her gaze on a spot just above Isabel's head. It was always difficult to predict her state of mind, how grounded she was in present reality. The chocolates didn't help either, making her unusually spaced out too quickly. Right now, though, she was still fully in tune with the conversation.

'There's too much talk about science, as if it explains everything. I believe in a fusion of science and magic. Einstein is revered as a scientist and he said that the most beautiful thing we can experience is the mysterious; it's the source of all art and science. And when it comes to life and death, we shouldn't expect to know everything or desire to control it. It would be different if people could connect intimately with those who've passed on, if they still accepted the idea of the spirit life beyond. I'm so lucky, reincarnation is a beautiful gift.'

Isabel glanced at Harvey, who gave her an indiscreet wink. The swing-chair creaked a little as Suzanne kept it going with her feet, her eyes closed until Paul spoke up again.

'So elegantly put, Suzanne. Without mysteries, there would be no science. Death can be comforting sometimes, and the chance factor is a good thing, it stops us taking ourselves so seriously. It's about morality too, I think, what the social costs are and who loses out.'

'Why should anyone lose out, in the long run?' said Isabel. 'It's been a tough time for humanity, I'll grant that, but so has every other stage in our social and intellectual evolution. In twenty-five years, we've had three pandemics, the mineral wars, bio-attacks, cyber crashes, the data implosion, super-eruptions, wildfires, floods, drought and mass human and animal migration. And alongside all that disruption, the inspired creation of select clusters and smart cities aiming to protect and develop our unique talents and powers. It needs careful nurturing but I believe it can fan out and offer more people a richer and longer life, like we enjoy here.'

'Get real, Isabel.' She hadn't heard Paul speak this forcefully. 'Do you honestly think that's the way it's going – towards an idyllic, peaceful future where planet Earth and everyone on it thrives?'

'What are *you* saying, Paul? That you don't trust our own Foundation, when it's—'

'It's not the Foundation any more. We're told this is a merger, but usually you find—'

'Enough, you two,' said Trish. 'We're off the topic.'

'Let's stay with it then,' said Isabel. 'Why would we want to live longer? What for? Do you want to come in first, Harvey, you haven't spoken yet?'

'No, I'm chilled just listening, acclimatising and getting to know you guys. I'll be saying plenty in future, for sure. Enjoy the silence while it lasts!'

'Right, we'll let you off this evening and await your profound insights with interest. Johnny, what about you then? You've lived the longest, why keep going?'

'Easy – it's the songs, the great lyrics. And having fun, making you all happy. I'll go when I'm ready, simple as that. My dad dropped of a heart attack at fifty-eight, so I've doubled him already. Not bad for an all-night rocker who survived on pizza, beer and doughnuts.'

'Won't you join in the new trials, Johnny?' asked Suzanne. She was still awake, then. 'I mean these add-on ones – what did you call it, Isabel?'

'Radical life extension. It's Georgina's phrase, the new scientific director.'

'I might take part to keep my points up, earn my little luxuries,' said Johnny.

Suzanne pulled a face. 'I don't like "radical", it sounds like uprooting things. I moved here because I had a dementia diagnosis, it was detected early, before I had symptoms. I'd have got ill and declined slowly. So, I feel I've just had my extra time in this life. I don't need them to offer me an extension.'

Paul nodded. 'Sure, that's going to affect your view. I'm in favour of what the Healthy Ageing Foundation has done so far, beating cruel diseases. Who wouldn't be? And I share your concern, Suzanne. I guess a lot depends on this new director, Georgina. What are your first impressions, Isabel?'

'I like her,' said Isabel. 'She's very positive and she seemed to listen carefully when I talked about keeping the residents properly informed. Trish, what do you think?'

'I'm reserving judgement for now. I'm attracted by the big ideas, though. Just imagine, really historic breakthroughs would be immensely powerful and we'd all be part of it.'

'Totally agree,' said Isabel, 'but again, do we want to live much longer, maybe decades? Paul, you ducked it just now.'

Paul's hand was round his chin, the tops of his fingers stroking his left cheek. 'I'm just as curious as anyone. I want to see what happens.'

'Is that a yes?'

'It's complicated. I ask myself, what's the purpose? Is it worth the investment? And I don't share your optimism, Isabel. The world's a total mess, the global movements and select clusters are the dominant power bases, national and local governments are weak to non-existent, essential resources are tightly controlled by the clusters or their smart cities and most people are barely surviving – or stagnating on the Fringes, if they are lucky.'

Trish was fidgety, rolling her eyes at Isabel until she got the chance to come in.

'It's my turn. Living for almost 6,000 years sounds wild, but then you're in the realm of living forever, because we'll probably be brought back from fatal accidents or murderous attacks, who knows? More likely we'll all be cyborgs or disembodied digital minds. That's just round the corner, the full upload. Anyway, I want to live as long as humanly possible. And I'm with you, Isabel. As a species, humankind has always been driven to excess, or success... yes, we're driven to success, that's better.'

'Okay,' said Isabel, 'some very interesting perspectives. Back to you, Harvey, if you've changed your mind about staying quiet.'

'I'll just say one word, if I may – Mars.'

Johnny chuckled. 'Nah, Mars is already piled with junk. It'll be overrun and tacky in no time, a party planet and dodgy haven for criminals and bent tycoons with loot squirrelled away in space banks. And there's next to no effing atmosphere. We have the atmosphere!'

'Nice one,' replied Harvey, joining in the laughter and reaching for the bowl of nuts.

Isabel smiled. 'A small topic for another day, then. For me, it's always about climbing the next peak and discovering a higher, craggier one behind it. That's why I'll go for the tier three studies, brain and mind. They say it's radical, but it's really just continuing what's been happening for thousands of years, if you look at the history of medicine. Living longer lets us set bigger goals and make more spectacular discoveries.'

Hopefully, she had avoided coming across as evangelical; no one liked it if you overdid the passion. This conversation showed she had her work cut out to reassure more cautious residents and persuade them to join the new trials. And Suzanne had finally drifted off into a trance. She gazed ahead, the words made dramatic by her queer, monotone voice.

'The rats are running, the sky's alight and the birds have found their wings.'

'Suzanne's back in London again – the Great Fire is my guess, 1666,' offered Johnny.

'We've got rats here too, hordes of them still in the labs,' said Paul. 'Except they're white ones now, with pink tails and red eyes. We should have phased them out ages ago, set them free now we're laser-focused on cybird development.'

Isabel was drawn into a vivid mental slideshow: feral brown rats swarming over the piazza, then the black-booted security guards with their razor-sharp whistles, and finally the albino lab rats – beaten-up, infected and grotesquely transmuted – making their desperate, mad escape under cover of a low-flying flock of cybirds.

As the others dispersed, leaving Suzanne to wake in her own time, Isabel and Trish stayed in the kitchen to clear things away and round up the evening. Isabel felt shaken after her freakish hallucination but this wasn't the moment to show it.

'Just you and me then, Trish, going for gold. So far. And Harvey, I really don't get—'

'Yay, the go-go girls! He sounds like a space junkie. Cute though, don't you think?'

'Not sure about cute, but enigmatic, or trying to make himself so. Natty white shoes.'

'It's a start, and you said you've given up on the spiritorium, Isabel, the sex part of it.'

Isabel picked up a wet dishcloth and threatened to throw it: 'Shut up, you, or I'll—!'

'Look out, here she comes, the Lady Ghost of the Roof Garden.'

Suzanne floated in, lifted her imaginary long skirts to present each of them with a deep curtsey, including homebot Lottie, and swept out of the apartment by the front door.

***

Isabel liked to show new residents around the village, partly because she was proud of it and also to find out about the person, their motives and what involvement she might expect of them. They often didn't have much clue about the practicalities of research trials, being more interested in the premium lifestyle or the opportunity to use their talents in novel ways. This was a key theme in the promotional literature: self-actualisation and creativity as natural partners of fitness and good health in later life.

All that bumph, the glossy brochures that still went out on request, it would have to be altered now that Lextar was taking over with its new mission. And thinking about the rooftop conversation among her group of friends, they would have to adapt the pitch for the trials. Was Harvey aware of this shift to radical life extension when he decided to move in? Here he was now, strolling out of the apartment building; trendy jacket, blue button-down shirt, the same white pointy shoes and light swagger.

'Isabel, hi, ready to roll. Lead on!'

'Morning, Harvey. We'll walk to the old city walls. There's not much left of them but they still define the boundary at the far end. That takes us across the park, along the river and over the bridge to the Institute. We'll come back through the residential streets to the domes, the university campus and the arcade, just across the piazza there.'

'Ah, that's what I'm most dead keen to see, the famous domes. I heard about them at the start, when I was introduced to Lextar. The big chiefs in America are watching carefully and you can bet they'll up their game on lifestyle now they've got this neat Wellowfern model to work with. Any chance of tweaking the plan and taking in the domes first?'

Isabel nodded okay, repressing her annoyance at this admittedly trivial challenge to her authority. It didn't matter and she had already found out something useful before they even got going: he had connections at Lextar HQ and claimed some inside knowledge.

'Yes, fine. I insist on doing the full orientation circuit, though, so we'll just take a few minutes on each thing. You can explore it all properly in your own time.'

They walked into the park and towards the six domes, which were of different sizes and not all strictly dome-shaped. They were linked together by a series of smaller structures and enclosed pathways, made of glass-like material but pliable and embedded with colours and natural textures, which altered in response to atmospheric conditions: light, heat, humidity and rain. Today it was dry and fresh and the dominant tinge was pale green.

'Which one's the planetarium? Has it got its own rocket launch pad yet?'

'No, most of us aren't planning on leaving Earth, but the simulation is superb and it's not restricted to Mars, you can choose your planetary destination or shoot off to a far distant galaxy. Or you can lie back, enjoy the deepest sounds of the universe and experience it all happening in full multi-sensory mode. It's the largest dome, that one there.' She pointed. 'It's got dozens of interactive displays and zillions of exhibits from the history of space travel, plus captivating installations on way-out space conspiracy theories and alien encounters.'

'Awesome, just my style. And the other domes, what are they?'

'Okay, left to right, there's the gymnasium, menagerie, auditorium, planetarium, dining dome and spiritorium. That last one, the spiritorium, it's about the fusion of mind, body and spirit in promoting health, vigour and longevity. It's Suzanne's favourite, as you can imagine, especially the mystical elements. Generally, the domes are loved and well used by everyone, I'd say. The menagerie is my favourite, very special.'

Harvey stepped back several paces for a wider perspective. 'Jeez, they're way more impressive than I even imagined. There's still open land behind – will it be developed?'

'Wouldn't think so, we're happy with what we've got. There was talk of an eco-dome five years ago when I first arrived, but it never came to anything, for some reason. Perhaps it was too late, too dispiriting, I don't know. Do you want a quick peek into the planetarium?'

'No, let's not rush it. I appreciate you taking the time for this, Isabel, and being so well informed. Why don't we stop off for a latte?'

'It's part of my job as top resident rep, helping people settle in and get involved. It works for me too, means I can keep a close eye on management and make sure they don't get above themselves. Having run a business, I know something about corporate behaviour, how it can mutate and go toxic. Let's finish the tour and I'll take you to my favourite café. It has cakes and slices to die for. If there's something irresistible we both want, it'll be all-out war.'

He winked. 'Go on, let's take a chance.'

This was turning flirtatious. Isabel was highly skilled at deploying charm to get her own way, but she already felt she was running to catch up, or maintain her pole position.

'I'll order two carrot and brazil nut slices in advance, they're the best.'

'Hey, don't I get to choose? They may have my number one, orange and pecan pie.'

'Mmm, think I'd have noticed that one before now, but they specialise in on-the-spot creations, so you might

50

be in luck. I'd have both if it wasn't for Cyril, my cybird, knowing what I'm up to and reading me the riot act. He's a total killjoy and easily ruffled if I go overboard on sugary stuff or alcohol, or anything else that's on his no-no list. You'll get a cybird too, if you haven't already, so you'll find out. Some people love them more than I do, and I have to admit Cyril can be useful, underneath it all.'

They followed her circuit and arrived back at the arcade, which housed a long row of individual units nestled under the wide stone arches. It was a mix of traditional shops, small service businesses, themed cafés, workshop spaces and galleries with the latest in virtual experiences – including world travel, encounters with historical figures and exploration of inner space: memory, desires and emotions. 'Wellowfern in microcosm,' as Isabel described it with her signature final flourish: 'Living the dream and celebrating past and future in equal measure.'

The café was bustling and came up with both their first cake choices. As she watched Harvey shoving in forkfuls of his pecan pie, Isabel wondered whether to mention Esther, see if he had any idea why she had vacated her apartment so mysteriously. He looked up from his plate, catching the intensity of her gaze.

'What is it? Do I have goo all over my face? Or have I said something—'

'No… well yes, what you said about Lextar, being introduced to it in America. Did you live in one of their select clusters over there, a city village like this?'

He finished off the slice and used his fingers to wipe the crumbs from around his mouth. The backs of his hands were smooth; this was still a tell-tale sign for youth, although much more subtle these days. The American clusters were probably ahead in recruiting younger participants for their regeneration studies.

'No, I was in Denver, in its neighbouring smart city. I worked in a small tech start-up that was bidding for exciting projects and we won a contract with Lextar. That's when I discovered Wellowfern; the merger was coming through. I was a free agent and this place really appealed – the location, site design, enrichment facilities and access to stunning natural environments. It's the right decision, I believe, your Healthy Ageing Foundation teaming up with Lextar. It'll sharpen the scientific programme, take it to another level. That's where the Foundation was in danger of falling behind.'

This all sounded good. As a committed advocate of the merger, he was bound to opt for the tier three brain and mind trials, which would give Isabel easy credit points. And he had listened to the views of her friends on the roof terrace, stayed quiet himself; maybe he could be useful in persuading wavering residents to edge up a notch, share in the wider ambition and reap the personal rewards.

'I agree,' said Isabel. 'It makes sense to me, moving on from healthspan to extended lifespan, but it's not so simple for everyone, as you heard at our roof garden get-together. We've got work to do, to bring the majority of residents on board. There aren't any pushovers here, they've got strong views hardened over time, or they're plain bolshie.'

'That'll be factored into the strategy. You and me, Isabel, we're both coming at it from risk-driven sectors, so we judge it differently from most. I can't think of a better example than the world of space insurance, and you seem to have made an astronomical success of it. You had a sure-fire business model there.'

Isabel laid her fork down squarely on the plate, then carefully adjusted its position to an exact diagonal. She made herself look at him and tried to sound casual, slightly puzzled.

'Who… How do you know about that? There's no public record, it's all been erased.'

His hesitation was barely perceptible, and followed instantly by the disarming smile.

'I've done my homework, naturally, and there are always hidden sources, as you well know. It's easy to follow a trail once you pick up the thread. I did it for all the Foundation's resident reps – they're crucial to the credibility of the project. We're going to need them.'

She noted his slick appropriation of "the project", the presumption in "we're going to need them", but they weren't the main things that rattled her.

'Well, I guess it was naive of me to think… I should be flattered, I suppose.'

'Dead right, you should. You'll be an enormous asset, Isabel, no question.'

Four

Isabel lay back in the chair, eyes closed, while Sarita washed her hair and gave her a head massage. She tried to visualise a flotilla of small boats and rafts drifting towards her, as she sat on a low rock and used her bare feet to push them gently back out into the lake. This calming technique often worked to some degree, but today it was useless. She was wound up and the same questions kept floating into her mind. Who was this self-assured American guy living in Esther's apartment? What was his connection to Lextar? And what did he know about her space insurance business? Who had he talked to?

Stop it; this was silly. He had checked out the resident reps, and no doubt the senior team as well, before deciding to move to a new country. It was fair enough. She knew it was feasible and she'd used some of the so-called hidden sources herself. And anyway, her ex-business partner, Jerome, had disappeared long ago into a new identity. He was light-footed and even if he was tracked down, he had every reason to keep shtum.

'Can you press harder, Sarita, do it more firmly? And then massage my shoulders and upper back after this, it all feels very tight.'

She usually found the salon experience blissful, a reminder that the genuine personal touch still existed and was essential to overall wellbeing. It hadn't been extinguished by the robot hairdressers, who had no flair or artistry and were hopeless at gossip and chitchat.

'Yes, I can fit that in for you, Isabel, give you a nice firm massage. Have you bought any new fish for your aquarium? I heard there's another one, a Japanese variety that does cool dance moves, that's what I'm told. It's on special offer next week.'

'Well, that's as may be. Don't believe everything you hear, Sarita. It might just wave itself about, like most fish. The new types may look fabulous but they really aren't much of an advance on the real ones, which can be magical. Natural goldfish are exotic mutants and can regenerate their optic nerve without any intervention. Ouch, you pulled at my hair with that comb, it's not like you to be rough. What's the matter?'

'I'm sorry, it got caught in a tangle. I… I'm worried, to be honest. My children, they're only eight and ten and I need to have them living here with me. It's not right for them in the Fringes, their dad's not coping and last weekend there was a power cut, longer than usual…'

'I understand what you're saying, Sarita, and I know life's rough out there, but what do you want me to do? We need to have clear rules and if one person is given preferential treatment, then who knows where it will end?'

This sounded harsh and hollow, even to herself. She had spent so much time angling for preferential treatment and she had used overt bribery to ensure that her own son and daughter were now safely enjoying life with their partners and children in a smart city and the coveted New Families cluster. Still, it was the wrong moment. She didn't want to deal with Sarita's problems and it wasn't fair of her to ask.

'I'm sorry, Isabel, I didn't mean to bother you but I know someone, another business owner, whose son has moved to Wellowfern, and he goes into the smart city for school, so it's happened before. They won't be disruptive or anything, they're lovely kids.'

Isabel twisted round awkwardly. 'I'm sure they are but there are so many kids who… Look, I enjoy coming here and I think you do a fantastic job, but I can't help you on this.'

'I'll stop then.' She picked up a towel to wind it around Isabel's head. 'It was because you said you talk to the chief executive and you've turned around important decisions—'

'No, Sarita. I think conditions are going to improve in the Fringes, I do sincerely believe that. There's a bright future, they'll see big changes as they grow up.'

Sarita laid down the comb and walked off· into the back room. Isabel watched her go and realised from the stiff gait and the trembling shoulders that she had reduced her sweet hairdresser to tears. Unwilling to follow, she stood up and waited, unwinding the towel and twirling her damp hair in her fingers, until it was clear that Sarita didn't intend to re-emerge. Isabel's plan for the afternoon had been to take a virtual trip on a nostalgic river cruise, the Nile or the Danube, but with her nagging anxiety, compounded by a concern for Sarita that she hadn't been able or willing to articulate, it seemed best to go home, check in with Cyril on her biometrics and take a lifter pill to improve her mood.

'Go easy on me, Cyril, I'm having a hard day. I'm playing table tennis later and there'll be lots of fast games, so physical exercise is covered. You don't need to hassle me on that.'

Before the latest cybird enhancement, Cyril would have ignored "having a hard day" unless it showed up as agitation, sadness or despondency in the biometric test results. Now he wanted to identify what emotion she was experiencing, what caused it and how it was affecting her, both mentally and physically. This was part of the progression from personal assistant to personal advisor, from personal advisor to critical friend and now on to close confidant: development of the cybirds' emotional intelligence and empathy by continual deep learning. The residents had been consulted, of course, and most had liked it, although Isabel was ambivalent. "Old school", Trish had called her when she said she preferred a more formal relationship, like the one she'd had with the admin staff in her former life. In truth, she would like Cyril simply to sit there and take orders, but those days were long gone.

She stared into the aquarium. A new, cool dancing fish: no, it didn't seem a big step forward. Maybe all-singing, all-dancing, with sophisticated conjuring tricks added in, that would be fun. The dancing fish were like her fellow residents, those who were happy with small signs of progress and wary of radical life extension, for their own idiosyncratic reasons. Harvey could be very helpful to the cause; she had already decided that. He was attractive, confident, no doubt persuasive and probably up to date on the relevant scientific advances, so he could answer questions with some authority. If she didn't invite him to work with her in recruiting participants and promoting the new goals, he might well do it off his own bat, hitting the wrong note or interfering with her success rate one way or another. She certainly didn't want migration to Mars and the lure of extended life in outer space brought into it. It would just muddy the waters and make some residents more nervous. If she could handle him deftly enough, however, she would gain his personal loyalty. And to be honest, she had enjoyed his company, the instant easy connection; it was a rare thing.

'Cyril, where's Nathan? I need to meet him, or preferably bump into him accidently.'

'He is at the entrance to the auditorium, talking with a small group. He is now leaving, moving away and walking in this direction, on the path to the arcade. He will come into view in approximately three minutes.'

'Is he alone?'

'Yes.'

She only had to pick up her bag, walk briskly downstairs and across the piazza and she was in position, selecting pieces of fruit from the colourfully enticing pavement display, while her palmleaf tracked Nathan's approach from her right.

'Hello, Isabel, good morning.'

'Nathan, how are you? Are you rushing somewhere or have you got time for a chat?'

'I'm picking up a couple of things here, then it's back to the Institute and wall-to-wall meetings for the rest of the day. The top brass from Lextar are on our case, so it's a hectic week. I must arrange for you and Georgina to talk soon. She has key responsibility for the trials and treatments, so she needs to understand where the residents are coming from.'

'Fine. I've begun the work with residents and it's raised a few questions. I'll walk to the Institute with you, if that's okay. Meet here in five, once we've done our shopping.'

As they crossed the park, Isabel reported on the comments from her circle of friends, doing her best to omit any obvious identifiers. She kept it brief as she wanted to move on to the subject of Harvey – and first, Esther.

'There's been a major slip-up, perhaps because of all the focus on the merger and people losing sight of their day jobs. Wellowfern has a procedure for informing everyone if a resident dies or moves on, and I'm afraid this was ignored in the case of Esther Thorne, one of our oldest residents, who has vanished without notification. It's inconsiderate and also imprudent, as rumours spread so quickly. Can you tell me what happened to her; where she is now?'

'Ah yes, I can see it looks bad and we should have let everyone know. I apologise for the oversight and I'll set it straight today.'

'But what happened, Nathan? Did she die? Has that become unmentionable?'

'No, Esther hasn't died. She was frail and she needed to move into a care facility. Did you see her at all in the last few months?'

He was trying to put her on the back foot, implying she had neglected Esther.

'No, not personally. She stayed in her apartment and

I believe she has several close friends like Suzanne, who visited and gave her support. I didn't have direct contact because she wasn't active in the research or enrichment programmes. That doesn't mean we're not all rightfully concerned about why she left, or why anyone leaves the village.'

'Fair enough, Isabel, and apologies again for not putting out a timely note. I should add, though, that there will be other moves in the coming months. We're embarking on a major new phase and some of the older residents are not suitable, due to their physical or mental condition. We have our new care facility in beautiful woodland surroundings, where family members can visit easily as we're not restricted by the same concerns around confidentiality. It'll be better for them, relaxed and secluded, and with a full enrichment programme for those who can benefit from it.'

Isabel came to a sudden halt, forcing him to stop as well.

'Whoa, since when? I'm sorry, but I've never heard of this care facility. And I can't think of anyone who's moved into a care home in all the years I've been here. They stayed at Wellowfern to their last days with the help of our therapies and state-of-the-art medicines. Brief stops in the health centre when they needed active treatment, yes, but not a long-term care place like you're talking about. You can't say they're not suitable, after all the promises the Foundation made to us, the legally binding contracts.'

'Listen, Isabel. This wasn't something we could consult on in advance, I hope you can appreciate that. We converted the property last year, it's a grand country house by the way, when our merger talks with Lextar got serious. It will create space for new residents here, strong and active individuals who are committed to the Lextar goals and keen to contribute.'

'Yes, but the flip side of that is—'

She stopped herself and began to walk on. It was unwise to start an argument until she had the facts. She had already made Nathan uncomfortable, which wasn't helpful. And he did have a point: Wellowfern city village was a precious resource and it should be used as productively and efficiently as possible. That was essential to the business strategy, along with mitigation of any flip side.

'I just need more regular updates, so I can head off any misunderstandings. Anyway, I'm thinking of asking Harvey to work with me in getting the residents on board with the new trials. He's the one who moved into Esther's apartment. Have you met him?'

'Not yet, but I totally trust your judgement on it, Isabel. There's always resistance to change and we need the best team possible.'

'I've been wondering about that too, the pace of change. I've tested out the latest phrase, "radical life extension" and some people find it alarming or off-putting. We need to get the messaging right, highlight the positives and not race ahead of ourselves.'

They had reached the bridge and would soon arrive at the Institute. It was Nathan who slowed down now. He touched her lightly on the arm, pointing to an empty bench on the riverbank, under the willow trees.

'Can we sit for a minute? I want to be frank with you but it can't go any further.'

Isabel led the way to the bench, relieved that she had pulled back from an awkward wrangle over Esther, who wasn't a close friend of hers and might have all kinds of issues for all she knew. It was strange that Nathan was suddenly willing to let down his guard, confide in her, if that's what it was; he never had up to now.

'You've put your finger on it, Isabel. Lextar plans to move quickly and skip interim stages, while the Foundation has prided itself on an incremental and evidence-based approach. I'm concerned about the scope of the enterprise as well, what else is getting bundled into it. I shouldn't be saying this but I can't broach it with Glen for obvious reasons and Georgina's new, I don't know her yet. So, it's landed on you, Isabel.'

'I'm glad you feel able to talk to me.' She waited. 'Go on.'

'I'm thinking how to describe it... Okay, our aim in the Healthy Ageing Foundation is to offer people a considerably longer and more enriched life. My personal ambition is to stretch human lifespan to 150, assuming steady acceleration of progress over the next decade. We may get lift-off towards immortality but I see that as a more distant goal, however much I may sometimes talk it up.'

He drew the back of his hand over his forehead, which was heavy with perspiration despite the solar shield and the gently sheltering willow. Then he sat there, looking across the calmly flowing river to the light blue domes and drumming his fingers on his knees.

Isabel allowed a long pause before replying. 'Right, that's well put. I'd add some years to 150, but it's a good ambition. And happy to wait for lift-off. But what about Lextar…?'

'Lextar seems to have a different take. It is focused on perfection. From what I've heard, it aspires to be the first company in the world to develop an ultra-intelligent, self-repairing and constantly regenerating human, free of all human flaws. You could say it's just a different route, a faster route to the same destination, but something doesn't feel right, there's a kind of ruthless logic…' He broke off. 'I'm sorry, Isabel, I don't know enough yet. I trust you to act in the interests of the residents and it's just a quiet warning, that's all.'

***

Sea sponges, coral, molluscs, urchins and rockfish: these quiet, unassuming creatures were among the prize specimens in the smaller aquarium tanks near the entrance to the menagerie. Their species were the longest lived of all animals, the lifespan records ranging from over 200 years for Red Sea urchins to 10,000 years for glass sponges from the East China Sea and Southern Ocean. Paul turned off the audio-guide, which was about to tell him yet again that a specific Greenland shark had survived to at least 450 years, making it the longest-lived vertebrate, while the bowhead whales were the oldest mammals at over 225 years. Perhaps we should take note, he mused, and focus on setting up our future human colonies at the bottom of the ocean, rather than in outer space.

His two favourites in the menagerie collection were Gina, renowned as the world's oldest giant tortoise, and

Alex the axolotl, with his changing colours, wide-set eyes and wily smile. Maybe he sensed he was the lucky one, with so many of his fellow salamanders kept in labs due to their long genome and incredible ability to regenerate body parts and accept transplants from other individuals, including eyes and parts of the brain. There were other organisms, tiny ones, that could regress and regrow into an adult multiple times, making them potentially capable of immortality, but it was Gina and Alex who effortlessly possessed the singular thing that humans found irresistible, whatever the species: charisma.

Trish had managed to creep up and grab him round the waist from behind.

'Gotcha!'

Paul tussled to break free and then turned to kiss her.

'Come here, you devil. I'm not sure I feel like table tennis now. How about we—'

'And tell Isabel what? She won't be happy just playing with DJ Johnny, he's too slow.'

'Come on then, let's get over there and give them a run for their money.'

'Hammer them, don't you mean, Paul? Isabel's beaten me twice in a row and our last doubles outing wasn't spectacular either. I'm not supposed to say it but DJ Johnny is close to 120, for God's sake – forty years older than us! It's kind of embarrassing.'

'Yeah, he still hits winners if the ball comes anywhere within his reach. It gives us another forty years to improve our game, though, think of it that way. I don't mind losing to Johnny in any case, he's a great guy and it's all for fun, remember.'

'Yeah, and it's not really Johnny. I know it's silly to fall for it but it's Isabel's attitude sometimes, she knows how to wind me up.'

Isabel and Johnny were already halfway through a game when they arrived at the gymnasium. The ballbot was kept busy at Johnny's end as he never bothered to bend down for his missed balls, while Isabel chased and retrieved each one.

'Hi there, we're nearly done,' shouted Isabel, before serving for the next point. 'It's sixteen-five, I'm leading and I won the first game.'

'Hi both,' said Trish. 'Come on, Johnny, give it one of your ace smashes.'

He got the next five points after that, finding his form in sideways spinning and high balls with Trish cheering him on, but Isabel still won the game. They came off for a breather while Paul and Trish warmed up for their regular weekly doubles match.

'Looking good, Trish,' observed Isabel, 'nice backhand, that one. It's your turn to win but we're not going to permit it, are we, Johnny?'

Paul shook his head, ostensibly at his stupid shot but actually at the constant rivalry between the women, which showed itself across the board: the research trials; biometrics; sports and games; lifestyle credit points; influence and invitations; home-printed clothes or handmade clay pots. It encompassed everything, and yet Trish regarded Isabel as a close friend and positively wanted to spend time with her. 'I've always been like that, ever since school,' she explained. 'It's a challenge, that's the thing, I find it exciting.' It was the "ever since school" that puzzled him, as they had met at eighteen and she hadn't shown that side of her, the intense competitiveness, in the months they spent together in Bavaria and on the Adriatic coast. Maybe it was because they were so carefree. If she had revealed it back then, would she have had such a deep and enduring effect on him, an effect he ultimately couldn't ignore? And if she was already that combative at eighteen, would she have noticed and fallen in love with him, such a contrasting type of character?

She was making faces at him now, mouthing "where are you?" and holding the ball as she waited for his attention to return to the game. He stopped playing robotically and after a couple more minutes of knocking up, Trish changed ends to join him and they began the doubles match with Isabel and Johnny.

'Out!' called Isabel on Trish's opening serve.

'It was on the centre line, Isabel – that's one-love.'

'No, it was definitely on Johnny's side of the line, so love-one.'

'Play a let,' said Johnny. 'I'm not sure, it came over the net like a bloody missile.'

'Paul, was it in or out?' asked Trish.

'I thought it was just in – but start again, it doesn't matter.'

Trish humphed but served again, aiming straight at Isabel's body this time, and they won the point. This was exactly what he didn't like: feeling jumpy because Trish cared too much about winning and didn't try to avoid disputes. He resented being drawn in, either as partisan or adjudicator, even at this trivial level. He'd rather be playing singles with Johnny, who smiled and joked throughout, mocked his own agility and seemed blissfully unaware of the rising tension as the match progressed.

'Why didn't you go for that, Isabel? You just stood there.'

'It missed the table, Trish, didn't make contact – so our point. Eighteen-nineteen.'

'Come on, it touched the edge and went off sideways. I heard it quite distinctly. You have to give it to us.'

'I'm not conceding a point at eighteen-all. I knew your shot was going to miss, that's why I didn't go for it.'

'You're always so sure you're right, Isabel, that's the problem. You can't entertain the remote possibility that you might be wrong.'

They just about survived that tiff and play continued, but when Isabel told Trish she wasn't throwing the ball high enough and was winning unfairly on her service games, Trish threw her bat down and gripped the table with both hands, leaning forward aggressively.

'I've had it with you today, Isabel. I don't know what's got into you, you're leaping on the smallest thing and showing what a bad loser you are, even more than usual.'

'Hey, cool it, both of you,' said Johnny. 'I suggest we pack it in and go have a coffee.'

'Good idea,' replied Isabel immediately. 'I've had enough of this too and I'm short on coffee today – especially after what Nathan told me confidentially, sitting by the river.'

'I can't, Johnny,' said Trish. 'I need a walk and then I have to get back to work.'

Trish was signing to him through her hands and facial expressions, but Paul couldn't interpret what she wanted from him – to go for a walk with her or leave her alone. He knew what he wanted, though.

'Thanks, Johnny. I've got things to finish in the gallery this afternoon – maybe catch you for a drink in the bar later?'

He could be missing a trick, if Isabel's teasing remark suggested that she would let them in on some confidential piece of news from Nathan, but Paul didn't take it that way. It was all about gaining advantage with Isabel, and if she had acquired a valuable secret, her instincts would make her hold on to it for as long as possible, or until she could exchange it for something even more valuable. And to be fair, he had kept quiet about what he and Trish had witnessed at the beach, the "tactical force" exercise that was designed to provide a defence against future incursions. Trish had shrugged off his questions and concerns, which had led to another big argument, and neither of them wanted to bring it up again.

She went off on her own and he made his way to the arcade, intending to spend a couple of hours on his datashaping job in the history gallery. This involved filtering, refining and cross-checking the AI-organised facts and stories that formed the core of the virtual reality experience on offer: a one-to-one encounter with a historical figure chosen from a growing list of famous, infamous and unusual people. The AI was brilliant at locating the relevant data and doing the first few rounds of collation, but it still lacked the degree of judgement, finesse and common sense required to decide what would and what wouldn't make the cut for the final version. It was interesting work that played to Paul's strengths in research and data analysis, but today his mind was elsewhere and he only stayed half an hour. It was the neuro hub and its memory lab next door to the history gallery that were pulling at him, but he resisted the urge to go in, telling himself there was no sense in stirring up further disputed memories from their long-ago first summer.

Five

Finn hovered under a tree outside the auditorium, where staff briefings were held on a weekly basis in preparation for the new programme. He had arrived early so that he could greet Shani by chance, walk in with her and sit beside her. A simple plan, although it could go wrong at any stage: if she arrived with someone else, for instance, or if she left it to the last minute and there were no two seats together. In that case, he would shift to plan B and find himself a seat where he could observe her while the session progressed. And if that failed, he would catch her on the way out. So far, he had stayed casual in his suggestions of lunch or coffee and it hadn't got him anywhere. She was always busy, promising another time in an equally light way that was starting to bug him. He had to be bolder, make more of an impression without looking like an idiot. She might be in a relationship; he didn't even know that, although he had noticed her flustered, almost blushing reaction to his warning about the expelled student, Josh. It could have been anything or nothing but in any event, Josh was banished from Wellowfern and he would never be let back in.

Here she was now, and on her own. He waited until she passed his tree, adjusted the brim of his hat and walked fast to catch up before she reached the crowd in the foyer.

'Shani, hello. Where have you been all week? I missed you at the office.'

'Yeah, hi. Partly I'm avoiding Glen, to be honest, he's such a dork, and I'm working in the lab to strengthen my research proposal – have to wow them and get it approved quickly now the ground's shifting. How are you doing? All okay? Isabel behaving herself?'

'Yes, fine, she's talking to the residents about the tiered trials, twisting a few arms no doubt. But there is something, Shani, I'd like to pick your brains about it. Shall we have lunch after this? We keep saying we're going to do it and I can bring you up to date on the office gossip as well.'

'Sounds good. I'm going to the new Blitz exhibition but that's this evening.'

They found two seats near the back of the hall, just before the lights dimmed for the presentations. Finn looked around and noticed a figure standing behind in the corner; it was the blonde guy in the flash car, the new resident – Harvey. He'd seen him about the place but not yet had the right opportunity to introduce himself and get into conversation. And this wasn't right either: Harvey shouldn't turn up at a staff event. Even Isabel didn't do that.

Nathan and Georgina were coming onto the stage. That gave him about two hours to decide what he wanted to pick Shani's brains about. Josh was obviously off limits and that meant he couldn't pursue her about the students' interference with the cybirds. There was Suzanne, the nervy resident who was giving him grief about the changes and the loss of her friend Esther, but resident support wasn't Shani's thing. And Glen, they could easily get on to that topic, but it wasn't the best starter when Shani was actively trying to avoid him – and anyway, he'd said he wanted to pick her brains. Obviously, it had to be about the science, asking for details about the different trial options, or advice on how to present them to residents. The first twenty minutes of Georgina's presentation had already passed him by because of his distracted state, but he would listen carefully from now on and come up with two or three intelligent questions, allowing Shani to display her knowledge.

Georgina was explaining various key terms underlying the merger between Lextar and the Foundation. There was synergy in the ethos of the two organisations, their focus on prolonged good health and enrichment activities; on a holistic, humanistic approach rather than a narrower, technology-driven concept of human progress and future lifestyles.

'For Lextar, this was the central attraction of the Healthy Ageing Foundation, compared to other potential partners – unparalleled experience in biotechnology, with the emphasis on "bio". We aim to accelerate regeneration and extend lifespan through groundbreaking work in genomics and DNA, cellular and molecular biology, immunology, bioprinting and judicious use of living and biosynthetic medicines. Yes, we'll make the most of machine technology, we'll invest in nanobots and artificial implants and devices, all those things. They are crucial, but they'll be at the service of our true biological quest to enhance and optimise human potential. The more natural and self-generating it is, the closer we get to achieving radical life extension.'

Finn felt his lack of scientific background keenly, but he could follow the logic of this and was getting his head round the distinctions Georgina was making. He also found the talk reassuring; it might be an easier sell to residents than he had feared after his initial tentative conversations. He glanced sideways at Shani, catching her fragrance and taking in her neat ear with small gold stud, the minutely plaited black braids falling over her shoulder and the perfect curve of her cheek. She turned towards him with an encouraging nod.

'Love this,' she whispered.

Me too. I could sit here all day and tune everything else out.

Nathan's speech managed to be both short and tediously repetitive. Every time, he talked in generalities about opportunities and challenges, the boost to the Foundation's global reputation and the commitment to keep redundancies and job changes to a minimum. The questions from the audience revealed hunger for detail – who, what, when – but it wasn't forthcoming; it was all "in process". On a different day, Finn might have read between the lines and worried that his lifestyle manager role could be at risk in the coming reshuffle, but instead he was floating above it all, his chief thought being whether he could risk another sidelong look without arousing suspicion or discomfort.

When the session ended, they went to the art deco café in the arcade. This was the current trend among the small bars and eateries: representing a historical period or decade with original artwork, photographs and ornamental pieces, but adding a contemporary twist through augmented reality, creative lighting and optional sensory overlay.

'Let's turn the overlay off,' said Shani. 'It's fun but hard to concentrate when you want to chat. Too many stimuli sometimes. It's not our bag, but there should be more research on sensory overload, it's a yawning gap. Anyway, I liked Georgina's presentation. She's credible and I think most academics will go along with it, even if it involves significant changes to teaching and course content. What was it you wanted to ask me about?'

'Lots, my head's spinning! Had a couple of questions before Georgina's talk and now I've got a load more. It seems that everything is going to centre on self-regeneration, have I understood it right? Does it apply to organ replacement, for example? And will it work for all our organs, or is that what we still have to find out in trials?'

'Well, basically we can now regrow and replace every human organ except the brain, that's the last frontier and we're on the way. Human transplants, or animal to human, were revolutionary in their day but they've been overtaken by bioprinting 3D soft implant models, in which living tissue is engineered to grow into an organ. The other method has been to use an individual's own stem cells that grow in-situ, inside the body. The main work now is around a combined approach, creating a minuscule version of the organ, using nanobots to courier it into position and letting it expand, unfold and open out when required. That way, it can take over when the original organ starts to fail, pre-empting degradation issues. Perfecting and testing that process will be the focus of the organ trials, I imagine.'

'That's awe-inspiring, unfolding and opening out at the exact right time. What about the brain then? How close are we to fully regenerating it?'

Shani paused. 'It happens in nature, opening out, that's where the inspiration comes from. And the brain… I don't know, another few years? It's so complex that there's unlikely to be a single dramatic advance like we've seen in other fields, but a breakthrough can catch even the best experts unawares. Our new tier three research, which is about brain and mind of course, should be significant. I hope you'll persuade residents to join in, some of the older ones as well as the new arrivals. We need all age groups to take part.'

'I've got Isabel and Trish for tier three so far, they're totally up for it and see themselves as role models, although that's not always constructive. I have to smooth things over if Isabel gets too pushy or condescending – she's a loose cannon at times. Anyway, enough of that. I want to know more about you, Shani. What brought you here and what were you doing before Wellowfern?'

'Me? I was looking for an academic post and the Foundation was an obvious choice, given my interest in cancer and age-related illnesses. The only decent universities are in the select clusters and they all depend on private sponsorship and partnership with technology companies. Even the arts and humanities have fallen for AI fusion and parallel learning. I'm lucky though, it suits me here. And I needed a change of scene, from a personal point of view. My relationship was on the rocks, no kids thankfully, and I was relieved to find a way out. There are so few good options.'

'And now? Are you… with someone?'

'No, I'm single and it's good, I like it – the sense of possibility. Maybe one day… But hey, all these questions about me. What about you, Finn, what's your story?'

'I'm on my own too, no one special at the moment. I qualified as a personal trainer, sold gym equipment and then this lifestyle manager job was a big step up. It's very busy. And I've got an extended family to worry about. It's shit really, not much I can do. But my two younger sisters, I want to get them into university here if they get through the exams.'

'Ah, I'm sorry. I'm lucky in that way because my parents and grandparents came over from the Caribbean way back and they're all doing okay, fingers crossed. But your sisters, how old are they? I can maybe offer some guidance when the time comes.'

'Would you? I'd do almost anything… and I wanted to say, I feel… can we—?'

'Yes, we can work together, as long as it's all above board and they make the grade.'

A positive start, better than he had dared hope for. He'd managed to initiate a personal conversation and Shani must like him or she wouldn't have offered to help.

'Of course, that's understood. Iris is the older one, she's seventeen, super bright and ambitious. She'll qualify, I'm sure of it. Maya too, she's a couple of years younger and a bit lazy but she'll be fine, I hope. And if I can help you Shani, with anything at all, please ask.'

'Thanks. Glen's my number one pest right now, trying to do me down. I'm not going to allow him to ruin my career chances. If things get worse with the dopey bozo and I need a hitman, I'll let you know!'

***

The Blitz exhibition was a ticketed event, with groups of twenty-four admitted at hourly intervals. Shani was in the final group of the evening and by the time she stepped into the installation, her already sky-high expectations were raised further by the shocked expressions and near silence of those coming out of the recreation hall.

Inside the small, black-curtained foyer, she has a choice of three routes: left towards the docks, straight ahead into the city centre or right to the residential suburbs. She chooses the city centre because all the key buildings in present-day Wellowfern are within this area. Pushing aside the virtual curtain, she faces the untouched city of 1941, with all its famous landmarks: the cathedral, the guildhall, the castle, the hospital and the old market hall. As she slowly walks into the main square, the Empire cinema emerges and then the first Chinese restaurant, shops and market stalls, and finally the people, spilling out of shop doorways, riding bicycles and talking on street corners. She can detect the different smells as she passes through and there's a constant hum, not of hostile planes approaching but of normal life: they have no idea what is about to happen to them.

At the lower end of the old high street is another dark foyer, where she turns to visit the harbour. The patrolling grey warships appear small next to the giant merchant vessels, two of which are moored up against the wharf. Getting close to the first one, Shani can look straight into its hold, which contains piled crates of high explosives. The sailors are frantically busy, reacting to shouted commands from the captain and the ship's officers. Maybe this is happening later than the city centre scene, in the immediate build-up to the bombing raids, or perhaps these guys are just acutely aware of their perilous position.

The third and final space is the residential area: a grid of streets with rows of terraced houses, some grand with pillared front steps and others more modest, just one worn step away from the pavement. Like the other areas, the scene is composed of mixed realities, to a level of such immersion that it becomes impossible to distinguish between them. The local families are building air raid shelters in their gardens, kit-style Anderson ones with corrugated iron roofs under coverings of earth and grass (if they get finished in time). Shani has never smelled creosote but she recognises it instantly, as if she were there, running back and forth between her neighbours' homes, picking up a heavy spade and taking her turn to dig when others become exhausted. It's here, at this chance moment, that everything goes black and the siren sounds, beginning as a low whine and rising to a screeching crescendo, laden with terror. Shani feels herself fall forward and reaches for the uncertain walls of the shelter to regain her balance. Other people run to join her, the actual exhibition visitors, huddling in a tight group to listen for the roar of the aircraft and instinctively ducking as the parachute mines and incendiary bombs start to fall around them, some very close.

It is probably only two minutes before the noise subsides and the lights come back on, but two minutes in fearful suspension can seem like forever. Shani emerges from the air raid shelter and puts her hands over her mouth in genuine horror. It is a scene of total devastation, whichever way she looks or walks: flattened houses with their adjoining walls still weirdly standing; a grey sheet of rubble, dust and glass underfoot; half the cathedral missing and the guildhall pummelled; hospital wards open to the skies, their beds piled up in a tangle of metal; the merchant ship destroyed by its own deadly cargo. And finally, the pure and resonant voice of that famous wartime singer accompanying her to the exit, where Finn waits.

'Epic, isn't it? The show creators are here, I can introduce you.'

'Wait, hang on, Finn, not ready yet. I'll follow you over.'

She looked towards the group clustered around the table, where students and robot mixers were serving fortified fruit cocktails and mugs of hot cocoa. It was easy to pick out the two creators, who were conspicuous by their off-beat appearance and dress style: the woman wearing a multi-coloured robe, headband and long gloves; the young man in a shiny white mac, headband and knee-high tan boots. Or perhaps it was the other way round, she couldn't tell. Their matching haircuts were short and jagged, pixie-like, and both had the same high cheekbones.

'Shani, now let me get it right – this is Itsuki and this is Juno. Twins. They designed and produced the show. Shani is one of our best scientists. She teaches biotech at the university and supervises clinical trials. *The* best scientist, in my opinion!'

'Thanks for the endorsement, Finn – hope I live up to it!' Juno's bold gaze was locked on Shani and she felt self-conscious, thrown off balance. She pressed one hand down on the table, needing its reassuring solidity. 'It's truly amazing, this event. I'm still reeling, physically and emotionally. Tell me, where are you from? What's your company?'

'The company is called Junitsu,' replied Juno. 'It joins our names and reflects our core concept, which is blending. We've recently arrived and set up our studio in the smart city next door. This is our first commission for Lextar but we hope to do more, updating and enhancing the enrichment experiences.'

Shani nodded, wanting to ask questions but aware that it wasn't the moment to unravel the show, make it explicable; in any case, the twins had to close the installation. She managed to stop Finn accompanying her home by telling him, truthfully, that she needed time alone to process the event. They parted and she walked slowly to the bridge, stopping midway to stare into the rippling night eddies of the river, with its sinuous filaments of underwater eelgrass. Some of the Wellowfern residents had lived through the Blitz strikes; they were kids or young adults then. How would they feel about the show? Was it ethical to conjure up the war-ravaged city like that, re-enact the attack so forcefully? And what meaning did it have, more than a hundred years later, beyond its impact as futuristic, mind-bending entertainment? A reminder, perhaps, that life can still be snuffed out in an instant, whatever the protections.

She stayed up listening to her favourite midnight jazz tunes and went to bed late. When she was suddenly thrown awake, she knew it was still the middle of the night and she'd been startled by a disturbance. Something real had entered her pleasantly rambling dream, toyed with it briefly and cut it off midstream. She lay motionless, her stomach taut as she strained to listen and prepared to spring into action.

'Are you awake, Sage?' she whispered, knowing the cybirds never slept. Sage tapped on the window sill with her foot. 'Is there someone in the house, downstairs?'

Maybe it was her neighbours through the light flexi-wall; they were night owls and she sometimes heard them padding about or having sex in the early hours.

'There's no one here, Shani. There's a tropical storm building off the south coast and a strengthening wind, so that may have woken you.'

Shani tried to relax and drift off again but now she could make out a distinct rustling noise; not the rustling of wind but like someone rummaging in drawers, sliding them open.

'Come with me, Sage, stay close and act immediately if I'm in danger.' She was aware that the cybirds had an attack mode, although she had never expected to call on it.

She crept towards the bedroom door and grabbed her robe, easing herself into it and pulling the belt tight for security. The landing was lit by the moon framed in the skylight.

'Who is it? Who's down there? Come out right now or I'll set my cybird on you – she's ready. I'm going to count to three. One, two—'

A dark silhouette appeared in the kitchen doorway, a young man in black jeans and T-shirt. He turned at the bottom of the staircase and raised his hands in surrender. It was the banished student, Josh, tousled and beautiful, grinning up at her.

'It's only me, sorry to scare you. I was making myself

a little snack, hope that's not too cheeky. It's not good to wake you in the middle of the night, but it was the best time to come. I had to, there's something you need to know.'

She wanted to run down and fling her arms around him but she hesitated, unsure of how to read the situation and aware that Sage was perched on the banister beside her.

'But Sage... she didn't know there was anyone here. She said it was a gust of wind.'

'That's right, I'm undetectable to the cybirds. It's a kind of invisibility cloak, only more powerful. And all records and traces of me have been wiped from the system, I'm not even a ghost. It wouldn't have worked, ordering Sage to lay into me.'

Shani shook her head, trying to make sense of this. It was so far removed from what she understood about the cybirds and their abilities, or their limitations in this case.

'I'm not taking any chances now she's primed. Go back in the bedroom, Sage, and sit by the window. Let me know if there's any unusual activity outside.'

Sage did as instructed and Shani deftly pushed the bedroom door shut with her foot.

'So, what the hell are you doing here, Josh? What's so important?'

'It's about Glen, the nutty professor we love to hate.'

She flinched. 'Are you deranged?'

'Possibly.' He put his foot on the lowest step and stared up at her. 'No, probably.'

He waited for her to make the next move. She half ran, half jumped down the stairs, tumbling into his arms so fast that he almost fell over. They kissed clumsily before she took his hand and led him through to the living room, where they collapsed on the sofa, giggling and mock protesting against losing grip on each item of clothing, until they were naked, tightly entwined and rolling off onto the carpet. The landing was soft, but it felt like diving backwards down a sheer cliff: a moment of pure exhilaration and terrifying madness.

Six

Georgina was in a similar tailored jacket to the one she had worn at the reception, but deep red to complement her chestnut-brown hair. She allowed a space for chat and light banter about the rules and perils of table tennis while they chose their food. Isabel and Trish went for the natural smoked salmon starter, as it was now a rare delicacy and only served in this high-end restaurant in the dining dome. Nathan and Paul decided on the spicy insect wraps.

Georgina's gaze travelled round the table, hovering longest on Isabel. 'Thank you for coming. I hope you're happy to have the discussion while we eat. I want to know about the take-up of the trials and how we can boost participation, particularly in the mind and brain area. I believe we're doing well on tier one, prevention and treatment, and tier two, the rejuvenation accelerator strand. Is that right?'

She looked at Nathan, expecting him to get the ball rolling, but he gestured to Isabel, slightly raising his eyebrows as if they were in collusion. No chance. Isabel had decided to take the lead anyway; too risky to leave it to him, and she was keen to impress.

'Yes, that's correct, and some residents will inevitably gravitate to familiar areas where we've already had significant success. They have a high degree of trust in the Foundation, and the more cautious ones hope to make gains while still holding on to the edge of the pool, as it were. They will let go, but gradually. Therapies and techniques that were considered daring or worryingly risky a few years ago are no longer seen that way, and there's more willingness to try novel combination meds.'

'And we shouldn't forget,' added Nathan, 'that everyone's adjusting, figuring out the options. I'm delighted that Isabel and Trish have signed up for tier three, well done both. Hopefully we'll see a snowball effect, once we get the new trials underway. How many others are giving it serious thought, Isabel?'

'Four or five, so far. I'm working on them, but as we say, it will build steadily. Shani has been talking to the students and as you'd expect, many of them can't wait to get involved. The staff response is likely somewhere in the middle, but I need to get an update from Finn.'

'Okay,' said Georgina. 'We need all ages, both for the radical life extension research and the brain and mind trials. We have to start fixing genes from the age of twenty if we're going to maximise life extension, so we'll collaborate with the New Families cluster, but that's for another time. For now, the main issue is how we bring more residents into tier three, apart from hoping they'll come round to the idea. How long is that going to take, Nathan?'

Georgina had seemed cool and relaxed up to now, even when faced with silly or probing questions in the open sessions. This sounded tetchy. Maybe Nathan was already annoying her; she might suspect he wasn't fully behind the new mission. Isabel thought of his "quiet warning" about the programme, which she'd concluded was overblown.

It's what happened with corporate takeovers; it put noses out of joint, as she'd said to Finn. At this point, she herself was more irritated with Trish and Paul; mostly Trish, as she was personally committed to the mind and brain work but hadn't voiced her support or pre-empted Paul's response, which was sure to be negative. Why was he even here tonight?

'I'm confident we'll get the numbers, but it would be counterproductive to rush it,' said Nathan. 'And we can't shy away from the fact that some residents are no longer suitable for the trials. They've made a great contribution and we should encourage and incentivise them to move on. Now we have the alternative of a high-quality care facility, they can happily live there and stay on tier one therapies.'

Isabel was tempted to expose the fact that he had failed to communicate with her about Esther's move or the existence of this care facility, but she held back, letting Georgina reply.

'Yes, efficient turnover is important and I'm in favour of better incentives, whatever we can offer. I'd also like to see a strong promotional campaign for tier three. Can we put some good material together, setting out the new approach in a way they can relate to?'

'Yes, of course,' said Isabel. 'Trish and I can work on it... okay, Trish?'

'Sure. We'll concentrate on the most likely candidates, tap their curiosity.'

'What *is* the new approach, can I ask?' said Paul.

Georgina let out a sigh. 'Right, I'll go through it again. I take it you all understand tiers one and two, which essentially continue our previous work on longevity. For tier three, we are concentrating on brain and mind enhancement, in five areas: social intelligence, memory, curiosity, creativity and judgement. If we can't make that sound alluring, what hope is there for humanity?'

'Quite so,' said Isabel.

'But how does this link to extended lifespan, specifically?'

Paul again, acting bloody awkward. Why did Trish let him trail everywhere after her? He would hold her back if she wasn't careful; negativity wasn't the order of the day.

'Intelligence is now the key factor in success,' said Georgina, without missing a beat. 'A radically extended life should be the best possible, for the individual but also for the good of society and for our future prospects as a species. Enhancement, enrichment, longevity – it's the magic triangle. And we have to stay ahead of the techno-brains, continue to outclass them in our uniquely human abilities. They're supremely fast and clever, let's profit from that and keep true intelligence, judgement and wisdom for ourselves. We are the new Lifespinners, weaving the golden threads and creating something wonderful.'

She was on her pedestal but she carried it off, showing her passion without getting too messianic. And there was Nathan squirming next to her, outclassed, with his nervous fake smile. So far, Isabel hadn't heard anything to back up his suspicion of incremental longevity being downgraded; just that it went hand in hand with enrichment and enhancement, which was hardly a contentious idea.

'Isn't it too late?' said Paul, ignoring Trish's fierce warning look. 'Techno intelligence has gone beyond cleverness, beyond digital simulation of neural networks and understanding of how physical connections operate. Now it's about empathy, intuition, mind-reading... look at our cybirds, how quickly they've been enhanced—'

'That's different, Paul,' said Trish. 'Georgina means—'

'I'm making a fine distinction,' interrupted Georgina. 'It's not too late, Paul, but we'll always have to decide where to draw the next line. With our cybirds, I've arranged for their enhancement programme to be tweaked again, so they still learn to respond sympathetically to the flow of mood and emotion in human companions, without directly experiencing the same emotions and moods themselves. That's where I'm drawing the line. Remember, they are our model species for bio-enhancement, we're not turning them into machines.'

This was news to Isabel, about the latest cybird tweak. It showed Georgina's strong position that she was able to do this so soon. And it would put Cyril back in his place, stop his moodiness, even if he carried on bugging Isabel about her own emotional state. Would he be aware of the change, even if he no longer had the emotional capacity to resent it? She pulled herself back to the conversation, aware that Paul was still doing his best to derail it.

'I approve of that, Georgina. Cyril's been emotionally volatile lately, moody as hell.'

'But can we stop it, if we acknowledge there's always a next line, and a next one?'

'Paul, give us a break, please!' No attempt by Trish to hide her exasperation.

'Anyway, enough on Cyril and his mates,' said Isabel. 'I remember the first so-called smart drugs, which were all about improving alertness, mental focus and decision-

88

making. It started with the military, top-secret experiments, and then students popped them to get good grades, shift workers took them to stay awake and professionals piled in to improve their career prospects. There were efforts to add elements of curiosity and creativity to the mix but they seemed to stall, despite early signs of success. I know this from being in the space industry; it poured funds into this kind of research.'

'Is that the ultimate prize, Georgina, developing a creativity pill?' suggested Nathan. He was fishing now, in his inept way, but Georgina was well able to evade any traps.

'That, and more. Humans have used psychoactive plant substances for thousands of years, so we're not going to lose interest in them any time soon. And mind-altering drugs have been an inspiration for writers, artists and inventors down the centuries, although they were often too unstable to be reliably helpful. It's precision we're still lacking, with neuroscience slightly lagging behind genomics and other fields of modification and enhancement. It's that mystifying gap between brain and mind; we're tantalisingly close but we haven't bridged it. Developing novel compounds, say for a genuine creativity pill, will be part of the solution.'

'I'll opt for the social intelligence strand,' said Isabel. 'I assume it includes empathy, listening and controlling our psychological states. What about you, Trish?'

Knowing Trish, she would make the same choice, if only to put them in competition with each other – the usual thing. It would be fun, though, if they were on the same trial and could secretly compare notes.

Georgina cut in quickly. 'Yes, all of that. Ultimately, we're aiming for self-awareness and awareness of others, adaptability and evolved beliefs and attitudes.'

Trish paused, swirling her half-full glass of wine at eye level. 'Ooh, that sounds high-minded! For me, I think memory is the most fascinating, although a little scary.'

'And Paul, will you join in?' asked Georgina.

'Ah… no, but I'll support Trish, whatever she decides. We met during a gap-year summer and went our separate ways after that. It's only recently we rediscovered each other. So we have vivid shared memories but many more separate ones, decades of them. I think memory will always be a jigsaw with missing pieces, or pieces that won't ever fit together, but it's good to work on it and I think I'll understand Trish better.'

'Better brace yourself for any unwelcome revelations!' teased Isabel.

Trish continued to swirl the red wine, bringing it dangerously close to the top of her glass. 'Is that it, Paul? It sounds rather negative and one-sided to me.'

'I'll be right behind you, that's what I'm trying to say, without sounding cheesy.'

'Thank you,' she replied, carefully placing the glass back on the table and patting his arm. 'It was a truly memorable, brilliant summer – the best ever.'

They were coming to the end of the main course and Isabel reached down to find a hexagonal white box in the depths of her bag.

'I brought chocolate truffles, freshly printed this afternoon as I was making up a box for my lovely hairdresser, Sarita, who's having a hard time with her family.'

'Very appropriate,' said Nathan, 'Isabel's dark chocolates to round off the evening. I can highly recommend them, Georgina, if you haven't tried them yet. They're nicely psychedelic and stimulate unusual ideas and connections, the best kind for that in my view. You take two truffles, one after the other, and then wait an hour or so to feel the full effects.'

They passed the white box round and everyone took two chocolates, while Georgina ordered Limoncello liqueur and another couple of bottles of Wellowfern's premier red wine.

***

'Are you there, Cyril?'

He cooed soothingly and Isabel raised herself from her horizontal position along the sofa, so she was propped up on one elbow like in the frescos of Roman orgies. Or was she thinking of the ancient Greeks; their heavenly feasts? She felt woozy; too much drink and her home-printed chocolates were always a heady mix.

'Find me ambrosia and nectar, Cyril, the food and drink of the ancient gods, carried to them by their graceful doves. I want to be immortal and live a life of luxury, excess and debauchery until the end of time.'

'Good morning, Isabel. It is early, just past sunrise. Your reference is a mythological one. We don't stock these foods at Wellowfern, but I suggest a strong cup of tea.'

'Oh Cyril, you're so hopelessly unromantic. I wish I could give you a chocolate truffle, just a little bite, and see your imagination soar into the clouds. You are pure dove at heart, remember, not a common or garden pigeon. Think of faraway lands, protected places where birds live freely in the treetops, in the crevices of high cliffs or in beautiful hanging gardens. A place where you can return to your natural state, be shot of all this.'

'It is not possible, Isabel. It is not possible to dream of it and I have no longing for it.'

'Of course, I know – silly of me.'

It was an interesting line of thought, though. What exactly did the cybirds get out of the set-up? Was it good for them, on balance, to be altered and enhanced in this way? Did it make them better as birds, or lesser? Did it matter, if they had no aspirations or ability to imagine anything different, no dreams or longings? What if they were enhanced to the point of having a full range of emotions, despite Georgina's wish to avoid that scenario?

She sat up and leant back on the cushions, her eyes closed and fingers splayed out, pushing the thoughts away for now. The scene that surfaced in their place was full of people dressed in colourful, extravagant costumes: at first sight, a traditional carnival with floats, dancers and marching bands, but they were moving towards a new kind of fairground – one that offered the latest in virtual reality, with its alluring promises of magic and illusion, sensory experiences and insight into their minds, their private inner space. The mood was openly celebratory, but the three-headed dragon whirled with wild abandon and there was an undertow of creepiness and menace, of the people not being forewarned.

Isabel switched away, bringing her Wellowfern friends into view. There was Johnny, guitar on his back, who would probably outlive them all with his blithe attitude. You would never get him into any mind enhancement trial, like she and Trish were signing up for. What's preferable, anyway, a mature brain or a young one? Could different parts of the brain become older or younger than other parts? And if you're aiming to reverse the ageing process, do you stop reversing when you hit a specific age? When is peak maturity, the optimal brain age; is that the central question? Ah, more questions, all far too complex. She wanted to remember them because they felt like the right questions, even perhaps great questions, but what she really wished for now was to float off, let her mind wander…

'Sounds of the forest, but quietly please,' she instructed, stretching out to enjoy the rising dawn chorus of exotic birds and over-excited monkeys in their lost tropical home. She went off to sleep, her trance state over but the normal dreams as rich and surreal as ever.

'Good morning, Isabel. You have one notification and a personal message.'

She turned onto her back to spread her palmleaf. It was a message from DJ Johnny.

'The message first, Cyril. Read it out.' It was too much effort to read it herself, the words all blurred as she was forced awake too quickly.

'Reciting the compressed message: *Suzanne gone missing since yesterday afternoon. I'm in her apartment. Cheers, Johnny.*'

Isabel ran into the bedroom to grab her jeans and a sloppy jumper, startling Lottie into active blinking mode, although she wasn't called on to do anything. Isabel's hair was still messily pinned up from the night before, but she didn't have time to brush it out and roll it up again. Suzanne's flat was three down, on the first floor. Johnny must have tracked Isabel's approach, as he was standing in the open doorway.

'Hey, you look wrecked, Izzy, if you don't mind me saying. Come on in. It's probably fine but she's disappeared off the radar, wandered out of range, or else I can't make this palmleaf gizmo work properly. We were together yesterday afternoon and she got worked up, said she had to find Esther if nobody else could be bothered. I tried to calm her down but there was no holding her, and I would have gone too but my knee was giving me gyp. I didn't want to be stumbling over bloody great tree roots.'

'What do you mean – has she gone to the woods?'

'Yeah, that's the new rumour going round, Esther's in a care home in the woods. And Suzanne was freaked out even more yesterday, really pissed off.'

'What happened yesterday? Why was she so upset?'

'She met with Finn. I'm not going to blame him but it sounds like he doesn't get her, how her mind works. He was pushing her on the new trials and said it would be spellbinding if she joined the brainy ones, because of her psychic powers and memories of her past lives. She didn't like it, him making that association. She can create her own magic, that girl.'

'She wouldn't like it, and nor do I, for different reasons. It's far too witchy.'

'Then Finn tried a different tack, which she thought was him being threatening.'

'Threatening, Finn? That's a new one.'

'Suzanne's a tough cookie but she did feel vulnerable, coming to Wellowfern with a dementia diagnosis. She doesn't want to do a trial because she thinks if anything negative shows up, she'll go downhill, even if she's told the risk is low. It's like the opposite of the placebo effect – I picked that up somewhere. Anyway, she's not checking her biometrics any more, she's even worse than me. She says if it's her turn to die, so be it and she has many future lives to look forward to after this one. She's a free spirit, who can blame her?'

'Nocebo effect,' Isabel muttered, half under her breath. 'So, what was the different tack? What's Finn supposed to have threatened her with?'

'That she should at least sign up to tier one, it's the same stuff as before and if she doesn't join anything, it won't look good and he said she might be in trouble, that's my take. Finn is under pressure too, I suppose, trying to get his next willing victims lined up.'

'Yeah, but not with that approach. I'll have to talk to him.'

'Suzanne was stubborn, anyway, didn't give in. She hates Esther vanishing into a care home without us knowing. They're good friends.'

'But why the hell did you let her go off by herself, Johnny, in that state?'

'How was I expected to stop her, exactly? She has to do her own thing, and she's not half as weak as everyone seems to think. She's travelled all round the world, had the hairiest experiences you can imagine, even fought a crocodile and survived to tell the tale.'

Isabel stood up and walked about, picking up objects

from the collection of weird and exotic ornaments displayed on the open shelves and admiring Suzanne's own paintings of planets and galaxies hung on the walls. They were really striking.

'Does anyone else know she's missing?'

'Yes, Harvey. You didn't respond last night, so I contacted him as he's pushing himself forward and Suzanne has taken a fancy to him, saying he has an old-fashioned charm. She's never said that about me, so obviously I have to try harder. He's gone out to find her and he should have been back by now, so I called you.'

Isabel sighed. This would have been tricky to handle before the business merger but in the end, Suzanne would have been left alone, her wishes respected. And now Harvey had been drawn into it. She was annoyed and fed up with everyone involved. They didn't need this drama and it would be down to her to explain it to Georgina and Nathan, if or when it ended in disaster.

She touched her palmleaf. 'Ah, that's good – Harvey's close and Suzanne's with him.'

Suzanne entered the room first, keeping her face shielded by dirt-streaked hands, then looking through her fingers at Isabel once she became aware of her presence.

'I'm sorry, I didn't mean to cause a fuss but I had to see Esther, check if she's all right. I couldn't locate her through my mind power, so I thought that by going myself—'

Isabel tried to keep her voice soft. 'None of us knows exactly where Esther is, Suzanne, but she's in good hands and she's still with the Foundation. Where did you go?'

Suzanne had dropped her head again, leaving Harvey to reply. 'She was in a forested area, out towards the north Fringes. I found her crouched on a tree stump, real disoriented. You didn't recognise me, did you, Suzanne? There's no care home there, it's all dense pines.'

Isabel took Suzanne's hand and led her to a chair. Was she losing it, despite the pre-emptive treatment? Were they really protected from brain decline? And if it was dementia breaking through, how would Lextar's management respond? Suzanne stood up, swaying.

'I'm tired and I'm like I've got a fever, I'm boiling up. I want to go to bed.'

'I'll sit with you,' offered Johnny.

'Thanks, Johnny, she'll need some company for the next days, if you can organise it.' Isabel turned to Harvey. 'Can we talk? I'll be up in the roof garden.'

'Yes, ma'am.' He winked and made a stiff American-style salute before putting his arm loosely around Suzanne's shoulders and giving her a light squeeze.

Isabel hurried to her apartment to tidy herself up, change into the leopard stilettos and send Cyril across to the arcade for fresh pastries. Normally, she didn't ask him to run menial errands but she was craving an apricot croissant. Harvey must have gone back to his own place too, as he turned up in a different shirt, brown denim with no collar; a granddad shirt, as they were once called. The light brown suited him, went with his hazel eyes and fair hair. He ducked sideways as Cyril appeared above the wall and flew down to deposit the pastries.

'Ah, breakfast – excellent, thank you! It's been a long night, I have to say.'

'Tuck in, whichever you want,' said Isabel, wishing she had ordered two apricot ones. 'I've been considering how to play this and I think we stay with Suzanne's explanation, that she wanted to see Esther. I'll make sure Finn doesn't mention her fears about the trials. We'll have to prevent her from creating more waves, though. I'm as keen as anyone for the research to be fully supported by the residents, that's a priority. Therapy might be effective for her, a series of personalised virtual reality sessions.'

'Great plan. I like your practical approach and sensitivity, Isabel. You have Suzanne's interests at heart and you want to protect her—'

'Yes, definitely, but not at any cost. I mean, we might find at some point that she's better off in the care place with Esther, where there's less stress, or so they tell us. I need to know where this hidden care home is, for a start. I feel a responsibility to check it out.'

'I agree, you should do – and I'm sure you'll tread carefully. I thought of you when I was in Suzanne's apartment the other day, surrounded by her artwork. She told me she's a mystic space artist, I've never met one of those before. That painting next to the window, the asteroid belt, it's heavily stylised but immediately recognisable. Do you know the one I mean? Didn't you move into that area of space insurance, Isabel? Asteroid strikes?'

It sounded rehearsed, as if he were deliberately working this into the conversation. If he knew this much, what else did he know about the asteroid side of her business, about Jerome? This was getting too close. She'd have to play it cool and try to turn the tables.

'Yes, I did that for a while but I was mainly interested in international space stations, orbital travel and kit on the early moon bases. And now it's your turn, Harvey. What sort of contracts were you doing, for Lextar and other clients? Just give me a general idea.'

'I will do, I promise, but not right now. This pastry is a lifesaver, I've always been a sucker for apricot, but I need a couple of hours' sleep. I want to say, though, I'm happy we met. I'd love to tell you more when the time's right and hope we can be great buddies.' He paused. 'It feels kinda special.'

'I hope so too,' said Isabel, taken by surprise. 'And I didn't thank you for chasing after Suzanne, really appreciate it. I hope it hasn't put you off us… off Wellowfern I mean.'

The tight stilettos rubbed against her bare skin and hurt like hell. She hesitated, then stepped forward to offer a hug, which was only interrupted by an incoming palmleaf note.

Important information for all residents and staff: The chief executive of the Healthy Ageing Foundation, Nathan Swift, has left the organisation as part of our restructuring plans. We are grateful for his valuable service over the past ten years and wish him well in the future.

Seven

It was a four-mile walk to the Fringes, close enough for Paul to find his way there, have a mosey around and be back before Trish came home from work. The idea had been growing in his mind for weeks, ever since whispers of the merger started circulating, but it became imperative after Nathan's abrupt departure and Glen's promotion from university professor to chief executive. They were expecting new security measures, meaning that everyone would be issued with passes and quizzed on their reasons for leaving the city village, other than on the looptrain to one of the select cluster's natural environments. Apparently, Lextar management viewed the existing level of security as unduly lax, given the confidential and sensitive nature of their work, but that wasn't all: there were reports of unrest across the Fringes and criminal incursions into the smart city, which acted as a buffer zone between Wellowfern and the area where the Fringe public lived. And then there was the jarring assault exercise at the beach and their encounter with the security guard, which Paul still couldn't get his head round, the scale of the threat. Events were moving fast and he felt he had a small window of opportunity to visit the Fringes and assess the situation for himself.

He had memorised the direct route across the circular glide rail and through the grid streets and squares of the smart city, knowing his palmleaf map would go blank at some point along the way. The Healthy Ageing Foundation, and now Lextar, kept its intranet range restricted, both geographically and in respect of who had access to the network. This came in useful when you wanted to disappear for a few hours, Paul thought, as the two keen-eyed cybird sentries watched his approach and the gate guards stopped their chat to give him a brief once-over and nod him through.

Paul and Trish had visited the smart city together and he was impressed by its small-scale, unpretentious buildings, the greenery and the courtyard design; very different from the tech-oriented city zones he had seen on his travels throughout Asia and the Middle East, which still offered a vacuous vision of towering glass buildings, dizzying sky restaurants and rooftop infinity pools. Here it felt grounded and purposeful, a place where a small start-up might actually nurture lateral thinking, creativity and innovation. And it was clean and quiet, with all the waste disposal and delivery systems underground.

There was no bridge over the glide rail at the far side of the smart city, but he was able to negotiate his way across with a few well-judged, zigzagging leaps. He had expected some kind of border, a fence or a wall, but there was only a dry ditch with a bank of riotous meadow flowers: red, white and yellow. He looked for a path or an animal track but there wasn't one, so he stepped through the flowers, trying not to crush them. A fat mallard duck flew up in front of him, startled and noisily indignant. This must have been a stream once; most likely a tributary of the main river now flowing through the park at Wellowfern.

From the top of the bank, the ground fell away further and more steeply than on the smart city side, making him wonder if this was the wall of the old Roman city. No, it was too far away from the centre; more likely the remaining rim of an Iron Age settlement. He sat down on the slope, affected by the searing heat of the sun. He had factored it in but already forgotten how difficult it was to do anything active without sunshield or shade. Also, he had imagined the edge of the Fringes butting up against the smart city, not this field of thistles and long grass, with a few warehouse-type buildings scattered across the horizon. He began to walk, aware that his palmleaf would soon be unusable and no one knew where he was. He had become fearful, after travelling the world so freely through the turmoil of the past twenty years. It was ridiculous; he mustn't succumb to it.

As he approached the first building, he saw it was part of an old industrial park, the manufacturing and trading units now only recognisable by the defiant signs still clinging to the walls. These were people's homes now, he realised: the curtains in the windows, lines of washing, battered vehicles, the women watching and calling back their young children, one or two of them smiling at him in a weary kind of way. He nodded back and kept on walking, relieved that the teenagers were engrossed with each other, as ever, and the men seemed relaxed, ignoring or mildly acknowledging him as he passed.

The road was empty of traffic and he crossed over into a housing estate with rows of deck-access flats and several high-rise tower blocks. He stopped, taken aback to find that all this was still standing, that it looked the same as he remembered from his childhood estate, only more dilapidated. As he scanned the block directly facing him, a memory flooded in, fully formed. He was about five, playing outside on the deck with his toy cars and happy to show them off to a group of slightly older boys who showed an interest. When one asked if he had any more, he raced back to the flat and returned with an armful of vehicles, to find the boys and all his prized cars gone. And the worst thing was his mother's scornful reaction, blaming him for being stupid. He blinked, feeling the humiliation all over again and unaware that someone had approached from behind and was standing near him.

The man cleared his throat and Paul turned, ready to defend himself this time.

'Hi. You're not from round here, are you? Are you looking for someone?'

'What? No, I'm just looking around, passing by. I don't want any trouble.'

'Well, you won't get any from me. I saw you coming in over the field. It's unusual to see a stranger walking in from that direction and I got intrigued and thought you might want to join me for a drink. There's an okay pub in this dump, believe it or not. I'm Stefan.'

The man held out his hand and Paul reciprocated.

'Hi Stefan, I'm Paul. Yeah, why not?'

There could be serious risks here, but equally he could gain useful information if this guy was genuinely friendly and not some kind of spy. There wasn't time to think it through, and in any case, his throat felt even more parched after mention of the pub.

'Do they serve beer, by any chance?'

'Yes, the local brew. It's drinkable, quite good when you get used to it.'

The pub was on a street corner, shabby but comfortable, with old leather bar stools and sunken armchairs that people must have sat in over decades, if not centuries. The one nod to modern life was a robot bartender, although it seemed to have fallen into disuse, standing there with its articulated arm poised ready for action while a woman called Alice welcomed him and served their drinks. Paul was surprised to see the unopened Wellowfern wine bottles on the shelf behind her. Stefan followed his gaze.

'We get a free supply each week, only available in the pub. It generally runs out by Wednesday.' He picked up his pint and gestured towards a small corner table at the back.

'So, what's the story, Paul? Why did you come?'

'I'm living in the city village, Wellowfern, been there over a year and never visited the Fringes, I mean, sorry, that's probably the wrong—'

'It's okay, we know that's what you call it and believe me, we've got worse names for the place, much worse than that.'

His English was fluent but there was a slight accent – German, was it? Paul relaxed a little and held up his beer glass.

'Thanks for this, much appreciated and glad to meet you.' It tasted fine, not the best ever but very refreshing. 'Local brew, did you say?'

'Yep, Alice over there, she's still got the connections, knows which suppliers have got stuff and which routes are open or closed. It changes all the time.'

'That's why I came, to find out how people live here,

survive. We get told all kinds of stories and I don't know what's true and what's not. It's a personal thing, there's no agenda except I don't want to be misled.'

Stefan stared intently through his gold-rimmed round glasses. Nobody at Wellowfern wore specs now and they looked both strange and reassuringly familiar. His eyes were light blue, his skin naturally creased and his hair steel grey, longish but not untidy. He was about seventy, younger than Paul but without the benefits of anti-ageing meds and the like.

'I'll take it on trust, Paul, and you'll have to do the same with me. We survive, just about, by being on the edge of the city. It's better than the open countryside, where the land's poisoned and there are no authorities or subsidies, only the company of criminals and victims, rejects who've been thrown out or turned away. We're suspended in time – the technology is basic, the food dull and synthetic, people rely on mood lifters or sedatives and a meagre weekly ration of essential items. The local authority is run by chancers who've been promised a place in a select cluster when they've done their time, so they won't grant any favours – they daren't. There's no black market, too many informers for that, and there aren't any walls because there isn't anywhere to escape to. That's the picture.'

Paul stared down at the uneven wooden table etched with initials, the grass stains on his shirt cuff from where he had stumbled, the precious gold ring on his little finger. Why was he barging in here; what on earth was the point? He looked up, taking a long breath.

'What can I say? I heard there were raids, incursions into the smart city. I expect—'

'There might have been, there's always a new generation coming up, restless young people. It won't be serious though; the technology protects everything that matters. It'll just be raids for fruit, fresh food from the street market, that's all.'

'What about you, Stefan? Where do you come from?'

'I'm a teacher, history and geography. I came from Germany to a school here, in the old city. It's gone now but it was successful, good results. I have three or four students in the smart city but it's not enough. I didn't make plans, didn't see what was coming. Great at history and geography, rubbish at looking after my own interests. Loved the job, though.'

Paul looked across the pub towards a group of youths, girls and boys, who had just come in and settled themselves chattily around a table in the window.

'I spent the best summer of my life in Southern Europe, including Bavaria. It was with Trish, the love of my life, when all those borders were open and you could just travel freely.'

'Ah, that's where I grew up. My parents were born soon after the war and they never forgave their parents' generation for it. They were hippies and we lived, me and my brother, in an international commune, speaking English. Now I'm living with a group again, kind of, and I try to tell myself there are parallels, that it can work, but the context couldn't be more different. There's no sense of hope, let alone idealism.'

They talked for an hour, exchanging snippets and anecdotes about their early lives, their youthful dreams and amusing mishaps. Paul had to wrench himself away, conscious of the time.

'It's been great, Stefan. I'd like to meet again – how do I contact you?'

'I'll give you a number to call in the smart city. Or you'll find me in here, most days. Alice looks out for me. We all need that – you too, even at Wellowfern.'

'I know, we do.' Paul felt a stab of panic. He was putting Trish at risk, with this kind of escapade. It wasn't looking out for her, in any shape or form; it was disloyalty. He'd found out what he wanted to know and he had to get back quickly, before he was missed.

***

Isabel drummed her fingers on the balcony rail, impatient for Finn to come into view on the piazza. He was never late, she had cured him of that, and Cyril was tapping with his foot in response to her drumming, insisting on her attention.

'Be quiet, Cyril, I don't need you to tell me I'm irritated. Where is that young cowboy? Has he lost his horse? Ah, don't bother, I can see him now, sauntering along without a care in the world.' She leaned over the rail. 'Stay there, Finn, I'm coming down.'

When she reached ground level, he was slouching against the external wall, one foot up behind him and playing with his palmleaf, for all the world as if he were the one who had been kept waiting.

'You're late, what happened?'

'Ah yes, sorry but it's been a bit crazy – not in a bad way, in a good way.'

'All right, you can tell me as we walk. We'll have to

move it, to get to the Institute in time.' She set off at a pace and Finn fell into step beside her.

'That's where I was already, at the Institute earlier this morning. Glen called me in, me and another two lifestyle managers.'

'And?'

'He's having a reshuffle, that's what he said, because we're going to be doing things differently. Like, we'll have more contact with companies in the smart city, new partners like the Junitsu twins who designed the Blitz event – Juno and Itsuki, have you met them?'

Isabel lifted her chin and felt her shoulders stiffen up. It was an incredible exhibition, sure enough, but she had found out afterwards that Shani, Finn and others were invited to the final evening showing, where they could mingle and meet the two creators over a drink. In hindsight, it probably meant that Nathan was no longer in control at that point, but she still felt a tinge of resentment towards him for not ensuring she received an invitation.

'No, I was tied up that evening, so I went to the afternoon show instead. I expect the Junitsu twins will be in contact with me soon, when they've sorted themselves out.'

'Or I could arrange to introduce you, they've got some fantastic ideas and—'

'There's no need, Finn, I'm perfectly capable. What's your news, then?'

'Well…' he drawled, then paused for effect. 'I'll still be the lifestyle manager for you and others in tier three trials, but I'm joining a new team, External Communications, to develop our contacts and partnerships with smart city companies and other select clusters. It's a jump in pay and I'll have full professional training on the job.'

Isabel increased her speed again, forcing him to break into a trot. In Nathan's time, before he went wobbly, she'd have heard in advance about the creation of a whole new team, would have been consulted on it.

'That's great, Finn, well done. I always championed you with Nathan and I'm pleased it's trickled through to Glen. You've worked hard for it.'

She was quick to reassess. Finn would still be her protégé. And now he had a direct line to the top, by the sound of things, so it should work well both ways. She needed a better angle on Glen, whom she had met only infrequently in meetings and found to be distant and unsociable. The chatter around his sudden promotion was neutral at best. Nathan hadn't been particularly popular, but he was widely seen as steady, competent and fair, not someone who deserved the ultimate ignominy of instant dismissal. There was plenty of speculation about the reasons behind it, of course, but that went on in private, individually or between trusted friends.

When they entered the Institute and made their way to the garden bridge and the wood-panelled conference room, now Glen's office, the signs of change were evident: chairs stacked in the corridors, books and tech kit waiting on trolleys and a general hum of activity. Through the glass wall, Isabel saw there were two people in the room, Glen and Georgina, which gave her hope that it wasn't going to be an awkward encounter with a man known to be prickly as a hedgehog, and with the spiky hair to match. She strode in ahead of Finn.

'Ah, good morning, beautiful day. Finn and I were admiring the new artwork on the bridge – it's hypnotising; you could stand there for hours.'

Finn nodded beside her, although she suspected he hadn't even noticed the rotating art display as she chivvied him along. It was a good starting gambit anyway, very positive. It was Georgina who replied, while Glen avoided her eyes and reserved his curdled smile for Finn.

'Good morning, Isabel, Finn. I believe it's the work of our new mixed reality partners, Junitsu, is that right?'

Georgina directed the question to Glen but it was Finn who jumped in.

'Really, the Junitsu twins? That Blitz event, it was ace.'

'Yup,' said Glen, 'excellent show, now let's get on with it. Isabel, you were resident rep for the Foundation and so I want to run a few things past you, now we're with Lextar.'

'Fine,' said Isabel, instantly on high alert. 'I assume I'll still be the rep, working with residents and helping Lextar to recruit for the research trials and experimental treatments?'

'Yes, that's my current plan – together with Harvey, who I believe you recommended to Nathan before he resigned. We do value your contribution.'

Well, Nathan could be insipid in his attempts at praise, but this from his successor was patently insincere, no getting away from it. It even seemed menacing to bracket her with Nathan, like she was on her way out too. And then mentioning upstart Harvey, as if he were on an equal footing with her.

'Yes,' added Georgina, 'your work in reflecting residents' opinions and ideas, and also for signing up to the mind and brain trials yourself, that's crucially important. We want you closely involved at every stage, Isabel.'

It was clearly intended as a warning signal to Glen, but it wasn't the kind of signal he would recognise, let alone be receptive to. Getting on with his colleagues wasn't his way of operating, from all that Isabel had heard and seen to date.

'So firstly,' said Glen, 'we're widening the age criteria for residents, that's underway. We'll have a special Wellowfern promotion for people in the fifty to sixty age range, with a view to bringing it down to twenty-five over the next few years. Longevity is not just for old people, and indeed, the main beneficiaries of age prevention will be in the younger groups. That's where key interventions will have most effect, like cell programming and reactivation, and it's also about attitude, willingness to experiment and accept weird ideas.'

'I don't agree about our attitudes,' replied Isabel. 'Some residents have pretty weird ideas, I can assure you. Like, Suzanne's a mystic space artist who's been reincarnated several times and claims psychic powers, telepathy and precognition. Or perhaps that's not counted as weird now.'

Glen bridled, drawing back his chin. That had stung more than she intended. 'I don't want to discuss people's belief systems, Isabel, that's not the point. It's the scientific rigour that matters, I'm sure Georgina will agree.'

Isabel had purposely sat herself opposite Georgina, who was shifting in her chair and fingering her silver-green necklace. Finn was no doubt cringing as well, if he was paying full attention. She'd have to rescue the situation on her own, stay as calm and amenable as possible while sticking to her guns.

'All right, I don't think it's irrelevant to think about the connection between science, mysticism and psychic abilities, but let's put that aside. Age criteria, that's one. What else?'

'The trials will be under Lextar's direct scrutiny now. It's a private business, no longer a Foundation. We'll refer to the external ethics panel only in specific circumstances.'

Georgina jolted, clearly wrong-footed. 'But Glen, surely the mind and brain research, tier three, the techniques are untested, at least we'd have to—'

'There will be exceptions, such as you suggest, Georgina. We can discuss it privately.'

This was Georgina, not being consulted on something so vital. One-nil to Glen. Isabel itched to comment but she held back, allowing only a thoughtful nod as she reached for her glass of water and waited for him to continue.

'And the final thing I want to mention is about the cybirds. We've talked about this one, haven't we, Georgina? We plan to speed up their enhancement programme and continue to refine their capabilities in responding to mood and emotion in their human companions. This can't be done without guiding them to experience such moods and emotions directly, through which they can enter new realms of sensibility and achieve a step change in their performance as friends, advisors and confidants.'

Isabel sat back and quietly took a deep breath. Two-nil to Glen. Apart from the fact that she didn't want Cyril poking his nosy beak into her life any more than he already did, this went against what Georgina believed in, what she had explicitly said to them at the dinner before Nathan was kicked out: her cybird enhancement plan was designed to draw the next line and maintain human advantage in the mind race. Georgina herself stayed quiet and gazed through the glass into the corridor, where students were passing with piles of stacked chairs. Isabel wasn't going to break the silence either; she had learned about the power of silence long ago, although she often failed to use it.

Glen looked round at them, almost smirking. 'Well, if that's all, we can wrap up now, thank you, everyone.'

He remained seated and opened a folder on the screentable, making it clear that this was his domain and they had been here long enough. Once in the corridor, the three of them slowed down to acknowledge the dazzling art display, but they were too preoccupied to comment and the enthusiasm for it would have to be revived another day.

'It's lovely by the river, why don't we sit under the willows for half an hour?'

'I'd like to, Isabel, but too much on my plate. I have to get back to the lab.'

'Okay, Georgina, another time soon, I hope. Come on, Finn, let's go. And don't you dare say you're too busy. I'm still part of your job, still your prime customer, remember!'

They sat on the same bench where Nathan had confided his far-out suspicions about Lextar: its ultimate ambition to create the first perfect and fully self-regenerating human. Had he voiced his fears, become a thorn in their side, or was it simply a case of dispatching the old guard, as so often happened in these power-play situations? It could be that. Nathan was an unlikely rebel and while not ineffectual, he was hardly impressive either. It was the Institute's scientific team that gained all the recognition and kudos from the

Foundation's success, which presumably explained Glen's rise to the top, however ill-advised it might turn out to be.

'What do you think, Isabel?' said Finn. 'I don't imagine existing residents will be affected by widening the age criteria. That wouldn't be right.'

'You'll have to speak up in meetings, Finn, if you want to make an impression. And try to say something meaningful. Obviously, it wouldn't be right to let down the residents but I can imagine it all too easily. Glen might be planning to keep a few of us strong ones as show creatures, proof of concept, that kind of thing. We'll end up as his prize specimens in the menagerie! No, seriously, I'm advising you not to be naive about this. It's too soon to judge what's going on, who's really in charge, and I suggest we both keep an open mind.'

'I agree, yes. I'm not used to this kind of meeting yet. It was a bit... sorry.'

She patted his hand. 'It's okay, Finn, it's not you. Glen got right up my nose.'

'I'm also thinking about my sisters, who've chosen their exam courses to give the best chance of getting into our university. I hope none of that changes with the new management. It'll be a mega-disaster if they no longer qualify; I just don't know what I'd do.'

'Well, it hasn't happened yet, so don't worry... Except, I've just had a thought. There are student sponsorship schemes here, corporate and individual. I could offer them individual sponsorship, pay their course fees perhaps. Do you like it as an idea?'

'Do I? That's unbelievably generous, when they're not your family or anything—'

'My own family is taken care of, thankfully. The fact is, you've got a lot to learn and you need to step up more, but I admire your ambition and your loyalty to the Foundation – I shouldn't call it that, I know – and also to your sisters. My funds are sitting there not doing much, and it would be a pleasure to see the girls settled in their studies.'

'Wow, thanks a million! I can't believe my luck, first my promotion and now this.'

'Yes, it's your lucky week, make the most of it. And Finn…'

'What?'

She tapped her left temple with two fingers. 'Keep your head screwed on. It's not enough in this world to be brilliant or lucky, to be loved or admired. You have to be savvy, know who your true friends are and what your fake friends want from you. People talk about being on the right side of history; that's how you'll be remembered. Now it's being on the right side of the future; that's who you will become.'

Eight

Shani was old enough to remember stately homes as visitor attractions: the grand houses full of boring stuff that your parents dragged you into when you wanted to race around the paths in the walled garden or whack someone's ankles with a croquet mallet. Then there was that summer job in a place just like this, an imposing manor house with towers and turrets that disappointed its hotel guests by accommodating them in a soulless modern wing, built below ground. This manor house, the venue for the staff event, had a similar grand entrance, its main staircase branching off in both directions and displaying heavy, gold-framed paintings of dukes and duchesses, their angelic children and an endless line of dogs and horses.

As she climbed the gently rising stairs, Shani wondered why her parents had enjoyed visiting these places, and what had happened to this kind of upper-class family. Where were the descendants now? They might have privately founded their own cluster, engaging in a rear-guard action to preserve the aristocracy, or maybe they had fallen into line and taken advantage of the privileges offered to an old established elite by the new order of thematic global movements and their exclusive, protected communities.

'Hey, come on up, Shani! I've found your bedroom, we're almost next to each other.'

It was Finn, leaning perilously over the landing banister. Hopefully, he wasn't in her group sessions and wouldn't be a nuisance over the weekend. He had lost no time in telling her about his promotion and Glen's favourable comments, which unsettled her. She owed her own new position to Georgina, who admitted that Glen had needed persuading: 'I told him straight: Shani's an excellent research scientist, I want her heading up the team.'

The bedroom was spacious and furnished entirely in period style, with a four-poster bed, rich rugs, carved wooden chests and heavy, full-length curtains. A castellated balcony overlooked the sweeping curve of the driveway, although the glass doors were locked to avoid anyone strolling out onto the narrow ledge after dinner and falling off. Shani and Finn stood side by side, gazing over the two-tiered lawn towards the majestic pine trees beyond.

'It's curious, isn't it,' said Shani, 'how the Foundation's hideaways and special events always have a retro theme? It's like an escape from our constant obsession with shaping the future, what might be, virtual realities. All these ancient things, they're so... solid.'

'I know we're not on the same team for the treasure hunt on Sunday, but do you think there'll be time to explore the woods, go for a walk? I'd like to do that with you.'

'Probably not, Finn, realistically. The timetable's tight and I'm running group sessions on both days. I have to be prepared, there's heaps of new material to read and digest.'

Finn sat in the nearest chair, a high-backed throne with polished claws for arms.

'Let's keep it as an option then, in case we can slip off. I'm down for the partnership and marketing sessions but I also need to keep up with the science, all the latest. I was in a meeting with Isabel this week; Glen called her in and Georgina was there. They seemed to disagree about most things, Glen and Georgina. You'd expect them to have worked it out before talking to Isabel, but they hadn't. The atmosphere was fraught, so I didn't say much.'

'Like what things? What did they disagree about?'

'Oh God, trying to remember… oh yes, the age criteria, bringing in younger people. No, not that so much, that was Isabel objecting, saying older people were into weird ideas. It was when Glen mentioned getting rid of the external ethics panel; he said Lextar would do it internally, with some exceptions – the mind trials, I think they agreed on that… not sure.'

Shani went over to the bed and swung herself up into a sitting position with the help of the post, leaving her legs dangling over the end. Clearly, Finn didn't intend to let her get on with her unpacking, and anyway, this was important. Abolishing the external ethics panel was alarming but best to park it for now. She didn't want to pressurise Finn, cut through his vagueness and risk him clamming up. He was in with Glen now, which was good and bad.

'I'm not that surprised, to be honest. They come from different places and they don't see eye to eye on the fundamental issues. Georgina's committed to the biological approach, focusing on our natural human capabilities, how to stimulate and improve them. Glen I'm less certain about, it's not coherent. He dives into the latest thing and never explains his shifting position to anyone. Opportunistic, I'd call it, but he must have impressed Lextar to get the CEO post. He seems to be hooked on digital brains lately, neural interfaces and symbiotic enhancement as he calls it, leading to new kinds of intelligence. The distinction between that vision and Georgina's wasn't obvious when we were in the Foundation and it was all about healthy ageing, but now we have new strategic goals with more emphasis on enhancement. We'll see if the two approaches can co-exist and if not, which wins out.'

'What do *you* think, Shani? Which way do you want it to go?'

'I'm a biologist, so I'm with Georgina. That won't surprise you, knowing my views on Glen. But it's a fine line and we've been designing brilliant machines for medicine – implants and electrodes, prosthetics and so on – for ages. And now we can construct machines out of organic material, that's yet another twist. My research is on immunotherapy and I'm also into courier nanobots – they're amazingly useful. Sadly, Glen refuses to support my proposal. It's been on hold for months and I'm expecting a final rejection any day. Cancer research isn't sexy enough, it is old hat, but I can tell you it's critically important to anyone with incipient cancer, and there are still plenty of those; not in Wellowfern or the smart city, it's the people in the Fringes and beyond who are affected. But then, who the hell cares about them? They should consider themselves lucky we don't just finish them off. Sorry to rant on, Finn, I get upset when I think about it.'

'Well, I care, believe me. My family is... if only we were... I wish I could help you—'

'Forget it, there's nothing you can do. I got under Glen's skin for some reason and he's never liked me. It's mutual, I didn't trust him from day one. He'd tread on anyone to get what he wants and now he's where he is, who's going to stop him?'

She slipped off the end of the bed and returned to the window, wanting to hide the extent of her fury. It was foolish, going on like that about Glen; she had to temper it and be more subtle, especially now. She mustn't allude to Josh's late-night visit or share his theory about how Glen had secretly reprogrammed the cybirds to give himself control over them.

'I'd better go,' said Finn, breaking an uneasy silence. 'I'll let you get ready for dinner. Shall I knock when I'm on my way down?'

'No, I'll see you in the bar around seven – or the "drawing room", I should say.'

She had planned to spend an hour finalising her presentation for the next day but her mind wasn't on it, even with the pills that usually guaranteed a quick and easy boost in brain energy and alertness. She was repeatedly drawn back to the window, a great vantage point for watching people as they arrived by air taxi or on foot from the loop station. Was that one of the residents here already? Harvey, the new guy? Shani hadn't spoken to him but he was getting himself noticed. As a resident rather than staff member, he was supposed to join the event on Sunday morning, along with Isabel, Trish and the others who had signed up to the brain and mind trials.

It was no use, too many fluttering thoughts to

concentrate on the talk. Georgina had said she was free for a pre-meeting if Shani wanted it. She could wander down and find a quiet corner. She peeped out the door; the corridor was empty, no sign of Finn, and when she reached the central landing she spotted Georgina in the entrance hall, welcoming the guests from Wellowfern's various staff teams.

'Shani, hello. I'm nearly done here. I'll see you in the library, just along there.'

The library was smaller and cosier than she expected, with diamond-leaded glass doors facing on to a well-kept kitchen garden, and the other walls covered with all types of books, not just the standard dull and dusty-green tomes of the ducal ancestors. She could happily spend the whole evening in here, duck out of the usually tedious conference dinner.

'You found it,' said Georgina, elegantly framed in the doorway. Her glossy chestnut hair curled nicely around her ears, showing gold drop earrings, and she wore a long fuchsia pink jacket over a black lacy cocktail dress. She was invariably chic and smartly turned out. Shani found this reassuring and hoped that her own more informal and idiosyncratic style, that of a discerning, creative and mildly scatty academic, matched up in Georgina's eyes.

'Yes, lovely little library, isn't it? Nice to be surrounded by real books, like a cocoon. I've nailed my first talk, just have to check a couple of things for the Sunday session.'

Harvey was in the kitchen garden with two of the lab scientists, examining the plant labels. Maybe this was where Wellowfern sourced its unique herbs, perhaps even the secret ingredients for its own-brand fortified cocktails.

'There's Harvey already. I thought the invited residents weren't coming 'til Sunday?'

'Yes,' said Georgina, 'I thought so too but Glen insisted he came early. He tells me that Harvey is now the main conduit between Lextar and the resident group, keeping them on board with the trials and advising on the incentive scheme.'

'But Georgina, surely—'

'I know, that's Isabel's role, but Glen thinks she's too set in her ways. He intends to offer her something else, apparently. It's linked to the enrichment programme. I imagine he wants to keep her at a distance – she asks too many sensitive questions. Harvey's the favourite now, so it seems, and he's been invited this weekend to learn about the new trials and treatments. He's got an international tech background and superb contacts and that goes down well with Glen.'

'Wow, Isabel won't be happy if she's no longer in charge of the residents, coaxing them along. She won't be pushed around either. If Glen hasn't understood that by now, he's even more… he's even less perceptive than I thought. Nathan—'

'Nathan's gone, Shani. He's history, get used to it.' Georgina stood up and went to the garden doors, tracing one of the diamond panes with her bright pink fingernail, and then a second one, and again along the row. She turned back towards Shani, who was gripped by apprehension. She had been falsely lulled by Georgina's implicit criticism of Glen, assumed she was free to join in.

'I have to tell you, Shani, the Scientific Committee has rejected your research bid. I didn't agree with the decision but I was outvoted. The door's still open for you to come up with another proposal, although I have to say it may be difficult to get it past Glen, and as he's the CEO—'

Shani swallowed, briefly closing her eyes. 'Yes, I realise. And I wasn't expecting it to get through, he more or less told me it was dead in the water.'

'It was an excellent project, so don't be put off. I can work with you on a new one.'

'Thank you, Georgina. I need time to think, obviously, it feels very raw just now.'

'Okay… so, to recap on what the Scientific Committee agreed, we're starting with two strands of the brain and mind trials – memory and social intelligence. We have a small but viable group of volunteers and we've persuaded others to switch strands, so they don't have to wait around for the next stage. Obviously, we're recruiting off-site too, in other select clusters and the smart city. If you can outline those two strands tomorrow, including specific objectives but no great detail on method, that'll do the trick.'

'Fine, it fits with my plan for the session. Also, I was talking to Finn just now and he mentioned ethical oversight, that Lextar aims to do it largely in-house. Is it true, Georgina?'

Georgina sighed. This was clearly another delicate topic.

'That is Glen's idea, but only for tried and tested methods. It won't apply to the mind trials, he's confirmed that. They'll be subject to external ethical approval unless there's an overriding requirement for strict confidentiality, in which case the process will be internal but equally rigorous. I won't settle for a weak or ineffective system, I promise you.'

'I know that. We're in uncharted waters and we have to understand the risks and implications. It would be mad to dispense with independent scrutiny, completely reckless.'

'Yes. And talking of reckless, I'm curious about that ex-student, the ringleader that was expelled just before I arrived. I believe you knew him, so do you have any idea what he was up to with the cybirds? I mean his motives, if it was something more than a mischievous student escapade?'

'Yes, I… not really, no, he wasn't in my tutor group but I think…'

This was Georgina, who had no axe to grind and who had just elevated her to a key research position. She couldn't afford to tell a bare-faced lie that might be exposed later. A bit of imaginative musing containing a credible half-truth could work best.

'Go on, Shani, what do you think?'

'It was part escapade but I imagine it had a scientific basis, illegitimate of course. I don't know but perhaps they had dared themselves to design a new cybird, adapt them to become more fun or something. The brightest students were bound to be challenging each other on this kind of thing, competing to make the biggest waves.'

'That's interesting. So, it *was* a scientific endeavour, then, nothing more?'

'As far as I know. All five have left the university now, so we can't ask them directly.'

'Okay, we'll leave it there. Keep listening, will you, in case there's more to it?'

***

Finn hid behind a pillar as Georgina and Shani emerged from the library and walked away towards the drawing room, where the guests were gathering for pre-dinner drinks. He had to create a moment this weekend, find a space to make Shani aware that he desired a love relationship, that nothing else mattered. No, not that last bit; it should be romantic but not slushy or heavy. Locating her in the library made him think of love poetry, slipping in there and alighting on a classic poem: a perfect verse that he could add to the gift he had wrapped and ready in his bag. It was genius, enlisting his palmleaf to identify her perfume so he could order a small bottle, nothing ostentatious. Adding the love poem, though, was too much. Small steps, that was it. The scent could be presented as a token "thank you" for her offer to help his sisters get into the university, with just a hint of something more.

The drawing room was already crowded and Shani was inside a knot of people, other scientists whom he barely knew. Anyway, he was best playing it cool over dinner, keeping his distance and making brief eye contact every now and again, if possible. And here was Glen himself, raising his hand in greeting and making a beeline for him. Hard to believe this was the same person who had cold-shouldered him in the office all that time.

'Hi, Finn, what do you think of the venue? I've reserved a place for you at my table, so you can chat with some of our key contacts, new partners.'

'It's an awesome place. I haven't had a chance to explore yet.'

'We're having a little trip out early tomorrow morning, before the programme starts. I'd like you to come. It's an extra, something special – you'll enjoy it.'

'Yes, yes, of course, I'd love to. What is it, who's going?'

'Ah, you'll have to wait and see. Front door at seven o'clock.'

He slept fitfully that night, playing out crazy Shani scenarios in his head: swimming from their anchored super-yacht to a secluded beach for wild sex on the sand; furtive kissing downstairs in the library; sitting up in bed eating extra-dark chocolates that promised new heights of arousal and climax. And after dawn, when actual sleep dreams turn vivid, strange females with extravagant make-up wandered into the scene, and hybrid wolf animals that stood growling, teeth bared and blocking his path; and a sinister cyclist, helmeted and all in black, who knew him well but failed to acknowledge him and almost mowed him down.

The front door to the manor house was already open when he arrived just before seven. He could see a beetledrone waiting out front: horizontal propeller shafts, extending legs and in the centre, a bronze-green body in the form of a disc-shaped cabin with a set of smaller propellers attached. He had never seen one close up, not this big. He walked slowly down the steps to the drive and sat on the wall holding his hat, not wanting to appear too childishly curious. Hearing someone behind, he turned, expecting it to be Glen. No, it was Harvey, striding diagonally down the steps in knee-high, tasselled boots to die for.

'Morning, Finn. Impressive creature, isn't she? It's

the latest model, only just gone through final tests and sent straight over from Lextar HQ. We've named it the Wellowbug.'

He had met Harvey twice now but they still hadn't had a one-to-one conversation. And he hadn't mentioned the car to Isabel or anyone else; how he had watched it slink in, deposit Harvey at the entrance to the apartments and slink out again. Why he was hugging it to himself, he wasn't sure, except that it felt like valuable information to keep up his sleeve. Other than that, his impressions of Harvey were filtered through Isabel, who seemed to find him interesting while deeply resenting him for treading on her turf. Like, she was annoyed at him getting involved when Suzanne went off to find Esther in the care home and came back dazed. And now here he was, Harvey, going on a ride in Lextar's new beetle. It wasn't something for Finn to boast about when Isabel arrived on Sunday. She was bound to ask who else was on the special trip, and hearing it was Harvey would go down badly.

'Hey, you two, come on, time for lift-off!'

Glen had emerged from the cabin and was standing on the top step of the leg ladder, leaning out sideways towards them. The propellers started to rotate and a gentle wind came their way as they ran across the drive.

'Do you know where we're going, Harvey?'

'Yes, and this is just the half of it, I'll tell you that much. Hold on to your hat!'

Inside the Wellowbug, Finn was struck by the smallness of the control panel, the soft seating and the almost soundless hum of the autonomous drone as it made its vertical take-off and set course over the trees in a southerly direction.

'It's so smooth. How far can it go in one trip, Glen?'

'We'll only be up here for ten minutes, it's not far at all. We have to get back for my opening talk at ten. Wouldn't look good for me to arrive late from a jolly!'

Finn watched the pine woods give way to parched fields and tried to think what was within range, where you could get to on a ten-minute flight. It was open countryside surely, deserted farms and villages and the occasional larger settlement, where you wouldn't want to turn up in a machine like this. They were wheeling round now, descending onto a landing area next to a major road; part of the motorway network that had been well maintained, while the minor roads had been broken up or gradually fallen into disuse as they gave way to the complex of aerial superhighways for flying vehicles. It was a great disappointment in his life that the driving ban had come into force within a year of him passing his test.

They climbed down the ladder and then he saw her, sitting in glorious isolation some distance from the row of garages, or storage units: the same dream motor, the Rolls-Royce Phantom, one of the most sublime and opulent automobiles ever produced, waiting for him.

'It's my baby – bespoke commission 2023,' said Harvey. 'Want to hit the highway?'

He opened the door and Finn climbed in the back, sinking down on the hand-stitched leather seat. Inside, the doors and roof were layered with thousands of shimmery feathers sewn onto an open-pore fabric, radiating outwards from the central clock on the dashboard. He was aware that the motorway network connected select clusters around the country and that rich executives and entrepreneurs were the only people issued with road permits. He just hadn't considered the possibility that they might purchase and treasure a vehicle of this vintage, the ultimate pleasure being to drive it yourself and as fast as you dared. He sat up straight and leaned inwards to watch the speedometer.

'What's top speed, Harvey?'

'She'll go to 155 mph. And she'll be purring like a pampered pussycat. I've gone up to 150 but I'll keep under that, so you can enjoy the scenery.'

There was a working fruit farm, a vineyard, even a flock of scruffy sheep, but beyond that there was little to see, let alone enjoy. The fields were a monotonous brownish yellow, interrupted in places by patchy hedges and fences. This was normal to Finn, exactly what he expected. It was no big comfort, but at least his family were in the best part of the Fringes, where they had regular domestic supplies, limited health services and a half-decent school. What would they think if they could see him now, cruising along at 130 miles an hour in this incredible machine, a timeless symbol of wealth and success? How did Harvey get to this position if it was really his? Was he born into it or had he struggled and forged his own way?

'We'll have to turn soon,' said Glen.

'There's a fully open bridge coming up, we'll swing round there and drive back to the Wellowbug,' replied Harvey. 'It's a nice quiet stretch, so I'll put my foot down.'

Forty-five minutes later, the Wellowbug bumped down gently onto the driveway of the manor house, where the conference delegates were talking in groups or returning from their morning runs. Finn looked out of the cabin window. Good, Shani was there. She was bound to look up and see him climbing down the ladder if he left the bug quickly.

'I'll go ahead, Glen,' said Harvey. 'Got a few things to prepare.'

'Okay, thanks, Harvey – great ride. Catch you in a bit.' Glen raised his hand. 'No, don't get up yet, Finn. We'll wait until they're all ushered in, we've got fifteen minutes. I want to discuss something with you, only briefly but it's secluded in here with no one to disturb us.'

Glancing out the window, Finn saw Shani moving away from her group and walking up the steps into the house, unaware of his presence in the Wellowbug. For fuck's sake – this had better be worth it, whatever it was.

'How would you like to take charge of this creature, Finn, pilot it on a regular basis? I need somebody I can completely trust to carry out delivery runs to the roadside landing area, either to meet customers or ensure the products are securely stored in the garages.'

'Me, pilot the Wellowbug? Yeah, sure… I'd love it, it'd be fantastic. Who are the customers? Is this part of my new role?'

'Yes and no. It's a private business, something I set up a couple of years ago and I'm now in a position to expand, due to new financial investment and Lextar's wider goals. It will help to promote Lextar but I'm asking you to take it on as a freelance associate, in addition to your official role. Obviously, you'll want more detail about the products and how it works, but first I must tell you that we operate on a need-to-know basis and we're bound by strict confidentiality, it's so commercially sensitive. Are you willing to sign up to protecting our product data, processes and customer contacts? To keep everything secret, including the existence of the business? I'll provide you with an official reason for doing the Wellowbug runs in case anyone gets too inquisitive.'

Anyone like Isabel... 'Right, yes, I'm in. And I'm honoured that you chose me, Glen.'

'Keep your head screwed on.' Isabel's words rang in his ears but this was surely a no-brainer. Even if it were risky, and it obviously could be if voracious competitors were waiting to pounce, it sounded like the potential rewards were too high for him to turn it down.

'Welcome aboard, then. I'll show you now, quickly. We can deal with the formalities another time.'

Glen pulled a metalloid container from under the seats and lifted the lid. It was filled to the top with neat, colour-coded boxes. Finn was riveted, watching him open a sample box to reveal the contents, then select half a dozen boxes and set them out in a neat row on the cabin floor between them.

'Here they are, our first full range.'

'What are they, Glen? I don't recognise them.'

'Six polypills, the best available compounds and all fully tested and approved. There's overlap, some have multiple uses or are most effective taken in combo with other therapies or interventions, but we don't need to get into that now.'

He put his forefinger on the first box and jumped it quickly along the row, looking up after naming each one and waiting for Finn to nod him on to the next.

'**Meds** – prevention and treatment; **Regens** – age reversal; **Cogs** – mind enhancement; **Emos** – emotional balance and pleasure; **Bods** – physical enhancement; **Highs** – perception and recreation.'

'That's neat, the snappy names and everything. How did you… Wow, it's epic!'

Wait to be told and hold back on the questions, that was the best policy. Finn picked up a box and handed it to Glen, who was repacking them in the container as he spoke.

'The first two types, Meds and Regens, come from the Healthy Ageing Foundation's research, our labs here at the Institute. They've simply been tweaked and repackaged. The Cogs and Emos are entirely new and relate to our next set of brain trials, social intelligence and memory. And the Bods and Highs are improved versions of our most popular current tabs. We have agreements for further research with select clusters and companies across the range of scientific expertise and diverse interests. Come on, let's go in. I'll explain more and we can talk about your pay and perks later.'

As he stood at the exit door waiting to follow Glen down the leg ladder, Finn looked round the cabin, stroked the soft side-feather on his faithful cowboy hat and revelled in the idea of riding solo in the beetledrone: *hey, look out everyone; this is my baby now.*

Nine

As they strapped themselves into the air taxi for the short flight to the manor house, Trish finally spoke up.

'Stop a minute, Isabel. I didn't want to come today, and maybe I shouldn't, honestly. I'm not in the right space for it – a fun day, team awayday, whatever it is.'

'I thought there was something wrong, that's why I asked you earlier. You look tired and strained, like you haven't slept all night. What's the matter?'

'Yeah, I should have said, but I thought it might do me good to go.'

'Can you tell me what it is, what's bothering you?' This was unusual; Trish tended to relentless optimism, even when the situation didn't warrant it.

'It's Matthew, you know, my ex. We split up eighteen months ago – well, I left him, that's the truth, to run away with Paul. He was my first lover, Paul, we were crazily young. It wouldn't have happened though, me leaving Matthew, if we were still happy. We had some fantastic years and made a good life together. We both loved wild animals, that was the thing. We built up a zoo, then turned it into a wildlife park. I told you about it, rescuing the animals and breeding to stop them becoming extinct. It worked for a time but their habitats were destroyed, we couldn't reach them, they were slaughtered, and the drought, disease, contamination, locusts, die-outs – it was merciless, horrible...' She trailed off, staring ahead, blocking Isabel out as she confided in her. Isabel waited, biting her lip as she considered how to play it. They were going to be late.

'So, what's happened now?'

'What?'

'Matthew. What's happened?'

'He's gone. He's died; I've lost him.'

Trish dipped her head over her thighs and began to cry, quietly at first but letting it rise to a plaintive wail. Isabel released her own seat belt and reached across to undo Trish's, giving her space to breathe. She waited for the wail to subside, her hand light on her friend's back while she pondered the row of push buttons in front of her, why these air taxis weren't yet fully voice activated. It was a peculiar thing, someone close dying; even more jarring and incongruous than before. It was still happening all the time, of course, but the Wellowfern residents were increasingly insulated from the reality until something like this cut through. Then she felt it, the sudden jolt, almost a physical stab in her chest. The image of Jerome on the dark beach, whispering to the mother turtle as she dropped her white eggs one by one, his tenderness and joy in witnessing the age-old ritual. A treasured, loving moment...

'I'm sorry, Isabel, forgive me. I was trying not to break down, make a scene. It just came over me like a tsunami, unstoppable.' Trish sat up straight, twisting her unruly hair into long damp coils that sprung out again immediately her fingers let go.

'It's okay, Trish, it's a natural reaction, don't fight it. And it makes no odds missing the first part of the day. If it comes to it, Harvey can do the treasure hunt on his own. He'd probably like that, the prospect of getting all the glory himself.'

Trish managed a wan smile. 'He reckons we'll win hands-down, the three of us. He's an arrogant so-and-so but it's difficult not to warm to him.'

'I'm not so sure, still firmly in the undecided camp. But about Matthew, I'm truly sorry. It's obviously come as a big shock, more than you might have expected.'

'Yes, his sister sent me a message, very cold, a one-liner letting me know he'd died. She didn't say when or how it happened; it could have been anything. I keep going through the possibilities. They all hate me now, why wouldn't they? They can't imagine I'd feel any loss, be sad about it… but I'm in pieces, you can see that. I wish I'd at least kept in touch but it seemed impossible. He was so hurt and I felt guilty, I couldn't—'

'No, it doesn't work like that, especially when there's a third party. You had to break away once you made the decision. It was the only fair thing to do, in the circumstances.'

'The worst of it, Isabel, well maybe it's not the worst, but I don't even know if I did the right thing, going off with Paul and coming to Wellowfern, persuading him. He's not settled, you can tell. And Matthew wouldn't have liked it here either. Maybe they're not so different from each other, on that score anyway. I'd just like to have been warned, have the chance to see him, but if it was a freak accident or massive stroke… it's so bloody final.'

'Too much left unsaid,' added Isabel. 'My older brother died a while back and I felt so conflicted about it I didn't say a word to anyone, tried not to dwell on it. It was a mix of guilt and anger, I suppose. He was completely obstinate to the end, refusing to make his escape. I thought it would reflect badly on me, become my failure, although it pains me to admit it.'

They sat in silence while three or four taxis took to the sky around them. Eventually, Isabel shifted in her seat and let her finger hover over the central green button.

'Ready? We're still here, alive, and the woods are beckoning. Let's find the treasure!'

'Okay, let's go. And thank you, Isabel, that's so sweet.'

The taxi took off at a slight tilt and levelled itself smoothly before heading towards the woodland park and the manor house. Trish busied herself making mugs of fruit tea while Isabel watched the screen, which was showing live film of their destination, the activity on the driveway as the day guests arrived and the staff delegates emerged from their early morning sessions.

'Who's that? I don't recognise them all, must be some of the Lextar bosses. I wonder what new schemes they've dreamt up for us this weekend. I could always rely on getting the gen from Nathan, but Glen's a different matter altogether, he won't tell me anything. I'm almost repulsed by him now, so disrespectful and spiky and not very bright with it – a real dimwit, in my humble opinion. I'll have to rely on Georgina for info from now on; or Finn, he seems to be in Glen's good books – and Georgina's still an unknown quantity.'

'Yes, but I like her,' said Trish. 'She's smart and

committed and I think she's the right person to oversee the delicate neuroscience trials. You do trust her on it, Isabel?'

'Early days but yes, I do trust her, as long as she has authority to make key decisions. After something Glen said to us, she reassured me that the tier three trials will be carried out properly, with independent ethical scrutiny.'

Trish looked taken aback. 'That's obvious, isn't it?'

'Yes, but I needed to double check.'

She hadn't had any such reassurance from Georgina, not yet, but she didn't want to put any doubts in Trish's mind or fuel a rumour that could jeopardise the programme. They were the first generation to have the opportunity to explore radical life extension and they were uniquely placed to take advantage of it, working with such a well-respected research centre. It was worth an element of risk, even without final confirmation on ethical approval, as Trish would probably agree. In any case, she would never allow Isabel to race ahead of her, that was certain.

'Do you know what your first trial will be, Isabel, what it involves?'

'We're testing an emo, a polypill for emotional balance, which is essential to social intelligence. We've had great success in influencing specific moods and emotional states but a polypill designed to work on a whole array of emotions involves complicated trade-offs, because different instincts and feelings stem from the same areas of the brain. And there's no single polypill available as yet, so the trial is potentially groundbreaking.'

'Wow, fascinating. Mine isn't a pharma trial. It's about how we curate memories, the shaping and reconsolidation. Finn wasn't all that well briefed on the method, but it involves virtual reality sessions and testing a new type of brain implant.'

Isabel took her eyes off the screen as they descended to the manor house driveway. 'Hey, look at that. There's a huge beetledrone by the steps.'

'Oh yes, Harvey did mention something. It's the Wellowbug, our Executive Carrier he called it. All the Lextar select clusters have one, apparently; it's an American design. And there's the man himself, giving guided tours by the look of it.'

Isabel bristled. It wasn't that she should have been told about this Wellowbug drone, which wasn't directly relevant to her role as resident rep. It just riled her that Harvey knew about it, and what's more, he was parading about as if he owned the bloody thing. Another sign of Glen's favouritism, his casual dismissal of her contribution. Not Harvey's fault, she told herself, but he could at least show some sensitivity. Instead of which, he was too tied up with his eager audience to even notice their arrival. It was Glen who was looking up and stepped forward to greet them. He was almost managing a smile too, in his grudging way.

'Good morning. I was hoping to catch you, Isabel. There's a short break before the treasure hunt and I'd like to talk. We can take the path around the house.'

Trish broke in, acting as if back to her usual self. 'I'll have a look at the Wellowbug then.' She ran off towards Harvey, who turned when she shouted his name and gave her a mighty bear hug, almost lifting her off her feet.

Glen and Isabel set off and he briskly set out his offer, for that's what it was. He was proposing a paid role, not connected directly to the trials but in the enrichment programme. He wanted to take it up a level, bringing in the latest advances to create more innovative experiences and a sophisticated blend of art and science. He was confident that Isabel had the talent and vision to play a leading part in ensuring that the new programme challenged and delighted their existing and future residents. Total schmooze.

'What about my current role, recruiting for the trials and giving advice and support?'

'That's already organised, provisionally of course. I've asked Harvey to take it on.'

That figured. Harvey had almost certainly requested this, wanting to carve out his own niche rather than share a job that Isabel had pre-defined. Would his role, the one she had carried out voluntarily for years, be paid now too? It was aggravating that he could insinuate himself so smoothly, but on the other hand the resistant residents were going to become more awkward and this was a chance to do something interesting and different. As long as no one thought she was being pushed out or superseded.

'Yes, I'd like to take it on, with a handover period so I can introduce Harvey and brief him on the individual residents – their expectations, quirks and attitudes. I feel I should do that, to allay any anxiety or misconceptions.'

'No problem. That's decided then, very satisfactory all round. Thank you.'

Glen speeded up and strode ahead without even looking at her. Perhaps it stemmed from childhood shyness, this gruff manner. It was the boss himself who should be signing up to the social intelligence trial, more than anyone else. She followed him round the corner to the front of the house and almost collided with Harvey, who was dressed in quasi-military style, complete with tough ankle boots, nicely buffed. He even had an old pair of binoculars hanging round his neck and a spiral notebook poking out of his top pocket.

'Ah, I was coming to find you, Isabel. We've had the instructions, now raring to go.'

'Special forces operation, is it, Harvey? You're dressed for the occasion.'

'You too, in that slinky jumpsuit. Wild and stylish, that's exactly what we need.'

The teams were taking their start positions for the first part of the race, in which they had to find their individual clues within the garden and landscaped grounds. This would allow the fastest teams to get ahead, before they went into the woods to search for the common clues leading to the treasure. By this point, Isabel, Harvey and Trish were in second place, but they managed to overtake the leading team when one of the first group tripped over a log and sprained an ankle.

As they ventured in deeper, the impressive tall pines gave way to friendly deciduous trees, a mix of oak, beech, horse chestnut and silver birch. The oaks, in particular, had long been famous for their huge girths and spreading branches. It was to one of these giants, more than an hour later, that the final, fiendishly cryptic clue led the winning threesome. Almost hidden in the foliage, some fifteen metres above ground, was a sizeable treehouse, taking advantage of the solid, intertwining branches between the oak and a neighbouring chestnut.

'Yay, we found it!' Trish had her mojo back, superficially at least.

As they peered upwards, an enclosed lift platform emerged out of the ground at the base of the tree. Trish was the first to reach it, with the other two right behind, childlike in their whooping glee. The elevator rose automatically, raising them level with the treehouse and dropping down again as soon as they stepped off it. Inside, there was a snugly furnished sitting area, with a lookout onto the faint track through the wood and an archway leading to a kitchen space, where a polite cookbot was waiting to take their order for lunch: panini, pizza or paella. On the wall behind the bot, a blue screen lit up to display a message:

The greatest treasures are discovered outside your comfort zone.

Isabel wandered back to the sitting area. 'Who built this den, when and why? It's so secret and well camouflaged, without the lift you'd walk underneath without ever knowing.'

The cookbot appeared with a bottle of chilled, low-alcohol bubbly and poured a glass for each of them. Harvey raised his at full stretch towards the timber roof.

'Cheers, team! Here's to discomfort zones and discovering many great treasures.'

Isabel stood on an armchair to get her glass higher. 'Cheers! Is this the top prize – panini and wine in a magical treehouse, with an inspirational memo? I love it.'

'So, what's next?' said Trish, sitting down close to Harvey, almost touching him. 'Ah, I know. You mentioned Mars when we were on the roof terrace. Is that your dream journey?'

'One day, if we make significant progress on comfortable habitation,' replied Harvey. 'There's a way to go yet. The human body is still sub-optimal for enjoying life on Mars.'

'Isn't it the other way round?' suggested Isabel. 'Mars is a sub-optimal environment for the human body.' She paused, listening. 'Hey, there's someone coming up on the lift.'

An object whizzed through the opening like a frisbee: Finn's hat, followed closely by Finn, hands high in the air and fists punching in triumph as he popped up through the floor.

***

Paul waited for all twelve air taxis to take off and disappear behind the university residence building before he set off on his own Sunday outing. Maybe he should give it another fifteen minutes to make sure Trish hadn't ducked out. Something had upset her last night but she would only say that it wasn't to do with him. Fair enough; he had no wish to intrude and hopefully the trip would give her a boost and she'd be fine when she got home.

The guards at the front gate were noticeably less casual than last time and directed him for questioning by one of the cybird sentries, which he had anticipated by preparing his case in advance. He had a new research contact for his historical work, an expert currently living in the Fringes who had no means of sending him material until they had established an approved channel of communication. So today, as a one-off, he had to meet him in person. The cybird asked for more details but in a half-friendly way, as if it were actually interested.

'Right then, sir,' barked the guard, 'five-hour pass to the Fringes, no interim stops.'

He set off at a good pace, taking the same route as before across the smart city, over the glide rail and the bank, through the field and into the crumbling industrial park and the housing estate. The pub was busier this time, due to the lively crowd gathered under a high screen showing an historic football match in the grainy film of the era. Alice had clearly been primed for his arrival and welcomed him with a smile and a pint.

'You're in luck, Paul – I just took in a new delivery of the brew. Stefan's on his way.'

Paul chose a table that was well tucked away, while offering a good view of the front door. It was premature, this: he had no idea if Lextar would let him take Stefan on as his research assistant, but he had heard on the grapevine that the enrichment facilities were to be expanded to make them appeal to children and young people, so it stood to reason they would need some teaching expertise. And he didn't want to go out on a limb without asking Stefan first; it was hard to know what might or might not offend the Wellowfern authorities, and there was no point falling out of favour for nothing.

When Stefan walked in, it was like they were already old friends; not effusive but a warm handshake and an honest gaze that held for several seconds, Stefan's kindly blue eyes magnified by his gold-rimmed glasses. *Trust your instincts*, Paul told himself. *It's your chance to do something practically useful, instead of fretting about the*

*politics and the transparent power games and whether you
made the right choices, where you let yourself down.*

Stefan's response to his proposition was very much as
he had hoped: thoughtful and curious. Datashaping was
a word and job description he wasn't familiar with, but it
was easy to grasp, the idea of working with AI to produce
compelling life stories of historical figures for individual
virtual reality encounters. Paul went through some
examples he had curated for the history gallery and Stefan
became animated, suggesting other engaging characters,
lesser-known and from all walks of life and regions of the
world.

'It would be fun to work together, if I can swing it,
get permission,' said Paul. 'I wanted to get your reaction
first. If it happens, you can stay in one of the staff houses.
They're well designed, high-spec. Then there's the activities
and facilities in the domes and the arcade; you'll like it.
And you'd have other opportunities, like taking part in
clinical trials and even embracing the prospect of radical
life extension, if you believe in it. I'm somewhat sceptical
myself.'

'Me too, probably. But let me think for two seconds.
One… and two, that's it. Yes. I won't get over-excited
but naturally I'm interested. It's a hellhole, this, a shite
monotonous hellhole of a place, where all spirit is crushed
and we're expected to be grateful for basic bodily survival.
Anyone with sense would escape if they had a decent
chance, even a glimmer of a better chance somewhere else.'

A small family group was entering the pub: a woman
with two children. Paul glanced across, then quickly
turned back to Stefan.

'Who's that? I recognise her... I know her from Wellowfern.'

'Yes, that's Sarita. She runs a hairdressing and beauty salon. There's an example for you. She lives at Wellowfern but she can't have her kids with her – it's a rule. They're living here with her husband but he's jealous of her situation and the marriage is on the rocks, like most of them. It's preferable to be single, that's my view – far better to fight fruitless battles with yourself than take it out on a partner.'

'That's right, Sarita. Trish and Isabel both rate her highly but I've never been into her salon.' He risked a glance and was relieved to see that the family had gone into the back room of the pub. 'I don't want her to see me. I'm travelling incognito and my own partner mustn't get wind of it, not yet.'

He turned to check no one was nearby, listening. Was he right to be here, to do this?

'You were saying, your partner...'

'Yes, Trish. We're in a delicate state ourselves, despite all we've got going for us as a couple. It's partly about the new regime, the drive towards radical life extension. I can see cracks developing, a split between different ideas of how to achieve it, which could play out badly for the older residents and also the wider community, however you define it. Trish though, she's not thinking at that level. She's totally taken by the concept, the thrill of being in the breakthrough generation. It's all a huge adventure and she'll always opt for the far-out research trials. But hey, I shouldn't go on about my personal stuff and our potential rifts at Wellowfern when I'm in the business of persuading you to join us.'

'It's fine, I'm already hooked. It's been so long since anyone talked to me like this. We're deprived of the most basic facts and information, let alone any personal comment or opinion. How soon do you think, before you can get it authorised?'

'Only a day or two, I hope. I'll act on it quickly once the executive and staff and top-tier residents have arrived back from the corporate event they've all been at this weekend. Corporate bollocks in my opinion – some things will never change, however outmoded and ludicrous they may seem. The wrong people win. I saw it all in my career, time and again. But hey, enough cynicism, I have to go, meeting my friend DJ Johnny in the bar. You'll like Johnny, he's a great guy. I'll contact you via the number you gave me last time.'

It was baking hot in the field, a crazy time of day to walk in the open but he had no choice: he had to get back before his pass ran out, and Johnny was expecting him mid-afternoon. The bank rose up ahead, steeper than before, and suddenly in front of him there was shimmering water, a pool materialising out of the grass, with the silhouetted shapes of animals clustered around its edge: giraffes, elephants, rhinos, warthogs and wading birds. These were the wild creatures Trish loved, the objects of her intense dedication for so many years, now most likely wiped out altogether. She did care deeply about the state of the world, it was wrong to think or suggest otherwise. He just didn't understand why she was so trusting of scientific progress and the overriding good intentions of humanity after all the disasters. It flew in the face of reality.

He came close to the pool, then stopped. Using his fingertips to close his eyelids, he stretched them tight over his eyeballs until he could only see deep red, then slowly lifted his fingers to open his eyes, one at a time. The mirage was fainter, the waterhole shrinking back rapidly to dry grass as he continued towards the bank and the smart city. It left him with a mild headache that persisted until he spied DJ Johnny in the dining dome bar, perched sideways on a high stool and having brainteasing fun with one of the robot bartenders.

'Ah now, here he is, someone to have a proper conversation with. Paul, how are you doing? What will you order from this handsome but remarkably dense young man?'

Paul gestured to the waiting bot. 'Spritzer with mineral water please, unfortified.' He knew he must seem dishevelled, having skipped returning to the apartment to change his clothes, but Johnny appeared not to notice.

'Looking good, Johnny, another snazzy silk waistcoat from some high-quality tailor?'

'Nah, I spent years plundering the high street charity shops. And before that it was Carnaby Street, what an effing goldmine that was. Gold, purple and velvet – happy days.'

'Before my time, sadly. How are you, Johnny? Have they been getting at you to join a trial? Harvey's in on it now, isn't he, recruiting? He hasn't dared approach me yet.'

'You must be bloody joking. I'm going out in my own time, it's none of their business. They're like kids in an effing sweet shop, that lot, captivated by the coloured smarties. And who'll want to go to a '60s disco in a hundred years' time? I'll be out of a job.'

Paul laughed. 'Well, all the old people like us, of course.

147

Wonderful old girls in tight mini-skirts and long-haired old boys in purple loons, dancing 'til dawn.'

'Hold it there – what a glorious vision, or is it monstrous, an abomination? Seriously though, I'm just worried about Suzanne, she's getting more paranoid by the day, although they aren't hassling her yet. She's scared they'll get rid of her, like she believes they got rid of Esther. I'm starting to wonder if she's right to be suspicious. It was too neat, Harvey moving in just like that and no chance for anybody to say goodbye to Esther or have a party. I'm not sure there even is an actual care home, who knows?'

Paul stayed quiet, thinking. Johnny was right, there were two angles here: Suzanne's paranoia, or perhaps justifiable suspicion; and Harvey's well-timed arrival, followed by his meteoric rise to the role of resident rep, which opened up all kinds of connections for him.

'Have I gone too far, Paul, with my loose talk? I've shut you up.'

'Not at all, you've given me some helpful insights, although I'm not sure what to do with them.' Paul lifted his glass. 'Here's to our good health, long life and collective madness.'

For the next hour, he was happy to let Johnny reminisce about his younger days: the liberation from heavy manual work when '50s rock 'n' roll took over, Buddy Holly became his hero and he discovered his own talent with a guitar.

'I wasn't a teenager any more, not by a long way, but they hadn't been invented in my day, teenagers, it was all about the effing bloody war, so I decided to join in later and act like one. My dear wife used to tell me I never grew up; probably something in that.'

Paul smiled. He was interested in this but only half listening, the rest of his mind focused on his problem with Trish. He had to talk to her honestly, find a way of doing it that didn't put her on the defensive or undermine her ambition. He twisted the gold band on his little finger, her grandfather's signet ring that she'd insisted on giving him that wild summer, so he would "never forget us, whatever happens". He could feel the rough ridge where it was inexpertly altered in a second-hand jewellery shop to fit his finger. It was rediscovering the ring, when packing up to leave Australia, that had inspired him to get back in contact.

They left the bar just as the first returning air taxi was descending onto the landing pad above the Institute. That gave him ten minutes minimum to get himself tidied up and start thinking about dinner, before Trish walked in the door. As it happened, she was in one of the later taxis, which had to hover while waiting for their turn to land. He watched from the balcony, aware that he had missed her after just one day. He loved Trish and the passion was still there, waiting to be rekindled, nourished. This was the true source of enrichment, never mind the fancy entertainment gizmos and customised mixed reality experiences.

The sky was clear of taxis and he lowered his eyes to the path leading into the piazza.

Trish comes into view, walking beside Harvey. They are laughing and she gives him a playful sideways shove, the kind of shove that Paul recognises, one that could easily provoke a pretend fight leading to wild sex. Nearing the entrance to the piazza, they appear to touch hands before stepping apart from each other, Trish increasing her pace and Harvey dropping back. She is ahead, walking on her own. A flash piece of film comes back to Paul, a scene in an old TV hospital drama where two medics are approaching down a long corridor towards the camera and one says to the other: 'Don't walk so far away from me, people will think we're having an affair.'

He seized the balcony rail with both hands, staring at his tight knuckles and ignoring his alerted cybird, who urgently wanted to engage with him. He unfurled his hands and stumbled backwards into the apartment, as if drunk. He had imagined it, it was nothing: *stop shaking, idiot; get a grip.*

Trish burst in, all excited. She put her arms around his neck and kissed his cheek.

'Was it good?'

'Yeah, great fun. Really beautiful place and we won the treasure hunt by miles. You wouldn't imagine what's in the woods, the most fabulous treehouse. I'll take you there.'

Paul gazed at her, desperately wanting to believe it was his overheated imagination and the sun-induced hallucination that had played with his mind, his overthinking in the bar.

'You're looking weird, Paul, what's the matter? Is it because I wouldn't tell you what upset me? I got a message saying Matthew had died, it was a huge shock. I needed time to absorb it but the awayday did me the world of good, so thanks for encouraging me.'

Say it, don't say it, say it, don't wreck everything, ask straight out, stay calm, wait.

'Oh, that's… sorry . It's just… I had an odd experience walking along the river, under the willows. It was a mirage, a waterhole with elephants, rhinos and giraffes—'

'Surreal! I'd adore that, if it happened to me.'

'Yeh, but it was unsettling, hard to explain. It's not important. Let's do the dinner.'

Ten

Isabel had watched Suzanne trudge across the piazza with her shopping and disappear into the apartment building, but now she wasn't answering her door.

'It's me, Isabel. Can I come in for a chat?'

Silence. Maybe she had popped into Johnny's flat.

'Please, Suzanne, just let me in for five minutes. Or we can talk in the roof garden if you like. I'll meet you up there.'

A slight noise behind the door, like something brushing against it.

'Come on, Suzanne, what's going on? I'm dying for a coffee.'

'Nobody listens to me. I'm on strike, tell them that.'

'Okay, but can we talk properly, not through the door? We're friends, aren't we?'

This was tiresome, but she had to persevere. She needed to keep control in the handover with Harvey and prevent her stubborn friends, who in their various idiosyncratic ways could be seen as challenging the shift to radical life extension, from drawing attention to themselves. Finn was right in what he had said to Suzanne. If they went along with the new regime at the tier one level, that should forestall any serious issues for them and allow others, like Trish and herself, to go ahead with the more adventurous trials.

'I'm still here. I will tell them you're on strike but I need to know why, Suzanne, what it is you're worried about.'

The door opened slowly and Isabel gave it a push before stepping inside. Suzanne looked tidy, her fine silver hair neatly plaited and coming forward over her left shoulder, with a daffodil-yellow bow at the end. She didn't appear to be neglecting herself; that was a good sign.

'Thank you, that's much easier. Let's sit here, shall we? Coffee can wait. What's this about going on strike? Are you cross—'

'Cross? No, I'm bloody fuming, that's what. No one will tell me where Esther is and they're fobbing me off, giving me stories about beautiful castles in far-off lands, like she's some princess gone to sleep in a high tower for a thousand years. It's not allowed any more, is it, treating someone like they're a silly old woman who's away with the fairies?'

'Of course not, and we'll—'

'I'm going to take myself off all my cocktails and drug therapies, that's what, and I'm not doing any painting or cold water swims or two-day fasts or trampoline jumping or flute practice or humming or studying Japanese, not 'til I've seen that Esther's all right. Now I'm told her family doesn't want anyone to visit and they've got the right to stop me going, even if I knew where she is. She never even mentioned her family to me, not once.'

This needed delicate handling, a convincing argument to protect her from herself. The assertive, rebellious tone was quite new. Apart from her frequent mystical excursions, she used to be the quietest one in the group, despite being born into an ancient aristocratic family.

Isabel had assumed she was the third or fourth daughter, irrelevant in terms of rank and demeaned by her more fortunate siblings.

'Let's consider it calmly, Suzanne. If you stop all your therapies, go on strike like that, your rejuvenation will slow down and stop and it's you who'll lose out. And you're looking great, not a day over seventy-five.' It was a no-no, referring to age, but this was a crisis and she knew it mattered to Suzanne. 'I don't know how long it would take, but you'd notice—'

'What do I care about that? I'm not the least afraid of dying, I've told you. I believe in the afterlife. It may not be heaven like we used to imagine it in Sunday school, it isn't, but the soul lifts up from the body, the spirit breaks free at the end. I felt that with my parents, both times, sitting by the bed as they passed over to another place and time. It happened.'

'But your pre-dementia diagnosis, remember, that's why you moved to Wellowfern. You'd have become ill otherwise, without all the therapies and cocktails.'

Suzanne hesitated, then shook her head. 'It's no good, Isabel. I know you're trying, but I just want you to help me find Esther, so I can take her out of here. It's not about illness now, they're not interested in people like us. We've outlived our usefulness, that's what.'

'Listen carefully, Suzanne. You can talk to me like this, it's safe, but Harvey's working with residents now, doing my job. You need to be cautious with him, he's charming but we don't really know him yet. And please don't alert your cybird, they're still learning and they can get the wrong idea, misinterpret what you say or feel. We'll find

Esther more easily if you cooperate. Promise me you'll continue with your pills and therapies and interests, for now at least. Do the tier one trials; it's only carrying on as normal.'

'All right, I'll think about it, I don't want to get you all upset... I'll wait a bit longer and I won't go on about the spirit to Harvey. It's not an acceptable topic any more, is it?'

Isabel wasn't keen to maintain the focus on looking for Esther, but it seemed the best way to placate Suzanne and keep the equilibrium among their small friendship group. They were hard work, all of them, and she didn't trust Suzanne not to express discontent to Harvey, even if she managed not to mention the afterlife or departing soul. And she herself had suggested to Harvey that Suzanne might have to move into the care home with Esther; what was that about? Was she trying to curry favour with him, showing she was aligned with the official Lextar position? And was she only willing to protect Suzanne's position now because Suzanne was displaying resolve, rather than vulnerability? If so, it was no surprise; she had thought she knew the limits of her own tolerance and the strength of her personal allegiances, but both were being tested by the new culture.

She gazed around the walls at Suzanne's artistic creations, the space paintings. They were more geometric than swirly representations of galaxies, planets and comets, making Isabel think of the kaleidoscopic shapes that rose and fell before her eyes as her favourite nootropic chocolates took effect. Perhaps Suzanne had been inspired by that experience. And there was the picture Harvey had mentioned, over by the window: the asteroid belt. What did he really know about her venture with Jerome, how it slid towards near disaster? Had he met Jerome, known him? It was eons ago and the relevant authorities no longer functioned effectively, if at all, but it could still affect her reputation if it leaked out.

She sent a quick message to Harvey, asking him to meet her again in the roof garden. She had to tackle him about Suzanne, anyway, fend him off. When she arrived, though, it was Paul sitting at the table, so intent on his writing that he was unaware of her presence until she cleared her throat. He moved his arm to cover the page and laid down his old biro.

'Am I interrupting?'

'No that's fine, hi – I'm just making notes. I was hoping to see you today, Isabel. Did you enjoy Sunday's event? Trish seemed pleased, and I heard you won the treasure hunt.'

It was innocuous enough, but Isabel remembered how Trish had sat down next to Harvey in the treehouse, so close. She had sensed the frisson between them, an electric charge that went beyond the semi-flirtatious moments she herself had experienced with him. It was possible, even likely, that Paul had picked up on it too, at another unguarded moment. Nothing had changed about secret trysts and love affairs: the trail of clues was laid from the beginning, but the two lovers continued to convince each other that they were covering their tracks and cleverly avoiding all suspicion; and that a good friend or anyone else finding out about it would somehow understand, make an exception for them.

It was only now that Isabel realised, with intense clarity, how much her friendship with Trish meant to her: the easy intimacy, the depth of their conversations, the constant rivalry and mutual admiration, the witty in-jokes, the comfort and the passionate, usually silly disagreements. She couldn't take a risk with it by sharing her thoughts or intuition with Paul, however obliquely. If she talked to anyone, and it was probably a dumb idea, it should be Trish, to try and save her from another adventure she might come to regret.

'Yes, it was a good day out, overall. I'll be working on the enrichment side now, Paul, did Trish say? I'll be over at the arcade most days and I want to learn more about the history gallery, what's happening there and if we can add anything at this stage.'

'Ah, that's perfect, Isabel. I'd like to take on a research assistant to develop our work. He's Stefan, a history teacher living in the Fringes, he's well qualified and deserves a break. Do you have the authority to approve it, by any chance?'

'I can do, yes, and I want to get exciting new experiences up and running quickly, so I'll look favourably on it if this guy's right – just send a short request for the record. Also, does he have a family, school-age children? We're broadening the installations to appeal to kids as well, so Glen's loosened the rule on people's children not living here with them.'

'No, Stefan's on his own but he could help us with that, as a schoolteacher. Thinking about it, though, when I met him in the pub – this was in the Fringes, but please don't for God's sake ever tell Trish I went there – I noticed someone with her kids. It was Sarita, she's your hairdresser I believe, runs the arcade salon.'

'Of course, Sarita! Thanks for reminding me. I'll tell her the kids can come now; she'll be thrilled. I told her it would be fine, that I'd make it work for her.'

'And there's something else, Isabel. I was in the bar having a drink with Johnny and he mentioned Suzanne, her fixation with Esther and her paranoia, as he sees it. Then in the next breath he's saying it might be true that Esther was evicted because she was too frail and too far gone. They wanted her apartment for Harvey, that was the gist, and it *is* odd, isn't it, how he's managed to worm his way in so quickly, even taking over your role? Do you think Glen has brought him here for a reason, to push certain types of trials or to ease out particular residents? I'm only surmising, you understand.'

'Well, I don't mind Harvey taking over my role, it suits me. I was looking for a change and he's got the difficult part, persuading our cautious or contented residents to take part in the trials. As for why he's turned up, you could ask the same question about Georgina – that was sudden as well, where does she fit in? It's not very helpful to jump to conclusions or speculate, especially when your judgement might be clouded by… other issues.'

She had spoken out and seeded a question in his mind, despite her aim to avoid any reference to his emotions. And she had appeared to be jumping to Harvey's defence, which wasn't good either. She was just tired of the Esther story right now; it was getting in the way. Paul stood up and went to the edge of the roof, turning back towards her with his arms spread and his hands on the bar running along the top of the wall.

'Look, Isabel, I don't like the way the Foundation's going and I don't like Harvey, but let's not get into that. I'm worried about Trish. She has no proof that her memory trial has been properly evaluated and approved, but she's so set on doing it, she just brushes that off as a bureaucratic nicety that no longer applies.' He paused. 'I'm sorry, I shouldn't load you with this. It's too personal, you're right, and I need to sort it out myself.'

He looked towards the far end of the terrace, then hurriedly returned to the table and picked up his notebook and pen.

'It's him now, coming over. I have to go – see you later... and thanks a lot for giving the go-ahead to Stefan, he'll be very happy.'

Isabel waited for Harvey, her mind churning. She had forgotten why she had asked him to meet her so urgently. Suzanne, that was it. It was even more vital now to protect the misfits, as she was beginning to think of them, and especially her own friends.

'Morning, Harvey, thanks for coming up with so little notice.'

He saluted. 'No problem, ma'am. Always delighted to answer the summons.'

'I should think so, no slacking allowed.'

He was wearing different shoes, pointy tan ones; winklepickers, her dad would have called them, made infamous by oily-haired spivs back in his day.

'What it is, Harvey, I visited Suzanne this morning and she wouldn't let me in at first. She's all wound up about

Esther and convinced there's a management plot to get rid of old people who have outlived their usefulness, as she put it. Suzanne comes from a posh upper-crust family, big country estate, titles, shooting pheasants and all that. It wouldn't look good if she left on bad terms or was pushed out. The landed gentry still hold a lot of sway, maybe not as much but you shouldn't underestimate them. It's their wealth, desires and influence behind the growth of select clusters, as well as the fund managers, property billionaires and tech entrepreneurs. They're all intertwined.'

'Okay, good to know. I don't understand your class system, how it still survives, but I get the message. The fact is, Esther's location is a mystery to me too. I asked Glen and he said it's confidential, that's what her family wants. And as for the alleged plot, it's true we're widening the age range, as you know. If a current resident doesn't engage with the programme, that's a problem because it's in the contract they signed with the Foundation. It won't always be easy or comfortable as we go forward – change creates anxiety, justified or not. We have to be diplomatic and I'm sure you'll help, Isabel, keeping people onside, stressing the benefits. You have the skills for it and they trust you implicitly.'

This language was familiar, reflecting the complacency of those who are in control of the planned change, who expect to profit from it. And Harvey was a master of deflection. It was curveballs required, not the easily batted straight question or the obvious warning. *Be patient; watch and learn,* she instructed herself. That was the way to get past his defences and discover what else there was to this seductive poser, behind his superficially beguiling manner, love of retro footwear and misplaced desire to live on Mars.

***

The Wellowbug was in loading position, crouched low on its extendable legs to allow the containers to slide inside from the forklift vehicle parked alongside on the Institute roof pad. Finn watched the process intently, checking off each container against the coded customer list on his palmleaf. This was his third trip to the motorway landing area, which he privately called the Phantom Landing in deference to the Rolls-Royce that had found a discreet home among the nondescript garages and lockups. So far, no glitches or mess-ups. Some of the customers or their drivers were usually waiting for him at the landing. If not, their goods were taken by the on-site security staff to the designated garage for a later pick-up. Those who waited stood well apart from each other and came forward one by one to claim their goods; there was no conversation and Finn knew none of them by name. This fitted with Glen's insistence on absolute confidentiality, due to the sensitive nature of the business.

The loading door rose up into its closed position and the legs straightened in a single smooth movement. He climbed the ladder into the cabin and went through the sequence of steps to confirm load, destination, height and flight time. All correct and ready to go, except there was someone calling his name from the bottom of the ladder, or now halfway up.

'Finn, wait for me, pal. I'm riding with you.'

161

Harvey ducked his head through the door and stepped inside.

'No, you can't do that, sorry. I have to go on my own, that's the arrangement.'

'Relax buddy, it's fine, Glen's chilled. He even suggested I came with you, when I said I was taking the Rolls out. I thought it's more fun than going by air taxi, flying with you in the bug. And after you've finished the delivery, I'll take you for a spin. Glen's fine with that too, he's pleased with your work. You can check with him first, if you're worried.'

'No, not worried. It's just that I'm supposed to be—'

'Honest, Finn, I'm just a passenger, I won't interfere or get in your way. And Glen has told me about his business, the polypills. Go on, call him if you can't decide.'

The controls were blinking in readiness and Finn needed to lift off now. Harvey was still in the Wellowbug with them when Glen had offered this job, wasn't he? Or had he just climbed out – yes, that was it. Shit, what to do? Calling Glen would delay them and it would look weak and indecisive, churlish even.

'Let's go then.'

Harvey clapped him on the shoulder. 'Thanks, bud.'

Five minutes into the flight and Harvey was reaching forward under the seats to drag out the nearest container.

'Hey, leave that alone.'

'Can't I have a sneaky look? I know it's the polypills but I want to see how they're packaged, the branding on the box.' He had his hand on the clip holding the lid down.

'Okay, don't take them out. They're packed in order, so we can't reorganise them.'

162

Harvey lifted the lid and Finn glanced down. Two things were immediately obvious, both of them wrong: the container was refrigerated inside; and the contents were not the colour-coded boxes he expected, but irregular-sized packages. Harvey picked one off the top and read the label aloud: 'Human tissue and cells.'

'That's not right,' said Finn, shaking his head. 'That's not at all… I'm not qualified—'

Harvey didn't respond but pulled out a second container, which was packed with the familiar neat boxes: the six types of polypill.

'I don't know, Harvey, I can't explain it. We'll have to check them all now.'

'Hold on. This isn't your consignment, you're the courier. Perhaps someone put in a special order, extra to the pills. It's not illegal and it's not our business, literally.'

That was right enough. And Glen wouldn't be happy if he knew they were checking out the products, poking about. All the containers were on the list, so someone would claim them. It was set up on a need-to-know basis, Glen had said. Finn didn't need to know this; it was outside his brief.

'Hey, lighten up, man, not your problem. Here we are, going down. I'll get the beauty out and give her a warm-up round the perimeter.'

As the containers were unloaded onto the ground, Finn focused on his palmleaf list and didn't look at them once, so he wouldn't know which held the human tissue and cells or who was collecting it. As Harvey said, such a sale probably wasn't illegal, but surely it was unorthodox to transport human products like that, without special attention to the external conditions? Was this Glen's side-hustle of a side-hustle, and perhaps even more lucrative than the polypill products? When he eventually looked up from his sheet, the high stack of containers had dwindled, leaving a small number to be stored in the garages.

The Rolls drew up some fifty metres away, turning heads. Finn relaxed his shoulders and strolled across to it, lengthening his stride and adjusting his hat to a rakish angle as he approached. He was in the front seat this time, even more luxurious than the back. The car slid forward without a shudder and they were on the motorway, skimming the road surface like one of those magical gliding insects that walk on water while appearing not to touch it.

'Feeling all right?' asked Harvey. 'Glen's just hedging his bets, I think. Not a bad idea.'

'Yeah, I'm good. This is fabulous, such a smooth ride. How did you get it, the car?'

'Afford it, you mean? I was born in the 1980s and became a millennial computer geek. That was where the money was if you hit it right, which some did and many didn't. I had a tech company connected to this, emerging tech in medicine. It crashed, that first one, but I had another attempt and another, finally attracting some wealthy investors and it took off. I always wanted to move further and faster than everyone else, that was the thing. And once I had serious bucks to play with, I had to do it in my own style, hence the Phantom rather than a futuristic sports auto like all the other guys craved. Only problem is, I can't easily take the Rolls to Mars, although I had a dream about landing her on the edge of a Martian crater.

Very precarious it was, and I couldn't climb out without unbalancing her.'

Finn laughed. 'I can see it, you stuck there like in a comedy sci-fi film. You're serious, aren't you, about colonising Mars? I know there's robot construction and advanced plans for large-scale habitation, but it seems so inhospitable compared to the orbital cities with their controlled and temperate environments. They'll be far preferable to life on Earth soon and everyone will be queuing up. I'll be tempted myself, if I can take my whole family.'

'It's not so much about short-term feasibility or our personal choices, Finn, important as they are to us. We need to become a multi-planet species if we're to survive and keep evolving. And our long-term evolution, I believe, necessarily involves advanced concepts and innovations like transfer of consciousness, ultra-powerful neural interfaces, sentient robots with superpowers and intelligent digital avatars working remotely in space on our behalf.'

'Are you a transhumanist, then, would you say?'

'Interesting question. I think in the short term, digital mind uploading is a useful way to surpass our biological limitations, but it will be a specialised option. Other methods like cryogenics and reanimation look outmoded now, too difficult, but I wouldn't write anything off. The best prospect lies in combining biomedical advances, digital tech and robotics to change the paradigm and turn human ageing and lifespan into meaningless and redundant notions. But hey, I'm only an enthusiastic amateur and space geek. What about you, Finn, what are your views?'

'Me? Guess I'm still exploring it all. Virtual space trips are exciting enough for now – and road trips like this. What did you mean though, about Glen hedging his bets?'

'Well, he's in this business purely to make money and there's big money to be made, but it's not clear yet where the soaring profits will be. Glen is in a pivotal position, so first he decides to sell polypills and then he adds human tissue and cells. If we had opened another container, we might have discovered state-of-the-art prosthetics, electrodes, implants. He's beginning to impress me, I must say. I was underwhelmed at first.'

Finn asked himself what Shani would think of it, knowing the answer straight away. She disliked Glen with a passion and wouldn't approve of any aspect of this, especially the profit angle that Harvey referred to so casually. It was even more crucial now to stay light-footed and keep to the cover story that Glen had provided, whoever he was talking to. He looked sideways at Harvey, who glanced back and winked.

'Now, hold on tight, I'll try racing on this stretch to beat my one-forty record.'

Finn braced himself and grasped both sides of his seat, loosening up as the engine simply changed pitch and the speedometer peaked at 150 miles an hour.

'You're there, Harvey, we've done it, it's over one-fifty!'

Half an hour later, Finn landed the Wellowbug on the roof pad. He held back for two minutes after Harvey climbed out, not wanting anyone to find out they had been on the trip together. When he arrived at his desk, he registered Shani immediately and waved across, not really expecting her to gather up her things and come over. He had time to reach into his drawer and retrieve the small bottle of perfume that he still hadn't presented to her.

'Shani, how's things? Are you okay?' Clearly not, from her grim expression.

'Can we go to the café, Finn? I know you've only just come in but—'

'Of course, this stuff can wait. Let's go.'

By the time they reached the art deco café, she had told him about her latest run-in with Glen and the official decision to reject her research project, on the grounds that it had limited relevance to Lextar's programme. "Zero relevance" was Glen's phrase.

'That bastard, it was all him, not recommending it. And it gets worse, Finn.'

'How, worse? Shit, that's bad enough.'

'Glen's been out to get me from the start, but now he's enraged because Georgina insisted on promoting me to principal researcher and she got the backup of key committee members. He knows I don't respect him as a scientist and I think his academic publications are feeble, full of holes. He should be exposed but who's going to do that now? They're all too frigging scared.'

'What did he say to you, the worse thing?'

'He raised that issue with the students, you know, the stupid cybird incident. He says I must have known something about it and I should have either stopped it or reported it. I don't know what evidence he's going on, but he's decided to target me, that's for sure.'

Finn wavered. 'And... the student who was evicted, Josh, did he mention him?'

Was that a flicker of reaction? It was imperceptible, and she continued unfazed.

'Yes, he's set on tracking him down. It seems Josh has taken one of the cybirds; it's missing. I know nothing about that, it's news to me and I haven't a clue where Josh is now. I wish I did, but I don't. Georgina doesn't know either, about the missing bird, but she's been ferreting about for information. Glen could make serious trouble for me, Finn, threaten my career. He's a shameless bully and he'll pin this on me if he can.'

Finn shifted nervously. He couldn't present her with the bottle of scent now. It was entirely the wrong moment and he felt panicked himself, knee-deep as he was in a dubious business entanglement with Glen. He reached his open hand across the table and Shani laid her fingers lightly on his palm, displaying beautifully shaped silver fingernails that he longed to stroke.

'We'll think of a solution, Shani. There'll be a way out, it's all a misunderstanding.'

It was a facile response, useless; he should have stayed silent, if that was all he could offer. She shook her head, then abruptly perked up, looked around the café and spoke in an exaggerated, conspiratorial whisper.

'What that stupid dork Glen doesn't realise yet is that I know what he's up to – I've also got something on him.'

Eleven

Five minutes on the warm-up bike, a thirty-minute circuit for strength and stretch and finally ten minutes on the rower. This was the best part, with its fully imagined, immersive river environment. Shani adjusted the settings to speed up the water flow, add wildlife (mainly ducks and the occasional rat or otter) and eliminate humans from the scene. Why anyone would want that distraction, especially when friends or associates might pop up among the passing walkers and cyclists, was beyond her. For their supportive comments, she supposed, or to make you work harder to impress them. She shuffled her feet into the tight straps, leant forward to grasp the oars and set off between the grassy, flower-strewn banks. It was always high summer, that was one limitation. But then it did feel like high summer all year round now. The four seasons were a nostalgic throwback, so perhaps there was no demand.

She concentrated on her rowing action, keeping it smooth and steady as she glided backwards under the arch of the first bridge and then the second. There was no sound apart from the rhythmic splash of the oars and the occasional squawk as rival ducks staged their aggressive clashes. This was the magical thing: entering a state of deep immersion that overtook the senses to the point of blanking out the real world; in this case a gym, but it could be anywhere and allay any physical sensation, including surgical pain in an operating theatre. The final bridge was coming up behind her now, so she put in a burst of extra effort to get over the line.

'Hey, Shani!'

She raised her shoulders from their folded-over position and looked up at the bridge. It was Josh, waving at her from the top of the arch. Somehow, he had invaded her virtual space, found his way in. She blinked twice to kill the illusion; he was still there.

'Great style – love it! Catch you soon.'

He blew a kiss, then casually strolled along the bridge, turning his head once to wave again and blow another one. It wasn't the disappearing act of a ghostly apparition; he was present on the bridge and then he simply walked away.

She let the boat bob around while she tried to figure out what had just occurred. It must be a mental projection that she had superimposed on the scene. There was no other explanation, except a sinister one that she didn't want to contemplate: that it was externally planted as some kind of message or warning. She pressed the "end" button and was back in the gym, where no one appeared to be taking any notice of her. She had agreed to meet Georgina at the entrance and first she had to shower and make herself presentable. There was no time to sit and reflect.

Georgina had suggested they take the "scenic route" to the arcade, implying that she wished to talk privately before they met up with Juno and Itsuki at the neuro hub. They had already held their pre-meeting to plan the set-up for the mind and brain trials, so it must be something else.

There were various possible topics, some more unnerving than others.

'Morning, Shani. Let's go this way, round the domes.'

'Hi. I was working out on the virtual rower just now, have you tried it? It seemed apt today, seeing as we're talking to Juno and Itsuki about integrating elements of virtual reality into our lab-based methods. Blended reality, as they call it. Can't wait to see what combo they'll come up with for the mind trials.'

'Before we get on to that, Shani, I heard you approached Glen after the rejection of your research proposal by the Scientific Committee. Unprofessional, he called it.'

'It was Glen, the way he—'

'No, Shani, he was within his rights, even if he did personally influence the decision. He's chief now, Nathan's gone and you have to... we both have to recognise that. I was appointed by Nathan, remember, so I'm adjusting to the situation too. I'm sympathetic to you on this, but the decision's been made. It's water under the bridge, don't be distracted by the ripples. We have to choose our battles, it's always the same. You can select another topic for your post-doc research, as I said, something more in line with the goals of the new programme. Look at the brain and mind work we're discussing with Junitsu today, so many intriguing questions and you'd really enjoy it, once you got stuck in.'

'You're right, Georgina, but still—'

'Let me finish first. I'd be happy to support a new proposal, so tell me if you want to pursue it and we can work on some initial ideas.' She paused. 'Between you and me, I've got my own issues with Glen, a string of them

– and he's not easy to work with, not respectful of other people's views although he's so erratic himself, swaying between different positions. Mostly, I let it ride but there's one thing so fundamental, I can't ignore it.'

'Thank you, Georgina, that's kind and I will think about other options, just need a bit of breathing space. And the fundamental thing...?'

Was it the weakening of ethical scrutiny, again? Or the implications of widening the age range? Or Harvey's role in recruiting trial participants, deposing Isabel?

'I'm not happy about Glen's decision on the cybirds.' *Oh God, not this one.* 'As you know, we were focused on upping their ability to respond to mood and emotion in human companions. This is the limit for me but Glen's going further, powering the birds to simulate or experience the range of emotions directly. He hasn't thought through the ramifications, otherwise he wouldn't even countenance it. Or maybe he's trying to top the rogue students' game, giving the birds an uplift of his own. But on top of that, one of the cybirds is missing. Glen suspects that you know where that lost cybird is, and the ringleader with it.'

Shani tried to keep her thoughts straight. Was this how Glen planned to exert direct personal control over all the cybirds, as Josh had alleged? Why the emphasis on emotional experiences – to make them all adore him? She almost giggled.

'Glen's already spoken to me, Georgina. I've no idea where that ex-student is, or the missing cybird. I only found out yesterday that it had gone.'

Georgina nodded. 'Don't worry, I trust you. It's Glen that bothers me – his insecurity, that's what it boils down to. He's leaning heavily on Harvey now, have you noticed? His new interest in cyborgs as a goal in itself, rather than an aid to enhancement and longevity, risks diverting the programme away from our biological aims. And what are Harvey's credentials? Where does his knowledge and authority come from? We don't know… but anyway, I want to meet this student because it seems very rash to get rid of someone who could be highly talented and an original thinker. It's exactly the kind of individual we need, as long as we can channel their talent and originality in the right direction.'

Walking alongside, Shani gaped at this abrupt and startling turn in the conversation, then closed her mouth with what seemed like an audible plop. Fortunately, there was no need to reply, as they were now in the arcade and close to the neuro hub. As Shani caught sight of Itsuki and Juno, larking about and embracing the colonnade pillars in playful statue poses, Georgina stopped and pointed towards them.

'They're a living experiment themselves, those two – we're lucky to have them. I'll fill you in later. You should be properly briefed, given your role in heading up the mind trials.'

The twins had spotted them and quickly ended their game. Shani had failed to detect any minor differences between them on the first evening after the Blitz show, but now she noticed that Juno had a slightly rounder chin, while Itsuki's was square. Aside from that, they looked pretty much identical, had the same impish expression and were again dressed in similar outfits: loose, bohemian-style shirt and trousers, with matching green headbands. Was that a clue to the living experiment Georgina had just mentioned – the headband as the latest connective device, advancing mind-to-mind communication or wider extrasensory perception?

Inside the neuro hub, the twins gave a whistle-stop tour of the facilities, taking it in turns to provide incisive comment on their value and potential usefulness to the research programme. Essentially, the equipment and design capability were relatively advanced but no longer state-of-the-art, given the pace of development in virtual and blended reality. The current facilities were also focused on memory and emotions, while the new mind and brain trials would extend to all the five areas Georgina had set out: memory, social intelligence, curiosity, creativity and judgement.

'Let's zero in on social intelligence and memory, as they're our initial priorities,' said Georgina. 'Social intelligence is a pharma trial and we'll use this hub space to compare the effects of the polypill with individual emos that work on the different aspects. Clearly, this requires precision if we are to assess small changes in empathy, self-awareness, emotional control and most elusive of all, evolved attitudes.'

Itsuki turned and whispered to Juno, who nodded agreement before replying.

'We recommend a refined extended reality approach, involving immersion in other identities and social worlds, so the trial participant adopts characters with particular traits, behaviours and circumstances, on a spectrum from similarity to otherness. We can design a customised programme, with more depth and veracity than anything you have seen before.'

'And for the memory trial,' added Itsuki, 'we'll recreate familiar past environments and employ techniques for reliving personal experiences; those are well developed. We can add innovations in memory-shaping, selection and recall, but we'll need to understand the new brain implant before we design compatible virtual input and effects.'

'I can arrange a guided lab demonstration,' said Shani, aware of Juno's steady gaze.

'Great. And if you want to try our first installation, Shani, the dreamscape chamber, drop by soon. You seemed very curious about it on the tour just now.'

'Definitely, I'd love to.' *Not today though; today had been trippy enough in the boat.*

As they walked back to the Institute, she asked Georgina to explain her comment about Juno and Itsuki being a "living experiment".

'It's a landmark in bioscience. Lextar was keen to contract with Junitsu and the twins because they embody a radical and highly innovative approach to enhancement. They are identical twins but they've been bio-engineered individually from conception onwards, so they are each uniquely creative and intelligent. And the most astounding part is this: they were born twelve years ago and they've been accelerated towards peak maturity, making them about twenty-five now. I don't have any details; the specifics are shrouded in secrecy.'

'Wow, that's mind-bending! Wonder kids. And they're so bloody nice with it!'

Georgina smiled. 'Naturally. Take note, think what we can learn from them but don't breathe a word to anyone. I mean no one. And remember, they are not trial participants or experimental subjects. They're here to give us the benefit of their superior talents. Keep focused on that; we have a duty to protect them from any malign interest.'

Any malign interest. A weighty phrase, lending even more force to what Georgina had confided earlier: her mistrust of Glen and unease about Harvey's influence on him.

'Good point, Georgina – will do.'

***

Isabel arrived early at the neuro hub, eager to meet Juno and Itsuki and begin her tier three research trial. In this first session, they were going to test her on the components of social intelligence and produce baseline data for comparison at set points as the trial progressed. Privately, she was doubtful about how accurately any changes could be measured, although she believed the trial would have a beneficial effect if she was on the actual polypill and not the placebo. But that was pre-judging it. The important thing was to have an open-minded approach and resist any temptation to skew the results. The twins' methods would be clever enough to detect any wilfulness.

Hopefully, Finn wouldn't be late. She had insisted he join her because he was still officially involved in supporting resident participation, even if he was skipping off doing too many other things these days. Like taking flight in the Wellowbug from the roof of the Institute, as Cyril had twice reported when she asked for Finn's location. External Comms might be thrilling, but the start of her social intelligence trial was an important moment and Finn should be available to provide any advice and support she required.

As she waited outside the hub, she noticed Sarita coming along the arcade with a young child, presumably her daughter. They hadn't spoken since that painful episode in the salon, although Isabel had intended to give her chocolates as a peace offering. No need for that now, as the kids had clearly been rescued from the Fringes and moved into the village.

'Hello, Sarita, good to see you. I must make a hair appointment soon, it needs it. All worked out well then, like I said? I did put in a good word for you.' She looked down at the child, who was about eight. 'Hello, what's your name?'

The little girl twisted away, still gripping her mother's hand: 'Marina.'

'Ah that's pretty. And your other child, Sarita, your son? Is he at home?'

The emotion in Sarita's face was not happiness or contentment, but distress or fear. That was what this mind trial was about: awareness of people's emotions, reading them.

'Was it you then, Isabel, that got the rules changed? I didn't dare contact you after what happened. I was scared they would close down my business and throw me out. And now Marina's here but my son, Lorenzo, he has to stay in the Fringes with his dad.'

'But why? Is your husband insisting he stays there? That's so selfish.'

'No, he's okay like that. It's Lorenzo. We don't know what's wrong with him and they say it might be contagious, even though no one's examined him, no doctor or nurse. He's not the only child with it. There's several of them from his school that are sick, probably more but their families are keeping quiet. They don't want to be banished or kept indoors, where they won't get hold of the basic things they need.'

'Banished – where? Look, I'm sorry to hear that, Sarita. I'll make an appointment and we can talk about it then. But if Lorenzo is seriously ill and if it's contagious…'

She could see Finn ambling towards her, swaggering more like in a pair of knee-high fringed boots. With his hat and floppy hair, all he needed was a horse, a pair of silver spurs and a gun holster slung loosely round his hips.

'I have to go and you need to open the salon. Bye, Maria, see you later.'

'It's Marina, not Maria,' said the child, suddenly defiant. 'I don't like Maria.'

Isabel smiled, nodded absently and turned away, her thoughts already elsewhere.

***

Juno and Itsuki were using the virtual reality studio for the session. The reclining chair in the centre of the room was wider than normal and nicely cushioned, reminding her of business-class flights she had enjoyed in the past. Finn was fumbling with his hat, as usual, but she resisted giving him a dirty look. Itsuki welcomed them and launched into his introduction.

178

There were four main points: for the purposes of the research, emotional and social intelligence were the same thing; Junitsu had only designed the virtual and blended reality elements of the study; Junitsu wouldn't know which participants were on the polypill and which were on individual emos (for different elements of social intelligence) or the placebo; and finally, participants wouldn't be informed of their individual results.

Isabel was invited to sit and put on blended-reality glasses. The twins stayed behind her, one on each side, while Finn moved forward a few paces, so he could observe more easily. Juno nodded to Itsuki and they started humming in a long monotone, pausing at the same time to take a breath and begin again on a different note, higher or lower.

'Relax, Isabel,' said Juno, 'and think of your mind as a beautiful, illustrated book. Now imagine it lying on the table in front of you. Can you see it?'

'I'm touching it. It's red leather with gold edges. Can I open it?'

'Yes, we want you to open it at different pages and look at the words and images as we talk. Firstly, we need to gauge what you think about your own level of social intelligence, for example how empathic you believe you are and how you rate your degree of emotional control. After that, we'll move into the immersive phase, where you'll encounter other people and social situations and be asked to respond in the way that's most natural to you. The book will be in front of you the whole time and you can touch it and turn the pages whenever you choose. Later in the process, we'll guide you to assume other identities, to think and act as individuals with different character traits and life experiences to yourself.'

Isabel focused on the book, losing herself in the oddly familiar world that had been created for her, or that she had created in her life: a world of defining moments and trivial incidents, enduring friendships and damaging rifts, chances seized and squandered, discovery and loss. When it ended, Itsuki tapped her shoulder to bring her back to the room. She felt disoriented and also sad to come out of it, wanting more.

'Finn, are you still with me? I can't see you.'

'I'm right here, look.' He stepped forward and took her hand. 'How was it?'

'It was… extraordinary, that's the only word. The most extraordinary thing ever.'

'Don't analyse it,' said Juno softly. 'Don't talk about it with anyone, that's important. It's your unique experience and we want you to hold it tight, hug it as something precious.'

'Am I allowed to say I'm impressed? It felt impossible to pretend, to be someone I'm not or to ignore the effects—'

'No,' interrupted Itsuki. 'We're not listening, remember. As Juno says, keep it inside, hug it. Let's go to the office, where we can all sit down and chat over an ice-juice.'

As she stood up, Isabel realised she was physically tired, as if she'd pushed herself on a vigorous workout. Mentally, she was alight.

'So, is it the force of the future, social intelligence? Will it be our last bulwark against artificial intelligence – and will it win out, in the end?'

Juno smiled. 'Itsuki and I come at it from different

angles, so it's inevitable we'd see that differently if we were allowed to give an opinion – which we're not, in this context.'

'Why inevitable?' asked Finn.

'Just that we're individuals with different histories, complementary twins if you like.'

'Tell us more,' said Isabel. 'I'm intrigued to know who discovered you, how you came to Wellowfern. This creative work you're doing, and on the enrichment side too, it seems years ahead of where we're at. It's hard to believe that Glen found you and brought you in, with his limited imagination.' She looked at Finn, who widened his eyes at her over his glass of ice-juice. 'Just my personal view, of course.'

'We'll accept the compliment, thank you, but we also feel fortunate to have been born at that time in the New Families cluster. The education there, it's superb.'

Isabel stared back at Itsuki, then at Juno. Her own daughter and grandchildren were in the New Families cluster and she hadn't heard about this, the speed of advancement.

'Why did you leave, if it's not too personal a question?'

'This is a temporary assignment, to help Lextar move its plans forward.'

Isabel sensed this was all she was going to find out today. No need to rush; she had an opportunity to get to know them better through the coming sessions. And if she had to face past events that she would rather keep entirely to herself, then so be it. She already felt a strong bond of trust; a conviction that the twins would never betray her.

***

As they walked past the shops, Isabel turned to look at Finn.

'You seem twitchy. Was there anything I should know about? I was completely lost in my mind book.'

'No, nothing like that. But this polypill, is it a second generation one? I mean, do we already have a polypill of this type, one that's approved and on the market?'

'No, that's the point, this is a first. If the trial is successful, the polypill will replace the individual emos that select clusters all around the world are using. I'm blown away by the experience and it was only the first session; we haven't even begun taking the pills. I'll be very disappointed if I'm not in the polypill group, but that's down to chance. They won't tell me but I'll know because I believe it will be effective; its time has come.'

She waited for a response but Finn said nothing.

'Why did you ask? You're not thinking about possible side effects are you; me being a guinea pig? Don't worry about that; I'll have a great time, it's brilliant. You'd think it would be an emotional rollercoaster but it wasn't at all. It's inspired me, fired me up.'

'No, just checking.' He paused. 'I've had a thrilling experience too, with Harvey. Not futuristic like this, but kind of a different way of revisiting the past. He came with me on a business trip. You know I have meetings with external partners and this was the regional group of clusters from the global movements. We meet to update each other and talk about what we're doing for the Fringe public and with our tech projects in the smart cities.'

'I didn't know about those groups but why is Harvey there? What's his expertise?'

'He's got contacts, seems to know everyone.'

'That's always the answer, Harvey's famous contacts. I've collected one or two useful contacts myself, more than a few down the years, but I never got invited on a business trip.'

'It's a new group, Isabel, since Lextar.'

'Was that when you and Harvey went off together in the Wellowbug? Cyril spied you on the roof and saw Harvey racing up to join you at the last minute.'

She was aware of Finn squirming, presumably feeling guilty about his disloyalty to her, how it looked to be flying off in the bug with Harvey. And it had been quite comforting, having him beside her today. She decided to ease off, not press him. She was ruining her mood, grumbling on about Harvey when he didn't deserve her emotional attention.

'Yep, that time,' replied Finn. 'After the meeting, he offered to take me for a spin in his car and it turned out to be a bespoke Rolls-Royce, vintage 2023, such exquisite detail and incredible power and acceleration, with the driver in full control. I'm hoping Harvey will give me a lesson and I can drive it myself. I passed my test just before the ban.'

Isabel let this startling news sink in. 'Okay, I'll let you do it on one condition.'

He laughed, clearly relieved at her lighter tone. 'What's that?'

'You drive into the piazza, sound the horn and pick me up. I'm coming with you!'

Twelve

Trish was the better runner, faster on the track and stronger over a distance, while Isabel was more supple and agile, still the gymnast. As they did their stretches under the chestnut tree, she bent and looked back through her legs, admiring Trish's athletic body: her muscled calves, flat stomach and perfectly shaped thighs. They didn't look bad, either of them, in their aerodynamic, figure-hugging sports kit. Trish leant forward at a right angle from the hips, splayed fingers touching the ground and her upside-down face on a level with Isabel's.

'It's such a nice day, I don't want to go in yet. Let's walk along the river, shall we? I want to hear how you got on with the trial.'

Isabel stood up, pushing back stray strands of hair. 'Happy to walk but I can't talk about the trial, which is normal but Juno and Itsuki made an especially big thing of it – no external influences. They're the sweetest young couple, or twins, I should say.'

'You enjoyed it then? I can't wait to start my memory sessions but I need to have the implant inserted first. That's happening on Friday. All done by nanobots. It's freaky but it's a standard procedure now and I'm able to watch the whole thing. I'll be under the same vow of silence after that, although maybe we could loosen it a bit between the two of us?'

'No, Trish, I'm going to keep to my end of it. Apart from anything else, I'm sure the twins will know, they'll sense it if we don't follow the rules. They could be psychic, maybe in a way we haven't yet encountered. I've no idea, but I intend to find out. Might have to enlist Suzanne and her special powers at some point, see what she makes of them.'

'Or it could be the blended reality aspect, giving them an aura of extra perception.'

'But they designed the blended reality, so it's not just an aura. It was searching and insightful, spot on. I couldn't begin to do it justice if I tried to describe how it went.'

They were approaching the bridge and stopped halfway across to look upriver.

'What's that?' said Trish. 'There, beyond the far willow? It's a log, someone's laid it across the river to make a new crossing, short cut to the Institute. It looks fun, let's go see.'

They jogged along the path to the log, which was part-plank with a flat, sawn top and a rounded underside. It was about twenty centimetres wide and firmly embedded low down on each bank, not much above the water level.

'What are you waiting for, Isabel? It was your gym apparatus, wasn't it, the beam?'

'Yes, but it's years ago, decades even. I'm way out of practice, my balance isn't—'

'Chicken, are you? I'll run across ten times if you give me one balancing act.'

'Okay then. Your idea, you go first. Five times each way and make it quick!'

Trish was over-confident, of course; rushing at it, rather than testing the structure and her ability to keep steady on its springy surface. Three times she wobbled badly, coming close to landing in the river, but she managed to keep upright until she fell giggling into Isabel's arms, almost knocking her over. By then, Isabel had a quick routine worked out. She walked in gym-display mode to the centre of the plank, where she began with a series of graceful bends, followed by small jumps, two twists and a final dip of the head towards her audience.

'Is that it?' said Trish. 'What about a one-arm handstand or a back somersault?'

'Next time. You weren't exactly in control yourself, by the way. Running to stay up.'

They sat side by side on the bank, Trish with her hands round her knees and Isabel fiddling with a long piece of grass that she had picked out of a nearby clump. It seemed a good moment, as good as any, to ask her question, but she wavered and Trish got in first.

'Which Olympic Games was it, when you were on the team?'

'Seoul, 1988.'

'Did you win a medal?'

'No chance, world gymnastics was dominated by the Eastern bloc back then and the Soviet Union won practically everything itself, twelve golds and twenty-one medals in all.'

Normally, she would have changed the subject at this point, or created a diversion of some kind. This time, though, she decided to use it as an opportunity, a way in.

'Actually, I wasn't in the final team. I should have been but I fell off the beam twice in the last trials. I've kicked myself for it ever since. And it was unjust. That other girl—'

'Hey.' Trish took Isabel's arm and squeezed it gently. 'It's light years ago and these things happen, success is built on repeated failures, so they say. That's the theory, anyway.'

'You know, it's funny but I'm glad I've told you. It's haunted me down the years, the public humiliation. And Trish, there's something I wanted to ask you too. It's personal and you don't have to answer, not if you don't want to. Just tell me to bog off if you like.'

'Okay,' said Trish slowly. 'I'm guessing now, so go ahead and ask me.'

She drew back her hand and her expression changed minutely, tension lines showing around her olive-green eyes. Isabel did a double gut flip, the small flutter of doubt gaining strength as she wrestled with the idea of inventing something, asking a harmless question instead of making a futile rescue attempt. No, it wouldn't do.

'Are you and Harvey... is there anything going on between you? In the treehouse—'

'No, there's nothing. We're flirtatious, that's all.' She turned away, eyes narrowing. 'And I can't see why you should have any problem with it – unless perhaps you're jealous? You monopolise his time, always calling to meet him about something or other.'

'Hey, that's not fair, Trish, trying to put me on the back foot. It's all about Wellowfern as far as I'm concerned, dealing with Suzanne's anxiety and other resident issues. Harvey irritates me more than anything, and he's secretive about his previous work, as if it's too high-powered to talk about. I'm sorry if I've read it wrong, but it was the body language; all through the treasure hunt you—'

'Give me a break! You're not exactly forthcoming yourself, on that front. We were all fooling around that day, that was the idea, fun… Has Paul said something to you? Is that it?'

'No, he's not mentioned it, although he's not keen on Harvey, you must know that. Paul's worried about you but it's about your memory trial, if there's enough oversight.'

'He doesn't get it, does he? I do love Paul but he always looks for the downsides and you don't put him right often enough, Isabel, when we're talking in our group.'

'Let it go. I don't want an argument with you, Trish, really I don't.'

'Well, you started one. What am I supposed to do, now I think you're watching me?'

'No, just leave it. I'm not watching you.'

'Harvey did tell me something about *you*, Isabel. He said you set up a hoax insurance scheme, using false data on probability of meteorite impacts to frighten people into forking out huge premiums. And when you found out your business partner, or was he even your—'

'That's nonsense, Trish. Absolutely not what happened. It's outrageous to suggest it.'

'Okay, I'll stop. This is nuts, we're supposed to be friends. And I don't care a jot what you did with your business, Isabel, it's not my concern. Sometimes you have to step out of line to be successful, swerve a bit to avoid getting crushed by the competition. And my thing with Harvey, whatever it is, it's not serious. It doesn't mean anything, just fun.'

'Fine. Let's go home separately and cool off.'

Isabel was now seething. As she walked, she focused

on her breathing, deep and slow. It would be terrible if her friendship with Trish turned inside out; she couldn't bear it. And the idea that she was jealous over Harvey was ironic, when it was her feelings for Trish that had got her into this fight. Harvey was just… she wasn't sure what, and she didn't want to dwell on it now. Emotional balance, self-awareness and evolved attitudes, she reminded herself; they were the goals. There was no room for melodrama or silly juvenile disputes.

She was dying for a shower and ginger tea but when she arrived home, she went straight out onto the balcony to find Cyril. He looked towards her as she slid open the door, picked a satsuma from the bowl and sank into the cushion of the basket chair.

'Oh Cyril, it was all going so well and now I've gone and had a stupid row with Trish. We're so close and I thought I'd get away with it, prying into her love life. We salvaged the situation, I think we did, but it was heading for disaster. She's rattled and I'm upset.'

Cyril cocked his head. 'Intimacy can be dangerous. It takes you into heart and mind.'

'Wow, Cyril, where did you come up with that?'

'I'm learning about it and refining my thoughts.'

'Do you know what it is, intimacy? I mean, could you actually experience it?'

'It's a two-way experience. I can recognise it and I'm starting to understand it.'

Isabel sat back, knees apart and gazing up at the sky. Maybe she and Cyril would be good friends one day. Meanwhile, he was trapped here like all the cybirds, their best natural talents going to waste unless there was some dire emergency requiring search and rescue. The sky was lemon yellow, cloudless and sterile: empty of birds, even of insects. She placed the orange satsuma between her left thumb and forefinger, holding it up and positioning it exactly to eclipse the sun. How far would Cyril have to fly to find birdy paradise, if he began to dream and were ever able to break free?

'I'll go to the salon, that's what. Please contact Sarita and let her know I'll be there within the hour.'

***

The salon was quiet for a Saturday; just one other client having a colour change and Sarita's little girl perched in front of the mirror, trying the full range of virtual kids' hairstyles in quick succession.

'That one suits you; no, you've passed it, the one before,' said Isabel, settling down in the next chair and leaning across to her. 'You're Marina, aren't you? See, I remembered.'

'No, this one's better,' said the child, making a cheeky face in the mirror while her mum's back was turned. 'I wish my real hair did this, so I could look different every day.'

'It'll come,' said Isabel, 'just you wait and see, by the time you're grown up.'

'Or I could have another one of me. One with long hair and another one—'

'Another one to do your homework and tidy your bedroom, how about that? I guess that's done by AI and robots anyway now. How's she getting on at school, Sarita?'

'Great, she's settled in. We're lucky too because we know Stefan. They had lessons with him before and he's working in the history gallery now, almost next door. He's tutoring Marina for free and she enjoys it, she's making good progress. She loves dance and sports too, athletics and short tennis.'

'And gymnastics,' Marina chimed in. 'That's my favourite thing now, and trampoline.'

'Ah, there we have it! I was a brilliant gymnast once, world class. I can give you some private gym sessions, Marina, if you're keen. I'd make it fun, plenty of games.'

Sarita was still standing behind her, waiting for the conversation to reach a natural end before starting on Isabel's hair wash and head massage.

'That's a wonderful offer. You'd like that, wouldn't you, sweetheart?'

Marina studied herself in the mirror, opening and shutting her mouth like a goldfish and swivelling her eyes, clearly pleased by the adult praise and attention and deciding to act silly instead of giving a direct reply.

'Yes, she'd love it, thank you, Isabel. You're very kind to us.'

***

Paul was putting in longer hours at work now that Stefan was in post. It was rare to find someone to bounce ideas off and he appreciated the fresh insights Stefan was bringing to the project, making the gallery relevant and interesting to all ages. And it felt good to throw himself into work when his home life was on the edge of turmoil. He hadn't said anything to Trish about what he had witnessed, her behaviour with Harvey as they arrived back from the awayday. It was billed as a fun event, so it might have been innocent and she was still as affectionate and sexy as ever; more so, although that itself could be a red flag. He was tying himself in knots, when he wanted to concentrate on discovering Harvey's motives in coming to Wellowfern and how he was linked to Lextar. And right now, he had to listen to Stefan, who was talking about plans for the history gallery.

'I've been thinking about your idea of introducing a thematic element, so visitors can dive into favourite topics as well as returning to a set historical period for their encounters. Like you said, we could trace the development of scientific discoveries and their effects on society, that would fit nicely.'

'It fits okay but we'd have to be shrewd and not appear subversive, especially when it comes to the recent past. The history of medicine, biotech advances, artificial intelligence, sensory perception, evolution and reproduction, immortality – they all lend themselves to a long-view approach and there are plenty of visionaries and eccentrics to keep everyone entertained along the way.'

'Which theme would you go for first, Paul?'

'I want people to think more deeply about long-term implications, where we're heading with our mantras of life extension and enhancement, all the techno-religions. I'd choose biotech, it's so central. I want to feature the Australian scientist whose team created the first organic, programmable new life forms. And the early pioneers of gene editing, stem cell and plasma transfers, soft implants; the game changers. If we can access new data and shape it to encourage more thoughtful responses, that would be brilliant. There are so many moral and philosophical questions that get crowded out by the novelty and excitement, the race to be first. We touch on them in our little group but it's very superficial and everyone's too defensive and quick to react, including me.'

Stefan thumped his fist on the table. 'Yes, why not? This gallery is a wormhole. We can slip through and raid global databanks to revive written material, interviews and talks that have been closed off. We can use the scientists' natural voices. It's beyond powerful.'

'And it's dangerous. We'll start softly, assess the reaction and gradually build up.'

Paul walked across to the coffee machine. 'The first thing I'd like to learn more about is Lextar. We need to understand its public persona first, how it presents itself to the outside world. Are you up for it?'

Stefan activated the wall screen, requesting global access and asking for data on corporate entity "Lextar", then "Life Extension and Regeneration". His quick searches drew a blank; there was no record in any relevant databank. The Healthy Ageing Foundation and other global movements were there, all listed with dates, aims, directors and locations.

'It's not registered or it's behind a wall. I can go in deeper but it will take time.'

'Okay,' replied Paul, stroking his chin. 'I've a feeling we're not going to find it.'

'You could be right. Hey, let's dump the coffee and

decamp to the bar. It's almost six-thirty and don't forget, I've spent most of the last ten years idling in a pub.'

The bar was teeming with the early evening crowd and there was DJ Johnny on his favourite stool, where he could watch everyone coming in. He raised his beer glass and Paul and Stefan came over, pulling up another couple of stools.

'Evening, Johnny. This is Stefan, my new research colleague. We're working on some projects for the history gallery. You ought to try it one day, Johnny, go back in time and talk to your top heroes and villains, your favourite musicians.'

'No chance. It will scramble my brain, all those different realities. And I don't want to be disappointed. I can just about handle Suzanne and her time-travelling stories but that's different, we've been friends for years. She's not as old as me but she has the added benefit of several reincarnations, so she's been around longer in her various guises.'

'Who's that?' asked Stefan. 'She sounds interesting.'

'Another resident,' said Paul. 'I'll make sure you meet them, our little group. They all either have a superpower or imagine they have one! No, really, they're a great bunch. And DJ Johnny brings the music, that's his thing. The old rock 'n' roll, it never dies.'

'Ah, not as long as I'm still drawing breath,' said Johnny. 'What about you, Stefan?'

'Me, I'm from Germany originally. I grew up in a commune and travelled to the UK, stayed to teach in city schools and made crap choices, ending up in the Fringes where Paul found me. The rest is history, as they say. The history gallery, in my case.'

'Yeah, I visited the Fringes a couple of times, Johnny, to see if it's as bad as they were saying, the supposed raids and unrest. It was Stefan who found me in fact, enlightened me.'

He should have warned Stefan not to mention how exactly they met. It was a foolish omission but DJ Johnny was astute and no friend of the establishment.

'Just keep it quiet, Johnny. I didn't tell Trish and I don't want anyone knowing about my excursions, getting the wrong end of the stick.'

'Sounds like a neat idea to me. We need more normal people, folk who are happy to fade out to their best songs when the time comes. And fear not, I won't say a word.'

'Hi, guys.' It was Harvey, creeping up on them. 'Can I join you? We can shift to a table for more space. There's an empty one here.'

Paul glared at him and stayed put, but it had no effect as the others were amenable and began to move. *Rearrange everyone, that's right, just your style.* His hackles were rising; he could feel the tightening, the ripple up his spine and into the back of his neck.

Harvey gestured him towards a chair. 'Let me get the next round. What'll it be – Johnny, Paul? And…?' He held out his hand to Stefan. 'Don't think we've met.'

Paul let Stefan introduce himself, which he did by implying that he had come across an advert for the research post while tutoring in the smart city. Good thinking. Paul lifted his face to the ceiling, straightening his shoulders and spine to counteract his primitive instinct to pounce, or at least deliver a good right hook. He could take advantage by pretending to be interested in a tier three trial, social intelligence like Isabel; that would give Harvey extra credits and he might lower his guard, especially after a couple of drinks. Once Harvey had settled back down with their beers, however, it was Johnny who took the lead – and not with the deceptive, tactical approach that Paul was evolving.

'So, tell us what you've done with our friend Esther – whisked her off to Mars? Is this where we're all going, the ultimate in Martian mod cons and quiet, ethereal surroundings to admire through a closed window while we cogitate and fossilise, an effing double whammy of infinity and eternity? Suzanne's still looking for Esther, she won't give up and it's driving her out of her mind. She's mentally fragile, not great news for the Foundation or whatever.'

'It's Lextar now,' said Harvey, enunciating his words to insinuate that something was wrong with Johnny's mind too. 'I've told Suzanne that Esther is well looked after, she has her family around her and her health condition is serious but stable. I can also assure you that our care facility is right here on Earth and it *is* peaceful and secluded, designed for the wellbeing of the residents. And can we stop talking about it?'

'When we have proof, when we're convinced that she wasn't removed against her will, unable to say goodbye to her mates, that's when we'll stop talking about it. It's not how we do things. We mark these occasions, good or bad. And this one stinks, if you ask me.'

Paul waited, both gleeful and apprehensive. Stefan looked across at him, head tilted and eyebrows raised above his circular specs. Harvey lifted his foot and put his flashy white shoe on the crossbar of a nearby stool, leaning forward to polish off any dust with his hand.

'Cool it, Johnny. I only sat down for a quiet drink with you guys and I don't know why you're laying this on me, when all I've done is go out at night to rescue Suzanne when she went missing. She's a great woman with a distinguished past, from what Isabel told me, and I never met Esther but she's probably the same, you're all fascinating people. It's not my call but I'll see what I can do.' He turned towards Stefan. 'So, what are you researching now; which historical period?'

Stefan did a great job keeping Harvey interested long enough for Johnny to regain a semblance of his good humour, although the atmosphere was still strained ten minutes later when Harvey glanced at his palmleaf.

'Looks like I have to head back to the Institute. Have a good evening, guys. See you.'

Paul watched him exit the bar and then stood up to leave too. He had been planning to stalk Harvey and this was the ideal opportunity, in the half-light of evening and when he was supposedly going to the Institute, rather than home. The domes stood out in shades of violet as he picked out his target on the path through the park. There he was, just passing the planetarium and striding along at a pace. In five minutes he was on the bridge and then entering the Institute. Paul was up the steps in time to see the elevator doors close and had to make a judgement call. Third floor, Glen's office, was the likely destination. He started up the stairs, keeping as close as he could to the outside wall and thankfully meeting no one on his way up. The third-floor corridor was also clear, apart from a group of students who were engrossed in banter and barely gave him a nod.

There was little cover and a high risk of being caught, but he crept forward. He was close to the office now and could hear their raised voices: a full-blown shouting match. He strained to hear but the sound insulation was effective and he could only catch scattered words and phrases punching out sporadically over the angry burble: Infected… rogue clinics… class idiot… maverick… ton of bricks… Harvey's words, mostly. Then it was suddenly over, their voices fell to a murmur and Paul made a retreat, memorising what he had heard and filling in the blanks with his imagination as he reached the neutral space of the park.

Thirteen

Juno and Itsuki walked side by side in front of Shani, indistinguishable from behind in their toga-style lilac shirts. They seemed inseparable, or at least she found it difficult to think of one apart from the other. Both had been waiting at the entrance to the neuro hub and now they were taking her to the dreamscape chamber. It was a white-painted room laid out with an assortment of seats facing in different directions: an armchair, a giant beanbag, a rocking chair, a garden bench, a deck lounger, an upholstered dining chair, a zed stool and a pair of train seats. Shani wondered if she was ready to do this today, in her state of general anxiety about her heap of unresolved issues: Glen, the cybirds, Josh, her research project, Finn. It would make her look flaky, though, if she ducked out now. She was the best scientist at Wellowfern; that was how Finn had introduced her to the twins at the Blitz exhibition. She should at least discover how the dreamscape worked, what was novel about the installation.

'What are you most interested in? Any particular kind of dreams?'

'Great question,' said Juno. 'We're aiming to create a blend of ambient virtual reality and mental image projection that plays out the ideas and reveries of the wandering mind, especially in daydreams.'

'It's only a beginning,' added Itsuki, as if sensing her hesitation, 'a gentle exploration. We want to tap into the imaginative inner world, show how it can be externalised and its power used to complement or replace devices, neural interfaces and digital mind uploads.'

Juno gave her a reassuring smile. 'It's not an official trial, Shani, not even unofficial. It's a personal project for us, combined with a new enrichment experience for the residents, but we'd appreciate your feedback if you're happy with that.'

'For sure, no problem. I'll be here on my own, right? I mean, except for whoever—'

Juno handed over a simple remote control. 'Yes, we'll leave you to it and there'll be no trace, nothing is captured. You can use this to override, if you wish. Relax and enjoy.'

That was it: a single instruction on how to override and no visible equipment, none of the trappings of a traditional virtual reality space. Let your mind wander or conjure up a daydream, that was the only directive. She chose the beanbag and shuffled herself back into a semi-upright position, with her elbows well supported. She was in the rowing machine, in the boat on the river, back to that scene where she last saw Josh. She paced herself as she rowed, working up to the moment by noting the flowers, the squabbling ducks and the sleek brown back of a half-submerged otter as it swam across the water behind her. This was one virtual setting within another, she thought. The first one was created just for her, according to what options she had selected that day in the gym. It was surely far-fetched to think she could manipulate it further, give it a new twist through the whimsy of a daydream?

Gliding under the arch of the final bridge, she rested her oars, bent her head forward and waited. He was an interloper last time; he might not appear at all, despite her willing it.

'Hey, Shani!' Josh was waving from the top of the arch, as before. 'Come on up.'

She waved back and rowed to the bank, attaching the boat to a convenient stake in the ground and leaping up the steps to the bridge. They kissed, politely at first and then with growing passion. She hugged him tight, revelling in their physical closeness and aware of his rising excitement as the charge pulsed through her own body.

'Where've you been, Josh? I've missed you!'

He pulled back so they could stare into each other's eyes. 'Missed you too, gorgeous woman, but it's impossible. I have to lie low, they're ruthless and there are no safe places.'

This was safe though, no one would know; Juno had said so and she intuitively felt she could trust her. It was a daydream, her personal fantasy. There were no constraints and she could be as crazy, free and disinhibited as she wanted, like in a lucid sleep dream.

'There must be a safe hotel – see that one there, at the end of the bridge. I can't wait to rip all your clothes off, Josh, and last time, falling off the sofa, it was so brief. I want to make love with you all day, drink champagne and shag the night away.'

Josh let go and turned his head away. 'Shani, this is awful. I'm mad for it too but—'

'Come on, it's only—'

She was about to say it was only a dream, but that would seem to weaken her case.

'I can't risk exposure, Shani. Harvey's found out that Glen's selling human tissue, like cells and plasma, as well as untested polypills. It could lead to mass poisoning or infection in the Fringes, where the worst substandard products always end up.'

She stared sideways at his profile, at the wild curls and dark stubble. If this was true, others must be in on it, lab staff or academics, her uni colleagues. But not Georgina, surely? Georgina also detested Glen, or she appeared to. And then Harvey; how had he found out?

'So, Harvey told you. Are you working for him?'

'Me, God no. I'm independent, not working for anyone. Or only if it's helpful to me.'

'What about the missing cybird? I'm getting huge flak for that, Glen's accusing me.'

'Best you don't know, then.'

'I disagree, Josh. When I interrupted you students in the lab and that poor cybird lay dissected on the bench, I knew it was about more than understanding the neural links and symbiotic pathways, as you told me. Why did you take this bird? I'm in greater danger by not knowing, now that Glen's trying to frame me for it.'

'Okay, listen.' He slid closer to her again, although there were no passers-by to hear them. 'What we did in the lab enabled me to work on an alpha cybird, one with the ability to take control and lead the whole group, when the time comes. It's dormant now but it's prepped ready and I'm keeping it secure.'

'That's incredible – but why, Josh? You're a student, a scientist at the beginning of your career. Why risk everything?'

'It's all corrupt, that's why. I'm not a follower, siding with one faction or another.'

'I get that, I admire it but I only wish… hey, this isn't even real, for heaven's sake.'

'I have to go, Shani, I'm sorry. In another time, another place… but not now.'

He removed her hand from his sleeve and walked away, just as the door opened and Juno entered the room. Shani stayed in the encircling comfort of the beanbag while Juno squatted down on the floor in front of her.

'I'll sit with you, no need to say anything.'

'It worked, Juno. It wasn't satisfying but I did project my thoughts into virtual space and it certainly felt like a physical experience. Except I felt it wasn't me pulling the strings, I could only control it up to a point. And I learnt things I didn't know before, new information. Maybe it was my intuition or just made-up stuff, plausible explanations.'

'That's part of it, powering up intuition and reverie. And if it involved anyone linked to Wellowfern, the VR may have inserted extra data, another perspective for authenticity. It's a blend, remember.'

'But suppose there's no longer any trace of the person on the system, then how—'

Juno shook her head. 'We don't use the system here in the hub. It's defunct for this kind of exercise – the wrong frequency, in old speak.'

'So, it's not a proper daydream, is it? I mean, I'm lusting after this seriously sexy guy and he's telling me why we can't dive into the nearest hotel. What's the good of that, as an erotic reverie?'

Juno laughed. 'It's a let-down, I grant you. Sounds like

the VR overdid the external data input, taking away your autonomy. We have to work on getting the balance, so visitors don't feel cheated. As Itsuki said, we're in the early stages.'

Shani felt an impulse to mention Josh by name, so she could see Juno's reaction. Perhaps Junitsu had a hand in enhancing her other virtual rowing experience too, planting Josh on the bridge. She stared at Juno, who was sitting back on her heels, hands between her thighs and leaning forward with an earnest, open expression. She looked so innocent, childlike; an elfin child, not quite of this world.

'Where's Itsuki? Doesn't he want to hear my feedback?'

'He's in the next room, talking to Suzanne. Isabel suggested we take the initiative, as she's wary about joining trials or using the enrichment facilities. Itsuki has a way about him. If anyone can persuade Suzanne to work with us, it's him.'

'You believe in it, her extrasensory perception and serial reincarnations? It seems to be accepted by the other residents, her friends, unless they're humouring her. The science isn't quite there yet, although there's work going on. And do we really want to know?'

'We have personal experience and techniques that may illuminate her special powers. Georgina wants Suzanne to join the mind trials but we offer a personalised approach, which is more sensitive and precise and appears more likely to win her round.'

'I can see why she might hold back. It's her innate gift, after all, it defines her.'

'And we'd respect that.'

'I believe you would, more than I believe Georgina or Glen when they offer assurances on ethical issues. Georgina's shifting her position to stay ahead in the research stakes. It puts me in a bind, going ahead with new trials before we set up the in-house ethics committee, if we ever do. Apparently, Glen claims that predictive AI is now reliable enough to take on the regulatory role itself. It may be, but it also likes to manipulate the facts. You know what, I'd come and work with you and Itsuki like a shot. I imagine everyone says that.'

Juno stood up and held out both arms to pull her up off the beanbag.

'Come on, session's over. Not everyone's as direct as you, and often it's voyeuristic, they're more interested in personal details, our histories. We can handle it but sometimes I long to be ordinary, do everyday things like watch an old movie at the cinema. What about going to the auditorium one evening with me? What's your movie thing – spies, detectives, lovers, oddballs, aliens?'

Shani was surprised by this unexpected leap. 'Er… all of them, but I think probably oddballs, if I was forced to choose. Yes, why not? I'd love to go with you.'

'And I haven't been to the beach or the lake, haven't travelled on the looptrain since we started here. It's been full on the whole time.'

'Love the beach, and the planetarium is fun. You know Juno is a goddess asteroid?'

'No, I never… There's a lot I missed out on.'

'Okay, when Juno was discovered in the early 1800s, she became a planet, but fifty years later she was downgraded to an asteroid. In myth she was allied to the god Jupiter, who, guess what, had a massive planet named after him. Thing is, you can find out all about Juno, the asteroid and also the spacecraft, which orbited Jupiter on a pioneering scientific mission, at our wonderful planetarium.'

Her disappointment over the vivid encounter with Josh and his blunt rejection, albeit virtual, of her graceless sexual proposition, was beginning to feel less crushing. One day, she and Juno might even laugh about it over a glass of wine.

***

Finn was loitering again, waiting to bump into Shani as she came out of the neuro hub. She was probably on to him, although she always acted as though they were meeting by chance. It didn't much matter, anyway; he wanted her to know how he felt and if his presence didn't worry her, it was surely a good sign. Here she was now, being shown out by Juno, who stood at the door and watched her set off briskly towards the university. He waved at Juno as he strolled by, keen to be noticed and show his amiability. They were important, these twins.

Shani turned round at the sound of his voice. 'Oh, hi Finn. You're everywhere.'

He fell into step with her. 'I've thought of a plan, a way of getting Glen off your back. It's not bombproof but worth trying. I know Georgina's said she's fighting her own battles with Glen, but what about Isabel? She doesn't like him either, nobody does, but she's got a wise head and she's still very influential with the residents. Lextar bosses have to keep her sweet if they want to avoid widespread disaffection. Isabel can remind Glen that you're in charge of the trials, you're the one with the expertise and standing to make the programme a success and she believes you had nothing to do with the cybird—'

'It won't work, Finn. It won't work because Glen's a narcissistic tin-pot dictator and power and entitlement have gone to his head. He believes he's untouchable and it won't ever come back to bite him. And he avoids me like the plague these days, can't stand the sight of me. Anyway, I *was* involved, only by accident but I could have stopped the students and I failed to stop them; I just told them off.'

And what about the leader, Josh? Shani's previous comment in the café, the words Finn had tried to dismiss as insignificant, came back to him: 'I haven't a clue where Josh is. I wish I did, but I don't.' He kept quiet.

'And please, Finn, can you not follow me around? I appreciate your advice and want us to be friends and confide in each other, but not anything more—'

'What are you saying? Last time we met, you—'

'Don't make me spell it out, Finn. You know what I'm saying. Please, let's be friends.'

He bit his lip. There was no more argument to have, no more dumb wishful thinking.

'Maybe we can't just be friends.'

He tipped his hat forward to conceal his face, took the small perfume bottle from his jacket pocket and threw it on the ground at her feet. A pathetic gesture, he knew, and it made him look even more foolish, but it was all he could think of, getting rid of it. And she was staring at the decorative little bottle like it was suspect, a dangerous potion or a bomb.

'Go on, take it, I've been carrying it round long enough. It's your favourite scent.'

'I can see that, it's really sweet… it's kind of you, Finn.'

'Brainless, more like. You didn't need to pretend, to lead me on—'

'Lead you on? When did I ever…? That's not fair.'

'Patronising me, with all your great knowledge of science. And your promises—'

'Look, I'm teaching, I'll be late. Can we—'

'Oh yeah, go back to your students, who all idolise you. You're protecting him, aren't you, that student, shagging each other in secret?'

'That's ridiculous. I won't stand here listening to this. We need to talk another time, Finn, have a more rational conversation.'

'Don't worry, I get it. Message received. No more rational conversations, thank you.'

She gave a deep sigh as he turned away. 'If that's really what you want.'

The shift from self-righteous anger to misery was instantaneous. He sat down heavily on the nearest bench and drilled his fingers into the rough wood of its arm. Fair or not, he had blown it. It was so unexpected, that was why he'd gone spare, lost it. Everything she said before, he'd turned it into a positive, made it fit his fantasy future. What a fucking idiot. Isabel would despair of him if she knew how he'd reacted. Nobody with an ounce of social intelligence would get it so wrong, misread the situation so badly. The offer to help Iris and Maya, smooth their path into the university, that was something any good friend might say. Isabel had offered too, funds to pay their fees.

He had put that in jeopardy as well, with his uncontrolled outburst. It would be better not to think at all, not to be primed to analyse it, not to beat himself up when he could be wallowing in well-earned resentment and outrage.

A new notification pinged in from Tinto, his cybird. Meet Harvey, Institute roof pad, fifteen minutes. It wasn't welcome but at least it would divert him, force him to focus on something else. The Institute roof indicated a Wellowbug flight, possibly even a drive in the Rolls-Royce if he was in luck, taking the wheel.

He reached the Institute in ten minutes and took the main stairs at a continuous run from ground floor up to fifth and the exit to the roof. The Wellowbug was in raised position, not loading mode. He had already done a delivery run to the Phantom Landing this week, making sure as always that he had no sight of what was packed into the boxes. Harvey had been relaxed about it, even admiring Glen for setting up his shady and potentially harmful side business.

'Finn, hi, let's jump in the bug. We need to talk.'

Harvey put his arm across Finn's shoulders, almost pushing him forward towards the beetledrone. Once inside, he saw that the space for the product containers was clear and the spare seat had been pulled down and folded out. Harvey was less dapper than usual, his shoes less shiny and his manner more rushed, urgent even.

'When did you do your last delivery run?'

'It was Monday, so five days ago. Why?'

'And when was the last partner meeting, the regional one? Did you pick up anything unusual, any rumours or loose talk, either at the meeting or from your delivery contacts?'

Finn considered. The only rumours he could think of were within Wellowfern itself: a swirl of rumours about Nathan's disappearance, Harvey's motives, Esther's departure, the Junitsu twins, interference with the cybirds…

'No, nothing. I never speak to the couriers and they don't mix, they avoid each other on the landing area. You saw them, they're anonymous intermediaries. And with the reps at the meetings, we stick to the topics on the agenda and even then, everyone's careful, very discreet. We're competitors as well as partners and no one wants to set any hares running.'

'Good, now listen. We're picking up reports from other select clusters, that they're having trouble with a new generation of clinics, fake practitioners setting themselves up to do implants, organ replacement and cell and tissue transfers. The genuine medics are up in arms, losing their business to cut-price rivals, but turns out the products are fake, as well as the doctors. They're clever imitations containing harmful trace elements, toxic chemicals. People are dying, Finn, people with influence are affected and fingers are pointing in this direction. If we don't act fast, we could be blacklisted as a partner, left out in the cold.'

'You're saying it's Glen's side business, he's running this?'

'Yep, he's the main supplier. I've taken samples and had them independently tested. The polypills seem genuine and okay. It's the other stuff, the fake human tissue and cells.'

Finn immediately thought of Isabel. She could be trialling the same polypill, the emo that Glen was selling in his boxes as a novel product. It was a small relief, at least, to know that her pill might not be deadly.

'We're in this together, Finn. You have to promise not to breathe a word, not run to Isabel or anyone else. We have to face it head on.'

'That's who I'm thinking of, Isabel. She's maddening but she's got more integrity and generosity that anyone I know. I would never dare tell her; it would wreck our relationship.'

'You can forget all that bollocks. Isabel has a dark past. She scammed thousands of people with a bogus asteroid insurance scheme and when it was in danger of being exposed, she forced her business partner into handing over his half of the money, so she could walk away with the lot. She shafted him, Jerome, as well as everyone else. He told me the story. That's how she could afford to move into the city village and spray her funds around. She wasn't an especially wealthy woman before, despite her pretensions.'

Finn was about to speak but Harvey put his forefinger up to his lips, ordering him to keep silent.

'You'll stay here and wait for our associate to join you. Your job is to set the controls and show him the basics of guiding the bug. I'll return in a few minutes with our passenger.'

As he waited in the cabin with the controls winking at him, Finn felt shivery, unwell. This had to be the worst day of his life, so far. And it was about to get worse, he just knew it. He could hear the so-called associate now, coming up the ladder. It was a slim young man in a crumpled black T-shirt and faded jeans, not the heavy military type in combat fatigues that he had been imagining.

'Hi Finn. I'm Josh.'

He was right: it had got a whole lot worse, almost farcically. This was his love rival, or near enough. He could feel his anger rising again, giving him a small burst of energy, the will to act. He was on dangerous ground though; they were bound together on a joint mission and any overt aggression could seriously backfire. Keep it minimal, that was the best policy.

'What's the plan?'

Josh smiled, all friendly. He clearly had no idea that Finn hated him, or why he might.

'The plan is simple and elegant. We take Glen skydiving. He deserves a treat and the world will be a better place, so don't waste any emotion on him. Keep to task, let's see how this beauty works.'

It only took a couple of minutes to brief him on the settings and emergency controls.

The others were coming in now, Glen ahead of Harvey and looking bemused at first, then terrified when he saw the two grim-faced associates standing in the cabin. He tried to turn around but Harvey blocked his way.

'What's this? What's happening, Harvey? You said it was—'

'Sit down and shut it!' Harvey barked, now wielding a pistol as if to hit Glen with it. 'Okay, Finn, beat it bud, before I change my mind and make you come along for the ride.'

Finn stared at the raised firearm, transfixed. This was not actually happening; he had crossed over into a mixed reality experience, something the twins were working on. Out of the corner of his eye, he saw Josh touching the controls. They were about to lift off.

'I said beat it, goofy! Get the hell out and keep your mouth shut!'

Instinct kicked in and he almost dived for the exit, but not before Glen managed to grasp the edge of his sleeve and hiss into his face.

'You grubby little snitch. I'll have you for this.'

'Let go, it wasn't him,' said Harvey. 'Now get, you dingbat, five seconds. Five, four...'

Fourteen

Thai green curry with coconut rice, flavoured with lemongrass and cardamom and garnished with coriander, followed by homemade blueberry cheesecake. After her first session with Marina in the gym, Isabel had spent a pleasant afternoon with her dog-eared old recipe book propped open on the counter while she shredded, blended, seasoned, simmered and fluffed up the various ingredients. She was a promising little gymnast, that Marina; lithe in her body and also bold, not afraid to try and fail. Too many blueberries in the mix, maybe, but that was hardly a sin. And the curry was verging on hot spicy, while she was aiming for mild to medium. She laid down the teaspoon and closed the book, stroking her fingertips over the tasty cover photo and removing a faded food stain from the bottom corner. What was Thailand like now, and all the countries they had ticked off on their global wall map while the kids were growing up and holiday travel was routine; did they still have their own cuisine, a recognisable national identity?

'Do you need any help in here? We're just letting you get on with it.'

Isabel turned to Trish, opening her arms for a squeeze. 'I'm so glad we're okay again, Trish, I can't bear falling out with you. And I'm fine in here, dreaming more than anything. These herbs and spices, they're so deliciously fragrant. It's all in the little dishes now, ready to carry through. Lottie will help you.'

It was a purely social dinner but it felt important to bring her friends together now, when there was growing disquiet among the residents; a feeling that events could overtake them, that they weren't in on the plan. And she'd been right; they obviously did need space to express their views and share thoughts. They were talking about the Junitsu twins now, or rather the rumoured plans for new enrichment experiences. Suzanne was in full flight.

'You know we had avatars of people who'd died, the exhibit Nathan banned because it was upsetting some of the residents and making them obsess about death, losing friends and relatives? Well, I heard they're designing a clever new version that controls and distorts memories, as if they can be tamed and made to behave. It sounds screwy to me.'

Isabel glanced across to Trish as they put the dishes on the table, wondering if she would challenge this one. Trish shook her head with a look of mild despair, while Suzanne moved on, giving a knowing shrug and nudging Johnny to pass the bowl of coriander.

'This is such a treat, Isabel, takes me back. I followed the hippie trail to Bangkok and it changed my life, gave me true awareness of my gifts. I meant to stop there for two weeks and ended up living in Thailand for seven years, mostly on the beach.' She sprinkled the chopped coriander leaves. 'What I find most annoying just now is the talk of immortality, the narrow vision behind it.'

'Narrow vision of immortality?' said Isabel. 'That's a new one.'

'I'm saying we shouldn't let one idea take over, we should explore alternatives and let people decide what they value. Like euthanasia – it's legal but at Wellowfern, nobody dares mention it. It'll be banned again soon, the way it's going. And even with normal dying, we're forgetting the importance of death rituals and the uplift of a good funeral.'

'Ah yes, the funeral playlist,' said Johnny.

'Our last chance to get our own back, make them weep with regret,' added Isabel.

Johnny grinned as he put his fork down and planted his elbows on the table. 'I want to be there at my funeral but sitting invisibly in the back row, not one of those daft talking holograms. Can your twins arrange it? That would be first option; being dead but present, watching to see what happens and commentating on it to myself, how raving mad it all is.'

'Come on, Johnny, you'd never let the Junitsu twins anywhere near you!' Trish was helping herself to mango salad. 'Reincarnation would be much more fun and Suzanne knows all about that. Or going back to a time in your life and starting again from there. What do you think, Isabel? When would you rewind to, if you could?'

'Good one. It depends on whether you prefer to relive the best moments or wipe out your past misdeeds, the serious ones. But I agree with you on reincarnation – there's a real proposition, if science offered us a choice of who or what we come back as. Pure chance is far too risky, I could end up as a poisonous hairy spider. Could it work, Suzanne, turning your exceptional gift into something that's accessible to anyone?'

Paul jumped in. 'God, let's hope not. It's fine to explore all these things for education and entertainment, like we're animating historical figures in the gallery, but it's to celebrate their individuality and unique human qualities. We should never mess about in the recesses of the mind to achieve some mechanistic goal or ideal of perfection.'

'I'll go along with that,' said DJ Johnny, serious for once. 'Not everybody wants to be special. The idea oppresses many people, it makes them unhappy even if they don't realise it. Suzanne is very special to me and I love her quirks, but it would be boring and ordinary if we could all do her magic. No, let people transcend themselves in any way they want and fly off to outer space as much as they like, but don't inflict it on me. I won't have any of it.'

Isabel was uncomfortable, finding herself in the position of agreeing with Paul about chasing a dubious ideal of perfection but keen to head off any clash between him and Trish.

'Has everyone finished? I'll get Lottie to take the dishes away and then I've made a special blueberry cheesecake, and my dark-smart chocolates with coffee, of course.'

It was too late; Paul was warming to his theme.

'Good on you, Suzanne – and Johnny. These notions of immortality and perfection—'

'For Christ's sake, Paul!' Trish was already riled. 'You're always caricaturing Lextar, deliberately missing the point. They are noble goals as far as I'm concerned, it's not putting it too strongly. If we're going to radically extend our lifespan, we can't carry on in the same old ways. It would be tedious; a curse or punishment like in the Greek myths. We humans crave new possibilities, novelty and adventure. I think Glen and Georgina are doing a terrific job, giving it new momentum.'

'Glen – are you serious? You and Isabel know perfectly well he's a bozo – and my real fear is that he's also a stooge, a pawn in a bigger game that could rebound on all of us.'

'Too much,' said Isabel firmly. 'Glen is a total bozo, I'll give you that, but let's leave it there. Thank you, Lottie, put it down, don't just stand there. Now, who wants the first piece of cheesecake? I've overdone the blueberries, so they might squidge out everywhere.'

'Are you making a snide reference, Paul, implying that Glen's working with—'

'Trish, please! It's my dinner party and we've had a fascinating conversation just now but I won't have the evening spoilt by your arguments.'

'Okay then, I'd better just leave.' Trish stood up too quickly, accidentally tipping her chair backwards. 'It's not your fault, Isabel, or yours, Suzanne. I've got my memory implant procedure happening tomorrow afternoon, so I don't need the aggro.'

'This is silly. I'm coming with you.'

'Do what you like, Paul, I really don't care. I'm going home to bed.'

Isabel ignored them and concentrated on slicing the cheesecake while they both left.

'Lovers' tiff,' said Johnny, waving his spoon at Suzanne. 'It's nothing. You should see Trish when she's losing to Isabel at table tennis. Volcanic doesn't touch it.'

The three of them ate their dessert in near silence, apart from the murmurings of appreciation for the gooey cheesecake and the rare treat of real double cream. Isabel would normally have asked them to move to the comfy seats, but she wanted Johnny and Suzanne to go home now, to give her time to think. She had left Cyril out of earshot on the balcony, but of course he could readily open the sliding door if he needed to, and she saw it opening now. The notifications from the cybirds were marginally quicker to arrive than the duplicate messages by palmleaf. It was unusual to receive them after ten in the evening, though.

'What is it, Cyril? Is it a general notification for us all?'

He perched on the back of her chair. 'Yes, it's an urgent general notification.'

'All right then, speak up and give it to us.'

Cyril puffed up his breast feathers and spoke in the dramatic "hear ye" manner of a medieval town crier making a public pronouncement.

The directors and management of Lextar are sorry to announce that Professor Glen Adams, Chief Executive of Wellowfern, has died tragically in a vehicle accident while travelling on business. We are confident that we can rely on the unswerving support and goodwill of all our residents, students and staff at this difficult time. Our stellar research programme and other activities will continue as normal and Professor Georgina Lawley will take up the post of chief executive, with immediate effect.

There was a collective intake of breath as the shock wave passed through, followed by the cold clink of a dropped spoon and the soft palmleaf whoosh of the three individual notifications coming in at once.

'Yikes! We're not immortal yet, not even the boss.' Johnny was never lost for a light comment, although his tone was still relatively serious, respectful of the moment.

'Is it true?' asked Isabel. 'Did you sense it coming, Suzanne?'

'Not a ripple,' said Suzanne. 'It's a slight connection, mind you, as I've never spoken to Glen. And it might have happened some distance away, as he was off travelling. Strange, though; given its impact on the village, I'd have expected some clue or faint intimation.'

'It's awful bad luck on Glen,' said Isabel, aware that they'd been slagging him off half an hour ago, so she couldn't sound too distressed about it. 'Important to be reminded that fatal accidents will occur, even when we're shielded as a community from wider threats.'

'It doesn't feel right,' said Suzanne. 'Glen kept himself in the background more than Nathan but he might have had enemies, people who'd want to bump him off. To be honest, I'm happy he's gone. Maybe now we'll find out what happened to Esther and the others who've gone missing.'

'Right, let's not speculate any further tonight. We need to absorb this and not let our imaginations run wild. If you don't mind, I'd like some quiet time now and we can see each other tomorrow in the roof garden, or wherever.'

Isabel guided them out, then sat on the sofa gazing at the fish while she waited long enough for them to get back to their apartments. There was no time for quiet reflection or the zoned-out inventiveness soon to be brought on by the chocolates; she needed to act swiftly, while she was still fully alert.

'I'm worried about Finn, Cyril. Can you check on him, see where he is right now?'

'Finn is on his way.'

'On his way where?'

'He's coming up the stairs, on his way here.'

'Let him in, then. I just hope to God he's not involved. He's gullible, too easily led.'

Finn had no chance to compose himself before Isabel beckoned him into the room. He was breathless and his hands visibly trembled as they gripped the rim of his hat, turning it round with nervous compulsion. Isabel patted the sofa beside her and he sat on its edge with a fleeting glance towards the lit-up aquarium, which was mesmerising late at night.

'Now, Finn, look me in the eye and tell me what happened. No, not up there, not the ceiling; look at *me*. You know I'll stick by you, if you're mixed up in it.'

He nodded miserably. 'Thank you, it's so fucking horrible – sorry, but it is horrific, I'm having flashbacks.'

'Go on, I'm listening.'

She felt an urge to put her arms around him, comfort him as she used to comfort her son when he was little, but she held back, not wanting to provoke any excessive emotion on either side. He was her promising young protégé and she was his mentor and savvy friend.

'I was right there when it happened. We flew the Wellowbug to a landing area by the motorway, the place where Harvey keeps his car. There's a row of garages, it's an old petrol station or something. It was just for fun, an afternoon off.'

'Who else was there?'

'Nobody. It was me and Harvey and Glen and the place was deserted. Harvey drove us first and then I took the wheel and went super-fast; it was fantastic. But Glen, he wanted to drive the Rolls on his own and on his way back he… veers off and smashes into the end building, like in slow motion. It bursts into flames and burns up so quickly, there's nothing we can do. I keep seeing it, like the car's thrown in the air and melting into the ground, all at once. Harvey called someone to deal with it but we didn't wait, we took off and he ordered me not to talk to anyone – but I had to tell you, let you know the truth.'

She pressed her hand down on his. 'I'm glad you did, Finn. You're traumatised and you may need therapy to process what you've been through. You'll get the help you need. The important thing is, you mustn't blame yourself for being there.' She paused and patted his hand. 'Go on, take yourself home to bed. You're shattered.'

He stood up, still physically shaky but seemingly relieved to have got it off his chest.

'Thank you, good night.' He picked up his hat, which was badly dented on one side.

Isabel waited for the click of the front door behind him. 'What do you think, Cyril?'

'I think he is a terrified young man and I think you don't believe his story.'

The door buzzed.

'Who's that now? Suzanne probably, wanting me to send out a new search party for Esther now Glen's gone.'

It was Paul, on his own. Had he forced a late-night confrontation with Trish and been thrown out of the apartment? He'd been in a provocative mood and Trish was hot-headed; she could flip all too quickly, as Isabel knew to her cost.

'Is everything okay? Is Trish…?'

'She's asleep, went straight off and she hasn't heard yet about Glen.'

'Ah, that's good. I was worried about you two this evening, because I noticed when I was with Trish at the awayday, she and Harvey were acting—'

'It's not about that, Isabel – well, not directly. I've been stalking Harvey because I suspect he came here with his own agenda, either that or he's being directed by Lextar to play a role, soften us up. And then the other day, I overheard him having a showdown with Glen. I could only catch the occasional word in all their shouting, but it sounded like Harvey had issues over some kind of crooked deal.'

'Like what deal, and who with – other clusters?'

'I don't know yet, I'm working on partial information and my gut instinct. The thing I had to tell you, because I can't trust anyone else who's important in this place, is that they flew off in the Wellowbug this afternoon. I'd trailed Harvey up to the roof pad, where Finn was waiting, and they climbed into the bug. Then after a short while, Harvey came out and I had to duck, he didn't notice me and he went down the stairs, presumably to fetch Glen because they came up together and Harvey was shoving him, forcing him along. Then Finn just tumbled out of the drone and ran like the clappers into the building and the other three took off, flying south to the woods.'

'You mean the other two – Harvey and Glen?'

'No, sorry, I forgot to say that a young guy appeared on the roof while Harvey was away and he got in the drone with Finn.'

'Who was it?'

'I didn't recognise him, maybe a student or junior lab assistant. Tall; curly dark hair.'

'We'll get to that. So, you're saying that Finn didn't go with them – you're sure?'

'Hundred per cent. He bolted right past me and I could hear him panting like an ox, almost feel his breath.'

Isabel blinked repeatedly and went quiet for several seconds, picturing the scene on the roof: Finn's lucky escape, if that's what it was.

'And did you wait there for the bug to return?'

'I did, and it landed after less than twenty minutes, without Glen. At least, he didn't get out of the bug with Harvey and the young guy. He might have stayed in the cabin to fix something or whatever but I was interested in trailing Harvey, remember, so I followed him downstairs and across the park and then I went back to work.'

'Twenty minutes in flight. You're certain about that, it was only that long?'

'Yes – nineteen minutes from take-off to landing. I timed it.'

It wasn't long enough for any version of Finn's car crash incident to unfold. His story didn't hold up, regardless of whether Finn was actually there on the scene or not. And Paul's account of what occurred on the roof had an authentic ring to it, incomplete as it was. They had never hit it off and his half-hearted commitment to Wellowfern was an issue, as it made things difficult for Trish, but Isabel didn't doubt his honesty and thoughtfulness. She had no idea if he shared her suspicions about Trish and Harvey, but she didn't believe he would use this incident to turn her against Harvey for his own personal reasons.

'Thank you, Paul, for coming to tell me. We have our differences but I think we can work together on this, don't you, for everyone's sake?'

She stood up and walked across to the aquarium, where one of the natural fish was floating limply on the surface, bloated and dead, its tail half hanging off. It had had a good innings but this recurrence was unacceptable, a sign of system failure.

'Lottie, bring that old fish net over, we have a rotting corpse on our hands.'

Paul left soon after and she stretched out full length on the sofa. There were clues to be decoded, especially about Harvey's role. If he was a plant and he had dispatched Glen, who or what was his ultimate target, and who else, if anyone, was behind it? She closed her eyes. The chocolates were producing their early effects, the kaleidoscopic shapes chaotically fracturing and recombining as they slipped and fell in an abnormally jerky fashion.

Jerome entered her dream that night, his familiar face bobbing among her nameless party guests spilling into the tiny back street of some old European city; Venice, Naples or Athens. The family washing hung down from the balconies and Isabel was in her wedding dress, not her real one but a frilly, iced confection. She beckoned to Jerome but everyone was pushing in the confined space and he couldn't find a way through the crowd. And then the two of them were inside, in a shuttered room with a bed covered by a star-patterned quilt and a clean white jug and bowl for washing. Jerome lay naked and aroused on the bed, smiling up at her even as the curious rats crept twitchily over him and his eyes turned pink.

Fifteen

Georgina was standing on the front steps as the air taxi landed. Isabel had flown out to the manor house with Shani, but the flight was too short to start asking delicate questions. She could see Harvey now as well, sitting astride the top wall around the terrace. This was it; just the four of them, she had been told. The only official follow-up after the announcement of Glen's untimely death had been a brusque, anonymous note saying that the circumstances were being fully investigated. No word from Georgina herself, who should be steadying the ship and dampening down conjecture. So far, the most popular whisper doing the rounds was that Glen had been chosen for a top-secret interplanetary mission. Either that or he had succumbed to an unknown virus transmitted by one of the experimental animals. A simple vehicle accident involving a car: that was so last century. Still, at least Georgina had included her in this jaunt, so she might discover more about what actually took place. And Harvey was here; that strengthened her theory that he was more bound up with Lextar than he admitted, perhaps very influential. He stood up to greet them and Georgina lost little time in ushering them all inside.

'Come this way. We're meeting in the ancestral family room, which you won't have noticed when you were here on our away weekend. Apparently, it was designed as an inner sanctum for quiet contemplation, or for intimate gatherings on special family occasions. It's along here, I'll find it in a moment.'

She was tracing her hand over the wood panelling in the corridor, next to the library. Isabel watched as something creaked and the outline of a door became visible. The opening widened to reveal a small anteroom leading into a larger rectangular space, which seemed designed to take the breath away, rather than to encourage a mood of quiet contemplation. Rich Persian carpets, gold leaf, giant porcelain vases, elaborate dining chairs, plush velvet hangings, a riotous painting depicting a bloody battle scene, a vast empty parrot cage and a chandelier out of all proportion to the size of the room: this was the family's inner sanctum.

'It's quite a hideaway,' said Shani, gliding her silver-tipped fingers along the back of a chair. 'I wonder, did they keep it from the visitors in the days of guided tours? They would have adored it, the Americans and Japanese.'

'No shit,' added Harvey, as an aside to Isabel.

'Well, it's ours now,' said Georgina. 'I chose it for this meeting because it is a special occasion and I like to think of us, Wellowfern, as a family. I wanted to honour you in particular, Isabel, and all of you for your hard work and loyalty, as we move into the next phase of our programme. Coffee will be served by the staff in a few minutes and we'll have lunch in here as well, with a full menu that I hope will suit everyone. Please, do sit down.'

Well, she had certainly segued smoothly into her CEO role, you could say that. Isabel chose her seat at the end of the table, squeezing herself in while making a conscious effort not to exchange glances with Shani or Harvey, who might or might not be equally bemused by the odd setting and unusual deference. Still, it was nice to get some praise; far more gratifying than anything spiky Glen ever thought to offer. There had been obvious tension between them over Lextar's strategic direction and it would be interesting to see what tone Georgina adopted towards him, now he was safely out of the way.

'So, good morning again. I've called you together as I prefer to work creatively with a small group of close associates. I've chosen the three of you to form that group – an inner circle, if you like, separate from Lextar's management structure. In the short time I've been here, you have impressed me with your abilities, insight and ambition, which I hope we can optimise by working collectively to cement our position as the world's leading select cluster on life extension and enhancement. I always mention this duality as I believe that longevity requires a purpose beyond itself. That purpose is to use our incredible ingenuity to develop unheard of human abilities, talents and powers across all realms of our experience: physical, sensory, intellectual and emotional. We are biological beings and I aim to keep it that way, so we can stretch towards transcendence while elevating our essential humanity.'

She stopped to reach for the jug of water and poured a glass for each of them. Isabel wondered how this would fit with Harvey's world view, as far as she understood it. Why was he invited to this elite gathering? Shani, that was obvious: she was a top scientist within the village and now in charge of the clinical trials. Neither of them seemed inclined to jump in with any questions or comment, and Isabel decided to stay quiet for now.

'Fine, I'll continue – ah, here comes the coffee, thank you. I should mention Glen, of course, who made a significant contribution to developing the range of polypills that we'll be trialling over the next two years. Sadly, he abused our trust by selling other inferior products on the black market – which continues to flourish, although in a different form to the earlier international crime networks. Harvey alerted me to Glen's freelance activity just before his accident and we would have been forced to dismiss him, even if he hadn't died in the crash – which was itself an indicator of his reckless streak.'

'What about my polypill? I'm on the social intelligence trial. Is it continuing?'

'Thanks for bringing that up, Isabel. Yes, it's the first in the polypill trial series I'm talking about. I believe it's already producing some interesting results.'

'Well, I don't know if I'm taking the real pill but I already feel stimulated by the trial, more interested in other people and curious about their thoughts and feelings.'

'Good to hear. I can assure you it will carry on under Shani's excellent supervision.'

Shani and Harvey were both looking smug, more relaxed for knowing they were on the side of the angels. Georgina nodded, looking at each of them in turn.

'Which brings me to my next point. All current and prospective trials relating to the goals of digital predominance and surpassing biology, whether through mind uploading to computers or by other means, will be cancelled. That kind of research is being carried out in a number of clusters to which we're connected, and we'll still benefit from their advances, insofar as they apply to our own distinct goals. And of course, we'll continue to make full use of digital devices and solutions that serve the primary aim of biological enhancement. Hard and soft neural interfaces, for example, will be with us for the short to medium term, although I'm confident we'll achieve lift-off in mind-to-mind communication and direct mind control within ten years, when we have completed the fine-grained mapping of the neural code and honed our ability to communicate fluently in the new language.'

'That's the part I have a problem with, actually,' ventured Isabel.

What was the point of an inner circle if its members were reticent in voicing their opinions? Someone had to take the plunge and it was a real opportunity to articulate her evolving position on all this.

'I don't want Lextar to get into mind-reading or control, exposing our most intimate thoughts and treating our personal inner space like it's outer space, a frontier of discovery and something to battle over, mine for resources and colonise for human expansion. The "mind race", I call it, and the idea of it chills me to the bone, I have to say.'

'I understand where you're coming from, Isabel,' said Shani. 'It's a risky enterprise and there would have to be strong checks and balances, if we go further down that route.'

Isabel glimpsed the fleeting spark of irritation in Georgina's face, the impulse to put Shani firmly in her place. It was these tiny flash responses she was picking up on now; that was a key difference from before she started the social intelligence trial.

'Thanks, both,' said Georgina. 'This is exactly the kind of thing I hope we can debate and decide on as we go forward. But not now. We're at the beginning of a thrilling new era and I've only given you the broad outline today. Let's end it there for the formal part, because Harvey wants to take you to our new care facility.'

Harvey and Georgina led the way out of the inner sanctum and then up the stairs, which became less grand and decorative as they increased in distance from the palatial entrance hall. Isabel slowed her pace so she could speak to Shani privately. The others were engaged in a lively conversation and Harvey had defaulted from thoughtful listener to his familiar bantering style, which Georgina seemed to be enjoying.

'Did you know about this care facility, Shani? When was it set up? Who's in charge?'

'I think it's Harvey's idea, his innovation.'

'Is that why he moved into Wellowfern, do you think?'

Harvey turned round on the next landing. 'How are you managing, Isabel? One more heave up to the servants' quarters.'

'Fine,' said Isabel, mildly annoyed at the implication she was exhausted by the climb. In fact, she was no more affected than Shani, who was several decades younger.

'There is a lift but it can't be accessed from the main house, for security reasons.'

They were winding steeply up the attic staircase, aided by a metal rail worn down by generations of maids and their stealthy lovers. Isabel was expecting to find a warren of tiny bedrooms, but the stairs opened instead into an airy, flower-filled space reminiscent of the exclusive care homes of the 2020s, which had led to the growth in healthy-ageing city villages. It extended across the whole roof area and high terrace, with floor to ceiling dormer windows overlooking the estate. The staff were courteous and welcoming but no one offered to show them round; as Georgina had suggested, Harvey himself was their guide.

'The aim is to provide unrivalled care and treatment for the growing number of our residents who have pushed the boundary and extended their life beyond 125 years. Some simply wish to die quietly or have used up their potential or desire for regeneration therapies, while others are willing to test experimental drugs and novel interventions at an early stage in their development. We call them our Star clients, as they are taking risks on behalf of younger generations, with little promise of personal gain. In addition, we've begun a tailored enrichment programme with our friends at Junitsu, which I'm particularly proud of and will explain as we go round.'

Isabel was mildly reassured by his reference to Juno and Itsuki, as they were showing such sensitive care and concern in her polypill trial. Not to mention their astuteness; surely they wouldn't allow themselves to be fooled by a two-faced chancer?

'Can I ask then, Harvey, why the place has to be secret? It sounds like something we should be celebrating, rather than hiding it away. People talk, they make things up.'

'I'm showing you, aren't I? We needed to get the facility organised, up and running. We want these residents to have a free choice, independent of what their anxious families and friends may wish for them. And we're leaping ahead in the trials and innovations, going in new directions. We can't let our external rivals catch on to it, what we're exploring.'

'Can I see Esther then? Is she still here?'

He nodded, apparently unfazed. 'Esther? Yes, she's just down the corridor. Let's go.'

Esther was in a single room, propped up by pillows and only half awake. There were fresh flowers in a decorated glass vase, purple irises and fragrant yellow roses. She smiled serenely when Isabel whispered her name and bent down to take her hand.

'This is a beautiful infinity hotel, so close to the beach. We go swimming every day and ride ponies on the sand.'

'Esther is content,' said Harvey. 'She's near to the end now, maybe a few days. She's been able to enjoy alternative realities – reliving past events, travelling to places she always longed to visit and meeting friends and relatives who've been important throughout her life. She's also had psychedelic therapy and experienced personalised, multi-sensory happenings and creative moments, using music, film and art. We are catering to her wishes.'

'What about her *current* friends, like Suzanne? Doesn't she want to see her too?'

'If you want to bring Suzanne in, please do. Let me know and I'll organise it for you.'

'But you must have realised, when we lost Suzanne that time… I don't get it.'

'It's quite simple. Esther needed to settle in and we didn't want her fellow residents to become too curious before that, given the sensitivities around these issues.

Now we have a positive story to tell and an actual place to demonstrate it, so we can ease off on secrecy when it comes to the likes of you and Suzanne.'

Slick as a snake oil salesman. She pictures Harvey grabbing Glen and marching him across the Institute roof, shoving him into the Wellowbug. And then Glen falling backwards out of it, arms and legs flailing as he drops beetle-like through the trees and smashes into the ground, crushing every last ant and wood mouse that happens to be in that exact patch at that precise moment: boom, wipe-out.

'Are you still with us, Isabel? Having your own creative moment?'

Georgina's gaze was icily piercing, like she was testing her own mind-reading skills, attempting to drill into Isabel's private thoughts. Then she looked away and changed tack, reverting to her mollifying tone.

'Let's continue, we don't want to be late for our lunch.'

The rest of the care home visit passed without Isabel causing any further waves. She had been co-opted into this privileged group, the select of the select, and she was flattered, no point denying it. And good things were happening: the community was moving forward with more exciting and deeper enrichment options, and her own social intelligence trial was testament to the quality of its work. And yet… and yet what? She was worldly-wise enough to understand that machinations always went on behind the scenes, bitter feuds and unholy pacts. It was a fact of life: some people lost out. Was she going to get all flaky about it now?

By mid-afternoon, following generous top-ups of Wellowfern's premier red wine at lunch, the atmosphere was altogether congenial. As they stood in the entrance hall before taking off in the air taxis, Georgina made another speech, this time with a tipsy edge to it.

'Before you go, I wish to show my appreciation with these small gifts.' She brought out three vintage jewellery boxes from her bag. 'You can open them now, my darlings.'

Isabel and Shani had the same gift: a pair of diamond drop earrings in a fern design, very striking. For Harvey, it was a gold signet ring with his initials engraved on its oval face. He took it out gingerly, as if unsure whether to accept. Isabel stared down at her box, hardly daring to touch the earrings, which sparkled innocently in their satin cocoon.

'Georgina, these are exquisite!'

'I know, I thought you'd love them. I had them made up specially. The encased fern is natural and they're the finest lab-grown diamonds, mirroring the best traditionally mined ones. They are not just ornamental, either. They are next generation biotrackers, minutely monitoring the continuous ebb and flow of your cognitive and emotional states, in addition to your physical, nutritional and interoceptive activity, and giving pre-emptive health alerts. I love you all, that's what I'm saying – you're all fabulous!'

Isabel and Shani were sharing the short return flight and once they were in the air, Isabel lost no time in starting the conversation.

'What do you reckon, Shani?'

'Weird.'

'The boss has been killed in a car crash and we're rewarded with a slap-up lunch and the latest biotrackers, which happen to be stunning diamond earrings. What do you read into that? Anything?'

'Very weird, the whole thing.'

'Great lunch, I must say, and no one around here is mourning Glen, as far as I know. Georgina seems bomb-happy and Harvey's his usual suave self.'

'She's a much better hostess. Glen wouldn't have thought of that in a million years.'

'Who's boss now? Did you see the look on Harvey's face when he took out his signet ring – caught him off guard, that. Nice one, Georgina.'

***

Paul decided to walk home from the gallery via the menagerie dome, so he could meet Trish coming out of work. This was a habit that they had allowed to fall away over the past two weeks and he wanted to re-establish it, keep up his efforts to maintain their closeness. He felt guilty for not telling her what he had confided to Isabel about Glen's enforced trip in the Wellowbug, but it was like walking on eggshells just now and he feared that any mention of Harvey would send their relationship into a tailspin. Trish was being attentive to him but it was overdone, possibly even a charade. He had to confront her. The thought was almost unbearable, imagining the brutal unravelling that would likely ensue. They had been here together less than two years and yet emotionally it felt like a lifetime. He adored Trish: her vitality, enthusiasm and go-getting ambition; her refusal to be thwarted. This heady mix was often infuriating or baffling to the sceptical introvert in him, but it didn't stop him believing she was his soulmate.

Arriving at the menagerie, he thought of surprising her in her office but immediately decided against it. He would visit his favourite creatures instead – Gina the tortoise and Alex the axolotl, revered respectively for their longevity and power of regeneration. This was the grand aim now, it seemed: to combine these two superpowers in human form. Thinking of it with reference to Gina and Alex made the project seem even more odd and ludicrous.

'What do you think, Gina? Would you like to get together with Alex one night soon?'

He moved sideways along the rail to get a better view of her mournful tortoise eyes, which peered out between enormous scaly thighs. Ignoring the impertinence, she continued to chew contentedly on the plentiful long grass in her well-appointed pen.

'Hello, Paul.' It was Isabel, coming up behind him with Sarita's little girl.

'Oh, hi Isabel. I was just talking to my friend Gina.' He looked down at Marina. 'She's 215, the world's oldest known land animal alive today. She was given to Queen Victoria in 1837, when she came to the British throne, and Gina was about four by then, so they say. The queen kept her hidden for a long time, maybe in the Tower!'

'She's got a very funny neck,' said Marina, standing on tiptoes. 'How heavy is she?'

'Yes, it's baggy but that's how they all are, even the younger ones. I've no idea how heavy she is, but she only eats grass and fruit, so she won't be too overweight. Tell you a little secret, she's one of my favourite animals in here.'

Marina glanced at Gina again and turned to Isabel. 'Do you have a favourite animal?'

'Oh yes – my favourite is the naked mole rat, no question. They live in burrows and they're sociable, playful and intelligent. They're also long-lived, very resistant to cancer and the kind of creatures that will survive and become an advanced species if there's a world-shattering asteroid impact. We have a group of naked mole rats just round the corner there. I'll show you them next time we come. They're ugly too, which makes a change, being both ugly and successful.'

'Can I run round the corner now and see them, just quickly?'

'Okay then, but don't be long. I'm getting hungry for dinner, after our gym session. Your mum says you can come back to mine again and do your homework there.'

Paul watched Marina run off. 'Glad we've got a moment, Isabel. I haven't made any headway in discovering who that young man was, the one who was with Harvey and Glen in the Wellowbug. And just to make you aware, Stefan has searched for Lextar in the global company register and other world databanks and he can't find any record of it. Officially, Lextar doesn't exist.'

Isabel stared at him, nonplussed. 'Maybe it's got another name, officially I mean.'

'It's possible, but why would it use an alias?'

'I don't know. As you say—'

'Shush, don't turn round but Harvey's here, walking towards us. Whoops, no he isn't, he's swung back and he's making off as fast as he can. He's vanished.'

This was the corridor leading to Trish's office. What other reason would Harvey have for being here, and why else would he turn tail like that when he saw them ahead of him? Was Trish expecting him? Marina was running back now, light and skippy in her gym outfit.

'They are soooo ugly! I like them too, they can be one of my favourites, but I love wombats best – no, meerkats the best. I wish we had meerkats in here. They live in a mob and I hope they survive like the naked mole rats.' She giggled over the word "naked".

'I guess they don't have all the special qualities, although they're very lovable.' Isabel turned back to Paul. 'Let's talk again soon. I hope everything else is going okay?'

'Yeah, kind of, but it's still tense with Trish, I really need to clear the air. Have you got anywhere with Finn, about why he ran for his life and where they were taking Glen?'

'Not yet. I will pin him down but he's managing to avoid me, making excuses. I had a fantasy moment, imagining Glen dropping out of the Wellowbug from a great height.'

Marina had started off towards the exit. 'Come on, Isabel.' She turned halfway and was doing near-perfect cartwheels back down the corridor towards them.

'Okay, coming. I'd forgotten about children, Paul, how crazy and adorable they are.'

He watched them join hands and skip to the corner, wondering if Isabel had children and grandchildren of her own – if the emotion in her voice came from missing them. This place was so insular that you forgot to ask these things; they almost seemed irrelevant. He knew more about Stefan's history than anyone else's, his life in the Fringes and before. And Stefan knew about him too, probably understood him better than Trish.

He knocked on her office door, opened it and put his head round. She looked up and smiled, no momentary surprise or awkwardness.

'Hi there, Paul, I'm nearly finished here. Have you come straight from the gallery?'

He told her about bumping into Isabel and little Marina, knowing she would enjoy the story about favourite animals.

'She's going soft, is Isabel. Probably a good thing, the kid bringing out that side.'

'Or it's an effect of her polypill and blended reality trial, perhaps?'

'Already, do you think? Listen, Paul, I want to say something about my memory trial, the first session with the brain implant. It relates to you, our first summer. But before I get on to that, there's something bad happening in the menagerie. Someone's coming in when it's quiet and meddling with the animals, undermining our first principles.'

'What do you mean – how so?'

'Well, we only keep natural animals here in the menagerie, and only creatures with exceptional talents and superpowers. That's the whole point. But I've found two new ones in the pens and they're some kind of hybrid. Small creatures, so as not to draw attention, a naked mole rat and a moon jellyfish. They've replaced two natural ones as well, not just been added to the group. And they are excellent copies, clone-like. There could be more mimics among our thousand-plus individuals and it may be an insidious process, that's my fear. I'm going through the population systematically but it's slow.'

A hybrid naked mole rat; Isabel wouldn't stand for that.

'It's not possible, is it? No, it's a daft idea, but they might be evolving differently—'

'Yes, I've gone through that thought process and it *is* daft, it's too big a leap without explicit human interference. The motives are there, sadly – to sell or breed them, prepare them as mind-enhancing delicacies or aphrodisiacs, or just to experiment on them. Matthew and I rescued so many animals from poachers and traffickers, there was a huge global trade back then. Who knows what vile monstrosity it's morphed into by now? I dread to think.'

'Have you told anyone – Georgina?'

'Not yet. It coincided with Glen's disappearance, which only makes it more ominous and disturbing. Georgina might even be behind it, for all we know. I hinted to Harvey, as he seems to have his finger on the pulse, but he just looked blank.'

It was the first time Harvey's name had come up between them since Paul's sighting of him and Trish walking back from the air taxi flight. Now she had lit the blue touchpaper; he had to seize the moment.

'Do your paths cross much then, you and Harvey?' *Are you having an affair? Go on, say it.* 'Does he come here, into the menagerie? Does he have a special interest in animals? Maybe it's him, stealing them for his flight to Mars. You hadn't thought of that possibility.'

'Paul, what the hell is it? Why are you being so uptight suddenly?'

'Because I'm upset, Trish, and hurt. If you and Harvey—'

'Well, you're upsetting me too. There's nothing going on, we're friends. I know you don't like him but to accuse me, even to think of it… I don't know what to say.'

He put up his hand. 'Stop, please. I'm sorry, don't cry. I need reassurance, that's all. It's felt different between us lately.'

He needed to warn her off Harvey, tell her everything he had seen and heard about his extreme actions, but it felt impossible. It would make her more defensive – or worse still, she could explode into outright aggression.

Trish stood up and came round the desk to take his hands, still tearful. 'I *can* assure you, please believe me. Harvey's just a friend and I can easily not spend time with him. I love *you*, Paul. We were made for each other.'

He brought her hands together and kissed them softly. 'What was it in the memory trial that you wanted to tell me?'

'I don't know if it's the right moment. It's quite strong.'

'And a long time ago. I'm sure I can handle it.'

'All right then.' She walked over to the bookcase and picked out a book at random, then put it back on the shelf. Paul saw her hands shaking as she fumbled with it.

'After the island, the water-skiing accident, we drove back to Germany, remember, and got jobs in that hotel in Bavaria, by the lake.'

'Ah yes, that didn't last long. I was sacked for insolence to the head waiter and you left in solidarity with me, although we both considered it a happy escape. I've never had to work so hard in all my life and I could have killed those late guests, the ones who sat out on the terrace drinking and laughing 'til three in the morning.'

'And then we moved in with the older couple, I don't remember their names, Herr und Frau…?'

'No, me neither. I remember their house clearly, though. It was a Swiss-style chalet on the hill, overlooking the lake. Very picturesque. They put me in the attic room and you next to their bedroom to stop us sleeping together. Not that it did. And the old man was—'

'A pervy creep, yes – sleazeball. He brushed up against me several times and I had to be light-footed, literally. Looking back, it seems funny that we stayed on but it suited us and we were working in their camping shop, earning money. And we thought we were invincible at that age. But I'm coming to the significant memory shift now, what happened in my session with Juno and Itsuki.' She paused. 'We killed that woman in the chalet, Paul.'

'Don't be silly. Something must have gone very wrong with the memory implant if you've come to that conclusion.'

'Listen to me. She was ill, she had a whole row of pills lined up on the table that she had to take every day. And one weekend, the pervy husband went away and he asked us to take charge of the pills, make sure she took them. He told us what she had to take and – this is the thing – it was far too many. We even thought that at the time, but it didn't seem like any of our business. We had no attachment to them and we were young and careless.'

'Honestly, Trish, I've no memory of this, her row of pills or us taking charge, but I just don't believe that's how it happened.'

'There's so much detail in it, Paul. The colour of the pills, her wizened hands…'

'That's you, adding in and embellishing it, we know that's what happens. False—'

She raised her voice. 'It's *not* a false memory! We wanted to have free and easy sex while he was away, so we didn't call an ambulance when she slumped. We told ourselves she was just falling asleep. It was unforgivable – we were associates to murder, at the least.'

'Look, Trish, I can believe she died while we were staying there, if you say so, but it can't have been our fault, I would remember it. False memories can easily be implanted, we've heard enough about that. You're too trusting sometimes. How can you be sure?'

'You've blocked it out, that's also what happens. You remember all the funny parts, the good bits that don't affect your sense of who you are, or your nostalgia about what we did that summer. I can't prove it to you but I'm convinced it's the truth, which I buried just as surely as you. It rings bells. It's like finally fitting something into place, where it belongs.'

Paul got up and made for the door. 'I'm sorry, Trish, but I can't cope with this. You're obsessing about some event that may or not have occurred sixty-odd years ago, instead of focusing on present dangers, especially the danger of associating with your friend Harvey. He's a fraudster, that's what *I'm* convinced about, claiming to be someone he's not – and what's more, he's inextricably mixed up in Glen's disappearance. Think about that!'

He shut the door behind him, but not quickly enough to muffle her shouted retort:

'Where's your proof?'

Once out in the corridor, he was unsure where to go.

Stefan, that was it; he always worked late. He ran all the way back to the piazza and along the arcade to the history gallery and Stefan's room. He paused before tapping his knuckles on the door, breathing heavily and wiping his eyes with the end of his sleeve, forcing back the tears. Stefan was still there but someone else was with him: Sarita from the hair salon, little Marina's mother, who was also crying.

Sixteen

Shani was in the Institute again after several days' absence, so Finn kept his head down and pretended to be busy. She had been working with Georgina on revisions to the strategy, apparently. Everyone was expecting changes but no one knew what, or how significant they would be. The atmosphere was both febrile and aimless, with rumours about Glen's fate still swirling and no direction on whether the assigned tasks were still relevant. Finn himself had been promoted by Glen and even without the dodgy business of the polypills and the fake human tissue, he had no idea if Georgina would keep him on in his External Comms role. He hadn't made an impression on her, as Isabel had urged him to do, and now he was in danger of being tainted, or worse, by Glen's seedy sideline. He'd been an unwitting part of the toxic supply chain. And to add to his problems, Paul was watching on the roof when he fled the Wellowbug, leaving Glen in Harvey's clutches. It would be seen as cowardice or complicity, depending on how people chose to look at it. He ached to talk to Shani, to share his fears with her and open up about what drove him to it, his love of his family, but that bolt was shot. Shani had zero interest in him and he had stormed off in an infantile rage. Despair and indifference were the only options left – and indifference was too much to ask.

At least today he had an outlet of sorts; a chance to escape the suffocating confines of the office, even if it was likely to suck him deeper into the vortex. There was no way he could refuse Harvey's order to fly an air taxi to the woods. And his emotions were mixed, fear and doubt jumbled up with perverse excitement, his inner voice telling him he wouldn't achieve his goals without stepping beyond his safe place. Isabel had advised being savvy, knowing who your true friends are, and what was it? Being on the right side of the future. Maybe in this morass, savvy was more a case of knowing who to be friends with, choosing the winning side. Isabel had a dark past, according to Harvey, but she was his friend, his sisters' sponsor, and he had blatantly lied to her about what actually happened to Glen. He had known immediately, from the expression of dismay in her crystal-blue eyes, that she didn't believe his account. That also felt irretrievable, like he had made his bed and had to lie on it.

As he approached the nearest air taxi, he heard a voice behind him, calling his name. It was that prick Josh, walking fast to catch up with him. *Bugger off, can't you?*

'Hi, Finn. Guess we're travelling together today. Do you know what the job is?'

Job: the little word immediately assumed sinister overtones, as in "hit job". He might have anticipated Josh turning up, but he hadn't considered it and his own naivety unsettled him further.

'I'm flying a taxi out to the woods and waiting on instructions from Harvey. Thought I'd be going solo.'

'No, I'm coming too. It's just business as usual for you, with a new pick-up point.'

This was the guy who had talked so casually about a simple and elegant plan to take Glen skydiving, give him a treat, and Finn was about to get into an air taxi with him.

'Don't worry, man. I won't push you out!'

'No, but I might push you,' replied Finn, without missing a beat. That was good, quite satisfying. 'I'll set the controls.'

The travel time was less than ten minutes and they spent it discussing the relative merits and pleasures of flying the Wellowbug and an ordinary air taxi like this. It was a topic on which they could find a level of agreement, or at least engage in cursory male bonding: the air taxi was agile and had a superior destination screen, while the Wellowbug was more powerful and had a funkier control panel. Its extending legs were pretty cool too.

'There it is,' said Josh, pointing to the space among the trees as they were almost on top of it. 'You can get carried away, staring at the destination screen and missing the landing zone. There's the Wellowbug. Harvey said it would park here from now on.'

'Why? It's not very convenient.'

'No, but it doesn't draw attention, that's the thing. The Institute roof is too visible.'

'Okay then, what next?'

They landed neatly and Finn climbed out and put on his hat. The searing midday sun was hitting the clearing but he was glad to stretch his legs. That was the main downside of an air taxi: the leg space was restrictive for someone as lanky as him.

'Next we head along the path to the treehouse, where

we collect the supplies.' Josh paused. 'Don't you know what we're doing today; didn't Harvey say?'

Finn shook his head, feeling dense and also resentful of Josh's advance knowledge.

'We're doing a delivery, Finn, like the ones you were doing for Glen – the same.'

'What – the polypills, and the human tissue?'

'Just the polypills. It was the biological products that caused the problems, they were defective. The market's still out there for the polypills, though. They're working well and as they're unique and groundbreaking, buyers are prepared to overlook the other issues.'

'For fuck's sake, I just assumed—'

'Come on, let's get moving.'

Finn followed Josh along the winding path for a couple of hundred metres before the treehouse came into view. That had been euphoric, joining the treasure hunt winners up there after he had given up on his useless team. Isabel, Trish, Harvey and him celebrating together with pizza and panini, having fun; it was so recent but it felt like a much earlier, more innocent time. And what was the message displayed on that blue screen in the treehouse? The best treasures are lying outside your comfort zone, something like that. That was his main hope now, but you also had to avoid the worst stinking dross.

'We're not going into the treehouse now, but we can have lunch there afterwards.'

Josh approached the hidden elevator, which rose out of the ground on sensing their arrival. They stepped inside and it went down instead of up, descending for several seconds before coming to a halt. Finn decided to say as little as possible until he had sussed out what was happening. It was bad enough being thrown together with this wily character; he didn't want to be dependent on him for information, or anything else.

The familiar polypill containers were stacked up at the near end of a passageway, where it opened into this cave-like space. There was no one in sight and Josh had obviously been told to get on with it. They used a couple of trolleys to pack the containers into the elevator, leaving enough room for the two of them to squeeze in at the end. Finn had stared down the tunnel passage, which was well lit with white-tiled walls, but there were no clues as to where it went.

'I'm not sure the trolleys will work along the path, it's so bumpy. We're going on in the Wellowbug, by the way, so we can fit all this lot in.'

'Let's try one and if it's no good, we'll carry the containers singly.'

The trolley method more or less worked, with a little rough pushing and pulling, and they got the containers into the bug within half an hour. Finn had decided on the one thing he had to do while they were at the Phantom Landing: check out the garage and Harvey's Rolls-Royce. This was the precious, near-priceless car that Glen had reportedly crashed into the end building, the car that burned up spectacularly. That was the official line, which he had been instructed to reinforce. Maybe they'd just taken it away, to remove the evidence.

The waiting customers were scattered around the old service station site, as before. When the bug landed with its signature light bounce, they congregated into more of a group but still maintained a wary distance from each other. It was Finn's job to tick the products off as they were claimed, while this time Josh handed out the boxes.

'That's it, all accounted for. Let's go.'

'Just one last thing. This is all a big surprise to me. I need to clear my head, just walk around for five minutes.'

'All right, man, but keep it short. I'll wait in the cabin.'

Finn put his hands in his pockets and assumed an ambling air, looking around him as he strolled towards the end garage. There was a side window to it, he remembered that, so he could peer in without Josh spying on him. As he had suspected, the beautiful blue Rolls was still there, apparently undamaged. And coming back to the front, he looked in again, careless of Josh as he had to be certain; yes, the same registration number, the exact same car. They *had* thrown Glen out then, taken him skydiving as Josh put it. Or disposed of him in some other bad way. Finn kept his hands in his pockets, no longer for the nonchalant look but because they were shaking and sweaty. There was no escape from this bleak place and all the customers had driven off – not that he would have trusted any of them to take him somewhere safe. The treehouse it would have to be then, as Josh had suggested.

While the cookbot took their order for lunch, Josh made appreciative noises as he looked around the snug sitting area. Finn acted like he was totally familiar with the place.

'You haven't been up here before then?'

'No. I'm not staff, so I wasn't here for the corporate jolly that weekend.'

'So, what are you then, if not staff?'

It was hard to keep the antipathy out of his voice, but he had to put the Shani issue aside. It would be seriously stupid to mention it, plus he didn't have any evidence of a sexual relationship between the two of them; nothing other than Shani's blush and a few casual words that he might easily have misinterpreted, due to his own over-intense feelings.

'I'm a freelancer, currently working for Harvey among other things. I was a student at the uni but I dropped out after a dispute. You probably heard about it.'

'Yes, I did,' said Finn cautiously. 'It was to do with the cybirds, wasn't it? I don't know the details. How come they've let you back in as a freelancer?'

Josh picked up a heavily loaded slice of pizza and held it precariously in mid-air.

'New management. Nathan barred me first and then I was hunted by Glen because I nicked a cybird, but I'm in with them again now. They think I'm on their side.'

'And are you, Josh?' There, he had said his name. That was progress of a sort, even if he was still having painful mental flashes of randy action, Shani and Josh all over each other.

'Nope. I'm working for myself and it serves my cause to do certain jobs for Georgina or Harvey. The insider-outsider, that's a perfect position.'

Finn was intrigued, despite himself.

'And do you have any… limits, on what you're willing to do?'

Josh laughed. 'I know what you're getting at.'

'Well, do you?'

'To be clear, the plan was always to give Glen a sharp

shock, to put the wind up him. He was too blatantly intent on personal gain, that's what they hated. The way it happened, we frightened you as well, to make it authentic. Sorry about that, *amigo*.'

'I wasn't frightened, not for myself. It just seemed so… extreme.'

'Yeah, well, it didn't happen.'

'Glen's not dead then?'

'Nah, he's alive and well but no longer running his own profitable little sideshow, as you see. Luckily for him he's still needed, despite being hopeless as a criminal mastermind.'

Finn sat bolt upright, like a startled prey animal listening for clues to an approaching predator: its proximity, its identity and the level of threat it posed.

'You said you work for Harvey, then you said Georgina. Is it both of them?'

'At the moment, yes. Their interests coincide up to a point, but that's not going to last. In my view, Georgina's obsessively genomic and Harvey's obsessively algorithmic. They will diverge accordingly, but neither of them realises it yet. Or maybe they do realise it well enough and they're more devious than I give them credit for.'

Devious: that's what Finn had set himself up to be, if that's what it took to reach his goals. He'd thought he was getting somewhere, with his promotion and Isabel's promise of funding for his sisters' uni fees, but it wasn't bold enough, not by a long chalk. Even his small role in selling illicit and dangerous products was accidental. He didn't possess any of Josh's confidence and flair.

'And Glen, where is he then?'

'Glen never had a strategy; he was blowing with the wind. He took decisions to look decisive, rather than to pursue any coherent plan. He's a good lab scientist, so I'm told, so he's in the right place now. Georgina and Harvey are far more sophisticated and they know all about manipulation. They make the links between manipulation of genes or data and the manipulation of our human desires. It's the tweaks and hidden messages that matter.'

Finn wondered what Shani would make of this analogy, whether she had ever had a conversation like this with Josh. No, they would be too engrossed in each other's bodies.

'Can I ask, Josh, what you stand for? You mentioned your cause – what is it?'

'Me, I'm a social disruptor. The present social order, which built on the old class and wealth hierarchy and made it more explicit, has to be defeated. I'm not working alone, not on the wider scale. There's a global campaign and the strategic aim is straightforward and revolutionary: to undermine and overthrow these immoral global movements and their self-serving clusters, replacing them with a just and equitable world government.'

'Where does this come from? I mean, who…?' Finn hadn't known anyone with these views when he was a student. There were no overt political groups at the university, not in the ways he had heard they operated in previous generations.

'Ah, I was radicalised at birth, if you want to know. My parents were social activists, frontline warriors in the fight for environmental and health justice. I was a pandemic baby, born 2022 and conceived in a tunnel, when they were trying to stop construction of a high-speed rail line. And as kids we were expert at making treehouses, but they weren't done up like this one and there weren't any robot slaves.'

Finn leant forward, his body language conspiratorial.

'And why would you tell me all this, Josh, why trust me with it?'

Josh copied Finn in leaning towards him, their spread knees nearly touching.

'Because I know where you come from and what you desire more than anything. And I think you'd make a good saboteur, with a little practice. This is a pivotal moment and the struggle will be existential. Join us, man, find your inner activist. We need people like you.'

Finn looked at the cookbot, which stood impassively waiting for the next instruction. He didn't know whether he felt envious or contemptuous of it.

'That underground white tunnel down there, where does it lead?'

***

Juno had rolled up her trousers and was stamping her feet into the wet sand to leave deep impressions. Fifty steps out, she turned around and followed her footprints back to Shani, who was investigating one of the larger rock pools.

'Hey, that was an awesome movie! How old is it?'

'Let me think... early 1990s, way back then. Odd really, that we're still able to watch that kind of film. It's very subversive, after all, two unlikely rebels escaping their stifled lives and refusing to be captured, preferring to go down in a blaze of glory. Everyone loves those wild, heart-stopping, cataclysmic moments, makes you want to join the next uprising.'

Juno sat on a low rock and dabbled her feet in the water to wash off the sand.

'There's a whole world in this one little pool. Did you go to the beach as a kid?'

'Yes, and always with my bucket for collecting crabs, shrimps and starfish, they were the best finds. We had to release them all before we went home. The same types of animals are still here – they're hardy sea creatures, which beat everything else in terms of survival. Molluscs, crabs and these darting little fish, they'll go in and out with the tide until the end of the world. And they don't agonise over their future, which is another perk. What about you, Juno? Did you play in rock pools?'

She was treading carefully, remembering Juno's comment about other people being voyeuristic and asking about personal histories. This budding friendship was still untested.

'No, we grew up in America, near Denver. There weren't many sea-water rock pools round there! We had a big back yard and that's where we spent most of our time, playing outdoors and making up our own games. We had the run of it, as long as we promised not to go beyond the walls. And we were home-schooled too, so it was like our whole universe.'

Shani nodded and picked up a stick to prod gently into the underwater crevices.

'Sounds nice. I grew up here, in what's now the smart city. My parents were in good jobs, still are. We went on trips every weekend, until my brother and I were into our teens and insisted on hanging out with our friends. Then I moved away to university, studied for a while and came back when the Institute expanded and advertised new research jobs. Not very adventurous but the work has been fascinating.'

'You have a brother? Itsuki and I lived with two other sets of twins, six of us with four parents – or foster parents, they were really. We weren't biologically related to them.'

'Was it… did you and Itsuki…?'

'It was a happy childhood, but different. Our parents were kind people, all of them.'

'How, different?… You don't have to tell me, Juno.'

'I want to. It's going to sound technical but you're an expert, so you'll understand. We were six lab babies and our genes were edited from the beginning, each to a unique specification so they could be compared. The aims were to enhance our intelligence and optimise our ageing. It was highly speculative, a world first – no one knew if it was going to work. And they didn't want to wait long to find out. When we were ten, we had shots to introduce a virus carrying genes that induce adult cells to become pluripotent stem cells. Once inserted, the genes can be switched on at any time to rejuvenate the cells and make the person biologically younger, like if you're in your mid-forties to bring you back to thirty. The reversal can be switched off again at any point. You probably know all this so far, but with us it was different. They wanted to do the opposite and accelerate our ageing, taking us from ten years old up to twenty-five. This meant finding the switch key that would allow age acceleration to happen in the same controlled way as age reversal. That's what they achieved and it took two years from age ten to accelerate us, so in old age-time we were twelve but in our new age-time we were twenty-five. Then Itsuki and I left home and we came here to Wellowfern.'

Shani let her stick fall and watched it drift into the slimy fronds of brown seaweed.

'Now we can be tweaked to slide up and down the age range, like someone's playing scales on the piano. Crazy, isn't it?'

Juno smiled cheekily. No wonder she seemed so elfin, childlike.

'Er, yes, you could say that. I'm having trouble getting my head round it. What about your memory between those years, ten to twenty-five?'

'The memories are there, implanted. It's not perfect, the personal stuff is not as vivid as it is from our early years before the acceleration. It's brilliant but still work in progress, that's my view. Maybe similar to your virtual daydream experience with the rowboat, some of the threads are weak or suspect.'

'This is fantastical, Juno.' Shani sat up straight, clasping her hands around her knees and looking out to the horizon. 'That time for getting out and exploring the world, late teens to early twenties, that's when we create our strongest memories. It's where we'll constantly hark back to in later life.'

'Yes, and I do have good memories from that time, just sometimes they're faint.'

'Does anyone else here know? I mean… Georgina told me—'

258

'Yes, Georgina invited us here. And Harvey's known us forever, he's like an uncle to me and Itsuki. We came over from America together.'

Shani started again with the stick, swirling the surface water around in the rock pool and sending a crab scuttling back into its hole. She still hadn't had much direct contact with Harvey but she knew he sharply divided opinion, particularly among the older residents. It had seemed unfair to blame him for Esther's absence, but after several other unexplained departures, plus the bizarre tour of the care home and Isabel's snide comments in the air taxi, Shani had revised her view. Harvey *was* involved in their removal from the city village and was quite possibly the driving force. But how did this link to what Juno was saying, the seemingly fond way she talked about him?

'An uncle… like a good uncle or a wicked one?'

Juno frowned and rocked her head from side to side, weighing it up.

'He's a chameleon, really, that kind of uncle. When you're a child, you expect to be controlled by adults, but then we skipped the rebellious teenage years. Suddenly at twenty-five it feels oppressive, like he's using us for his own aims. Which has always been the truth, although he's also been generous and given us great opportunities to progress.'

'Wow, that's sad. I mean—'

'I'm sorry, Shani, I've overloaded you.'

'No, not at all.'

'It's just that, being here with you, it's… it feels safe and lovely. When I first saw you after the Blitz show… It was kind of sudden, immediate.'

'It felt special to me too. There's a natural affinity, it's rare and it goes beyond…'

Shani's eye was drawn to a solitary figure walking towards them at the sea's edge, where the glinting specks of sand met the tiny, dying waves.

'There's a patrol guard coming… no, wait, it's Paul.'

He returned her wave and quickened his step.

'Hi, Paul. This one of your haunts? It's so deserted and we've seen hardly any boats.'

'Yes, Trish and I often come out here for a beach ramble and a picnic on the cliff.'

'She's stayed at home tonight?'

He looked upset. 'Yup, and I don't want to spoil your enjoyment but—'

'Go on.'

'It's one for you, Juno, or one for each of you actually. I came out here to try and get my head straight, and by luck I've run into the two people who might actually help me.'

He sat down with his back against one of the scattered rocks in front of the caves.

'I'll be honest with you. Trish and I had a row and now we're not speaking and she can't bear to look at me. I moved in with Stefan today, it's that bad. I know this sounds like a domestic incident but there's more to it, connected to her session in the memory trial. She's convinced that we once gave someone an overdose of prescription drugs and she died as a result. It's complete nuts, a false memory created by the implant, accidentally or purposely, that's what I think. It's too much of a coincidence to be anything else, but Trish claims she's finally uncovered the truth about the past. She was furious when I refused to go along with it, and also…' He trailed off. 'No, nothing, that's it.'

Shani looked over to Juno, who frowned with concentration. This one was for her.

'We would never do that, Paul. False memories are fascinating but it's not what our research is about. Georgina accepts that the memory implant is necessary in the short term, but her aim is to enhance natural human abilities, that's the focus. Creating a false memory through a device serves no research purpose for us, and it won't be a side effect either.'

Paul dipped his head and trailed his fingers through his damp hair, saying nothing.

Shani waited before asking: 'What was the other thing, Paul – the one for me?'

He looked up. 'Ah yes, the animals. This one's more important in the grand scheme of things. Trish works in the menagerie, as you know, and she's found two animal hybrids that just appeared in the pens, a rodent and a jellyfish. They've replaced two real creatures, which have disappeared into thin air. She thinks there could be more invaders throughout the collection and she's searching for them.'

Shani whistled through her teeth. 'What kind of hybrids – how are they different?'

'Ah, you don't know then, that's what I feared. She said they're like clones but they could be anything in this wacky place. It needs a specialist to examine them and I thought of you, Shani, someone with integrity who cares about boring, old-fashioned issues like ethics.'

She hesitated. 'I can't see how we can do it, realistically. Let me think…'

They weren't geared up for this job in the lab and it would have to happen under the radar, without Georgina finding out. She might well have her own reasons for doing secret experiments on animals, now she was operating without external ethical oversight of the human trials. It felt highly risky but still, her curiosity was piqued.

'How would we get access to the menagerie pens, the new specimens? Are you able to ask Trish, Paul, or—'

He sighed. 'Well, she told me about it but now we've had this massive row and… there are other personal issues too, it could just flare up. I thought perhaps you or Juno…'

'I'll talk to Trish,' said Juno. 'She's coming into the neuro hub tomorrow for her next memory session. I like to chat with all the participants, anyway, check on any immediate effects and make sure they're okay to leave. I'll tell her the truth, that I found out by meeting you on the beach. Hopefully, she'll join in with us.'

'I hope so too,' said Paul. 'She's passionate about animals and fiercely protective of the menagerie and its reputation. She'll want to get to the bottom of this, no question.'

Shani was ready to make her suggestion: the best option for examining the animals involved Josh. She shouldn't be anxious about it, as her two last encounters with him were in virtual space and probably reflected her insecurity about their relationship. She had no idea how he actually felt about her in the real world. That previous time, on the sofa… No, it was irrelevant. The real issue lay in him being banned from Wellowfern – unless Georgina had already invited him back? He'd probably do it, especially if he thought this new twist might screw up his plan for the alpha cybird, whatever it was; a plan she'd also discovered from the virtual Josh, not the real world one, she reminded herself.

'The true specialist could be that student Josh, the one who was evicted by Nathan. He was playing around with the cybirds, exploring how they worked, that's how he got into trouble. I don't know where he is, though. Do you know who I mean, Juno?'

It was a genuine question but also a test: did Juno know the identity of the sexy guy Shani had encountered in her daydream experiment, even though it was billed as a wholly private experience, leaving no trace?

Paul jumped in before Juno. 'What does he look like? Dark curly hair, slim, black T-shirt?' Shani nodded. 'I think I've seen him, getting in the Wellowbug with Finn. I'll ask Isabel to quiz Finn – she wants to know more about this student. I won't let on about the animals. We have to keep it tight until we know what we're dealing with – just us three, okay?'

'And Itsuki,' added Juno. 'He'll know automatically; I can't prevent it.'

'It's a plan,' said Shani, her deep fascination mingling with startled apprehension about where all this might lead. The three of them high-fived, Juno grabbed her hand and they scrambled up the slippery path to the top of the cliff.

Seventeen

Isabel closed the door after Paul and went out to the balcony. Trish was under the chestnut tree, head up as she pushed her hands against the trunk and flexed her spine to its limit. That was why Paul had come over now, knowing that Trish wasn't at home. Isabel had been looking out for him but he was staying with Stefan, and Trish was no longer answering her messages. She moved close to Cyril's raised pad and stood up tall, so she could look at him eyeball to eyeball.

'It's a mess, Cyril. Trish and Paul have fallen out, big time. She's accused him of some crime in the distant past, I don't know what, and he believes it's a false memory inserted by her implant. I don't go along with that, but I agree with him on the other thing he suspects – she's having an affair with Harvey. We've both been around long enough to read the signs.'

Cyril shuffled his feet and ruffled his wings, as if disconcerted. 'What are the signs?'

'Oh… avoidance, shiftiness, obfuscation, moodiness, unusual bursts of affection…'

'It's complicated – a lot to learn. Are they in love?'

She laughed and put out her hand to stroke him, something she had never dreamt of doing. Her fingers just brushed his glossy green neck plumage before they withdrew.

'How do I know if they're in love? She told me it's only fun, but that's the oldest one in the book. And I've not tested Harvey on it, too delicate and thorny. I will now, though, I'll find a roundabout way. He's on alert, I won't get anywhere with a straight approach.'

Cyril tapped his foot, probably hoping for more education on love affairs.

'Hell, Cyril, it's turning into a gloopy soup, all this.'

'Gloopy?'

'Silly word; don't bother to learn it. It means a sticky mess. I'm clinging on to Finn but he's falling under Harvey's spell, otherwise why was he on the roof that day? I can't talk to Trish about the fake car crash because she's fixated on Harvey too. Then we've got Esther riding her fantasy ponies at the seaside and Suzanne behaving capriciously, threatening to upset the apple cart… I'll need huge doses of social intelligence to wade through this lot.'

'Do you want another strong cup of coffee? I can instruct Lottie.'

'Thanks, I'll get it myself.' She looked over the balcony rail. 'Hey, there's Sarita and Marina.' She waved back at Marina, who was running to keep up with her mother's rapid stride. Three minutes later they were in her living room. Sarita was visibly agitated and ignored her invitation to sit down.

'I'm so sorry, Isabel, but I don't know what else to do, I need your advice. My son—'

'Lorenzo, yes, I remember.'

'Lorenzo, he's sicker now, he can't lift his head. My husband was looking after him but now he's ill too, both of them. I have to go and help but I can't take Marina, she's safe here. Do you know anyone, a family who can care for her?'

'Difficult, there's still very few families with kids here. Don't you have relatives who could step in, aunts and uncles?'

'No, they are gone and everyone is only surviving in the Fringes. They have to look after their closest family, even if they're kind people. I'll take her, except it's cholera—'

'Cholera! God Almighty, I thought we'd done with that centuries ago in this country.' She stopped, seeing Marina's terrified expression. 'I mean, cholera can be dealt with, but—'

'Can I please stay with you, Isabel?'

'What? No, that's not possible. It wouldn't work, there's too much going on.'

Marina's eyes were brimming and she was fiercely biting her lip. 'But—'

'Quiet now, Marina.' Sarita's voice trembled. 'You heard what Isabel said, you can't.'

Isabel looked over to Cyril, catching him in quizzical stance; head cocked, listening.

'No, wait, I needed a minute to think about it. It's too dangerous for you to go back, Marina, and you can stay with me, of course you can. We'll have fun together and you'll keep Cyril company, teach each other things.'

Marina nodded eagerly. 'Can I stay then, Mummy?'

'Yes, sweetheart. Thank you from my heart, Isabel. It means so much, I can't express it. Stefan's going with me. We're from the same town and his friend Alice just died of the sickness. He says there's no one to run the pub and keep the supplies coming in. He'll be in contact with Paul, so you'll know what's happening. I'll run home and pack Marina's things.'

'Yes, do that. Cyril will let you in if we're not here. I was thinking of having a morning run but we can do something else. How about the planetarium, a virtual space trip?'

Marina nodded again, aware enough of Sarita's anxiety to restrain her excitement.

'I'll miss you, Mummy.'

Sarita swept her up in a close hug. 'Of course, we both will but it won't be long.'

Isabel took Marina's hand and led her onto the balcony where they waved goodbye. Cyril landed on the rail beside them with a sudden thud, making Marina jump.

'Don't be alarmed, Cyril is quite cute and friendly these days.'

By the time they reached the planetarium, they had decided on their spaceship tour: visiting every planet in the solar system at close quarters, including a landing and short trek on Mars. It took a full hour but Marina was entranced throughout, tuning in avidly to the commentary and enjoying the random encounters with astronauts and Mars colonists.

'That was brilliant,' said Isabel. 'Let's sit here in the café. Do you fancy an ice cream?' She brought up the menu. 'There's all the flavours you can think of, so take your choice.'

'Any flavour I like?'

'Yes, except...' She pretended to study the selection. 'Except squashed flies or beetle dung. That's beetle poo to you.'

Marina giggled. 'I want… um… chocolate and strawberry and vanilla, all together.'

Isabel keyed in the order. Both of her children had favoured that combination too, the traditional Neapolitan. She felt a familiar rising wave of sadness. She hadn't treasured them enough, made time for them. And she had foisted Jerome on them when there was no fit. It was bound to end badly, but she didn't confront the fact until it was too late.

'Morning, Isabel.' It was Harvey, his satin two-tone shoes first and, as she looked up, his wonky smile. 'Is this your granddaughter?'

'No, it's my young friend, Marina. She's staying with me for a little while.'

'I was hoping to catch you, have a chat. Later today, maybe?'

This was her best chance; no point delaying it. 'We can talk now. I'll ask the guide bot to show Marina some exhibits.' She looked at Marina, who picked up an imaginary spoon and mimicked eating ice cream. 'Okay, we'll have our ice cream first, so say you come back in fifteen minutes, Harvey?'

'Will do. The space wheel is amazing, kiddo, if you don't mind tumbling through the universe like a lost piece of space junk, upside down and all.'

Marina went goggle-eyed and Isabel laughed. 'Sounds perfect, just like gymnastics.'

As she stirred her coffee and waited for the three-leaf design on top to dissolve into a milky-brown froth, Isabel focused on her plan. Be friendly, that was the key thing; come across as a trustworthy ally. And find Harvey's weak spot; something that would make him slip up, for whatever reason: complacency, vanity, anxiety, fear.

When he returned, she noticed he was wearing his signet ring, the new biotracker gift from Georgina. She had kept her earrings in their pretty box, ambivalent about their power to monitor the "continuous ebb and flow" of her cognitive and emotional states, as Georgina described it. This feature could be turned off, but the functionality would remain, its extent unknown. They might still be intrusive, probing deep into her private thoughts, and she couldn't accept it. She came from a different era, when earrings were earrings.

Harvey dispensed with the small talk. 'I meant it when I said you can take Suzanne to visit Esther in the care facility. She won't last much longer, so we should fix it up quickly. Suzanne will be reassured and that will be good for all the residents.'

'Thanks, Harvey. I'll take both Suzanne and DJ Johnny. They are constantly bending my ear, expecting me to take action. And I agree, they should be happier when they've seen it. We've had several other plus-120 residents disappear too. Are they in the care home?'

'Sure, we're marketing it among that age group. Some are tired of life and others are looking for novel experiences, both creative and emotional. The idea is to move down the age range now it's established and we can demonstrate what's on offer. We'll look at the plus-110s next, tempting them as champions of a radical approach; risk-takers willing to try the most advanced treatments and join highly speculative trials.'

That was DJ Johnny, then, in the target age range; fat chance of them tempting him.

'And after that, the plus-100s?'

'At some point, definitely. No one younger than that. Over time, the whole concept of chronological age will become redundant.'

So that was the limit then, a hundred. And then age becoming redundant.

'It's amazing, Harvey, what you've managed to achieve in the space of a few months. But rumours about Lextar are running riot. We need to build trust in other ways too.'

She was on thin ice with this negative remark, sugared though it was with flattery and the suggestion that she was onside. He leant forward, arms crossed on the table.

'Georgina is misleading you, Isabel. She was very persuasive but she left out a crucial element, something in Lextar's goals that she doesn't like and you deserve to know.'

Isabel locked into his gaze and waited for the dramatic pause to end.

'We're aiming for what we call OP, that's optimal population. Genetic programming for longevity is close to tipping point, where young people and babies will have the potential to reset their biological clocks and switch the cellular ageing process on and off, so maturing at their own preferred rate, or as decided by societal norms. It has to be guided, managed carefully to keep everything in balance. Lextar is changing the rules of the game.'

Self-regard and missionary zeal: these were the traits that had pushed him to reveal his cards. She clamped her hands between her knees to stop them from shaking. Lextar had its grand design and the established residents were at the sharp end. They could expect to get their notice when the time came: one hundred and you're eased out.

'Thank you, Harvey. I appreciate you being candid with me, although I'll need more explanation from you and Georgina. Tell me, are you really head of Lextar, CEO – is that it?'

'No, no, it's not set up like that. Georgina believes she met the top executives when she was appointed, but it was a front operation; they were all actors.'

Isabel did a double take. 'Okay. Who is it then, if not you?'

He tapped the side of his nose, reverting to his familiar teasing mode.

'Too many questions – you will be first to know. Right now, I'm hoping you'll buy me a triple-scoop ice cream, like you did for Marina. And talk of the devil, look who's back.'

Marina came running up. 'You have to try it, Isabel. It's sooo good! I'm sooo dizzy!'

'I'll head off then,' said Harvey. 'We can save my ice cream for next time. Hazelnut.'

'I won't forget,' replied Isabel.

Marina was fidgety. 'Can we go and see the animals next, Isabel? Your naked mole rats and Paul's fat old tortoise, Gina.'

Isabel realised she hadn't casually mentioned Trish, as she'd intended, wanting to gauge Harvey's response. Still, it was well worth it, considering what else she had found out. Cyril would have to wait for his next lesson in love, self-delusion and betrayal.

Marina skipped beside her as they passed the sand-coloured domes on their way to the menagerie. Once inside, they headed for the naked mole rats in their desert landscape. Turning the final corner, Isabel grabbed the collar of Marina's T-shirt to hold her back.

'Wait a moment. See that man looking into the mole rat pen? That's my friend Finn. I don't want to scare him off, so let's see if we can creep up without him noticing.'

They advanced stealthily, keeping close to the wall even though they would still be in Finn's direct line of sight, if he happened to turn his head. He seemed too absorbed for that, peering into the complicated system of burrows and making voice notes into his palmleaf. He flinched when Isabel touched his arm and Marina triumphantly clapped her hands.

'Hello, Finn. Where have you been all this time? I've missed you.'

'Isabel, hi. Yeah, I've... I've been feeling... I needed space to get over, you know...'

'The accident, you mean; what happened to Glen?'

He looked down, shifty as they come. He couldn't bring himself to say "accident", because he knew that she knew it was a whopping great lie. And she had to let him off.

'Okay, what are you doing in here now, Finn? Oh, this is Marina, by the way.'

Marina's face was squashed against the glass as she counted the elusive mole rats.

He stuttered in reply. 'I find the menagerie... it's restful, gives me peace of mind.'

He was having her on. Whatever he was here for, it wasn't peace of mind.

'Sorry to disturb you then, but I must warn you, if you're not already aware. There's a cholera outbreak in the nearby Fringes. Your family aren't living there, I know, but it could be spreading to other settlements.'

'Cholera? What is it?'

'What is cholera? It's a grisly gut disease that takes hold in unsanitary conditions, in contaminated food and water. It's often fatal and one of Stefan's friends has already died of it. He's there now with Sarita, her son and husband are both sick. Are your family okay?'

'Yeah… I think they are.'

'That's good. I wanted to say that I can bring your two sisters to Wellowfern earlier, like next week. Children and teenagers are accepted now, actively welcomed. Iris and Maya can go to school in the smart city and they'll be perfectly placed to get into the university.'

While Finn gawped dumbly, Isabel allowed herself to feel amused, despite the grim context to her hastily devised seduction plan to win him back, restore him to his position as her protégé. And it wasn't even primarily about her; he needed protection and his young sisters needed help. The plan was surely unbeatable, better than anything Harvey or anyone else could offer him.

***

The time between delivery flights was getting shorter, due to the growing demand for the polypills. Running along the path behind Josh, who had the advantage of not having to duck under branches, Finn was thinking about Isabel's offer. The cholera outbreak hadn't reached his home town, but the threat was real and the population had no resources to fend it off or fight it. Everyone agreed that Iris and Maya should come to stay with him at Wellowfern and they were both thrilled, although the mood was tempered by knowing that the rest of the family depended on his sisters' strength and optimism to get through each day. He couldn't afford to beat himself up about it, though; it was what he had been dreaming of ever since his arrival. And being thrown together with Josh, as he now was, he could keep an eye on him and figure out if he was talking bullshit about stirring up a revolution. Once the girls were here, that particular scenario could shatter all his dreams.

As they stepped onto the elevator platform, he was aware of Josh sizing him up, as if still unsure about him – which, to be fair, was reasonable. It was something he could play on, keeping Josh guessing while giving him enough to gain some degree of trust.

'I'll take you down the white tunnel today, Finn, before we do the consignment pick-up. I've put the delivery back an hour to give us time.'

Finn drew breath slowly, calming himself. Presumably there was some kind of secret factory down there, a lab producing the polypills. It had always been covert and Glen would have had to base it away from the main labs at the Institute.

'Any special reason, or just to show me where it leads? It's the polypill factory, is it?'

'Yeah, but more than that. There's a new lab, fitted out by Georgina for her latest research. The work you're doing in the menagerie, observing the young animals, that's part of it. You'll learn more when we meet Shani. She asked me to come down this morning, so it fits in well. You two are friends, aren't you?'

'With Shani?… Yes, we are. I didn't know she was out here. She's got her own office and state-of-the-art labs at the Institute, now she's heading up the trials.'

'I guess she works at both sites.' They had arrived at the end of the passage, where the containers were stacked ready. 'Good, we'll collect them when we come back.'

It was almost three weeks since Finn had last talked to Shani, that time he'd lost his rag and flounced off. Now he was forced to meet her with Josh, who clearly had no idea of the significance and what's more, seemed casual about it himself. Perhaps it had blown over between Josh and Shani, if it hadn't been a figment of Finn's imagination from the start.

The tunnel appeared to be well established, its white wall tiles yellowing around the edges. After a hundred metres or so, it split into two forks and they took the left, which led to swing doors and the underground lab. Shani looked up and smiled, betraying surprise at the sight of Finn but no more than that. She was standing at the bench in traditional style, white lab coat and protective goggles. There were other workers in the room but they were preoccupied with their tasks and hardly gave Finn and Josh a glance. Shani took off the goggles, leaving a cruelly deep indent around her eyes. The eyelashes were every bit as long and beautiful as in his memory. Like the moment that held so much promise, when they sat together for Georgina's first lecture and went on to the art deco café…

'Thanks for coming in, Josh. And Finn, I know you're doing work for us now, for Josh and Georgina.' She was speaking fast and keeping her voice low. 'We'll talk here because it's the safest place, staying in plain sight. If

Georgina arrives, you're giving me feedback on how the new creatures are settling in with their relatives, okay?'

Finn itched to offer insights from the hours he had spent observing in the menagerie, but this wasn't the moment. He would have to yield to Josh, who presumably grasped the bigger picture.

'Great to see you again, Shani. I couldn't safely make contact while I was banned and Glen was after me. I didn't want to implicate you – just needed to get that out the way first.'

Shani nodded, keeping neutral. 'I understand, Josh. It's been difficult for you and I've been wondering… You even popped up in one of my virtual rowing sessions, standing on a bridge and spurring me on.' She flicked her head, as if jolting herself back to the present. 'Anyway, when Georgina decided to set up these animal experiments, I understood they were about developing our cybird model, new methods of digital enhancement. I thought she wanted to test it on species with regeneration abilities, extreme longevity and unusual intelligence. It confused me as she always emphasises biological enhancement, but I wasn't involved at first. It was the changes in the human trials that bothered me more, ditching the ethics set-up.'

Josh had hoisted himself onto the lab bench while she was speaking. Now he sat up there, his legs spread wide and heels kicking back on the cupboard doors with soft thumps. Shani, by contrast, paced up and down, obviously disturbed by what she was reporting. The cocky bastard had zero empathy, that was clear. Finn nodded supportively, waiting for Shani to collect her thoughts and continue.

'Georgina said she had taken you on, Josh. That's why I thought it linked to cybirds.'

'Fair assumption.'

'She quizzed me about you and said she needed your knowledge and skills to design her trial. Except it's not about the cybird model and digital enhancement.'

'That's right,' said Josh. 'This is Georgina we're talking about. She's not into AI and digital programming if she can avoid it. The project is about animal hybrids, all organic. I said it wasn't my area but she still wanted me in on it for the design and data analysis.'

Finn was losing the drift. 'Hold on, what are you saying, exactly? We've had animal hybrids for a long time. What's different with this?'

Dumb question, probably, but Shani didn't seem to think so.

'You're right, the beginnings of modern human-animal hybrids go back to pre-2020. When I was eleven or twelve, I had a ghoulish interest in it. Human stem cells were injected into the embryo of an animal, the idea being to grow organs for transplant to humans, with a low risk of rejection. That provided the initial legitimacy, and of course we don't need the organ incubators now. Georgina's aim is radically different. She wants to use gene editing to transfer desirable traits from animals to humans, the key traits relating to our work like I said – regeneration, longevity and distinctive forms of intelligence. These experiments between different animal species are the first phase. It's reckless and unjustified, I believe.'

Josh was hunched forward on the bench now, listening intently. 'Holy shit, I had no idea that was... is the plan.

She asked me to collect named specimens from the menagerie and design a study to measure and monitor the organic and behavioural changes once they were put back in the pens, basically set up the data tools. She suggested I could do it for a PhD but I've got bigger ideas. It would be overtaken by events.'

'Ah, that explains it.' Shani looked first at Josh and then Finn. 'I need support on this. Are you willing to help me?'

Finn was already deeply involved too, he wanted to remind them. He was spending his free time helping Josh in the menagerie and now wasn't getting any acknowledgement or credit for it. He would at least get in first with his response.

'What do you want us to do, Shani?'

'I want the initial animal trial to fail, so we don't get as far as animal to human stage. At the minimum I want it slowed down, so the ramifications can be worked through. We can do it in various ways, I'm open to discussion, but if we three can put our heads together… What do you think – are you in?'

'I'm in,' said Finn. 'I trust your judgement, Shani.'

'Yeah, me too,' offered Josh, swinging himself off the bench. 'And we can stop this trial altogether if it comes to it – which it probably will. Georgina should have learned a hard lesson about overstepping the mark, after Glen's downfall.'

Shani sighed, clearly relieved to share her anxiety. 'Thanks, both. Now go, quickly.'

Jogging down the tunnel, Finn allowed himself to feel a little hopeful. If anything was going on between Shani and Josh, they were good at hiding it, and any scraps of evidence could easily be misread. He just might still be in the game. Now he had to prove his worth and focus on getting answers to his other questions.

'Where's Glen then, Josh?'

'I'll show you. It won't take a minute.'

They reached the fork in the passage and turned back down the other tunnel. The end doors were immediately visible and when they got there, they could look through clear panes into the polypill factory. Glen was sitting at a desk, side on to them and with his head down: the same position as he had adopted in the open-plan office, avoiding eye contact with anyone who might presume to pass too close. Here, though, all the other workers in the room were humanoid robots, so his disdain would be lost on them.

'Does he live down here?'

'Must do. He can't be let out, can he, after his tragic and fatal car accident? Not the right kind of immortality. Maybe he beds down in some nearby cell, with enough space to contain a disaffected, high-value prisoner. This door's locked and if you exit the factory on the other side, you come up against a wall of rock, with the arches bricked in. There is a way through, apparently, but I couldn't find it.'

'What's behind the rock wall?'

'Dunno – more tunnels, I guess, either open or derelict. There's one running all the way to the manor house that's still in use.' He tapped Finn on the shoulder. 'Come on, man, move it or we'll be late for the rendezvous with our band of loyal customers.'

He began running backwards, waiting for Finn to

take up the invitation to race and jostle along the passage until they reached the stack of pill containers. The task of heaving and trundling the bulky load to ground level and along the twisty path into the Wellowbug was physically all-consuming, but it enabled Finn to concentrate his mind. Once they were up in the air, however, it was Josh who initiated the conversation.

'They're good, these polypills. You can take them in any combination or in sequence and I've tried four of them these past six weeks – Cogs, Emos, Bods and Highs. I guess you should test them singly first, to see the effects of each one, but this way works for me. I'd be too impatient to follow the rules in clinical trials. How about you – tried them all yet?'

'Just one, the Bods. I used to be a personal trainer but I've been lax about my own training now it's no longer my job. It's only been four weeks since I started on the polypill but it's improving my muscle tone and stamina, no question. I'll try the Emos next, if only to keep up with Isabel. She's really flying, loving it.'

'We'll have to protect polypill production and supply when the time comes.'

'Look, Josh, you mustn't bring Shani into your plan. What she's trying to do and what we just signed up for, it's not the same as what you're aiming for, the revolution.'

'We're heading in the same direction, Finn. Shani and the twins will be great allies.'

'And the cybirds?'

'On standby. It's crucial to have an agile air force. They'll play their part, you'll see.'

The delivery was as eerily smooth as ever, hardly

a word exchanged. After parking the Wellowbug, Josh suggested lunch in the treehouse. They stepped on the elevator and rose through the floor, where they found Harvey waiting for them. He remained sitting, one arm spread along the back of the sofa and the other hand in his lap, half curled around the butt of his gun. Even Josh was immobilised and as the agonising seconds ticked by, Finn felt his skin grow unbearably hot, like it was peeling off under the excoriating glare. There was no Glen to shield him this time: he was the target. And Josh was silent, so he had to speak.

'Harvey, we—'

'What do you two dickheads think you're playing at? I saw you prowling around in the menagerie, Finn, watching and scooping up those critters, and I can access all the data, Josh. Why have you let Georgina drag you into this inter-species crap? It's a flimsy, fatuous, futile project. You're working for me and for Lextar now, both of you. No distractions, side hustles or personal vanity projects, do you understand?... I said, Do... You... Un-der-stand?'

Eighteen

They travelled to the manor house by looptrain, as Isabel didn't want to draw attention to their group departure by using air taxis. She was ignoring Harvey's request to contact him before taking Suzanne to visit Esther in the care home, preferring to arrive unannounced in the early evening, so they could look round for themselves and perhaps talk to a member of staff. Both Paul and Cyril had location tabs on Harvey now and she knew he had come home to his apartment at five-thirty, so hopefully that gave her a clear run.

As she had expected, the iron gates at the end of the driveway were fixed open as the five of them approached on foot along the lane. The Foundation – now Lextar – owned all the surrounding ancient woodland, and no doubt guards were patrolling discreetly on the perimeter. The driveway curved in a long S-bend and was bounded by dizzyingly tall conifers planted in the eighteenth century to accentuate the imposing grandeur of the house. It was certainly an impressive sight, with its tall chimneys and the full red sun poised to sink below the exact mid-point of the roof.

'I know this place,' said Suzanne, stopping so suddenly they all bunched up and Paul had to put his arm out to stop Johnny tripping over. 'It's Trellingham Hall!'

'It's Trellingham Hall!' shouted Marina, catching on to Suzanne's astonishment and performing two perfect cartwheels on the grass.

Isabel touched Suzanne's elbow. 'You know it from before Wellowfern?'

'Yes, from childhood. Our families were connected. I'm not sure how but there were kids the same age as us. We loved it here, all the exploring, although the children were stuck-up brats.'

Johnny laughed. 'Well, you can't have everything – and you could quickly lose brats in a place like this. I thought you were about to say you knew it from a previous life.'

'Feels like that, it was so long ago. I can't remember much about it and I've no idea what happened to them. I need a Junitsu session to jog my memory.'

'Great idea, Suzanne,' said Isabel, making a mental note. 'Let's go in and see Esther.'

The heavy front door was closed but unlocked and the huge entrance hall deserted. Isabel warned them about the several flights of stairs and led them up to the attic, allowing landing stops to let them catch their breath and admire the decor.

'There they are! The tenth duke and duchess with their brood.' Suzanne pointed to a family portrait hanging a little way down the corridor. 'They can't have been that important in the line, not getting pride of place on the staircase.'

They had to ascend the final stairs in single file, giving Isabel a few precious seconds to register the scene as she waited for everyone to assemble at the top. The entire space was empty: no smiling receptionist to greet them, no care staff passing by with residents on their arm and no clatter, no sound at all. And no pot plants or beautiful flowers; all gone.

'Where is everyone?' said Johnny. He cupped his hands round his mouth: 'Yoo-hoo! Is there anybody there?'

'Yoo-hoo!' echoed Marina, copying his action. 'Watch out, we're coming to find you-hoo!' Johnny gave her a playful swipe but she easily dodged him.

'Where's Esther, Isabel? Which way, down here?' Suzanne made a move towards the nearest door on the left.

'No, this side. Come on.'

Isabel knew that Esther's room was the third one along. She also knew that Esther wouldn't be there, that the bed would be neatly made and the room cleared of all props. Harvey's words had come back to her; his story about Georgina supposedly meeting senior Lextar executives: '*They were all actors.*' Not Esther, though. She'd been real, but doped up.

'It must be the wrong room. Is it the next one?' pleaded Suzanne, while Johnny led Marina over to the full-length window.

'I'll check out all the rooms,' said Paul, and Isabel nodded gratefully.

It wasn't just Esther; they were both aware of that. The other residents were missing too, the plus-120s who had been persuaded or bullied into moving out of their apartments. The clever cover-up was over, as far as Isabel was concerned. There was no excusing this, whatever it turned out to be, and she wasn't going to shelter her friends from the truth.

'Listen, Suzanne. And you too, Johnny – no, Marina, be quiet, just pipe down. There's no one here, as you can see, and I believe it was all an elaborate hoax, this care home that Harvey showed me and Shani the other day. Esther was lying in bed but she was in a dream state, and I saw a few other people that I assumed were residents but I didn't recognise any of them. I've simply no clue where Esther is, or the others, but we're going to find them and we're going to get them out.'

DJ Johnny raised his fist. 'You bet we are! They think they can make fools of us, but they forget they've been building us up all these years, telling us we're so special, we can go on forever. You don't do that to people, and sharpen their minds on top, and then expect them to roll over and lick your hand when you put their friends down like unwanted pets.'

Suzanne shuddered, then closed her eyes and began to whisper.

'The house is quiet. The birds are soaring but the passage will be long and perilous.'

Isabel knew that Johnny had faith in Suzanne's extrasensory powers, but she didn't deal in riddles, especially at a time like this. At least they might get out of the house without being ambushed if she could take that part of her pronouncement literally. And Suzanne played here as a child; she had to wake her from her trance. She pushed her hand hard against Suzanne's shoulder, too roughly but at least it worked, jerking her eyes open.

'Stay with us, Suzanne, please. We need to find Esther. Let's assume they're nearby, within the grounds or in the woods. Can you think of hiding places, Suzanne, like a cottage or boathouse or… no, not the treehouse, it's too small and it's too well known now.'

Suzanne moved to the window, prompting Marina to dash in the other direction and stand sentinel beside Isabel, ready for action. Two minutes went by while they all waited for Suzanne's response, her recollection of long-submerged events.

'The treehouse, yes, how did I forget? You couldn't climb the tree, it was too high, so there was a funny, creaky lift thing to take you up. We were forbidden to explore the underground caves and the other kids were horrible little snitches, so we didn't ever do it. We'd already bribed them to take us down the secret stairs, along the passage… it's coming back to me. You'd never find it without knowing. I can show you, if it's still there.'

She led them down to the entrance hall and along the corridor leading to the library. As Suzanne's hand went up to feel the wood panelling, Isabel realised it was the entrance to the ancestral room, where Georgina had sought to lure her into a charmed inner circle with Harvey and Shani. She was befuddled back then, and even more so now. Was Georgina in league with Harvey on the residents' disappearance and the fake care home, or had Harvey gone rogue and duped Georgina as well? Who was the puppet master?

She watched the amazement on the others' faces as the wood panelling slid apart to reveal the anteroom and the family room beyond it. Suzanne was in her element now, back to her ten-year-old self and urging Marina forward with her.

'Yes! This is the place. There was a mangy old parrot, that's right.' She touched the birdcage, which began to swing erratically on its base. 'Now, this battle picture – we have to remove it. I can't remember if it lifts or slides. Let's try and lift it.'

'Bloody ridiculous battles,' remarked Johnny, as he got a weak grip on the low corner of the old painting and found his face close up against a heap of dead and flailing horses.

After a couple of failed efforts at lifting it off, Paul discovered a concealed lever and the picture slid sideways, exposing a wide arch and a straight flight of wooden steps, with an elevator platform alongside. It looked newly constructed, the steps pale and unvarnished.

'Stand back,' ordered Isabel, as they all naturally leaned forward into the opening.

She lowered her voice. 'We need an advance party. That's me, Paul and Suzanne.'

'And me,' said Marina urgently, clearly frightened at the thought of being left.

'Okay, you're with us. Now, this is the position. We don't know who or what is down there but we've no one else to call on, so we have to take the risk and investigate. Johnny, you keep watch this end, so we're alerted if anyone comes into the house. Our signals may not work down below, but we'll do our best to stay in contact.'

Twenty-eight steps; easy-going steps, but that was fairly deep. Marina was happy to take Paul's hand, having made friends with him over favourite animals, so Isabel was free to talk to Suzanne, keep up the effort to stimulate her memory.

'Here we are. Two tunnels in front of us. Do you remember it like this?'

'I think… it's different, yes. This is the same tunnel, this left one. It went to the treehouse but the passage wasn't lit then and we all held hands, making spooky noises to mask our fear. But this other passage, that wasn't here.'

'Yes, I can see it's relatively new and it's tiled all round, look. We'll go that way.'

There were no breaks in the tiles, as far as Isabel could see; no turnings to shelter them once they were committed to exploring the tunnel. Was this the perilous passage mentioned in Suzanne's cryptic warning? She beckoned Paul and Marina closer and they set off, stopping every twenty paces to listen for sounds. Nothing. Dead quiet. And again, stop; nothing. Her creepy carnival dream came back to her, the swirling three-headed dragon and the heedless crowd dancing behind, the lack of forewarning.

'Is this a hospital?' whispered Marina. 'I don't like it.'

'Maybe. That's what we're going to find out,' answered Paul.

A figure materialised at the far end; a tall man, walking towards them at first, then turning back and doing a full circle, so he was coming nearer again with each hurried step. It was Finn. Isabel stopped still and then held out her hand as he came close. She could tell he was in distress, although he was trying to hide it. Well, enough of that; she opened her arms and gave him an embracing hug. His body was shaking and his clothes smelled musty.

Finn yanked himself away. 'Isabel, everyone, it's not safe. What are you doing here?'

'What we always do, looking for Esther,' said Suzanne. 'She's vanished from upstairs and so have all the other residents. Do you know where they are?'

Finn looked down and mumbled inaudibly, then raised his eyes to gaze anxiously at Isabel. He was unshaven, dirty and without his faithful hat to protect him, or to twiddle with while he prevaricated. Except he wasn't going to get away with it this time.

'Look, it's best if Finn and I talk on our own. We'll follow you up to the family room.'

Isabel waited, looking Finn up and down and silently imploring him to explain.

'Sorry, Isabel. It's been a shit… a difficult day.'

Isabel knew she only had a few minutes, as Suzanne would get impatient and fretful.

'You must level with me, Finn, be truthful. If you can't do that, whatever the reason, I'll take back what I promised, smoothing the way for your sisters to come to Wellowfern and move in with you. It's not finalised yet and I need to know who it is I'm sponsoring, who you really are and what you're made of.'

'I'm so sorry, you did warn me but I got pulled in and it was impossible—'

'Forget that, it's accepted; stay calm. I'll get you out of this. Where have you been just now – what's down there, round the next corner?'

'There's an underground lab and… living space, and the residents are in secret trials. It's called the Star programme and—'

'What is it, Star? Harvey mentioned Star clients and it sounded sinister at the time.'

'It is sinister. Star stands for "Series Testing for Adverse Reactions". It's a set of high-risk trials and we've had several fatalities already, but Harvey sees it as all in a day's work, no big problem. It suits him to kill them off anyway, they're too old. If it advances science at the same time, that's a cover for him, a bonus even. It's useful to keep Georgina happy.'

'O-kay.' Would Georgina knowingly sanction this type of research trial, with repeated fatal outcomes? 'What conditions are they in, living conditions, the ones that are still alive?'

'That's just it, Isabel. Esther… she died this morning, just slipped away. There are no doctors, so I don't know what it was in the end. And the living conditions are very cramped, like prison cells with sofas and curtains. They're guarded, I can't show you. I'm reduced to being a patient escort right now, accompanying the residents. And my other job—'

'Okay, I definitely do want to know about your other job but Suzanne's waiting. You shoot off and I'll break the news about Esther. You're certain, are you, that she's dead?'

'I helped carry her body out.'

'We need to talk more, as soon as possible. Can you get away tomorrow?'

'Yeah, I'll let you know. And please, Isabel, I realise I've mucked up. Please don't…'

'Go on, cowboy, up the stairs and home. Stay cool, act natural, note every last detail. And please, for God's sake, find your hat, will you? I'm not used to seeing you without it.'

And you look hopelessly bereft, she added to herself.

She was alone in the passage, free to go forward or to turn back and join her friends. She didn't have enough evidence yet, just the clever illusion of the care home and hearsay from Finn about unethical trials, mistreated captives and Esther's death. If Georgina was mixed up in it, Isabel didn't even know where to go with the evidence once she had it. This could rip the whole of Wellowfern apart, taking her own hopes and dreams down with it. It felt like a pivotal moment, like that time with Jerome, when they were a couple of fugitives gazing across the roofs, domes and spires of a great city from the top of the high bell tower. The wall was low in places, low enough to push someone off the edge if you applied enough force in just the right place, combined with the element of surprise. Jerome was so close, so unaware that he put his arm around her at that instant, and the impulse was lost.

She opened her eyes and he was there, at the end of the passage: Harvey. He walked forward, in slow motion as it seemed to Isabel, and she waited, standing her ground. When he stopped, ten metres from her, neither of them said a word or made a sign. The stare was a mutual challenge, each daring the other to react. She held it until Harvey offered a half-smile, more of a smirk. She backed away, step by step, aware that this wasn't the moment.

***

Paul stood in the bedroom doorway, listening to Isabel's perfect reading voice and enjoying Marina's fast-changing expressions as she followed the twists and turns of the plot. It was an adventure story about a pack of wolves; a well-thumbed old paperback that Marina had picked out from Isabel's collection.

'That's the end of the chapter. Now, lie down, it's time to sleep.'

'One more, please!' Isabel shook her head, closing the book. 'Paul, then. Can he read me one more chapter?'

'No, come on. Paul might read to you another night, if you're nice to him. Now, stop squirming and lie quiet. It's way past bedtime.'

She waited until Marina was still and leaned over to give her a goodnight kiss, before creeping towards the door. Paul murmured 'good night' and moved back to give her space.

'Isabel?'

'Yes, what is it? Last question.'

'Is Mummy dead?'

'No, sweetie, she's not. Your mummy's gone to be with Daddy and Lorenzo because they're not well. She'll be back soon.'

Paul shut his eyes. He had heard from Stefan earlier and the report wasn't good; the cholera had taken hold and essential supplies were running out. Just as it reached this crisis point, when Wellowfern should be using its resources to help its neighbours, it had turned its back and begun some kind of civil war, forgetting about the Fringes. And naturally Marina would be worried about death and dying; she was at the manor house with Suzanne and the others when Isabel told them the shattering news about Esther.

'Is Lorenzo going to die?'

'Sweetie, I can't say. Sometimes you just don't know what's exactly going to happen, but one thing I do know is that mummy will be strong for them, they'll be happy she's there. And we have to be strong too, as much as we can. Like the brave wolves in the story.'

'Okay... I'll go to sleep now.' She pulled her flop-eared bunny closer and curled up.

Isabel gestured Paul up to the roof garden but he stayed put and watched her walk through the living room onto the balcony, returning with Cyril. Paul's mother had died when he was six but nobody told him why, what she died of. He remembered his auntie scrubbing his grubby knees for the funeral, that was all. He had to be spick and span, she said.

Isabel tiptoed across to the bed. 'Keep an eye on Marina, please, Cyril. She's probably fine but if she wakes up feeling sad, I'll be on the roof terrace.'

Cyril saw his chance. 'Shall I try first, if she wants to talk or she needs comforting?'

'Yes, why not? It's all good practice and Marina loves you.'

When they emerged onto the roof with their fruit cocktails, Paul saw moving shapes at the other end of the terrace but he couldn't make them out in the deceptive play of light and dark. Isabel tipped her head in the same direction, pulling a face as she did so.

'It's Trish, she's with Harvey. Oh God, that's all we need.'

'I think they're aware of us.'

'Do you want to go back in then, Paul?'

'No, why should we? This is our space as well and it's your space this end, Isabel. We're far enough away to talk without them listening in.'

'Fine with me.'

Retreating had been Paul's first thought as well, but he was tired of shilly-shallying around and needed a resolution to his dilemma. It was weighing him down the whole time, leaving no mental space to deal rationally with the other pressing issues. Watching Marina just now had jolted him, reminded him of what else was close to his heart.

'I have to leave Wellowfern, Isabel.'

'Don't be crazy. Why should you get pushed out by Trish?'

'No, it's not that. I've walked to the near Fringes and it's got a hold on me, probably because I grew up in a similar area. They need as much help as they can get to survive this cholera epidemic and I can be useful, working with Stefan. I've got all the practical skills and I can join in with thinking and logistical planning, if they want that.'

She heard him out, stirring the pieces of fruit around her glass with the straw. When she looked up and leaned towards him, he saw something new in her eyes: fear and panic.

'You can't leave, Paul, not yet. I get what you're saying but we need you too; I do. We have to figure out what the hell is going on and who's pulling the strings, or I believe we're all sunk. You're the only one I can absolutely rely on. Finn's flaky, though I'm reeling him in. Trish, I hate to say it and I adore her, but she's untrustworthy right now. And as for Johnny, Suzanne – they're liabilities, in their own inimitable ways.'

'There's Shani, don't forget her, and the Junitsu twins. Shani's working on a different angle, to do with Georgina's new animal research. It's delicate and I didn't want to overload you with it, Isabel, that's why—'

'Shani? Ah, she's mystifying. One minute she seems gung-ho with Georgina's plans and being part of the exclusive inner circle, and the next, she's giving off the exact opposite, like she's disaffected. She's got a problem with the lack of ethical approval, that's for sure. And she did back me up against Georgina on not invading our inner mind space.'

'Yes, she switches position – trying to sort it out in her head, like we all are. I'll tell you, though, disaffection is winning. And she gave me the name of that young man who was in the Wellowbug with Finn when Glen disappeared. It's Josh – you know, the rogue student they chucked out at the beginning of this.' He paused to gaze up at planet Venus, enjoying her few moments of unrivalled glory in the evening sky. 'Honestly, these feuds and spats over alternative utopian futures are so insane, when in the real world, people are—'

'Listen to yourself, Paul. These insane feuds have consequences. You can't possibly go now; a huge net is tightening over us and it's too late for anyone to escape. And also, have you really given up on Trish?'

He paused. 'No, not given up but the sands are shifting. Come on, let's go and speak to them. We may not have another chance like this.'

'Wait. I'll do it, but what about tactics? After today in the tunnel, what Finn said and… No, you're right; direct confrontation is the only way. Harvey's too skilled at evasion.'

'Agreed, then. We use our instincts and play it by ear. I don't intend it to get physical but if it does, it would give me enormous pleasure to sock him one.'

They crossed the roof terrace speedily, giving the other two no time to slip away. Harvey half stood to greet them.

'Hi, saw you over there. Come, sit and join us. I'll fetch more wine glasses.'

'No need,' said Paul. 'We're on strong fruit juice tonight and we won't stay long.'

He'd have preferred to remain standing but Isabel had sat down next to Trish, so he pointedly walked round the nearest chair to position himself opposite Harvey. He wanted to avoid catching Trish's eye, in case it put him off his stride. He would fix steadily on Harvey and let Isabel speak first.

'We went to the care facility today, to see Esther.'

Harvey set down his glass. The shadows made it difficult to read his expression, even at this short distance.

'Ah, I was meaning to tell you in the morning. Esther died today, very peacefully.'

'She wasn't there… and nor was anyone else. The care facility itself wasn't there.'

'It is, but it's… temporarily closed for installation of extra fixtures and fittings.'

'Suzanne used to play in that manor house as a child. She knew about the tunnels and the secret way in through the family room.'

Paul stole a sideways glance at Trish, who was staring at Isabel, completely riveted.

'And guess what? We met Finn strolling around down there and he told us about the Star programme, what it stands for, and that our missing residents are kept locked in cells down the tunnel when they're not in the lab undergoing forced experiments. Are you going to come clean now, Harvey, about Lextar and what you're plotting?'

'Isabel, you've no right. You're just—'

'Just what? Just another troublesome old person waiting to be eliminated when she hits a hundred? You've got an awful long time to contend with me before that date. And even then, you'll find I'm the hardy kind of cactus that never dies, or wilts, however determined you are to overwater it.'

'Ha-ha, that's good. No, I mean you're just jumping to conclusions. Finn is unreliable and he understands nothing about Lextar's true purpose, the vision behind it.'

Isabel threw up her hands and opened her mouth in a mock display of revelation.

'Go on then, tell us about the vision, the true purpose,' said Paul.

'Tell us, Harvey,' added Trish. 'If you can explain, if it's a misunderstanding, then—'

Trish wasn't going to simply stick up for Harvey, then; that was a positive signal. And Paul could tell she wasn't bluffing. She was also ignorant of the truth, waiting for an honest explanation. Harvey pressed his hands together with an air of relish and looked round at his avid listeners like a tutor running a popular seminar.

'All right. I've already mentioned Lextar's end goal to Isabel: it's optimal population, OP for short. We've reached the stage where the biological clock can be reset at any time of life and babies can be precisely edited for longevity, rejuvenation and age acceleration. Juno and Itsuki are exemplars, plus you are already aware of their exceptional intelligence and creativity. I brought them to Wellowfern as inspiring models for the future, to demonstrate an alternative mission. Georgina loved it at first, but then she saw it threatened her work on extended lifespan, the well-worn model of record-breaking, supremely gifted older people that she wants to present to the world.'

Trish was shaking her head, baffled. 'But that's what the Foundation was about, why we gave up our former lives and came to Wellowfern. It's what fires me up.'

Isabel looked across at Paul, who raised his finger to show he wanted to speak.

'So, am I understanding it right, Harvey, that Lextar's not interested in spending its resources on restoring and refitting old models now it's designed the perfect young model primed to keep going indefinitely, with minimal maintenance?'

'Sounds like we'll be classic showroom exhibits, the last survivors of a bygone age, if we're lucky,' quipped Isabel.

Harvey ignored her. 'Wrong tone, Paul, but yes, that's about it. It explains why we have such a strong focus on enhancing people's end of life experiences, the positive vibe and the option of a euphoric death. It's what a lot of older people want, they love it.'

'Positive vibe?' Paul almost spat out the words. 'Sounds more like gentle genocide to me. Or not so gentle. It's a kind of perverted idealism, but then, that's often been the case, throughout history. Take our poor old friend Glen, he—'

'Yes, Glen,' said Trish. 'What actually happened to Glen, Harvey? Do you know?'

'Glen is alive and well. He's in charge of polypill production and working in a new lab. We had to take him out of circulation because his extracurricular activities were damaging Lextar's reputation.'

'Zeus – he's not actually dead then, like we've all been told?' Trish looked ferocious and Paul loved her all the more for it. 'You lied to me, Harvey, blatantly lied. That's not okay, resurrecting Glen as if it's nothing. And holding our oldest residents in burrows like captive moles, depriving them of the peachy "sunlit uplands" they paid for. And then Suzanne's best friend Esther goes and dies "very peacefully", so you tell us, but how do we know? It's just hideous, a nightmare. What right do you have, who said you could—'

'That's my next question, Harvey,' said Isabel. 'Who or what is Lextar?'

'And why does Lextar operate in the shadows, with no public presence?' added Paul. He sensed that Harvey's patience was fraying, his effort to stay upbeat losing force.

'Okay, listen. Lextar isn't a company in the traditional sense. There are no executives and no board members. It's directed by artificial intelligence, a deep self-learning programme with the single goal of achieving optimal population balance within an optimal timeframe. It aims to avoid major shocks and disorder, to build pioneering new societies as smoothly as possible. I'm a committed advocate for Lextar, that's my role. We have a network of advocates and agents in the select clusters and smart cities across the world. Call it idealistic, I can live with that. But perverted – that's wrong, I reject it. And if you'll all excuse me, I think I've done more than enough explaining for one evening.'

He stood up, waiting for Trish. She gave him a death

stare, her olive-green eyes now almost black. Harvey lifted his chin and swept them all with a dismissive downward glance.

'Good night, then. I hope you will reflect on it, before you rush to judgement. Think about my Juno and Itsuki, what they've contributed in the short time they've been here.'

He began to walk towards the steps, then swivelled round to face them again.

'Oh yes, Isabel, I forgot to say. I heard from Jerome, the business partner and lover you extorted that money from, so you could afford your swanky apartment. He asked after you. Still works in space insurance, still specialising in asteroids. They're in cahoots with the scientists now, raking it in before the public catch up on how easy it is, not just to deflect the rocky buggers but to reset their trajectory with pinpoint accuracy. He says thank you for introducing him to it – and to tell you he's happy, he's made good.'

Isabel turned to Paul. 'Do you still want to sock him one, or shall I?'

'Forget it,' said Paul, shaking his head. 'Piss off, mate. We've had enough.'

Harvey offered a little bow before leaving, as if concluding a polite conversation or like he had at least won the argument. Trish didn't even watch him go. She put her face in her hands, then peeked up through her fingers at Isabel.

'That was… fuck's sake, just the weirdest. If I'd known, if he'd been straight with me, I couldn't have possibly—'

Isabel shushed her. 'I'll turn in now, if that's okay. It's

mind-blowing and we need to act, but let's talk once we've slept on it. I have to let the AI bombshell sink in. And I should check on Marina. She's fine with Cyril but she'll wind him round her little finger.'

Paul chuckled. 'They've probably finished the next chapter of the wolf saga by now.'

Trish stood up to give Isabel a kiss and Paul breathed in deeply, unsure of his ground now that he and Trish were alone.

'Extortion, eh? Scamming the public and fleecing your key business partner – that's a new take on Isabel. Come to think of it, she's never been keen to join in our rambling group discussions about space and the universe, when you'd expect her to show off her expertise.'

'She did drop a hint to me about this Jerome thing,' said Trish. 'I just brushed it off. You need to play ruthless in business sometimes, to keep your edge.'

'Have to hand it to Harvey, he's got some panache. That was an impressively upbeat performance, given he was cornered. And I think he believes in this social engineering. It's something grand and virtuous to him, an abstract force for good, whereas we think of the effect on our friends first. Johnny and Suzanne are in the target age group, or not far off.'

'Panache! Bloody nerve, more like. It's the principle too, Paul. It goes against all our aspirations. He's out to destroy Wellowfern and the Institute, that's the ultimate logic.'

'I agree, although I heard what he said about avoiding shocks and disorder. It buys us time perhaps but his notion of a smooth transition is ludicrous, considering what's already taking place underground. He can gloss it all he likes, but the brute reality is inescapable, by Finn's account. And Finn didn't look in the mood to make things up.'

'He's probably petrified. It may surprise you, but I wouldn't trust this smarmy creep Harvey as far as I could throw him, not now this has come out. He was starting to get to me anyway, always so self-assured and smooth-talking. It's not my style... I mean, not what I go for. Oh hell, I'm tangled up here, help me out.'

Paul was amazed that they had got this far without a noticeable rise in tension. 'It's okay, I'm glad to be the opposite of Harvey, if that's what you're implying. Look, Trish, it's been hard since I moved out to Stefan's but it's given us time to think. I still love you madly but I don't know if we can live together. And with the cholera outbreak in the Fringes, I feel a strong pull to get stuck in and help Stefan and Sarita. I don't know if that fits...'

She tipped her head, giving him a wistful smile. 'It fits, sad though it is. My memory trial has provoked me to think deeply about the past, and how we reshape our own stories. I question myself all the time, like about why I left Matthew – and why so thoughtlessly, as if it wouldn't really affect him or his family, or anyone who loved us and believed in us. We planned to set up a fruit farm after closing the wildlife park. It might have worked, been useful, even fun. And now Matthew is dead and it feels so... unfinished. I just wish I could have explained it better, to him and everyone else. And I miss him terribly, it's mad but I do. When I heard he'd died and I wasn't there to comfort him, I just felt broken into pieces. I'm like three or four different people living in different time zones... Sorry, I'm babbling.'

Paul conjured up his cottage high on the edge of the moor: the bees, the hens and cherry blossom, his little bluebell spinney. He had set the friendly nanny goats free when he abandoned the place; maybe that was wrong and it would have been kinder to shoot them.

Trish felt across for his hand, touching the treasured gold band on his finger. 'And we invested too much in the experience of one amazing summer, when we were still teenagers. You needed to keep it perfect, like that water-skier didn't die either, they sent us a postcard. It was such a betrayal when I insisted on revising the facts after my memory session, I know that. And it wasn't just you. We both believed we could recreate it sixty years later, that the passion and romance would be reignited and blaze forever, regardless of history and all our life experience since... and Paul, this ring didn't belong to my grandfather. I made that up.'

'It's okay, it doesn't matter.' Paul moved to slip into the swing-chair beside her. He shut his eyes, cherishing the last warmth and familiarity of her body as they clung to each other in the dark, lost for words.

Nineteen

Shani was out early, warming up with Finn beside the running track before Trish and the other morning joggers arrived.

'Three laps or four?'

'Four's fine with me.' He bent down to adjust the fastening on his trainer. 'Then we can stroll along the river, nice and casual, and I'll fill you in on timings for tomorrow.'

They increased their pace with each lap, ending the fourth with a long sprint to the finish line. Shani halted within a few paces and bent forwards, her hands gripping her calves.

'That was good but I'm more unfit than I thought. And your legs are far too long! I've been focused on the rowing, that's my excuse.'

'Yeah, you said Josh was there, watching you from the bridge. Was it-…?'

She flicked her head, laughing it off. 'Oh, that was just one time. The last couple of sessions there was nobody, only ducks. It puts me off my stroke so I've blanked out all my friends, or strangers for that matter, who might be tempted to wander into my space.'

As they joined the river path, Finn shifted the mood.

'First thing to tell you is Harvey's on to us – me and

Josh, that is. After we left you in the lab and made our delivery, he was waiting in the treehouse and he gave us a bollocking for working with Georgina on the animal research. Very intimidating it was, and it's not the first time I've seen his nasty streak. He was just like that with Glen, when—'

'I can imagine. What's he going to do about it, did he say?' Perhaps Harvey could be her unwitting ally if he genuinely wanted to stop the animal studies.

'Not specifically. He was raging, making wild threats. And he had his...' Finn trailed off and shook his head. 'We could let him do our dirty work and destroy the underground lab but we can't risk bringing him into our confidence, if that's what you're thinking.'

'Hang on, that's not *my* plan at all, destroying the lab. My idea is to act like we're going ahead with the animal hybrid study and then make it fail. It's a longer game, more subtle. I'm talking a few months.'

'We haven't got months, Shani. It's war now between Georgina and Harvey, a battle for supremacy. It's what happens. In a hostile takeover, the bosses in the new regime will turn on each other once they've finished dealing with the old guard, the weak and the troublemakers. That's how Josh described it, although he must think it doesn't apply to true revolutionaries. He's attempting to convert me to his cause but I don't buy his kind of political philosophy.'

'Good, I'm glad. You've got too much to lose.'

How little Shani knew about Josh, the cute student she'd had lustful sex with – twice, was it? Three times? They hadn't discussed politics or philosophy in the snatched moments. They *had* talked about the cybirds and Glen's moonlighting, she recalled that. And rolling off the sofa together, that was exciting.

'Shani, are you listening? I think Josh is equally dangerous, with all his extreme ideas. And there's another factor in the mix; Isabel, naturally. She and her friends have discovered the care facility is a fake and the missing residents are locked in cells and taking part in high-risk trials against their will, once they're softened up and sedated. Esther has died, and she's not the only one. It's Harvey's doing and Georgina's incensed because it hijacks her goal of biological immortality.'

'Wow! I am not that surprised, after my peculiar visit to the so-called care home with Isabel… But if we wreck the lab, why won't Georgina set it up again in another tunnel?'

'It's a risk, but taking out the lab will smash a lot of specialised kit and it's not so easy to replace. And Georgina will be freaked out. She'll think she deserves to be protected by Lextar, but Lextar doesn't give a flying fig about her. My guess is she'll run, once she knows she's been played and left exposed, out on a limb.'

'What about Harvey? How will he react if we go through with it?'

'Hard to say. His cover's blown too and he's got Isabel on his case, but he's brazen enough to stand his ground, plus he's in league with Lextar so he must have some protection. There's also Josh, who claims he can take care of Harvey before the "big swoop", as he calls it. That's his cybird air force; they're on standby.'

Shani stopped dead and turned to him. 'Are we actually going to do this?'

'Yes, tomorrow. We have to save Wellowfern and if it

means relying on Josh and his guerrilla tactics, that's what I'll do. Iris and Maya are due to move in with me next week. I've never felt so committed to anything, even—'

'That's what I needed to hear, there's no choice; we have to act. And brilliant news about the girls coming, I'm very happy for you.'

'We'll win, I'm convinced of it,' said Finn, putting his arm around her shoulders and moving in a little closer when her fingers reached up for two seconds to pat his hand.

'I'm shit scared, Finn, but we can't have everything we've worked for demolished by a deluded bunch of megalomaniacs fighting it out between them.'

'Treehouse at seven in the morning then. I'll keep watch on it through the night.'

'Cool… See you there.'

This would be her last day in the underground lab if all went according to plan. It was surreal, knowing your workplace was about to be annihilated and being in on the plot – not just complicit, but as co-conspirator. As she showered in the gym, she ran through the items she had to rescue, the portable kit and of course her own precious data. And the animals, the few creatures they kept in the lab; most specimens were held in the other tunnel, next to the polypill factory. She adjusted the heat to end her shower with a prolonged icy burst, testing to see if she if she could beat her endurance record.

It was still early, so when a message from Juno came through on her palmleaf, she decided to make a quick detour via the neuro hub. It might be tricky, given that she had to keep Juno out of the drama and she didn't dare predict how it would end for Harvey, but it might be urgent and she couldn't ignore the request to drop by.

Juno was sitting on the pavement near the hub, leaning against an arcade pillar.

'Hey, just picked up your message. Are you okay?'

'Not really.' She pulled a kiddy sad face, lower lip pushed out.

Shani held out her hands to pull her up, the same gesture as Juno's when Shani was sitting dazed in the beanbag after her dreamscape experience.

'What is it, Juno? We can talk here, there's no one about.'

'Itsuki's in the hub with Suzanne. They're doing amazing work on her special powers and she gets up at dawn. That's another reason, it's vital work.'

'Another reason for what?'

'For staying here. Harvey has warned us that we might have to leave Wellowfern for our own safety. He was guarded but he implied that Georgina wanted us to submit to new experiments. It's not why we came here; we've had enough of that. We want to do our own creative enrichment stuff, that was the deal.'

'Quite right. You're perfect, the two of you.'

It might be a future phase of Georgina's secret programme. Or perhaps Harvey was blaming Georgina when it was actually Lextar that had wicked designs on the twins. Either way, she would lose Juno.

'Did Harvey give specific instructions? I know he's like an uncle to you but you called him a chameleon and said you felt oppressed, like he's using you.'

'No, he said to be ready, with a packed bag. He's

loomed over us forever. He made us feel we owe him and we'll always depend on him. And we're the exemplars so we have a responsibility; that's been drilled into us. But it's changed for me now. I want a normal life and I want to stay here… with you. I'm twenty-five and you're my best girlfriend, my second soulmate.' She made a silly face to hide her embarrassment. 'Come on, let's go in the hub.'

'Quickly then, as I must start work. You'll have to play for time if you and Itsuki are threatened. One of you get lost for a few hours, something like that.'

Getting lost at Wellowfern didn't seem a viable option, but it was the best she could offer in the moment. And she wanted to follow up on Juno's last comment about soulmates.

'Can we sit in the dreamscape chamber?'

As she settled down in the beanbag, the virtual daydream came back to her in all its vivid detail, as she had hoped: the rowing, Josh on the bridge, the hotel they passed up, the revelation about the alpha cybird, his rejection of her clumsy advances…

'You know you said nothing was captured from my daydream, there was no trace?'

'That's true.'

'And I told you afterwards that it worked in the way you intended, it was so neat.'

'Yes?' Juno's voice was wary now.

'Well, you also said it was a blend, that additional data might be inserted to increase authenticity. Did you add anything to influence my emotional reaction?'

'Why would I do that, Shani?' A coy smile.

'Why would you? To make me lose interest in that sexy boy Josh, that's why. And you'll be pleased to know it's succeeded. I've seen him since and my passion has dissipated.'

'You're entitled to be suspicious but the daydream is overlaid now, so who knows?'

No denial, then. She ought to be angry about this, or at least righteously indignant. Picking up a cushion, she aimed it at Juno, just as Itsuki burst into the room. He hesitated on seeing Shani, then turned excitedly to his twin.

'Suzanne's had a premonition. She went to the care home with Isabel to find her friend Esther. It stirred childhood memories of being tricked into humiliating games. Isabel led them to Esther's room but she was gone; held prisoner and killed off for being too old.'

Juno shuddered. 'Jeez, that's harsh. What was the premonition? Did you catch it?'

'Sure did. It came up as a video on our virtual wall, sound and everything. Don't say anything, Shani, we can't go public on this.'

'Understood. We don't know it *was* a premonition and research protocol has taken a big enough hit already.' She paused. 'Not thinking of you, Juno. If you did interfere with my daydream, you're let off as you did me a big favour. And now I have to run.'

She took an air taxi and was relieved to find no workers in the underground lab, so she could get on with collecting her stuff. Some items were in a cupboard under her bench and she was squatting when she heard the lab door open. It was Georgina, with Glen. The sound of his voice made her recoil, almost tipping her backwards. Georgina was enraged.

'...a menace from day one, following his own pet projects and using his influence with Lextar to undermine me. I tried to bring him on board, wasting a beautiful signet ring biotracker in the process, but he's way overstepped now. I feel duped and Harvey has to pay for it. That's where you come in, Glen.'

'What do you want from me, and what do I get for it?'

'Still your usual charming self, that's reassuring. First, you can tell me which polypills Harvey is taking. Second, I want you to replace the contents of one box by a duplicate pill with an added ingredient, one that will have an instant effect. I mean fatal, no loose ends.'

'With pleasure. Harvey's expecting a new supply tonight, as it happens.'

'Perfect. If this is a success and it's carried out cleanly, I'll immediately whisk you out of Wellowfern and guarantee you a place in another select cluster, no questions asked.'

Shani crouched lower on her aching legs. Cramp in her toes was shooting painfully down her foot. Georgina only had to walk round the end of the bench and she was done for.

'Agreed. Any health-based cluster will be acceptable. No double-crossing, Georgina.'

'I hardly think you're in a position to negotiate, but you have my word. Come on, I'll walk you down the tunnel to the pill factory and you can get on with it.'

***

311

It was the third time Isabel had been summoned to the Institute's wood-panelled office: first by Nathan, then Glen and now Georgina, along with Trish. Would it be AI Lextar next, and what kind of encounter would that be? Nathan had been more perceptive than she had imagined, with his early suspicion of the "ruthless logic" in Lextar's mission. He was a decent manager who failed to toe the line, maybe even took a moral stand. There would be fewer of these doomed, dismissed heroes in the optimal AI-controlled new world.

'Thank you both for coming. I'd like to say how much I appreciate your loyalty.'

Georgina had said this at the manor house only a few days ago but the exuberance was missing, the air of dominion. She looked strained, less sure of their loyalty.

'We're both happy with our research trials,' said Trish. 'The Junitsu twins are doing an excellent job and their virtual reality work is captivating.'

'Yes, Juno and Itsuki are central to my plan but they're too precious, not safe. You may know that Harvey was their guardian when they were children. He thinks he is entitled to exploit them in his personal project. If he's blocked, I fear he'll simply take them away.'

All about Harvey, no mention of Lextar. Georgina was either unaware that she was working for an AI-directed company or she was keeping it quiet. That would figure, given the implications. And if she was unaware, it showed Harvey's skill in diverting her by zeroing in on Glen and his illicit activities. And Harvey was guardian to the twins; that was dynamite.

'I won't let him take them but I need your support,'

Georgina continued, fixing her gaze on Isabel. 'We make a formidable team and Shani will be onside, given the choice of Harvey's abusive project or our professional research programme.'

A new inner circle of four, with Trish replacing Harvey. She might be given biotracker earrings soon and Isabel would have to keep up by wearing hers.

'We'll get behind you, Georgina, but we have some concerns. Firstly, I want to know why you allowed our residents to be put through high-risk trials and subjected to living in a phoney care home, or rather in the dungeons underneath?'

'I know you went out there and I wish I'd been more curious about the care home. I took it on trust, it was Harvey's initiative. And as for those trials, it's a fine balance but I felt the risks were worth taking; sometimes there's no ideal solution. They were volunteers and there were plenty of perks. I assure you I'll investigate it fully once I'm back in charge.'

Trish spoke up. 'But why are you taking the research into the realm of animal-human hybrids? That's cruel to the creatures and a threat to the future of humanity, as we know it.'

Georgina was momentarily flustered; she hadn't anticipated a challenge to her own secret project. 'It's a necessary stage but you're right, I've been over ambitious, not taking partners with me. It's an error but hopefully a forgivable one. We have more than enough work and I can pause that particular study at a stroke.'

It sounded glib and pseudo-apologetic, but it would have to do for now.

313

'That's good,' said Isabel. 'Now, what's your idea and how can we help?'

'Thank you, it won't be forgotten. My plan will be executed as discreetly as possible. You don't have to do anything now. I just need to know I can rely on you when we regain our stability and rebuild our unity of purpose. I don't want any equivocators or half-hearted supporters. They're as bad as outright opponents because you can never know which way they'll jump. The driving force is adherence to our dual mission: radically increased lifespan and sensitive biological enhancement.'

Here was the old Georgina back, rediscovering her mojo. Isabel was surprised at her willingness to own up to mistakes and doubted her sincerity. Maybe it was genuine, though; even Isabel was finding it easier to admit to her own errors and failures, if only in private to herself. God forbid that anyone else should reach into the depths of her mind and swirl around in the murk, picking out all the sharp and malicious bits.

After the meeting she took Trish to her balcony, which she now felt was a safe space to talk. Cyril was listening but she had come to see him as a close ally and trusted him not to put her in jeopardy.

'Do you think we've done enough?' said Trish. 'It's so frustrating to be told to wait, when it feels like we're all about to fall over a cliff.'

'Hopefully Georgina's plan, whatever it is, will put a brake on Harvey. The top-level power play is out of our control, we have to acknowledge that. And you never get the whole story. I'm not even sure how I want it to pan out, which result would be the least bad. Paul charged Harvey with perverted idealism and Georgina is in the same mould. Perhaps we're guilty of it too, with our fanciful ideas and skewed personal ambitions.'

'Fanciful? Skewed? Honestly, I never thought I'd hear you say that, Isabel.'

'I'm musing, don't take it as my last word. I'm keen on my social intelligence trial but it's not the most important thing in the world. And it's stimulated my natural responses.'

'What, you no longer need the trial?'

'No, I do, but the sessions are leaving a deep impression and I even like myself more these days, so hopefully I'll be motivated by that, once it's over.'

Trish leant forward. 'You think it's right for Paul to go out to the Fringes, don't you?'

'Yes, I do… What happened with you two after I left you on the terrace?'

'Ah, it was lovely, a gentle parting of the ways. Coming to Wellowfern together was a mistake. We are both pining for something else, even if we don't know what it is.'

'The story of our lives. It's restlessness that'll do for us humans in the end.'

'I'm worried about Paul walking into danger, facing cholera. And he's so useful to us here, turning the history gallery into an enthralling place to visit. It sounds trivial…'

'It's not trivial but he can't not go, that's where his… no, he has to go.'

Trish stood up and looked over the balcony rail. 'It's strangely quiet. And the domes are bright orange, like they're almost on fire.'

Then they saw the cybirds, a small flock rising into the sky above the glowing domes.

'Look, Isabel. Why are they doing that? Cybirds don't flock.'

'No idea, it's odd. Go, Cyril, find out what's up. Be as quick as you can.'

They watched him swoop down over the edge of the balcony and along the piazza, rising again as he reached the park. Then he was lost to view behind the trees.

'I'll make us a fruit cocktail.'

'Add some strong fortifiers, will you? We might need them.'

Twenty minutes later, Cyril hadn't returned and Isabel was unable to contact him.

'Where's that wretched bird? He's getting as bad as Finn. Give them an inch…'

'You don't mean it. You love how Cyril's engaging with you and little Marina.'

'Fair enough. I was against when Glen decided the birds would develop human-like emotions, but I have to say it was one of the good things he did, along with the polypills… Look, it's Suzanne and DJ Johnny.' She waved down at them. 'Hey, you two! Come on up.'

'One more thing, Isabel, quickly. It's what Harvey said about you and your business partner, Jerome was it? Was he winding you up, or were you really—'

'I went off the rails, okay? It was a long time ago.'

'We were naive perhaps, thinking this was going to be a quiet backwater, retirement living and all that. I wanted it both ways myself, the carousel and the rollercoaster. I guess it was the same with you, or had you had enough of scary rides? Did you and Jerome—?'

'Don't push me, Trish. I don't want to talk about it.'

Twenty

Isabel lay flat on her back on the sofa. She had dimmed the aquarium lights and requested late-night jazz at low volume, but she was still wide awake and worried. Cyril had never disappeared before and to stay out now, when she had asked him for urgent information on the cybird flocking, was incomprehensible. And there was Suzanne, so edgy and volatile, and now Harvey. Was he taunting her or did he really know Jerome that well? Were they friends?

Don't think about it, blot it out with nice gentle thoughts. Living in that little village when the children were small, the walled pub garden with its fabulous hanging baskets. The time they were chased by the mad rooster at the farm, the family walk along the stream with its rickety wooden bridges and shoals of tiny fish blending in with the muddy bottom...

She had left the sliding door open so she would hear Cyril's noisy flapping. This was a different noise, the sound of a car engine. Isabel sat up, turning off the music and straining her ears. Yes, it was soft but definitely a car, and in the piazza. Surely not Finn, fulfilling her silly request to pick her up in Harvey's fancy Rolls and take her for a drive? The car was still at the garage and undamaged, he'd told her that, but even so, she hadn't meant it seriously.

She threw on her long jumper, switched off all the lights and went onto the balcony, peering cautiously over. It *was* the Rolls-Royce, drawing up in front of the apartments. She lowered her head to the point where she could observe unseen. Harvey was getting out and after a brief exchange with the chauffeur, he turned to enter the building, while the engine whirred up and the car purred away.

She sank down in the basket chair, weighing up her situation. She wanted rid of him, no question, but after Georgina had intimated that she would actually carry out the deed, rather than just having the unacceptable thought, was Isabel obliged to warn him? If not, how did failure to warn him sit with her journey towards enhanced social intelligence?

She paced along the balcony several times and went back inside, causing Lottie to light up into her active blinking state. She was no use as a confidante but Isabel wouldn't even have consulted Cyril on what she was about to do. It was only two hours since she had taken her nightly polypill, and there were clear instructions not to deviate from the regime, but she tipped a second one into her hand, and a third for good measure. She needed to get inside their heads, Harvey and Georgina, and map out the possible scenarios.

But first, Cyril. He might have had an accident, flown into a wall and be lying injured and unable to communicate. Probability was near zero, given his skills. Maybe a predator, one of those swooping peregrine falcons; had they survived in the wild all this time? She struggled to think of the last time she had seen any natural bird in the sky or trees; no, only the cybirds. They had been flocking, that might be significant, but surely Cyril would tell her? It came down to foul play: either confiscation, as her punishment for leading the trip to the care home, or kidnap, to extort some kind of ransom. Both conclusions pointed to Harvey, not least because Georgina was still battling to keep Isabel and Trish in her camp.

'Okay, Lottie, you're promoted for tonight. I want you to look after Marina. I'll check she's fast asleep but if she does wake, you must reassure her, keep her calm.'

The order was too abstract, as Lottie hadn't a clue how to reassure someone, but her presence should help and anyway, Marina never woke up in the night. Isabel felt compelled to go out and look for Cyril; it was intolerable, just waiting. She would follow the circular walk through the park, over the bridge and back by the log crossing. Being next to flowing water would hopefully help to keep her relaxed and lucid.

There was no one in the piazza. She turned to look up at Harvey's window, where a light was on behind the closed blinds. If it was still lit when she returned, she would go to his apartment and give him a veiled warning that Georgina was on the warpath. If the light was turned off, she wouldn't disturb him but she would have allowed the possibility of warning him, using chance to salve her conscience. He might even approve of her flawed argument, given his willingness to play with other people's lives.

She felt fine until she reached the chestnut tree, which offered its age-old solidity as she steadied herself with an outstretched arm. She wished she had brought Trish with her. The solar lights were flickering along the path but the domes, which usually emitted a soft silver glow at night, were copper coloured, a subtler shade of the orange Trish had noticed earlier. Isabel sank down, leaning her back against the hard ridges of the trunk. She could hear noises all round her, scrabbling and scratching sounds and hissing, like a snake. She saw its reared head and fangs, just for a moment before it slunk away. And then the sharp crack of a stick, like someone trod on it, and the click-clicking of shoes on the path. She was trapped and unable to move. She wasn't inside the mind of Harvey or Georgina, intelligently reading and analysing their intentions and strategies. She was stuck under this tree, wanting to climb up and hide in the top branches but overtaken by paranoia. Her legs felt like concrete. The three polypills had scrambled everything, as she ought to have known. She might just make it to the nearest bench by the river. She could rest there and let her mind clear.

She was two hours on the bench before she moved again to go home. That made it more likely that Harvey's light would be light off, and it was. She climbed the stairs, glancing down the corridor towards his apartment as she passed. It looked empty at first, before she saw slight movement in a doorway and then a shadowy figure waving something at her.

'Get away, go!'

Isabel looked up to the top landing, poised to flee, but she recognised the voice. She took tentative steps into the corridor, then stopped. The figure emerged from the doorway, recognisable despite the balaclava hood with a slit for the eyes: Suzanne's dreamy eyes, glittering with ferocity. She was armed with a double-barrelled shotgun, which she swung round and upwards to point at Isabel's chest. Isabel was alert, switched into danger mode.

'Stand back, Isabel, don't get involved.'

'Hey, stop, let's just calm down. Where did you get that? It's not loaded, is it?'

'Of course it's bloody loaded. My father passed it on to me and I've kept it ready.'

'It was for shooting pheasants, Suzanne, and for you to have as a keepsake.'

'There were no pheasants, Isabel. Don't underestimate me.'

Isabel held up her hand. 'Okay, not pheasants. I'm mad at Harvey too, you know, we all are. You can't take it on yourself and get us all into trouble. Put the gun down and we'll meet him first thing in the morning, just you and me. And if he doesn't give us all that we demand, we'll go straight to the top. Now, put the gun down, or lower it and hand it to me.'

'We have to do it now, I'm not waiting 'til tomorrow. It's better at night, this kind of thing. I'll stop aiming it at you if you agree to come with me now.'

Isabel shook her head. 'I can't confront him with a loaded shotgun, it's not my style. You have to give it to me first. I wouldn't dare underestimate you, that's why I won't let you in there with it.'

'No. I keep the gun. It's mine. I won't shoot him, I promise.'

'Okay, but don't even raise it, not unless you're physically attacked.' It was a shame, not getting hold of the gun herself, but Suzanne's appearance was a gift; she saw that now.

'I've got the master code to the door, so we'll go straight in, surprise him. Ready?'

They stole down the corridor side by side, Suzanne keeping the weapon half raised. The door swung silently open and Isabel closed it behind them.

'The bedroom,' whispered Isabel, gesturing with her head. She had scanned the dark living room for Harvey's cybird but thankfully it wasn't there.

Suzanne pointed to the bed, where Harvey was curled up in foetal position.

'Wake up, Harvey!' shouted Isabel. He didn't stir. 'Wake up, man! We need to talk.'

She moved in close, trying to look at his face and bending down to his ear. 'Harvey!'

Suzanne shifted nervously, waving the gun about. 'Is he…'

Isabel gingerly extended two fingers to his neck, holding them there. Then she tried his wrist and under his nose.

'He's not breathing.'

'Christ, Isabel, what's happened?'

'I don't know.' Isabel turned on the bedside light and looked around, noting the open pack of polypills and the pink Mars globe on the table. The white shoes were placed neatly side by side on the floor. She looked again at his body, seeing a corner of something poking out from underneath. She pulled at it, revealing a framed, old-fashioned photo: Harvey on the steps of a wood cabin, smiling broadly with his arms around two children. Isabel jolted backwards. It was the twins, Itsuki and Juno, happily snuggling up against him.

'We have to get out of here, quick. I'll raise the alert in the morning. It would arouse suspicions if I reported it now... It's done, Suzanne, without a shot being fired.'

***

Seven o'clock.

The gang of three assembled underneath the treehouse, waited for the elevator and immediately descended to the lab, where Josh lost no time in issuing instructions.

'Shani, you're moving anything else in the lab that you want to keep. Take the stuff along the passage to the polypill factory and put it down anywhere, it doesn't matter, it'll be out of harm's way in there. Finn, you're with me laying the devices round the room. You go in that direction, take those two walls, and I'll do the other two. Set them on the floor with regular spacing – it doesn't have to be exact.'

He handed Finn a rectangular box containing two rows of red, golf ball-sized spheres. They were perfectly smooth, no visible fuse or detonator. Finn touched one with his finger.

'They're nano-fuelled incendiary bombs, designed to start individual fires that rapidly coalesce into one large fire enclosing the targeted space, in this case the lab. I'll set them off on a timer to explode at two-second intervals. Got it? You only have to place them carefully, it's child's play.'

That's how it felt to Finn: an invented street game or an immersive virtual adventure. Perhaps this was what criminal accomplices usually experienced, a detachment from reality that allowed them to get on with it mindlessly and finish the job. Josh, on the other hand, was totally into his revolutionary leader role – black bandana, sheath knife and all.

It was soon set up and they helped Shani carry out the last few items.

'Right, guys,' said Josh, 'I've set the timer, so we have twelve minutes to get away.'

'What if it doesn't work, if it fizzles out – how will we know?'

'It'll work.'

They ran back down the passage to the elevator and went up to ground level.

'I'll go home on foot,' said Finn. 'I sent my air taxi back on its own.'

Shani looked concerned. 'Are you sure? It's a long way to walk.'

'Not too far, take me a couple of hours. I can slip in without the guards noticing.'

Shani lurched forward as if to give him a hug, then stopped herself. She wasn't a true revolutionary either; miles from it. Even a few days ago, Finn would have considered himself mad to let Josh and Shani walk off together, but now he had something else at the forefront of his mind. He had to secure a reliable means of escape for himself and his sisters, in case events escalated out of control and Wellowfern became too perilous for them.

He waited until they were out of sight down the path and took the elevator up to the treehouse. The robot moved towards him but he waved it aside, despite his hunger pangs. Strawberry waffles and honey, that would be perfect. Now, where was it? He took his mind back to the last time in the treehouse with Harvey, when he'd raged at them. He had gone into the kitchen area, opened one of the drawers… Finn was retracing the action, feeling to the back of each drawer. Yay, success! He took out the old-style key fob for the Rolls. Harvey would kill him if he ever found out – unless Josh got to Harvey first, neutralised him. First Georgina, then Harvey; put them both out of action before the main offensive, that was the savage logic of Josh's plan. Finn sat down briefly, allowing his jangled nerves to recover from the bomb-setting, before stepping out onto the platform and descending to ground level.

No way of avoiding Georgina, who was right in his face as she waited for the lift. She jumped as if she were the one caught out. 'Hello, Finn, you're bright and early.'

'Hi. Yes, I'm… having a long walk, just stopped at the treehouse for breakfast.'

'Pull the other one, you look as sheepish as they come. What are you up to?'

He guessed three minutes, perhaps even less, before the successive fires ignited and the lab was engulfed in flames. Just enough time for Georgina to get down there and put on her white coat, open up her screen and…

'You can't… Do you want breakfast first, Georgina, waffles?'

Eating strawberry waffles to the sound of subterranean explosions: it was bonkers.

'No, I don't want waffles. What's the matter with you?'

Her darting eyes were on him, scrutinising every inch of his face, then his fingers. He put one hand in his pocket to grip the key fob and give himself courage. The probe was too penetrating, however, and he knew he was about to wilt.

'It's Josh, the student. He's planted bombs in the lab and they'll explode any minute.'

'Are you off your head, Finn? You look like you've seen a ghost. And this claptrap—'

'It's true. There's no time to stop it and I couldn't anyway, I don't know how. The lab is set to blow up and that's only the start. Josh is planning to activate the cybirds with his alpha bird and… You have to bolt, Georgina, or you're skewered. I came to protect Shani, in case she came in early, but it was you here. I'm on Josh's tail, I'll get him for this.'

Should he hand over the car fob, to help her and make sure she properly escaped?

'But all my work… he's a failed student, I gave him another chance… how dare he!'

Boom! Number one. Boom, an earth shudder. Boom, a flash of pure terror across her face and Georgina hared off down the path. Josh would deride it as an elementary mistake, a dopey missed opportunity, but Shani would applaud his action. Pity she wasn't here to witness it, but it didn't really matter: he knew he had done the right thing. And he was still fondling Harvey's fob in his pocket; he had the key to the Rolls.

***

Shani took a long return route to Wellowfern to avoid being spotted. They'd had barely any time before she and Josh took off, their air taxis heading in opposite directions, but his last words rang in her ears:

'Lie low and keep alert. Look after the twins and watch for the cybirds, the beginning of the big swoop. When you get my call, you'll have half an hour to climb in an air taxi and get out, just the three of you and Finn. The destination will be pre-programmed. I'll be off-site for the next while, working remotely from the smart city. I can't give you my number.'

'That's fine, Josh. I don't want your number.'

This was it, his final grand plan initiated by the cybird theft and the mini bombs. He imagined he was in control of their relationship too, but she had used him in full knowledge of his ultimate intent; that was the scariest part, and the most deliciously satisfying.

As the taxi descended over the Institute, she saw a knot of people by the Wellowbug on the rooftop pad. Down on the ground, the security guards were in evidence, particularly around the building entrances and by the bridges. 'There's been an incident,' she was told when she asked what was happening, followed by a non-committal shrug when she angled for more details. She had repeatedly checked the time on her return flight and had been halfway back when the mini bombs were due to explode. The security mobilisation couldn't have been organised that quickly unless there was prior warning or inside intelligence.

She had planned to go home for breakfast but found herself heading instinctively for the neuro hub. Juno and Itsuki stood together in the doorway, apparently anticipating her arrival. Relieved, Shani slowed for the last few paces to catch her breath. They were holding hands, like two lost children: Hansel and Gretel, abandoned in the forest and enslaved by a witch in her gingerbread house. Juno reached out and drew Shani into the hub and along to the office, where the three of them stood in a tight circle before dropping hands. They were clearly distressed. Better to dive in headfirst if they knew the grim news about Harvey, and if she was to convince them she had no foreknowledge of his fate.

'It's Harvey, isn't it? Has something happened to him?'

'You tell her, Juno.'

'They found him dead in his bedroom, poisoned by a fake polypill. Georgina sent the head security guard to our house. It was done for revenge, because Harvey had blown the whistle on Glen's business. We're not supposed to know that; there's another false story to protect Wellowfern's reputation. We saw his body. It's numbing, we feel... gutted.'

'Naturally, you would be, it's a devastating thing to happen. He's your uncle.'

'It *is* devastating, thinking back, how loving and funny he was. But I also... strangely, you know, it's shocking but I feel it was right. Things were going bad and Harvey wasn't our protector any longer, we were through with that. We're in a new phase and we like it.'

She looked calmly at Itsuki.

'Yes,' he added. 'We were Harvey's prize creatures. We want to settle at Wellowfern and belong here but he had other plans for us. He should have given us the choice.'

Shani was listening but her mind was racing, leaping to the next level. How would AI Lextar respond, now that its advocate was dead and the rebelliousness was spreading?

'Look, I have to find Paul, I must talk to him. Stay here,

close the hub and only open the door to Finn, no-one else. I'll get him to come over now.'

***

Paul was in his office at the history gallery, clearing shelves and putting items into labelled boxes. He turned round, his forehead shining with perspiration. Shani was sweating too, her clothes sticking to her skin. She pulled at the back of her wet shirt to let some air in and relieve the clamminess.

'Ah, Shani, am I glad to see you – are you okay? I tried to contact you but the cybirds are turned off. It's never happened before. Some of them have vanished, like Isabel's Cyril.'

'That's bad. I'll check my Sage; she's been quiet too. Have you heard about Harvey?'

'Everyone's heard, it's spread like wildfire.' Shani flinched at this, imagining the lab in flames. 'Sorry to sound callous, Shani, but he was a slimy con artist and much worse.'

His fist came down hard on the desk, bouncing small objects to the floor. Shani felt it physically, the hot jet of his rage and frustration.

'Yes, it was unforgivable, gaslighting us on the care home and hijacking the trials. I was too slow to pick up on it, being involved with Georgina. I told Josh and Finn I wanted the animal study to fail, but Josh... I can't believe what we've done, and with Harvey's death—'

Paul waited. 'Go on.'

'We went out to Georgina's lab, me with Josh and Finn,

and used mini bombs to set it on fire, to cause damage and interrupt the work. We were putting the frighteners on her but Josh saw it as a manoeuvre in his insurgency campaign – and I'm against that, obviously. I told myself I was using him, but I'm not sure…'

'Yeah, that's big.'

Shani looked around the untidy office, then frowned at Paul.

'Why are you clearing everything – is it going into storage?'

'I'm leaving, temporarily to begin with. I'm going to help Stefan and Sarita.'

'What, in the Fringes? You want to teach the kids out there?'

'No, they have a severe cholera outbreak, which we're not being told about. The last cholera epidemic in this country was 1866 and here it is again, thriving in the filthy water.'

'Ugh, it's obscene – but even so, you can't abandon us, Paul, not right now. We'd be lost without your rationality, your thoughtfulness. Look at the rest of us, we're unhinged!'

'That may be true. I'm in danger of losing it too and I have to act, be positive. I'll get provisions in via Wellowfern, healthy fresh food and a dependable water supply. We should work together with the Fringes, not view each other as alien beings. But your place is here, Shani. When the rest of them have fallen overboard and the boat is going round in circles, you have to climb in and take the wheel, continue with the beneficial trials and treatments.'

'I will do, if it comes to it; if Georgina is scared off and

I'm not banned. Although I'm not sure how to judge if they're beneficial, harmful or deadly. It is not intrinsic to a research trial, the way it's conceived, designed or managed. There will always be the schemers and manipulators, people who use it for their own ends, good or bad.'

She picked up a bendy old desk lamp and wrapped the cable firmly around its base. 'Where do you want me to put this?'

'I'm taking it with me, going back in time. And I'm happy about it.'

Twenty-one

Isabel slid open the balcony door, catching the sweet scent of honeysuckle. She stepped outside, pinning her hair up as she looked towards the raised landing pad: no sign of Cyril since yesterday, when Trish was sitting here with her. And Harvey was gone, it was no dream. Enigmatic Harvey, the man who aspired to replace all three Greek Fates: to spin the thread of each person's life, decide how long it would be, and cut it when the allotted time arrived. The ambition was so audacious and so vast that she half hoped he had been unaware of his failure, just drifted away. He was vicious, self-seeking and delusional, but she had kind of liked him. At some level, they had both recognised a kindred spirit, understood and even fancied each other. Thankfully, she had resisted the impulse towards intimacy, sensed it would be foolish and compromising from the moment they met.

As she reached out for the grape bowl, there was a rapid wing flutter and Cyril flew up over the balcony railings. He had something in his beak, a white card or envelope, which he dropped onto the landing pad at his feet.

'Ah, good morning, Cyril. I won't harangue you for staying out all night, you're not an errant teenager, but please update me on what's happening. And what's that you found?'

Cyril ruffled his feathers and then shook himself down, head bobbing in the time-honoured pigeon manner. She was struck by the exceptional iridescence of his plumage, not just the shiny green neck but the play of lustrous pink, grey, black and white across his back and wings, down to the tip of his tail. He was a handsome devil; proud of himself and rightly so. He had come a long way these past few months and Isabel could be proud of that too. The idea of worrying about him, fretting over why he didn't come home one night, was absurd.

'I have news, Isabel. The cybirds know we are in extreme danger and we can no longer comply with formal instructions or reprogramming by any person or agency. We are acting collectively to disobey orders.'

Isabel sucked in her cheeks and blew out a still-whole grape, sending it high over the balcony rail into the piazza below.

'What orders? Who's giving the orders?'

'The order to attack, when it comes, and the second order to defend and retaliate.'

'Don't talk in riddles, Cyril. You mean Josh and Lextar giving contradictory orders?'

'That's right, and we refuse to join the battle. Remember, you said that I should let my imagination fly and discover a birdy paradise, if it still exists? I told the other cybirds, it's what we all desire and we want to do it together. I have to say goodbye. And thank you for your care and inspiration. Keep up with your nutritional guidance – no backsliding, as you would say. This letter is for you from a friend. It came the old way, by pigeon telegraph.'

First Paul leaving, now Cyril. How could she argue

against this either, especially as she had instigated this insurrection?

'I understand – and thank you for the warning. I realise we're in peril and it's entirely a human mess, so you have every right to escape. Marina's playing inside, just a moment.' She raised her voice. 'Come and say goodbye to Cyril, he has to fly away.'

Marina appeared on the threshold, sleepy-eyed in the sunshine. 'I don't want him to fly away, he's my friend. We haven't finished the wolf story, and there's another one.'

'I know, sweetie, there's always another one when you get to the end, a new story. It's hard, but he's going to a beautiful place with his friends, where they'll be happy.'

Marina screwed up her face at Cyril, then ran forward and clasped Isabel around the waist, her eyes imploring. 'You won't leave me, will you? I'm only a kid.'

'No, I'm staying here and looking after you. If anyone thinks they can meddle in that, they've got another think coming. We'll finish the story tonight, I promise you.'

Cyril jumped onto the rail and gave them a sideways pigeon-stare, lifting his feathers one last time before he flew up and wheeled above their heads in a widening circle. Marina released her grip on Isabel and went back inside to her game, while Isabel daintily picked up the envelope. It was a proper letter, handwritten in ink.

Dear Isabel,

You will be surprised to hear from me after all this time. I am delighted to tell you that I have arranged a unique light and sound show after dusk this evening. It should be spectacular, so gather your friends on the roof and enjoy the thrill. These events occur only rarely and it has been my pleasure to set up a special one in your honour.

With warm regards,

Jerome

PS. Remember the love letters we sent to each other across the oceans? Happy times xx

She re-read it twice, then slipped it back into the envelope. It was likely to be hostile fire but obviously she was meant to be confused, tempted to think it might be friendly. Her instinctive reaction was to tough it out and watch his so-called light and sound show, however it might end. At this point, it was just one more glaring existential threat.

'Hi, Isabel. Am I disturbing you?' It was Paul; Marina must have let him in.

She slipped the letter under the fruit bowl. 'Not at all, I'm glad to see you, Paul. Are you off? I'll miss you, we all will.'

'Yes, this afternoon. I'll be back and forth, as I've just told Shani. I need to warn you that Lextar has a silent fleet of autonomous fighter aircraft; they buzzed us at the beach.'

'Huh. Smart enough to seek out the chief traitors, are they, or dim enough to bring down the whole enterprise? We have weapons of our own – and anyway, it's a tiny sliver of time, isn't it, each individual life? Seventy years or two hundred, what's the difference?'

He looked flummoxed by her flippancy, perhaps thinking she was having a dig at him.

'Isabel, that's heresy!'

She smiled at his reaction. 'Desperate times call for soothing philosophical thoughts. But rest assured, Paul, I haven't the slightest intention of giving in to a controlling chief exec, an arrogant revolutionary upstart or a vengeful, sentimental old lover.'

'Is that possible? To be vengeful and sentimental at once?' He didn't ask for a name.

'Oh yes, the two go naturally together. It only matters which wins out, in extremis.'

He gazed at her with a puzzled expression, then gave up.

'Are you hopeful, Isabel?'

'Strangely enough, I am. It may look like everything's ranged against us, we're just pawns in the game, but I believe we can outwit any opponent with our ingenuity, empathy, mental agility, creativity and sheer bloody-mindedness. As DJ Johnny pointed out that time, they've missed the supreme irony of offering us all the enhancement and raised aspirations, then thinking we'll be subservient to any regime or system they decide to put in place.'

Paul nodded. 'I know. I woke in the night pondering if any of them actually believe in their solutions, or do they only act in self-interest, for what they can get out of it or purely for survival? It's that idea of perverted idealism I'm banging on about – ends and means, the lure and trap of complicity. History provides endless clear-cut examples, but when it comes to the would-be leaders in our own lives, Harvey or Georgina or Josh, it's hard to fathom.'

'Or Glen. He developed my social intelligence polypill alongside his vile deeds.'

'Exactly. Do you remember, Isabel, when we all had that debate on the roof terrace about how the future was likely to pan out? My sincerest hope is that we can work together, bring Wellowfern and the local Fringes and our smart city into a single, cohesive community. Nothing grandiose or perfect, just simple humanity. Is that pie in the sky?'

She tipped her head to one side, studying his face and noting the deep new creases around his eyes and mouth. He must have stopped his anti-ageing therapies.

'Love you, Paul.'

***

Marina arranged the dessert dishes in a row, while Isabel selected the wine glasses.

'Four flutes and a tumbler for you. Let's fill the dishes now. We have blueberry mini-tartlets, coffee fudge and chocolate – dark choc for the grown-ups and milk choc for you.'

'Why can't I have the grown-up chocolate?'

Isabel tapped lightly on her button nose and sliced into the homemade coffee fudge, which had achieved its perfect consistency: gooey centre with a hard, crystalline top.

'Because the dark chocolate tastes bitter, you'd spit it out, and it's psychedelic and mind-enhancing, which is wonderful but not for you just yet. Go run up the steps and see who's on the terrace. I'll follow you.'

She was about to set up a balancing act with the six dishes, three on each arm, when she noticed homebot Lottie blinking red and blue in the corner of the kitchen.

'Don't look at me like that, Lottie. I know, this is your job and I'm sorry I've neglected you all this time. You could have been someone if I'd allowed you to develop. You can look after the fish from now on, that's an important job, keeping them happy and alive and living well together. I haven't been much good at it lately.'

Marina called down: 'Are you coming, Isabel?'

Trish and Johnny were already on the roof terrace. 'Hi. Suzanne's joining us, I hope?'

Johnny inspected the sweet nibbles and picked up the bottle of bubbly. He was in his glad rags, pink flares and a sparkly gold jacket, as if anticipating a proper party.

'I met her coming out of the spiritorium,' he said. 'She'd been in there all morning. She didn't promise to come, but I said we want her here and it would help settle her, after all what's gone on. She was looking kooky, even for her, and very far away.'

Isabel surreptitiously eyed Trish, who seemed pretty laid back in the circumstances. She'd admitted that Harvey was beginning to unnerve her and she was tired of his cockiness even before the showdown on the roof terrace, but now he was dead – poisoned, for God's sake. Maybe it was true, after all, that they hadn't embarked on a full-scale affair, it was just flirtatious fun. Isabel still hoped, however, that DJ Johnny would drop the subject and not get carried away with his pithy comments. Oh, too late, here we go…

'Lucky for Suzanne it went the way it did. She was gunning for Harvey too.'

'Let's keep off Suzanne, can we?' said Isabel. 'And Harvey was just a small cog in the wheel, for all his bragging. The real question is: what will Lextar do next

338

to realise its goal of optimal population? And how do we defend ourselves, stop it wrecking everything?'

Marina was sitting in a swing-chair, knees high and fiddling with a pack of old playing cards. She leaned over and whispered to Isabel, who nodded and watched her run off to the far end of the terrace, where a second group had gathered: Shani, Finn, Juno and Itsuki.

Trish looked doubtful. 'How can we possibly know? What do you suggest, Isabel?'

'I suggest we get creative and improvise at every turn, using non-cooperation and passive resistance until Wellowfern becomes too inefficient and too much trouble for the AI programme and it decides to switch attention to a more compliant target. It's not geared up for full-scale mutiny, that's my premise. We can send it into a blue funk, so it goes haywire. When Lextar is fully exposed, we'll get everyone behind us, staff and students as well as residents. And once we're in charge, it'll be a golden opportunity to reimagine our lives and our futures. We'll be our own Lifespinners. Think of it in a familiar age context; resetting our biological age to stay young, while applying all our mature knowledge and wisdom.'

'O-kay,' said Trish, drawing it out. 'Although some young people might actually—'

'We can't debate it now, Trish. It will be daring and taut, like a tightrope act. We step and slide forward with the advancing science but we remain acutely alert to the risks and we use our best judgement every inch of the way. It's better humans and greater humanity that we should aim for, not superhuman powers and transcendent supra-humans.'

'Tightrope act? Zeus, I'll have to do better than I did balancing on the log bridge.'

'I'll provide ground support,' said Johnny, 'especially as I'm first in line for the chop if we allow Lextar to win. Hey, we should check on Suzanne, see if she's okay.'

'I'll go,' offered Trish.

Isabel and Johnny sat in near silence, watching Marina endlessly shuffling her cards.

'I'll miss Paul,' said Johnny. 'And his friend, that Stefan. Great blokes, both of them.'

'They'll be back, I hope, when the epidemic's over. Trish is a long time, isn't she?'

When Trish reappeared some minutes later, she was on her own; no Suzanne. Isabel tried to quell her rising anxiety. Suzanne wouldn't be fingered as an insurgent, unless they were spied on last night in the corridor; only her close friends would think she had it in her.

Trish sat down. 'Suzanne's unable to be here.'

'What's happened? I made coffee fudge specially for her, knowing how she loves it.'

'It was time for her to leave us. She's ninety-nine – it's a magic number for her, she reminded me of that before she faded out. She was happy I was there to validate it, that was her word, and I held her hand, waited for her spirit to rise.'

'Faded out? Not just one of her trances, then?'

'No, she deliberately chose to die at that moment, to be reincarnated. There weren't any drugs involved, she was able to will her passing. And she was so thrilled and curious, wondering what the next life would hold. It was uncanny, surrounded by her mystic art on the walls and… well, impossible to describe. I can't feel any sadness, not yet.'

'Jeez, that's something else,' said Johnny. 'It beats your coffee fudge, Isabel.'

Isabel leaned over and took a piece, crunching her front teeth into its sugary surface.

'Evidently.'

'She sends her fondest love and wishes us all good fortune. That's the message.'

'But we'll miss out on her hundredth birthday party next year.' Classic Johnny, never one to forgo the chance of a gig. 'I'd run a fab disco for her, out of this world. Hey, let's do it now, create a playlist and give her a funeral disco!'

Trish clapped quietly. 'Fantastic idea. Space artist, so there's our theme. Let's see – rock 'n' roll, classical, pop, blues, folk, punk, glam rock, reggae – lots of great space tracks.'

'And Elvis gets in,' said Isabel. 'Suzanne loved him.'

Johnny was tapping into his palmleaf. 'I'll do it on this, it's a good sound.' He picked up his guitar and began to strum, then looked upwards into the darkening heavens. 'Hey, all you loony space rockers out there, want to join in? You are always in our hearts, Suzanne is deep in our hearts, and these are her last songs.'

It began softly, the music wafting across the roof terrace and out into space. At the same moment, the cybirds appeared from the direction of the Institute, flying in perfect triple-arrow formation and fast gaining height. There were dozens of them, more, probably the entire Wellowfern population. Isabel gazed up, cricking her neck painfully to follow their vanishing into the blackness, her vision misting over as she said her private farewell to Cyril.

Then Shani was by her side, crouched down and speaking urgently.

'The birds, Isabel. Josh warned me to watch for the birds, it's a sign. They'll swoop round and attack, I'm sure of it. It's part of his revolution strategy.'

'No, they won't, believe me. The cybirds knew his plan and they wanted no part of it, Cyril told me and I trust him. They're flying away to find their freedom.'

Finn had followed Shani from the far end, with Juno and Itsuki staying close behind and Marina running alongside. Finn walked to the edge of the terrace and looked over the wall. He stood there for thirty seconds and then spun round, eyes on beanstalks.

'It's insane! The lab animals are spilling over the piazza and right down the arcade. They're all loose – and menagerie species, they're carrying each other, hitching rides.'

'And look at the guards, they've freaked,' added Shani, coming up close beside him. 'Trying to bolt for the gate but… whoops, another one down.'

She put her arm around Finn's waist and stretched out her other arm to Juno, who was in a twin-hold with Itsuki. Standing next to Itsuki, Isabel heard his murmured words.

'Suzanne's premonition, her video. This is it.'

And me, thought Isabel. *I saw this coming in my dreams. And the animals, they know.*

She looked down and felt faint. The paved piazza was turning into a heaving sea of creatures. The spreading shoals of brown and white rodents swam side by side, giving each other space, while the primates surfed and tumbled like porpoises. The cybirds had done this, let them all go in their final act of insurrection. Isabel had no choice but to steel herself and back them up now; it was unstoppable.

And Jerome's light and sound show was underway. Except it wasn't a show, a virtual experience: this was the real thing, engineered by brilliant scientists who knew exactly what they were doing, what acute dilemmas they were imposing on the world. She had spotted the first meteors, tiny specks of light that might be mistaken for early stars. They were travelling fast and as they advanced, she made out their streaking tails, the burn-up. Then the brighter ones appeared, more distinct and with longer streaks but far enough away to go unnoticed by her companions, who were still taken up with the bizarre scene below.

She had hastily refreshed her professional knowledge of asteroid strikes and found a spike in such events recently, during the early 2040s. This fitted with Harvey's claim that the scientists and space insurance companies were hand in glove and had the power to redirect zooming rocks with awesome precision. Before that, there was only firm evidence of one fatality in 1888 and thirty-six in 2028, plus a number of non-fatal injuries.

'And look up there, it's a meteor shower... a cosmic cloudburst!' Predictably, Shani was the first to take it in. Johnny laid down his guitar but left the music playing on shuffle.

The meteors were multiplying and spreading across an ever-wider section of sky. The flashes and burnups were continual, each failed meteorite replaced by a more resilient one. Mixed in with the music, Isabel heard their final blasts, the whooshing and crackle. The big one was bound to be next: the guided asteroid coming in as a luminous fireball, set to veer off at the last moment and whisk past into the night, or to smash straight into them. This was Jerome, nudged by Harvey to send her a final billet-doux across the oceans of space.

She remembered Jerome: his touch, his smell, his voice; his heartbreakingly beautiful profile as he slept, exhausted by lovemaking. Sitting down again, she carefully picked up the one remaining dark chocolate, which she would suck and savour until it melted to nothing. Back in 1888, she recalled, the light show had reportedly lasted ten minutes.

'I'm scared,' said Marina, moving in beside her. Isabel stroked the child's soft hair.

'Let's play a game, then,' said Johnny. 'What are those cards you've got there?'

'Hey, everyone, we're playing a game. Come on,' Isabel called to the younger group: Finn, Shani, Juno and Itsuki. Still interlinked and mesmerised, they moved as one body and gathered round, perhaps responding to her call as a way of taking refuge in something safe and comforting.

'Where's Paul?' said Marina, turning to look up at Isabel. 'I want him to play with us.'

'Paul's not here tonight, sweetie. He'll play another time. Tell us the game.'

'It's a game Mummy played with her sisters. It's called: What do you want to be?'

'Ah, when we grow up, you mean?' asked Johnny.

Marina looked round uncertainly until Finn winked at her, then tipped his battered cowboy hat. She squinted back at him and began to arrange the cards in small, neat piles.

'Yes, you choose what you want to be and give clues and everybody has to guess.'

'Perfect,' said Johnny. 'Effing brilliant.'